TALES OF THE
SHADOW

Volume 7: Femm

edited by
Jean-Marc & Randy Lo͟

stories by
**Roberto Lionel Barreiro, Matthew Baugh, Thom Brannan,
Matthew Dennion, Win Scott Eckert, Emmanuel Gorlier,
Micah Harris, Travis Hiltz, Paul Hugli, Rick Lai,
Jean-Marc Lofficier, David McDonnell, Brad Mengel,
Sharan Newman, Neil Penswick, Pete Rawlik,
Frank Schildiner, Stuart Shiffman, Bradley H. Sinor,
Brian Stableford, Michel Stéphan** and **David L. Vineyard**

foreword by
Xavier Mauméjean

portfolio by
Matt Haley

cover by
Phil Cohen

A Black Coat Press Book

ISBN 978-1-935558-44-6. First Printing. January 2011. Published by Black Coat Press, an imprint of Hollywood Comics.com, LLC, P.O. Box 17270, Encino, CA 91416. All rights reserved. Except for review purposes, no part of this book may be reproduced or transmitted in any form or by any means, electronic or mechanical, including photocopying, recording or by any information storage and retrieval system, without permission in writing from the publisher. The stories and characters depicted in this anthology are entirely fictional. Printed in the United States of America.

TALES OF THE
SHADOWMEN
Volume 7: Femmes Fatales

Table of Contents

MILADY

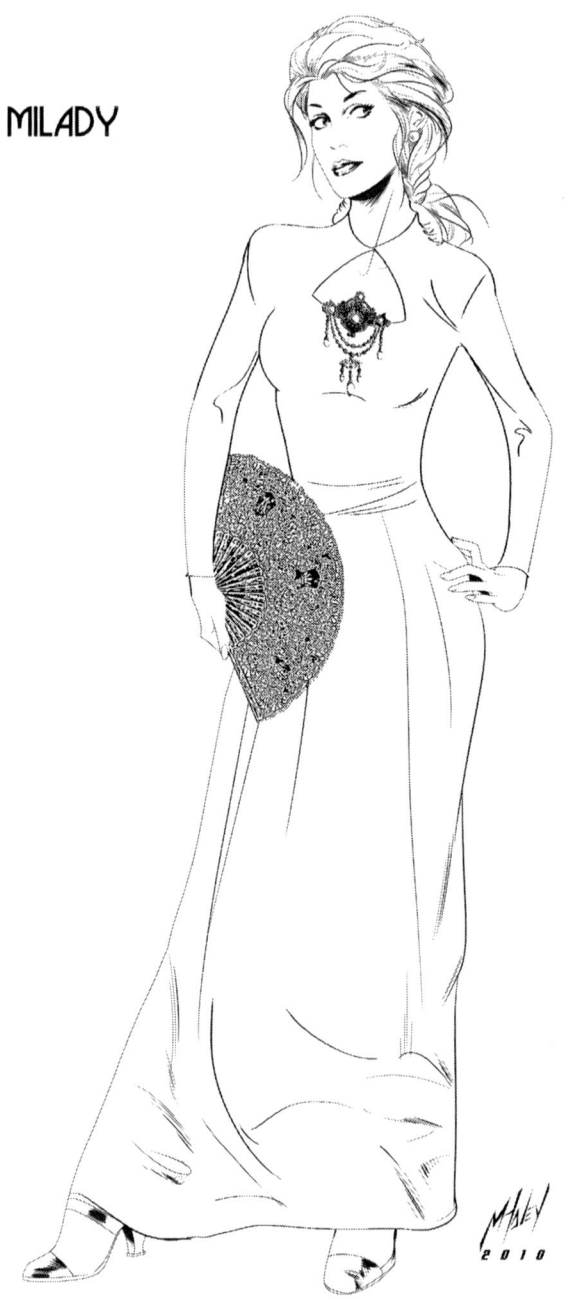

Matt Haley: *My Femmes Fatales*

Tales of the Shadowmen *periodically offers portfolios by renowned artists. To illustrate a volume dedicated to the concept of "Femmes Fatales," we could think of no one better than Matt Haley.*

Matt is a prolific and talented comic-book artist, illustrator and visual designer whose works include Alone in the Dark *(Image; written by Jean-Marc & Randy Lofficier),* Ghost *(Dark Horse),* Elseworld's Finest: Supergirl and Batgirl *(DC),* The Order *(Marvel), the* Badass *books (Harper), etc. He has also contributed artwork to Stan Lee's* Who Wants To Be A Super-Hero, Sanctuary *and* The Human Target.

Matt's Femmes Fatales *include a selection from the very best villainesses of French popular fiction. Ranked in chronological order, they are:*

1. *Milady*

Was she Anne de Breuil, the name she used when she met and married Athos, becoming Comtesse de La Fère? Milady Clarick de Winter, Baroness of Sheffield, through her subsequent marriage to Lord de Winter's brother? Or perhaps "Charlotte Backson," the name under which her brother-in-law tried to have her exiled? Created by Alexandre Dumas in 1844 for *Les Trois Mousquetaires* [The Three Musketeers], Milady is one of the best known *femmes fatales* in all of popular literature. She is a spy, a thief and a murderess. She has willfully seduced and killed several men, including at least one of her many husbands. She is scheming, conniving, deceitful, vengeful and unrepentant, except, perhaps, at the very end when she is about to be decapitated by the Executioner of Bethune. Her evil son Mordaunt did his best to avenge her death in the sequels.

2. *Baccarat (Louise Charmet, Comtesse d'Artoff)*

Like Milady, Baccarat is a commoner who used her stunning beauty and feminine wiles to pull herself out of a life of misery. Created by Pierre-Alexis Ponson du Terrail in his *Rocambole* saga (1857-70), Baccarat finds herself quickly on the side of the Comte de Kergaz against his evil half-brother Sir Williams. She is rewarded by marrying the kind Comte d'Artoff. Later, she destroys Rocambole, sends him to the labor camp of Toulon, and ultimately rehabilitates him to become a force for good. The archetypal courtesan with a heart of gold, Baccarat is an accomplished rider, swordswoman and sharpshooter. Ponson du Terrail speculated that she might even have traveled to the Far West and rode alongside Calamity Jane...

BACCARAT

MARGUERITE
SADOULAS

IRMA VEP

3. *Marguerite Sadoulas, Comtesse de Clare*

Marguerite Sadoulas is the very opposite of Baccarat. She, too, came from a poor family and used her beauty to become a high-priced courtesan. But where Baccarat's nature compelled her to do good, Marguerite's propelled her towards evil. She was created by the grandmaster of crime fiction, Paul Féval, in his *Habits Noirs* [The Black Coats] saga (1863-75). Marguerite succeeded beyond her wildest hopes by becoming, first the mistress of the cunning Lecoq, which eventally got her a seat on the High Council of the Black Coats, and then the wife of the brutish Comte Joulou du Bréhut de Clare, becoming herself Comtesse de Clare. While her scheme to seize the inheritance of her cousin was foiled, Marguerite thrived as one of the comspiracy's leading strategists, and even escaped death when she and others in the Council plotted to steal the Colonel's Treasure. Féval never told the story of her death. She just faded away...

4. *Irma Vep*

She is the mysterious, black-clad muse of the criminal gang known as the "Vampires," created by Louis Feuillade for his eponymous 1915 ten-part silent film serial. Her name is, of course, merely an anagram of "vampire," so her real identity may never be known. Played by actress Musidora (Jeanne Roques, 1889-1957), Irma Vep is identified only by her black tights and black mask, as she slinks down corridors and escapes over rooftops; she defined the popular archetype of the super-villainess for decades to come.

5. *Antinea*

Queen Antinea is a descendent of the Ptolemies of Egypt and lives in an ancient Atlantean outpost hiddem in the Hoggar Mountains of the Sahara. Created by Piierre Benoit for his 1919 novel *L'Atlantide*, Antinea keeps an undeground mausoleum filled with the numbered and labeled bodies of her former lovers, forever preserved in orichalcum. Unlike H. Rider Haggard's Ayesha, to whom she has been compared, Antinea is full of pride and without any shred of compassion. She is a female sphinx, a vampire of sorts, the ultimate *femme fatale*. She is not a victim of the gods, she *is* the gods.

6. *Joséphine Balsamo, Comtesse de Cagliostro*

Is she the immortal daughter of Cagliostro and Joséphine de Beauharnais, or merely their great-grandaughter, benefitting from an incredible family resemblance? Or is she possibly a mere spy and con artist? Introduced by Maurice Leblanc as the latest, and deadliest, adversary and lover of a 20-year-old Arsène Lupin in *La Comtesse de Cagliostro* (1924), Joséphine would today be considered a bipolar sociopath. She eventually died in Corsica in 1918, but not without having put in motion a plan to turn Lupin's son against his father.

ANTINEA

COUNTESS
CAGLIOSTRO

GEORGETTE
CUVELIER

7. Georgette Cuvelier, a.k.a. The Spider

Few adversaries have challenged the prodigious skills of Harry Dickson, the American Sherlock Holmes, more than once. One such foe was Professor Flax, the so-called "Human Monster." Another was his equally gifted daughter, Georgette Cuvelier. Outwardly a modestly-dressed schoolgirl, she was in reality the Spider, the iron-fisted ruler of a criminal gang. Georgette appeared in 1933 in *La Bande de l'Araignée* [The Spider's Gang] and *Les Spectres-Bourreaux* [The Ghost Executioners], fell in love with Dickson, and eventusally came to a tragic end.

8. Madame Atomos (Kanoto Yoshimuta)

A survivor of the nuclear bombing of Nagasaki, where she lost her family, Madame Atomos is a brilliant Japanese scientist with one, single obsession: to avenge herself on the United States of America by inflicting as much pain and terror as possible. Created by André Caroff in 1964 and starring in 18 novels published until 1970, Madame Atomos starts as an older woman, but soon creates a younger duplicate, Miss Atomos, who turns against her by falling in love with the FBI agent who opposes her. Then, she finds a way to rejuvenate her body and becomes a true *femme fatale*, using both charm and super-weapons to pursue her nefarious goals.

MADAME
ATOMOS

Xavier Mauméjean is the author of The League of Heroes *(which won the 2003 Imaginaire Award of the City of Brussels and was translated by Black Coat Press in 2005), as well as a regular contributor to* Tales of the Shadowmen. *Xavier has a diploma in philosophy and the science of religions and works as a teacher in the North of France, where he resides with his wife and his daughter.*

Xavier Mauméjean: *My Femmes Fatales*

Contrary to popular belief, the *femme fatale* is not a literary invention of the 19th century. Homer's *Odyssey* provided the first embodiment of the myth, with Circe who seduces Ulysses's crew before turning them into pigs ready for slaughter. From that point on, seduction, humiliation and death became the marching orders of a legion of literary figures. Not of a harem, for the *femme fatale* is usually a solitary figure. Far from the submissive "brides" of Bram Stoker's Dracula (1897), John Keats, Sheridan Le Fanu, Théophile Gautier and Leo Tolstoy preferred to create Huntresses lining up their collection of male trophies, foreshadowing the Vamp. Arthur Machen offered a first modern version in *The Great God Pan* (1894), in which surgery creates the Dionysian character of Helen Vaughan. The same year, Frank Wedekind perfected the criteria that make a *femme fatale* with the character of Lulu who appeared in two plays: *Erdgeist* and *Lulu, Die Buchser der Pandora*. Lulu, a terrifying ingénue, eventually dies under Jack the Ripper's knife. The story was adapted into an eponymous 1929 motion picture by Georg Wilhelm Pabst, in which the title character is brilliantly played by the sublime Louise Brooks—a stroke of genius by the director.

The archetype of the femme fatale was definitively set in 1911 in Hanns Heinz Ewers' *Mandragore (Alraune, Die Geschichte eines lebenden Wesen)*. The daughter of a murderer and a shameless prostitute, Mandragore, whose name is an homage to the mandrake, the flower "born of the equivocal tears of the innocent hanged men," is further subjected to scientific experiments. Conditioned from childhood to destroy men, Mandragore acts with complete innocence and is the epitome of ultimate perversion.

In Pierre Benoit's *The Queen of Atlantis (L'Atlantide*, 1919), Antinea pushes André de St. Avit to murder his companion, Jean Morhange, because the latter, a former Trappist monk, has not succumbed to her sulfurous beauty. The character of Antinea was inspired by the mythical Tin-Hann, Tuareg Queen of the Hoggar. H. Ridder Haggard's Ayesha, Queen of the underground kingdom of Kor, lit by flaming mummies, appeared in four novels following her first appearance in *She* (1887). Edgar Rice Burroughs' La, Keeper of the city of Opar, High priestess of the Sun God, could not bring herself to sacrifice Lord Greystoke in *The Return of Tarzan* (1917)—or in any of the sequels penned by the prolific Burroughs.

Fritz Leiber uniquely depicted *femmes fatales* as witches hunting in numbers in the exceptional *Conjure Wife* (1953) or as terrifying psychic succubi in *A Deskful of Girls* (1958). Bob Morane was able to successfully resist the charms of Miss Ylang-Ylang, a poisonous flower created by Henri Vernes (1965). Catherine L. Moore's spacefaring hero, Northwest Smith, a true pursuer of deadly beauties, encountered the vampiric Shambleau (1933) and the warrior woman Jirel of Joiry (*Quest of the Star Stone*, 1937). Science and technology only increased the powers of the *femme fatale*, as in Philip K. Dicks's *Do Androids Dream of Electric Sheep?* (1968). In 1977, William Kotzwinkle offered a more classical interpretation of the myth with *Fata Morgana*, with Lazarus Renee, Queen of the Ball of Harlots.

Of course, this brief review is not exhaustive. It is inevitably incomplete and biased. Certainly, Poison Ivy and other Dragon Ladies would be offended to not have been included. Lee Marvin had less trouble gathering his team in *The Dirty Dozen* than I had here. Ultimately, for me, the most troubling *femme fatale* of all, one who instilled love and fear in my heart as a child, was the Evil Queen from Walt Disney's *Snow White*. The history of the cinema did not record the name of the toon actress who played her, but to me, she surpassed even the legendary Jessica Rabbit.

Tales of the Shadowmen *prides itself on being virtually the only truly international anthology that opens its pages to non-English-speaking writers. We have in the past published stories by Belgian, French, French Canadian and Italian authors, and in this volume we are proud to present a tale by Argentinean author and current Chilean resident Roberto Lionel Barreiro, directly translated from the Spanish, which brings together two legendary figures who each hid their own secret identities under a careful mask...*

Roberto Lionel Barreiro: *Secrets*

Montreuil-sur-Mer, 1822

The day was almost done in Montreuil-sur-Mer when the mysterious gentleman arrived.

At first, his coach didn't draw any more attention than usual: too many aristocrats and wealthy people used the main road that crossed the town for a single carriage to be of much interest to the townspeople. Even though the Wolves' gang had recently been causing serious trouble in the region, there were still many people using that road. So the sight of one carriage was not enough to cause many people to notice—at first.

What did attract the town's attention was the horse attached behind the carriage. Or, more accurately, it was what was on its back: a wobbling body, still spouting blood from a single bullet hole to the forehead. The bullet had struck right between the eyes.

Surprised, the townspeople gathered—in increasing numbers—to discover that the corpse was that of Pierre Dumeville, leader of the Wolves, who had avoided capture for well over three years. The commotion caused by this realization eventually brought the Mayor, Monsieur Madeleine, to the carriage.

Madeleine approached the driver, a man with olive-colored skin who might have been Italian, or Greek, or even possibly Egyptian—it was impossible to tell.

"What is going on here?" asked Madeleine asked.

The driver merely stared at him.

"Unfortunately, Señor, my servant does not understand you," said a voice originating from inside the coach. The correct pronunciation didn't hide the foreign accent.

Madeleine looked at the man who stepped out. He was definitively a gentleman. His figure, from his perfect haircut and impeccably trimmed mustache to his expensive coat and trousers, and the embroidered handkerchief he held in his hand, testified to the exaggerated care for elegance that was a mark of mem-

19

bers of the Court or the very rich. In fact, the mayor found the visitor a trifle effeminate. Only his eyes contrasted sharply with the rest of his body: they looked around, scrutinizing everything with unusual sharpness, ready to suspect everyone. It was a look that didn't please Monsieur Madeleine.

"Could you tell me how did this dead bandit ended up on the back of your horse, Monsieur?"

"Of course. They tried to rob us on the road and discovered that my servant is an excellent marksman. As a consequence, this man died. I suspect that he was their leader, because when the rest of the gang saw him fall, they fled and left us alone. It seemed the right thing to do to bring the body and explain what happened to the authorities. At least, I hope it was…"

The visitor had told his tale as casually as if he had been telling a story at a dinner party.

"It was even better than that, Monsieur: you have done us a great service. This criminal was wanted by all the gendarmes in the region, and he and his associates terrorized travelers with their crimes. I don't know how we'll ever be able to thank you, Monsieur… Monsieur…?"

"Oh, please excuse my bad manners! I am Señor Alejandro Raposa, at your service. And I presume that I am talking to someone of authority in this town?"

"You are indeed. I am Monsieur Madeleine, the Mayor of Montreuil-sur-Mer. If I can be of any assistance…"

Raposa took some seconds before answering:

"Well… The truth is that this attempted robbery has delayed me, and I don't think I'll make it to my planned stop before nightfall. Also, I am a man who prefers to avoid unnecessary effort if possible. So I would like to ask you to recommend a place to stay for the night."

"Señor Raposa, it would be my honor to offer you and your servant the hospitality of my house—if you would accept."

"Thank you, Monsieur," answered the visitor with a brilliant smile. "I hope that my company will be pleasant…"

And, after a firm handshake, the man followed the Mayor inside his house, thereby beginning a night during which many long hidden secrets would be revealed…

Raposa tuned out to be an excellent guest. He easily entertained the many curious townspeople who had come to the Mayor's house to meet him. When they discovered he'd come from America, and that his servant was a native of that continent, the stream of people became almost continuous. Nevertheless, the visitor seemed perfectly at ease, tirelessly regaling the Frenchmen with stories of the New World.

"What brings you to France from so far away?" asked Mademoiselle Dunant, whose eyes had not left Raposa, and who would secretly have been happy to ask the gallant American to finish the night at her house, preferably in her bed. This was something to be expected of Mademoiselle Dunant, if one believed the local gossip.

"Ah, my dear young lady," answered Raposa with a smile, "I would love to tell you, but my mission is secret. I can only tell you that I must talk to His Majesty, your good King Louis, or one of his ministers, to discuss matters pertinent to problems in my home country."

A murmur of excitement ran through the parlor. What a fascinating personage this handsome American was!

Finally, after an evening that seemed endless, Monsieur Madeleine managed to convince his guests that the foreign gentleman needed some rest. Señor Raposa helped by emitting a few badly covered yawns.

Upon returning to the salon after saying good-bye to the last visitor, the Mayor noted that it was exactly 11 p.m. His guest was still in his chair, calmly lighting a cigar of prodigious fragrance. When he saw Madeleine enter, he took another cigar of the same size out of his jacket and offered it to his host.

"Your reception was most charming, *Señor Alcade*; I enjoyed it very much," said Raposa while Monsieur Madeleine sat down and lit the Cuban cigar.

"Thank you for the kind words, but I doubt that my humble home could appear so charming to someone who has known the King's court."

Raposa's laughter rang out like a crystalline stream.

"Don't you tell me that you believed all my stories, my friend?"

"So the reasons for your trip aren't so secret after all?"

"Of course they are. We all have secrets. We hide things that we don't want others to find out, afraid that they would emerge from under our respectable guises at the least appropriate moment, destroying the lives we have worked so hard to build for ourselves..."

Raposa seemed to speak distractedly, as if he was indulging in a bit of idle philosophizing, but Madeleine saw his sharp, attentive eyes moving from one side to another, and he felt a shudder deep in his soul. The American wasn't speaking idly: those words were directed at him. Or more accurately, to the man he had once been.

Raposa continued speaking as if his words were of little importance:

"Let's take an example... You, for instance, my dear Mayor. Tonight, I have heard how you are respected by your neighbors, all the good things that you have done in so few years... beginning on the very night you arrived in Montreuil-sur-Mer. A hero who, upon his arrival, rushes into a burning house to save people who are complete strangers to him... How can someone as good as you have anything to hide?

The stranger stopped for an instant and the knot in Madeleine's stomach began to spread its deadly coldness through his body. Raposa continued:

"Tonight, I saw your forearms, which appeared briefly from under the sleeves of your shirt. It was but a fleeting sight; none of the other guests saw anything, I'm certain; you pulled your sleeves diwn so quickly. But your gesture wasn't fast enough for the trained eyes of an attentive on-looker like myself, and I saw the scars—distinctive scars that look just like those that would result from having been chained in a labor gang... A rather rare and singular thing in a public servant, if you don't mind my saying....

Raposa exhaled a spiral of smoke; Madeleine looked at him hypnotized, like a bird watching a cat stalking it. What did the stranger know? Why was he tormenting him about his past? Had he not changed enough? What would he do next?

"My family was friends for many years with a venerable French priest," continued Raposa. "He was known as a kind and just man, who performed his Christian duties with goodness and love for others. His name was Monseigneur Myriel. For a long time, we exchanged letters, telling stories about what was happening to us, living on different continents. He passed away a few years ago... Did you know him?

"Yes... I knew him..." replied the Mayor slowly, growing very pale.

"I remember an incident which he described in one of his letters... There was a man who had recently left prison, whom Monseigneur Myriel received in his house. The man stole some silverware, and was later apprehended by the police, but the kindly Monseigneur not only claimed he had given the silver to the man, but further offered him a pair of candlesticks in order to extract his promise to go straight... In his letter, Monseigneur Myriel expressed the wish that the convict would manage to reform and become as honest as he was tall and strong. Apparently, this Jean Valjean—I believe that was the name Monseigneur Myriel gave me—was a bear of a man, just like you, Señor Madeleine..."

Suddenly, the sound of blows in the next room cut through the thick silence, surprising both host and guest, putting an abrupt end to the tense situation in which they had found themselves. Both looked in that direction. Raposa barely had time to grasp his cane when the door slammed opened and five, fierce looking, armed men entered the room.

"So you're here, pretty boy?" one of them shouted to Raposa. "Did you think you could escape our revenge after killing our leader? We'll teach you to meddle with the Wolves! I'm gonna..."

"...kill me with that smell?" Raposa's ironic smile enhanced his insult.

The bandit's face turned red and he advanced furiously toward the gentleman. Raposa pulled a sword from inside his cane and inclined it lightly; Madeleine understood that he was *en garde*, expecting the attack which he had provoked.

Raposa's hand was like a slash of lightning. Mere seconds later, the bandit dropped dead, the killing blade having unerringly found his heart in his chest with deadly accuracy.

What happened next was something that Madeleine would never forget. The foppish aristocrat suddenly turned into an elegant, exacting, prodigious killing machine. Raposa faced the remaining bandits, sword in hand, and attacked all four simultaneously. One of the Wolves fell with his neck slashed. Another received the point of the sword between the eyes, a blow which reminded the Mayor of the legendary *Botte de Nevers*. And all this happened while Raposa did not lose his sarcastic and contemptuous smile.

But as he attacked the third bandit, Raposa neglected the last man for an instant. Madeleine saw the Wolf ready to slash the American with a cutlass. If he allowed the bandit to do this, his secret would be safe again. For a mere second, the old Jean Valjean lived again, pushing the kind Monsieur Madeleine back into the recesses of his mind. He only had to keep still for an instant...

The Wolf couldn't stop the formidable bulk of the Mayor, who knocked him down with a swift, clean punch, leaving him unconscious on the floor. Then Madeleine saw Raposa disarming the other bandit with a quick turn of his blade.

They locked up the two surviving Wolves in the cellar, then looked after the servants, making sure that they were unharmed. When they were finished, Raposa took another cigar and offered one to Madeleine. After exhaling its rewarding smoke, he said:

"You know, Señor Madeleine, your town has some *extremely* interesting distractions..."

It was nearly noon the next day when the carriage left. Raposa and his native servant were ready to continue on their way, surrounded by villagers who couldn't believe what had happened. Between the handsome American and their sturdy Mayor, the bandits who had terrorized the region had been eliminated in a single night!

Before leaving, Raposa approached the Mayor. He spoke in low voice:

"Before we were rudely interrupted last night, I was going to tell you that my friend Monseigneur Myriel supposed that Jean Valjean was an honest man at heart who had suffered terribleluck. After seeing what happened last night, I heartily agree with him. Besides, as you probably suspect, I am not really in a position to expose anyone else's secret identity. I can assure you that double lives are an unbearable weight to people who live them. So, Monsieur Madeleine, Jean Valjean, or whatever you wish to call yourself, I only wish you good luck in this life, and I hope that your own secret identity does not burden you as much as mine sometimes does!"

And thus, Señor Raposa, a surname used by Don Diego de la Vega for his secret mission in France, left Montreuil-sur-Mer, never to return.

Matthew Baugh opened the first volume of Tales of the Shadowmen *in 2005 with a tale pitting the dark cloaked avenger Judex against the Frankenstein Monster. In his latest tale, he again uses Judex, torn from the silent serials, and places him in the charnel house of World War I (one is reminded of Abel Gance's masterful 1918* J'Accuse!*), facing even grislier supernatural horrors. Fortunately, this time, Judex is ably assisted by a very superhuman fellow...*

Matthew Baugh: *What Rough Beast*

The Western Front, 1916

"Monsieur Danner?"

Hugo looked up from his novel. The nurse was an angular woman in her 30s who he had never particularly liked. He knew the feeling was mutual; with so few beds to spare for the wounded, she didn't think much of accommodating one uninjured Legionnaire.

"There is a man wanting to see you," the nurse said. "Will you follow me, please?"

He put down the book and rose with the ease of a gifted athlete in perfect health. He was handsome, with his tanned skin, and his hair and eyes so dark that many of his compatriots mistook him for a "Red Indian." More than that, there was a sense of power about him, as if his personality was charged with electricity that made him the center of attention.

With a sour look, she led him through the rows of cots crammed into the ruined church that now served as a field hospital. Outside, the day was sunny and there was no sound of the fighting in the trenches, not five miles away. She left him in the shadow of an oak where an elderly man dressed in formal black waited. On the lane, just beyond the tree, stood an expensive Peugeot touring car.

"Legionnaire Danner?" the white-haired man asked, extending his hand politely. Hugo shook it, trying to size up his visitor. He was probably in his sixties, and possessing a quiet dignity that impressed the younger man. He wore no sign of rank or service.

"My name is Vallières," the man said.

"Do I know you, Monsieur?"

"No," Vallières said, "and there is no reason that you should. I am not a terribly important person; outside of the mission I have been given."

"And this mission concerns me?" Hugo asked.

"It does... At least, if you truly are the one they call *le Colorado*."

"I come from Colorado, in the United States," he replied. "Some of the men in the Legion called me that as a nickname."

"I have heard some remarkable stories about *le Colorado*," Vallières continued. "They say that you single-handedly resupplied your post during the recent German offensive. You carried 1000 kilos of food and ammunition on your back through no-man's land."

Hugo shrugged.

"Is it also true that you went into the trenches alone and, when your rifle was broken, slew scores of men with your bare hands?"

Hugo didn't respond. He wanted to like the white-haired gentleman, but he wondered where this was going.

"You were shot?"

"More times than I could count."

"And bayoneted?"

"The *boches* did their best. They managed to shred my uniform, for all the good it did them."

"You were not wounded?"

In response, Hugo stripped off his shirt revealing lean, hard muscles and unmarked skin.

"Why, then, were you in the hospital?"

"Exhaustion."

Vallières shook his head in wonder. "If all of this is true, then you are the man we need."

"It is true," Hugo said.

"Forgive me, but this is so remarkable. Can you show me something to convince me?"

Hugo walked over to the man's automobile. Taking a solid grip with both hands, he strained to lift the vehicle. The weight didn't bother him, but it was tricky balancing the big car, and he wanted to be careful not to damage it. After a moment, he found the right stance, and his feet sank ankle-deep into the grassy lawn as he raised the car over his head.

"How do you do that?"

"They grow us strong in Colorado."

Vallières smiled. "I think, rather, it has something to do with your father, the medical scientist, Abednego Danner."

Hugo scowled as he lowered the vehicle to the ground. He hadn't made a secret of his strength in his service with the Foreign Legion, but had never said a word about the treatment his father had used on him in the womb. He felt suddenly vulnerable, something uncomfortable for him.

"What else do you know?"

"You were liked in your hometown, even though your parents kept you rather secluded. You left to attend Webster University in Missouri where you excelled at American football. You left there…"

"I left when I accidentally killed another player in a game," Hugo said. "Monsieur Vallières, where is this leading?"

"Forgive me, Monsieur Danner, but it was necessary to investigate you. I regret that I have crossed the bounds of discretion, but I assure you, there is no need for concern. Your private history is safe with me; even should you refuse to accept my offer."

"What offer?"

"There is a mission you are needed for. It is most urgent and only you have the power to accomplish it."

What kind of mission was this?

Vallières had dropped Hugo in an abandoned farmhouse close to the front. He'd obtained the American's release from the hospital with a set of orders signed by General Broulard and brought him to this remote place.

"Wait here," the old man said. "You will be joined by three others shortly. Two men and a woman."

"Agents of the French government?" Hugo asked.

"Not exactly," Vallières said with an enigmatic smile. "I am a patriot, but trust me when I say that this is a greater matter than nation against nation. You will understand soon enough."

Hugo looked into the old man's eyes and saw the strength there. He could tell that he would not get any more from Vallières, except through force. He decided that he would rather trust that the man was an ally.

Vallières showed him where provisions and an oil lamp were kept, and the best way to blank out the windows so the enemy would not see his light and call down fire on him. Then he bade him good luck and drove away.

Hugo waited, impatiently, for several hours. There was some furniture still in the house, though most of the belongings had long since been looted. There were a round table and a few chairs, plain but made with painstaking craftsmanship. Hugo wondered about the hand that had carved them. He imagined a farmer, skilled with mallet and chisel, and the family he shared meals with, and wondered if they were still alive.

He made himself as comfortable as he could and ate some of the provisions, finding the bread stale, but the cheese good and the wine excellent. For a time, he tried to read his novel, but without much success. He was too anxious to focus his mind on anything for long.

Just past dusk, he heard the sounds of a car coming down the lane. Hugo extinguished his lantern and watched as the vehicle came to a stop and two shadowed figures emerged.

With the confidence born of invulnerability, Hugo opened the door and stepped out. The visitors walked into the light from the doorway and, if they were afraid, he couldn't see it. The first was a man as tall as he was; he wore a European suit but with the beard, turban, and sash of a Sikh. The woman looked to be well into middle age, though still very attractive. She had a wealth of black hair, shot with gray that framed a pale, lovely face.

"You are the people I am to meet?"

"Yes," the man replied.

"I was told to expect three."

"We are all here," said a voice from behind him. Hugo spun to see another man, this one dressed in a long black cape and matching slouch hat that partially hid his features. He had not heard or seen any movement, but the stranger had managed to enter the cottage.

"How did you…?"

"Pardon me," the turbaned man said, "but it would be more practical if we finished this conversation inside. Your light may be seen."

Hugo stepped aside, letting the man and his companion pass, then followed and shut the door.

"Now, perhaps you can tell me what this is all about," he said. "And who are you?"

"I am Sâr Dubnotal," the turbaned man said. "My companion is Mademoiselle Gianetti Annunciata. Our mysterious friend uses the name Judex."

Hugo scowled, puzzled by the men's odd pseudonyms. Still, this was secretive business and spies, he supposed, must have codenames. "Gentlemen, Mademoiselle," he said with a nod. "If someone can tell me what we are here for, I'd appreciate it. I've been on pins and needles all day."

"Of course," Sâr Dubnotal said with a polite smile. "Each person here has certain abilities that are needed to prevent the unleashing of a terrible weapon."

Hugo felt his heart begin to pump faster and his mouth tightened in a grim smile. This was the sort of thing he'd been looking for: a true challenge, a chance to make a difference.

Dubnotal produced a folded map and spread it out on the table. It showed France and the western front was clearly indicated by a red line.

"As you know, the war has been static for some time, with each side entrenched against the other. There have been offensives and counter-offensives, all without any real result. But recently something new happened, here."

The Sâr placed his finger on a point that Hugo judged to be about 20 miles north of the farmhouse.

"For the last three nights, the bodies of the fallen have risen from the trenches and walked."

Hugo glanced at the man's face, incredulous, but the turbaned man seemed completely serious.

"The dead walking? That's preposterous!"

"I have heard the reports," Judex said, his shadowed features grim. "They say that the soldiers walk or crawl in the same direction. It doesn't seem to matter whether the dead belong to our forces or the Germans. Some soldiers have

The Sâr seemed unperturbed by Hugo's outburst.

"I do not ask you to believe anything, Monsieur Danner," he said. "I simply offer information; it is up to you to decide how to use it. There is one more thing I must show you. If you will be seated around the table and join hands..."

"What is this, some kind of séance?" Hugo asked.

"Gianetti is one of the most gifted spirit mediums of our age," the Sâr replied.

Hugo nearly refused, but the appeal in the woman's dark eyes, and Judex's stern expression swayed him. He sat opposite Judex and joined hands with Gianetti on one side and Sâr Dubnotal on the other. The turbaned man began to chant quietly, using words that belonged to no language Hugo recognized.

A thin, faintly luminous mist was gathering on the table and dribbled off the edges. It thickened as Hugo watched and he seemed to see tiny figures moving through it. Slowly the insect-sized forms resolved into human beings—men in tattered uniforms—who trudged and crept through a landscape sculpted of mist."

"He calls them," Gianetti said in a hollow voice.

"Who?" Sâr Dubnotal asked.

"Von Meyer calls the dead to his home."

"Why does he call them?"

"That he may use their flesh and bone to sculpt a weapon; a colossus that will sweep away the forces of his enemies."

"By what power does he call them?"

"By the words of the grimoire."

"What grimoire?"

"The book of Nathare of Vyones."

The Sâr caught his breath. Even in the dim light, Hugo could see that his face had gone pale.

"Does he build the same abomination that once laid waste to Ylourgne?"

"He does, and no weapon forged of man shall be able to stop it."

"Show me!"

Gianetti gasped in pain. Her eyes rolled back and Hugo felt her hand spasm and grow cold. He looked at her in alarm, but the spell passed in a moment. When his gaze returned to the table, the scene had changed. The tiny soldiers lay in heaps while robed men and nude man-like things hewed the flesh from their bones with knives and cleavers. The flesh they gathered in a cauldron that simmered with a deep red glow while the bones they placed in a vat of sickly pale hue.

As quickly as the two vessels filled, huge bestial man-things ladled their contents into buckets which hooded men carried into another area where they dumped the contents on a great pile in the shape of a colossal, partially fleshed skeleton.

"The Colossus," Gianetti said. "Made from the flesh and bones of ten-thousand dead men. He will—"

Her words ended with a shriek of pain as she leapt to her feet, her limbs twitching with epileptic frenzy. Hugo and Judex both reached for her, but the Sâr's voice stopped them.

"She is in the power of our enemy," he said. "If you touch her, she could come to great harm. Please, leave this to me."

"*El Tebib?*" Gianetti's voice had changed into a deep and cultured male voice. "*El Tabib, ist dass Sie?*"

"I am here, von Meyer," Dubnotal replied. Hugo was amazed at how calm he remained.

"*You seek to spy on me, my old friend,*" Gianetti said. Her limbs no longer twitched but Hugo saw that her feet hovered several inches over the floor. The sight sent a shiver of dread through him. He glanced at Judex, wondering if the same fear he felt had penetrated those unreadable features.

"Release the woman," Dubnotal said in a clear, reasonable tone. "She is an innocent; your conflict is with me."

"*An innocent?*" Gianetti threw back her head and peals of masculine laughter came from her mouth. "*El Tebib, don't you know how much joy it gives me to torment an innocent? The jaded are so tedious, but the naïve can provide us with such exquisite entertainment.*"

Hugo saw the Sâr's hand dip into his pocket and emerge with a thick piece of chalk. Out of the corner of his eye he saw that Judex had drawn his Steyr, but made no move to point it at the woman.

"Danner," Sâr said. "Seize Gianetti."

Hugo leapt forward, his arms closing firmly around the woman's slender form. She struggled with inhuman strength, clawing and biting, but might have been trapped in a steel vice for all the good it did her. His only concern was to keep her from harming herself in her frenzy.

Dubnotal didn't waste a moment. He bent low and used the chalk to draw an even circle around Hugo and his captive. Then he drew strange glyphs, fourteen in all, evenly spaced around the outer edge. When he completed the last one, Gianetti screamed in her own voice and went limp in Hugo's arms. As gently as he could, he powered her to the wooden floor.

"What did you do?" Judex asked.

"I did not think he was so powerful," the turbaned man said. "He reached out with his psychic powers and overwhelmed her mind. The circle should protect her, but…"

He stopped as the woman's body convulsed violently and her mouth began to foam. Hugo caught her arms to keep her from hurting herself.

"She's like ice," he said.

The Sâr stepped carefully into the circle, taking care not to scuff the chalk. He knelt next to Gianetti and forced her eyes open with his fingers.

"Von Meyer is trying to break through my defenses," he said. "I must save her if I can."

"What can we do to help?" Hugo asked.

"Thank you, my friend, but this is something only I can do," Dubnotal replied. "While Meyer is distracted here, the two of you must go to his base. The colossus must not be allowed to rise."

Hugo gazed at the dark terrain far below. In the light of the full Moon, and from an altitude nearly a mile, the French country looked serene and beautiful. It was hard to imagine that this was the same land that was the battleground for tens of thousands of men in the daylight.

He rode in the front seat of Judex's plane, a Morane Type-L spotter. His mysterious companion, ever prepared, had hidden it in the old barn by the farmhouse. He and Sâr Dubnotal must have been planning this even before they contacted him.

His reverie was broken by the roar of diving engines and the whine of bullets. He felt a series of mild stings across his back and saw holes appear in the fuselage around him, then the aircraft rolled sideways and several dark shapes shot past.

Biplanes, he realized. *The Germans have found us.*

He strained into the darkness and counted three of the planes circling to come at them again. Judex didn't seem interested in a fight. He turned them away from their pursuers and began to climb toward a bank of clouds, clearly hoping to lose them.

It was a good strategy, but Hugo quickly realized that it wouldn't work. The German planes were faster, and could climb better than the Morane. It was only a matter of moments before they were strafed again.

As the planes began to fire, Judex took the Morane into a dive, picking up speed. The Germans followed as he dodged and wove in an unpredictable pattern. Abruptly, the aircraft rose into a steep climb, losing speed rapidly but rising out of the line of fire. It took only a moment for the pursuers to adapt and begin the climb behind them, but, as the Morane came close the stalling point, Judex turned the rudder and the nose dropped. In an instant, they were screaming toward the ground.

The Germans scattered to avoid the diving plane and, with a half roll, Judex leveled out heading back in the direction they had just come.

For a moment, Hugo thought they had escaped, or gained a few precious moments, but the squadron leader was an unusually talented flyer. He was back on their tail in an instant, firing his twin Vickers machineguns. Several shots struck the engine, for it stuttered and caught fire. Hugo could see Judex fighting with the controls, but the aircraft didn't respond. Despite his best efforts, the plane went into an uncontrolled spin and plummeted toward the ground.

The spinning, tumbling fall disoriented Hugo, but he knew he had only seconds to act. He reached behind him and grabbed the fuselage, his fingers tearing through the heavy canvas to find a solid grip on the plane's metal skeleton. He pulled himself from the cockpit, shredding his safety harness as he did, and made his way, hand over hand, back to Judex's seat.

He had just a moment to register the disbelief on the Frenchman's face before he ripped lose his harness. Gathering his ally in his arms, Hugo kicked out into space.

Once he was away from the plane, Hugo managed to orient himself. They were approaching the ground rapidly and he barely had the time to get his feet under him before they hit.

The Moon had risen to the peak of the sky, but its light barely penetrated the heavy canopy of forest. As far as Hugo was concerned, that was a good thing. It meant that the German planes couldn't see to strafe them on the ground, and even search parties on foot would have trouble finding them.

Judex stirred where he lay and opened his eyes.

"How are you feeling?" Hugo asked.

"Alive," he replied, rising cautiously to his feet. "Nothing seems to be broken, which is remarkable."

"I cushioned your fall the best I could."

"And how are you?" Judex asked.

"I'm right as rain. Jumping out of an airplane doesn't seem to be that much for me."

Judex smiled and shook his head. "Did you know you'd survive?"

"I suspected as much, but I couldn't be sure. That's not the sort of thing I do for a lark, you know."

"Your strength is an amazing gift."

"I suppose so," Hugo said. "I keep hoping I'll find a way to use it that'll make a real splash in the world, but no luck. I think I'd have been a lot happier without it."

"What do you mean?"

"I didn't have any real friends, or even pets, when I was a kid. My mother was afraid of my strength; afraid I'd kill someone. When I got away from home I thought it'd be easy to make my way in the world, but all I seem able to do is break things and terrify people.

"I thought the War would be the perfect chance to put all that destructive power to use. The thing is, as many Huns as I kill, it doesn't seem to bring the conflict any closer to ending, and the people around me still die."

"You have lost friends," Judex said. It sounded like a question, but Hugo could tell that the man already knew the answer.

"One friend, yes. Another American named Tom Shayne. He was a swell guy until the Huns dropped a shell on us. It deafened me for a bit but there wasn't much left of Tom...

"I kind of went crazy then. I went into the trenches and wore myself out killing them. Can you imagine? It's like stomping cockroaches until you're so tired you can't lift your feet. That's when they put me in the field hospital. You know the rest."

Judex was silent for a moment, then he took a small flask from his coat and passed it to Hugo. He caught the aroma of strong brandy and took a swallow. The liquor warmed his stomach but did nothing to lift his spirits.

Judex took the flask back and raised it.

"Tom Shayne," he said, then took a small drink and put the flask away. The sincerity of the gesture touched Hugo.

"Did it help?" Judex asked.

"What?"

"Taking vengeance on your enemies."

"Not really," Hugo said, after a moment of thought. "Tom's still gone, and I hate the bastards more than ever."

Judex was silent and Hugo could see that his words had stirred something deep within the man.

"Perhaps for revenge to truly make a difference, it must be applied carefully."

"Are you saying I shouldn't have killed those bastards?" Hugo asked, feeling a surge of indignation.

"No," Judex replied. "I would never deny any man his just vengeance. It is only that, if it is to achieve true justice, revenge must be applied as carefully as a surgeon's scalpel."

"Is that why you do this?" Hugo asked.

"This mission?"

"More than that. You have some amazing skills, and your own airplane, and there's this hat and cloak. What is all of this for?"

"Yes," Judex replied. "There is a man I must punish, not just for what he has done to my family, but for all those he has ruined."

"Maybe when this is over, I'll help you," Hugo said.

Judex smiled and nodded, but it seemed to Hugo that he was still troubled. The cloaked man pulled out a map and a compass and spent a few moments getting his bearings.

"Joiry is that direction," he said, pointing into the woods. "If we start now and walk through the night we should be able to reach it before dawn.

"We can do much better than that," Hugo said with a grin. "I can outrun a race car if I want to."

Half an hour later, the two men stood on an outcropping of rock where heavy forest opened enough for a clear view of the starry sky. The ruin of Joiry Castle stood on a jagged escarpment overlooking the countryside. An unhealthy red light shone through some of the gaps in the ancient stonework.

"There," Judex said pointing to a narrow trail that ascended the rock face. "Movement on the rocks."

Hugo followed the gesture. In the light of the full Moon, he made out an irregular trickle of human shapes shambling up the path.

"Men," he said, "but there's something wrong with the way they're moving."

"I wish I had my field glasses," Judex said with a rueful smile. "I'm afraid I left them on the plane."

"We were in a bit of a hurry," Hugo replied, returning the smile.

"The walkers aren't being challenged, but the forest has been cut back at the base of the rocks. I don't see a way to reach the place by stealth."

"There's no need," Hugo said. "There's no way they can keep me out of that place. You stay here; I'll go and smash their super-weapon."

"We should both go."

"No offense, but for all your skills, you're just a man. There's no danger for me, but you'd likely be killed."

"No danger?" Judex fixed an intense stare on him. "My friend, you are powerful, but it is foolish to make such an assumption. We need a strategy."

"I don't," Hugo said. "I hope you take my advice and keep to cover. *Au revoir*, my friend. I'll bring you von Meyer's head on a bayonet."

He made a huge leap, which cleared the treetops and took him to the edge of the woods, then he ran toward the cliff-side path. Hugo heard shouts from the ruins and, a moment later, the sound of rifle fire. He barked out a laugh as a lucky shot caught him in the abdomen, the bullet flattening against his unyielding flesh.

Hugo slowed for the narrow, winding footpath. He could make out the figures ahead of him now, soldiers in German and French uniforms marching together in single minded determination to reach the Château Joiry. Some of the men bore terrible wounds. A one-armed German, half his head a wreck, marched almost proudly, while another followed at a slower pace, limping but otherwise untroubled by his missing right foot. Hugo felt the fear tickle his spine from bottom to top. He knew that the walking dead couldn't harm him any more than the living, but the sight of them was horrifying. He decided to bypass the macabre procession as much as he could. He stopped running and looked up to where the trail doubled back to pass over his head. Gathering himself, he leaped to the next section, then repeated the process, using the switchbacks like a set of stairs.

A few shots caught him before he reached the top, but they barely registered. The joy of battle was on him as he came over the edge, and he was disappointed to see only a dozen terrified German soldiers and two men in black hooded robes.

He raced toward them contemptuous of their rifles. When he reached them, he drove his fist through the first soldier's chest like a spear. Hugo felt a brutal satisfaction as he saw the others blanch with fear. Several of the soldiers continued to fire, but most turned and tried to flee into the keep. Hugo grabbed a man and pitched him far over the side of the escarpment. Seconds later, he sent two more screaming after him.

By this time, all of the others had abandoned their weapons and were scrambling over each other in a frantic attempt to get through the narrow door. Hugo picked up a discarded rifle and hurled it like a javelin to impale one of the men. He caught two more by their necks and banged their heads together with such force that their skulls exploded in sprays of red. He pushed through the throng, lashing out with his fists, crushing a spine, collapsing a ribcage, ripping an arm from its socket and discarding it.

Ignoring the three surviving men, Hugo surged forward and caught the robed leaders and pinned them against the parapet wall, one in each hand.

"Where is your leader?" he yelled at one of them.

"*Ich verstehe nicht!*" the man cried, his voice frantic.

"Wrong answer," Hugo said. He tightened his grip, just a little, and was rewarded by the crunch of the man's trachea and, an instant later, the pop of his spine."

"Your turn," he said to the other hooded man. "Where is the Herr Doctor Meyer?"

"*Der Meister?*" the terrified German pointed to an archway that had once been a door leading to the inner castle. "*Er ist dort, durch diese Tür.*"

"Thanks, pal," Hugo said. He slapped his palm against the man's brow, turning his head to a mix of red jelly and bone shards.

He gave a glance at the three surviving soldiers, who huddled against the wall, paralyzed by fear. He nearly turned back to kill them, but something in him didn't want to.

"Not worth my time," he said, then headed through the arch into a broad stair that spiraled downward. The passage was dark but, as he descended, he discerned the reflection of a ruby glow. A moment later, three guards appeared around the bend, carrying torches that gave off the unnatural glow. They were roughly human in shape, but with distorted, dog-like faces and hooved feet.

Their inhuman appearance startled Hugo, only for an instant, but enough for them to leap on him, attacking savagely. They were strong—much stronger than men—but that was nothing to Hugo. Their claws slid harmlessly across his flesh. He grabbed one by the hip and shoulder and found that its flesh was unnaturally touch and rubbery. With a powerful wrench, he pulled the creature to pieces. He lifted the second and slammed it into the stone wall with such force that the ceiling threatened to cave in.

The third monster backed away from him, growling uncertainly. Hugo sprang forward swinging his stiff-fingered hand horizontally, like a sword. The blow caught the creature in the side of the neck, releasing a fountain of gore. The doglike head fell from the body to roll down the stairs.

Hugo emerged into the room he had seen in Gianetti's vision. Black robed men and naked fiends paused at their grim work so stare at him. One man, tall and bearded, his robe embroidered with strange occult symbols, stood at the far side of the room, supervising. Hugo knew instantly who he must be and strode toward him.

He was met by a surge of inhuman bodies as more creatures like those he had killed on the stair leapt on him. Others joined them: a bat-winged reptilian creature shaped like a giant ape, a small-toad-skinned man with tentacles lining his mouth, and many others whose bizarre appearance Hugo barely registered before they were on him.

Hugo flailed at them as their fangs and claws shredded his clothes and left scratches on even his steel skin. This was like the trenches again, except these things were far stronger then men and did not die easily. Like ants, they continued to attack long after taking wounds that would have killed a human being. Still, for all their ferocity, he smashed them down, one by one, until the floor of the chamber was steeped with a mix of blood, ichor, and foul smelling fluids.

Then the small demon with the tentacled face rose up with a bowl of pale liquid which it dashed into Hugo's face. It blinded him and he swallowed a bitter mouthful. A moment later, he felt weak and dizzy.

Hugo tried to throw his tormenters off, but his muscles wouldn't obey him. Under the unrelenting attack of the demonic horde, he sagged to the ground and darkness claimed him.

He awoke in a different room, a huge chamber that must once have been the great hall of the castle. The ceiling had partially collapsed and he could see the moon through the aperture.

Hugo was bound to the wall by heavy chains that held his arms over his head; his feet dangled above the stone floor. He tried to test the chains, but discovered that his muscles were paralyzed. The room was dominated by a gigantic human form, the colossus of Gianetti's vision now completed.

"Master!"

He had just enough mobility to glance toward the voice. It was the toad-skinned creature which, with the winged ape-thing and two of the robed men, stood near him, apparently acting as guards.

"Master," the creature repeated, "he awakens!"

The man Hugo had seen earlier stepped up to him. He was tall and massively built, with close-cropped red hair and a full beard. The softness of his body was offset by his eyes, which were a pitiless blue that made Hugo think of an Arctic sky.

"*Wer sind Sie?*" the man asked.

"Go climb a tree," Hugo replied in English. Speech was easy for him so he reasoned that paralysis rather than weakness was what held him motionless.

"Who are you, *Engländer*?" The man's English was slow and heavily accented but Hugo could understand him.

"What's it to you, Herr Doctor von Meyer?"

"Ah..." Von Meyer smiled at the sound of his name. "If you know that, then you are an ally of the Frenchman, Dubnotal. Was he the one who gave you such power?"

"Nuts to you."

"Are there more like you?"

"A whole regiment," Hugo said. "The 'Fighting Colorados,' they call us."

"But they only sent you?"

"One man is more than enough to take care of a freak show run by a two-bit sideshow magician."

Von Meyer's face darkened and he smashed Hugo across the face with a backhanded blow. He hardly felt the impact, but the sorcerer yelped in pain and nursed his hand.

"Ghouls," he yelled, "*Bestrafen Sie ihn!*"

Two of the dog-like men moved forward, heavy iron bars in their hands. They began to beat his torso with powerful, measured blows. After some time, they stepped back, breathing hard, and Hugo laughed.

"You are a challenge," von Meyer said. "We must see if there are more vulnerable areas." He barked an order to the ghouls. They stepped away to return a moment later. One carried a sledge hammer, the other held a glowing poker. Hugo closed his eyes, tightly, and braced for what was coming. The red hot metal pressed against the skin of his eyelid and he felt the heat. It was unpleasant, but no worse than what a normal man might feel when the water in a shower grows too hot.

He could feel the ghoul trying to wedge the point of the implement between his eyelids and strained to prevent it. It seemed to go on forever, then the iron withdrew and he felt rubbery hands grasp his ankles and spread his limp legs.

Hugo opened his eyes in time to see the second ghoul swing the hammer in an upward arc to strike him squarely in the testicles. It wasn't a damaging blow, he knew, more what an ordinary man might feel if flicked with a fingertip, but he no longer felt like laughing. Half a dozen strikes later his eyes were watering and the creatures released him as von Meyer stepped forward.

"You see?" the sorcerer asked. "Nothing can withstand the intelligent application of force. Even a diamond can be split when one knows how."

Hugo glared, but kept his mouth shut. As strong as he was, he knew that the man was right. Eventually they would break even his superhuman body and, long before that, the pain would break his spirit.

"Are there others like you?"

"No," he said, seeing no harm in the answer.

"Did you come alone?"

He thought of Judex waiting in the forest. It had been foolish to leave the man behind.

"I did. Sâr Dubnotal wanted to send others with me, but I thought I could do this myself."

"Perhaps," von Meyer said. "Just the same, I have sent some of my ghouls out. They will sniff out anyone within five miles of the castle and tear them to pieces."

Hugo said nothing.

"I shall enjoy learning more about you, my friend," von Meyer said. "A man who can slaughter ghouls and demons may be of great use to me. For the moment, though, I have far more important things to attend to. I leave you to the tender care of my creatures."

For the next quarter of an hour, the ghouls applied their ingenuity to the most vulnerable parts of Hugo's body. In the background, he could hear the sound of chanting in some language he didn't recognize.

Then it stopped.

As if someone had thrown a switch, the chanting, the torture, all sound in the movement in the great chamber went away.

Hugo opened his eyes and saw that everyone was staring at the colossus. The gargantuan body took a breath, then another, then opened its eyes; the same ice-blue eyes of von Meyer's face.

The creature rose to its feet—Hugo guessed that it was at least 100 feet tall—and stretched its muscles. The thing raised its face to the sky.

"*Meine Stunde ist gekommen!*" The voice was the sorcerer's, but augmented by a chorus of 10,000 others. The giant laughed and strode from the castle, sending demons, ghouls and black robed men scurrying to avoid the falling debris as it tore through the walls.

Many of the fiends followed in its wake, but one man, the ape demon, the little toad skinned man, and two of the ghouls remained to continue their work on Hugo.

As he waited for the torture to resume, Hugo saw something like a shadow move from the shelter of the wall and come up behind his tormentors.

Judex!

The caped man came silently, his pistol drawn. When he was almost close enough to touch, Hugo saw the nostrils of one of the ghouls twitch. The creature spun, only to receive two slugs in the chest from Judex's Steyr. The pistol spoke again and the second ghoul joined the first on the floor.

The ape-thing sprang at the man, but he side-stepped and it caught only his cloak, pulling it loose. He fired a bullet into the demon's heart and the creature dissolved into foul greenish smoke.

The little demon sprang at Judex then, tackling him to the ground. Though only four feet tall, with a scrawny build, the toad-skinned horror seemed to have inhuman strength. It slapped the pistol away and began to strangle him. Fortunately, for all its strength, the creature only had the mass of a child. Judex spun to the right, throwing it off balance, and swept its feet from under it with his leg.

The demon lost its grip and was thrown nearly a dozen feet. It sprang back up in an instant, but Judex was just as fast. He dove for his pistol and rolled to his feet in one smooth motion. As the demon leaped, he fired two shots, and it burst into flame and vanished.

Judex turned, gun still in hand and strode toward the black-robed man who was the last of Hugo's tormentors. He placed the muzzle of the weapon against the man's forehead.

"There is an antidote for the paralysis drug, is there not?" he asked in a calm voice.

"How did you get in?"

The antidote the lackey had produced seemed effective. Hugo had recovered his movement in a matter of moments and easily broken free of the chains.

"It was not hard," Judex replied. "I overpowered one of the walking dead and took his uniform. I copied the unfortunate creature's gait and entered the castle unchallenged."

He paused for a moment.

"I saw what you did to those soldiers outside."

"Do you have a problem with that?"

"It was not necessary. They could not have harmed you."

"They were enemy soldiers," Hugo said. "They're responsible for killing Tom, and thousands of other good men."

"They were soldiers in war. Our own troops have done as much."

"Why are you criticizing me? I hate those sons of bitches and I'll avenge my friend's death every chance I get. I'd think you, of all people, would understand that."

"We have different ideas," Judex said, "but now is not the time. We have to stop the giant."

"I don't think even I can do that," Hugo replied.

"We must try."

The colossus was moving fast, but Hugo was faster. He carried Judex through the woods at the same breakneck pace, only stopping when they reaches a clearing a quarter of a mile ahead of the giant's path.

"Stay hidden," he said. "A silver bullet won't do anything against that monster." Hugo moved to the center of the clearing where an ancient glacier had scattered an assortment of granite boulders. He lifted one that must have weighed five tons and, as the colossus entered the clearing, threw it.

The rock sailed at the giant's chest, only to be batted away like a tennis ball. The monster bellowed out his eerie chorus of laughter and stomped with a colossal foot. Hugo saw it coming, but not in time to dodge. The weight stunned him and drove his body into the ground like a tent peg. He thrashed and struggled himself free of the earth, only to feel a great hand scoop him up and lift him high.

He drove his fist into the palm of the hand, piercing the flesh and breaking a metacarpal bone thicker than his torso. The colossus cried out and flung him to the ground with stunning force. Hugo lay there unable to move, waiting for the final attack that would snuff out his life, but it didn't come.

"Can you stand up?"

Judex was at his side, helping him to his feet.

"I was afraid you were dead," he said.

"Too close."

Hugo shook his head to clear it and became aware of the sound of howitzer fire around them. "What's happening?" he asked.

"Several German artillery placements have begun to shell the creature. That was what distracted him from you."

"The Germans? But he's one of them."

"All they see is a monster," Judex said. "They do what anyone would do."

"Can they kill him? Is it even possible?"

Judex shook his head. "I don't know, but we must try to help them."

The big guns were still firing as the two arrived. Dozens of soldiers tried to augment them with small arms fire. The Germans had set up their position in an old stone church and the attached parsonage. As they watched, the colossus tore open the roof of the smaller building and scooped out a handful of screaming infantrymen. He raised the soldiers to face level, then caught one with his other and popped him into his mouth. Hugo looked away as the giant began to chew.

One of the howitzers fired. Hugo turned back to see an explosion open a gaping hole in the monster's chest. For a moment he felt a surge of hope. Then the wound began to knit itself closed and, in moments, it had disappeared.

The colossus laughed and tossed away the remaining soldiers. He strode to the big gun seized it by barrel and lifted it like a toy. He tossed the howitzer into the woods and set about stamping on the gun crew like ants.

"Keep him busy," Judex said. "I have an idea."

He darted away in the direction of the buildings leaving Hugo to stare incredulously after him.

Keep him busy? That's insane.

Judex ducked into the old church but the colossus saw him. He abandoned lone survivor of the gun crew and moved toward the building.

Hugo muttered a string of curses and looked around for something to use as a weapon. His gaze settled on an officer's staff car. He raced to it and hoisted the big vehicle to his shoulder just as the giant bent to peer in the church windows. He threw it with all his might and caught the colossus on the jaw, staggering him.

"Here I am!" Hugo shouted, throwing a German motorcycle good measure.

And here we go, he said to himself as the giant rose and began to move toward him. He raced toward it, avoiding a clutching hand and running between the towering legs.

He pushed himself to the limit as the colossus gave chase. With its long legs it could cover ground faster, but it couldn't turn or stop nearly as fast as he could. He moved into the woods, darting through clumps of trees like a rabbit while the giant stumbled after him, leaving a trail of destruction.

It must have been a dozen times that Hugo narrowly dodged a trampling foot; then he saw something ahead of him. He only caught a glimpse but he could tell it was a little town, with people in the streets. He couldn't lead the abomination there.

Hugo hesitated as he tried to change his course. It was only for an instant, but that was enough. A mammoth hand scooped him up. He struggled against the grip and managed to apply a variation of a wrestling hold to one of the fingers. He pulled as hear as he could and heard the gratifying snap of tendons.

The giant let out a bellow of pain and threw him with such force that he nearly blacked out. The ground shot past at blinding speed until he came to earth with shattering impact.

Hugo lay still for several moments before he could raise his head. His entire body throbbed with pain unlike anything he had ever known.

He looked around and realized that he had been thrown back to the artillery placement at the church. The colossus apparently wanted for all of his victims to be in the same place. Colossal footsteps echoed through the forest as the monster approached. Hugo rose, his limbs barely able to support him, but he wanted to fight, or at least to die on his feet.

The colossus came into sight, towering above the tallest trees. When it saw him, its mouth twisted into a bestial leer and it headed in his direction. Hugo found himself watching his approaching death with an odd sense of detachment. He was too weary to be defiant, angry, or even frightened.

The voice of a howitzer sounded and, a second later, a wound appeared in the giant's chest. Hugo waited for the hole to close, but it didn't. Instead, black blood began to flow from the wound as a look of confusion spread across the colossal features. It raised its head and ten thousand voices shouted as one, "*Nein!*"

The colossus collapsed with the sound of a toppling building. Hugo followed a moment later, sinking to his trembling knees. He heard someone calling his name and turned to see Judex and several German soldiers racing toward him. Then he breathed deeply and let darkness carry him away.

He woke in the same field hospital. His old nurse seemed a little more pleased with him this time, now that he was covered with cuts and bruises. The second day, Sâr Dubnotal came to see him.

"Is he dead?" Hugo asked.

"Von Meyer?" The Sâr stroked his beard thoughtfully. "It is possible," he said, "though with a thaumaturge of his power it would be foolish to assume so."

"I know that Judex found a way to kill him—the giant—but how?"

"He remembered what I said about the silver bullet and went into the church to try to find something made of that metal."

"He must have succeeded. What was it?"

"I believe it was a statue of St. Dunstan. He gave it to the gun crew and it became their bullet."

"So I own my life to the enemy?" Hugo chuckled bitterly. "At least, now I know there's some use for religion."

"I have a note for you," Sâr Dubnotal said, and passed him a folded piece of paper.

My friend,

I am grateful that you survived. What you did took great power and greater courage and I am proud to have fought by your side.

As for your generous offer to help me in my mission, I fear I must decline. The vengeance I seek must be dealt out coolly and precisely and you are a man of passion and turmoil.

A man of your gifts has much more to offer than to act as an instrument of revenge or a weapon of destruction. I hope that you discover a way to build up rather than tear down. More than that, I hope you find peace.

Judex

The nurse announced that Hugo needed his rest so the Sâr shook his hand and left. He didn't rest though. He remained awake staring at the note and wondering if there could be anything in his life that would mean more than death and destruction.

For the life of him, he couldn't think of a thing.

While Tales of the Shadowmen *doesn't force its contributors to draw inspiration from this year's volume's sub-title, it is fitting that the* femme fatale *starring in this story by Thom Brannan is none other than the iconic (and poorly named) "Bride of Frankenstein." Instead of portraying her as an innocent victim, as she was in James Whale's 1935 movie, however, Thom logically follows Mary Shelley's premise and depicts her as evil—perhaps unwittingly so. And which better adversary for this preternatural* femme fatale *than a mysterious traveler in time and space...*

Thom Brannan: *What Doesn't Die*

> *"I thought with a sensation of madness on my promise of creating another like him, and trembling with passion, tore to pieces the thing on which I was engaged."*
> Victor Frankenstein

January 15th, 17**

The Creature looked down on me, disgusted, as I lay on the worktable, lightning flitting through the skies and various alchemical equipment surrounding me.

"A failure," he said, rage twisting his features. "My bride is incomplete. Even in his absence, Victor defeats me."

I realized as I looked up at the Creature, my Creator, that his lips weren't moving. It was only a moment later that I realized this was out of the ordinary. Was I receiving his thoughts? I probed further.

I saw through his eyes as he waited by the lake while another man threw a basket over the side of his boat; I felt the Creator's rage at this act. Time shifted, and I saw and felt my hands, no, his hands around another man's throat, trying to wrench the secret of life from this man, to no avail. Time shifted again and I was--no, the Creator--was diving for the basket, retrieving it and bringing its contents here, to where I lay in pieces on the ground.

A mighty blow to my head shook me from my Creator's mind, and he proceeded to tear me asunder. In his anger, in his haste, he left the job undone, and painfully, over time, I thought myself whole again, this time using an image my Creator held in his mind as ideal. An Elizabeth, whoever that was. To no avail . . . as I did that, he had travelled to enact his wedding night vengeance.

These are my first memories. I have been called a monster, and were I to agree with that, this formative experience might be the reason why.

I do not agree, however.

October 8th, 1893

The woman in black and red disembarked from the railcar with grace and poise, oblivious to the stares drawn to her pale, almost alabaster skin. She took the railway conductor's hand for assistance, not deigning to look at the man, but more enraptured by the city she'd arrived in. Chicago: transit capitol of the United States, the bustling center of a web of steel and wood, powered by coal and blue electricity. The train station was well-appointed and new, being recently upgraded to handle the transportation boom the city was experiencing, and it was aglow with modernity.

As crowded as the station was, the pale woman was unaffected by the seething throng of humanity. She only had eyes for a large poster on the wall advertising the Chicago Day at the World's Columbian Exposition. She stalked towards the poster, stepping in the way of several people as she did, seeming to not see them, only taking in the poster's every detail. Her eyes traced the stars and stripes at the top right down to the grand waterway at the bottom, a smile growing on her lips. With the back of one pale hand, she caressed the image of the Sentinel of the Republic and spoke soundless words to no one.

She was tall, stately; the woman wore a flowing black dress atypical of the time, with red striping and lining. Against this background, the whiteness of her hands and face were an explosion of difference. Her high cheekbones were a perfect pink, matched by an almost wanton redness in her lips and fingernails. Her black, black hair was captured at the back of her head with a white rose, a blank tombstone for the grave of ebon hair that hung down and trailed behind. She eschewed the hat that was the norm of the day, but hardly anyone male noticed *that*.

Stepping back, the pale woman ripped open her oversized purse and dug in it. With a faint cry of victory, she pulled from her bag a small beige ticket, looking from it to the poster.

"Soon," she whispered, her rasping voice that of shifting sands. "Very soon, I will be complete."

Turning from the poster, the pale woman walked purposefully towards the main thoroughfare, intent on finding transportation. Unnoticed behind her, an elderly man watched, his white hair swept back over a wide and intelligent brow. He smiled as the woman in black and red strode for the exit.

He held an identical ticket.

Keeping a respectable distance back, the old gentleman shadowed the pale woman to a grand hotel and watched her interact with the clerk. He noted with interest how she furrowed her brow as she stared at the young man behind the counter, and that interest piqued when the pale woman received a key without payment, or even signing the ledger.

"Extraordinary," he whispered. After she left for the newly-installed elevators, the elderly man approached the desk.

"Excuse me, good sir, what are the rates to stay here through the tenth of the month?"

The clerk, however, was distracted, watching the woman in black and red retreat to the lift.

"I say, young man. Are you this habitually rude to potential customers as a matter of principle, or is there some deeper business tactic at work here?"

When there was still no response from the clerk, the older man shook his head and reached out, touching the clerk at a spot behind his left ear. With an audible pop, the clerk swung his head back around to face the gentleman at the counter.

"Sorry, sir, bit of a busy day today. May I ask your name, sir?"

"I am Doctor Omega. And you're welcome."

"Welcome for what? And your name was what, sir?"

"For what, indeed? Hardly a thing seems to have changed." Leaving the flustered clerk to his papers, the Doctor walked haughtily away from the counter, watching after the elevator.

"What are you up to now, Eve?"

The Doctor made his way through the grounds of the World's Fair Columbian Expo, a look of consternation on his face. He virtually ignored the glittering splendor of the White City, focusing instead on the program in his hand and the exhibits listed therein. The Expo was full this year, a grander experience than either the London or Paris Expo, a perfect example of the emerging American Exceptionalism. He shook his head . . . how was he to find--?

His thoughts were interrupted as bright electric light mercilessly outshone the dying light of the day. A sign lit up above the Doctor's head, reading:

WESTINGHOUSE

ELECTRIC

&

MANUFACTURING CO.

TESLA

POLYPHASE

SYSTEM

"Ah. Him."

Bypassing the gaudily-lit General Electric display, the Doctor walked through the Westinghouse area spread out over smaller exhibits, listening for a particular voice: Americanized but with a distinct Serbian flavor. Soon, he found the person he was looking for.

"...and as you can see, the opposing phases of alternating current create a rotating magnetic field, as evidenced by the gyrations of this copper Egg of Columbus."

After a smattering of applause, the man continued, a faint smile on his face contorting the dark mustache he wore as he indicated the machine before him, a spinning metal egg on a platform suspended over coiled electrical wiring. "This egg is turning at a very slow speed, only forty hertz. But, for a more dazzling, more spectacular demonstration of how my polyphase system might be applied, be sure to return tomorrow for the Chicago Day festivities."

To more applause, the man bowed and started other bits of equipment for the next crowd coming through. His thin frame moved amongst the equipment with purpose as he set machines up, the speed of his movements displacing his neatly parted black hair. His four-button cutaway of brownish-grey contrasted neatly with the surrounding electrical equipment. He was very clearly a man who gave his all to his work, and the gaunt, hollow cheeks under black and sunken eyes gave testament to this. As the crowd departed, another man came into the display area and the Doctor stepped behind one of the large polyphase generators.

The man was older, portly, white-haired, with a great mustache connecting to his sideburns. He approached the other man, and with a clap on the shoulder, began to speak.

"You've done it again, Nikola. I've been wandering the Expo, and people are talking about you and your wondrous machines. Tesla will be a household name."

The younger man smiled. "And I suppose, George, that the name Westinghouse will not be?"

As the conversation continued, the Doctor faded away, slipping out of the exhibit without either man noticing. He knew why she was here. He thought knew when she would make her move. The date on the ticket she held, the same as the ticket in his possession, obtained the same day as he shadowed her, was for the next day, October ninth. There was to be a grand celebration, and no doubt Tesla and Westinghouse had one of the Serbian genius' grand lightning shows planned. There was a pavilion, Doctor Omega saw, erected expressly for this purpose.

Eve would no doubt be there, though the Doctor knew not when exactly she planned to accost Tesla. As he made his way through the mass of people, taking in the layout of the sprawling Expo, the Doctor considered what he knew to come next.

October 9th, 1893

The Doctor haunted Tesla's exhibit area, always careful to stick to the shadows. He'd been around the other exhibits, taking mental inventory of the materials there, looking for anything that might be of use to him.

He believed he'd found something. There was only to use it.

The room darkened, signaling the beginning of another demonstration and the Doctor straightened. He'd been vigilant for hours and it was starting to tell on him. His perseverance was rewarded this day, however, as he looked out to the gathered crowd and saw Eve's pale face among the onlookers.

The room filled with the hum of high-frequency equipment and soon the air was electrified. Tesla himself walked through thick bolts of blue lightning shooting across space to thunderous applause. As he began speaking, the Bride rose from her seat and approached the stage, eyes aglow with anticipation. She reached the edge of the stage and put her hand out, fingers splayed, and laughed hoarsely as lightning arced out towards her, the audience behind screaming in astonishment.

She whispered words meant for Tesla; the Doctor, having touched her psyche before, heard a reflection of them.

"Your mind is full of wondrous things, Nikola. Come with me, be my consort and my savior. Restore me to fullness, and you--"

With a flick of a switch, the Doctor cut off her entreaty. A shining ray of red, brighter than anything presented at the World's Fair, cut through the room and blossomed on the Bride's torso.

"You are not wanted here, madam," he shouted over the crowd, and made an adjustment, increasing the brilliance of the light. As he did so, fingers of lighting from Tesla's machine caressed the red beam, at first tentatively, as a child testing something new. Eve's eyes widened.

"What is the meaning of this?" Tesla asked, and in a flash he had his answer: the arcs of electricity found the beam of red light and rode it full-force into the body of the Bride. With a prolonged scream of pure hate, she glowed, her body suffused with energy, then exploded, vaporized by lightning.

The crowd erupted into panic and headed for the exits, throwing open the doors to the exhibition and spilling out into daylight.

The Doctor caught Tesla by the arm. "Come with me, young man. You're not safe here."

"Preposterous!" the inventor thundered. "That woman, she . . . this machine is not meant to do that."

Pulling on Tesla's arm, the Doctor nodded. "Yes, I know. And later, you'll have to excuse me for borrowing your ruby button lamp and tinkering with it. But for now we must leave this place. That woman was not a woman, and you are in danger. Come on."

Tesla looked on the smoking remains of the woman, ashes that were swirling in the light, and to his eyes it looked as if they were dissipating. As the last of them faded away, his mind was filled with a scream, unlike anything he'd ever heard before. Reluctantly, and with many glances back, Tesla followed the Doctor.

Later, in a different part of the White City, Nikola Tesla sat with the Doctor and heard the strange story of the Bride.

"She appeared, almost one hundred years ago, young and beautiful in appearance but damaged beyond repair in her mind. Her soul is an abyss, bereft of even the spark of humanity that Victor Frankenstein gave to his first creation. And since that day, she has wandered the world with one goal in mind: life. A full life. She has flitted from university to university, from theorist to inventor to alchemist, draining each one of their ideas in search of someone to make her whole.

"As Eve is, she exists in some sort of half-life, moving through the waking world but unable to connect with any of it. The Creature's abortive attempt to wake his Bride only partially succeeded, leaving her with a vast emptiness that she strives to fill, somehow. For this, she travels and searches, leaving behind her a trail of broken men, near-mindless husks, shadows of their former selves, all for her.

"I came to her attention, early on in this life of exile from my people; she latched on and found me bursting with knowledge. I narrowly escaped her clutches, and in doing so I touched her mind.

"I know what blackness lurks there. I have shadowed her every move, waiting for the right moment to put an end to her reign of terror. I have vowed to bring an end to her wanton destruction of intelligence, and I would do so here, in this White City, one way or another," said the Doctor. "I just hoped that you would not join the chorus of the Bride's empty men. And I am glad to have prevented that!"

"But I saw her destroyed," Tesla said, his brows raised in incredulity. "And you did it with my coil. And my button lamp. How? That machine was calibrated to be a harmless showpiece."

Omega's eyes glittered. "Interesting, was it not? But she was not destroyed, as you say. Her corporeal form was reduced to its constituent components when her mind was overloaded by the jolt of current I gave her. But she is well-versed in piecing herself back together, and that trick will not work a second time. We must discover a way to put an end to her for *all* time, and yours is exactly the type of mind needed."

"But who are you? And how do you know of her actions a hundred years before?"

The Doctor smiled. He stood, straightening his coat and trousers. "I walk the pathways of time. Now come, Nikola Tesla. We have work to do, and little enough time to do it in, even for me."

October 9th, 1893, cont.

As Tesla bustled around the exhibit, a third figure came into the area. George Westinghouse's face was a bright red and he sputtered as he talked.

"Great Scott, what was that this afternoon? What in the name of . . . and just who are *you* supposed to be?"

Doctor Omega whirled on the magnate. "Who am I? What an excellent question. Let us go outside while Mr. Tesla sets up an experiment, hmm?" He walked to Westinghouse and, with sheer force of will, backed him out of the exhibit. There was a crowd gathered outside, still talking about the wild events.

"Now wait just a minute--" Westinghouse started.

"Congratulations, Mr. Westinghouse," the Doctor proclaimed loudly enough for all to hear, cutting him off. "Your experimental illusion projector was a wild success! I must say, I cannot wait until they go into production. However did you manage to make it look as if that woman had disappeared? Why, that was something straight out of a magic show!"

Westinghouse, his eyes looking about the crowd and seeing genuine curiosity there, took up where the Doctor had left off. "Well, as you know, these things are impossible to predict. Whims of the demand and all. Why, the science behind it is years beyond anything possessed by our most esteemed competitors."

One of the crowd members stepped forward. "Mr. Westinghouse! Was that a discovery of Tesla, sir?"

With a wink, the Doctor left Westinghouse to bluff the crowd. He turned back inside to find Tesla in the middle of the room, eyes vacant and staring into space. He knew what was happening inside the young genius' mind and dared not interrupt until the thought, whatever it was, was fully formed in Tesla's mighty brain.

Finally, when the inventor snapped out of his trance, the Doctor stepped forward. "What is it, my boy? Have you something?"

The gaunt and tired-looking Tesla shook his head. "I'm not sure. I was thinking . . . there was a second where she touched my mind, Doctor Omega. And it came to me that if there is a way for her thoughts to touch mine, without contact of any sort, then her mind must be possess of a frequency to send and receive messages. If we can find it, perhaps we can use that to our advantage."

The Doctor's face broke into a mirthless grin. "Yes, yes, you have something there. Have you the materials here to deduce such a frequency?"

Tesla looked about the exhibit and his eyes alit on the Egg of Columbus. "Yes, Doctor, I believe I do."

"Excellent. I shall return. I must try to find the exact reason Eve has sought you out specifically. She's become very selective these last few years, and I must know what it is."

Doctor Omega hurried into the hotel the Bride had arranged for herself, stepping past the same clerk as the day before without so much as a glance. He walked with purpose to behind the counter, his countenance stern and his stride swift, his hands firmly grasping the lapels of his coat.

"Show me," he said to the clerk in a tone that brooked no resistance. "Show me the room you're not letting out."

A look of confusion passed over the clerk's features. "I'm sorry sir, I don't know what you mean. The hotel is booked to capacity for the Expo; there couldn't possibly be--"

"Look at me," the Doctor snapped, his chin thrust out. "Look into my eyes. Yes, deeper."

Within seconds of locking eyes with Doctor Omega, the clerk's face had gone slack, his will quickly battered down by the force of the Doctor's own.

"Listen to me, now. I want you to tell me the room number that you are hiding from the manager and staff. That is the room that she has taken for herself and you are actively keeping a secret. Tell me the number."

Vacantly, the clerk rocked his head from side to side, eyes locked on the Doctor's. A small trickle of drool began at the corner of his mouth.

"Can't . . . tell . . . you. She won't return if . . . if I do . . . she won't . . . she won't . . ."

"She will not in any case. You poor man. Tell me the number, and I will take from you this burden."

The clerk's face softened. "1408."

Doctor Omega smiled faintly and grabbed the key out of the cubbyholes behind the desk. He then placed his hand on the clerk's forehead. He spoke a word sharply and pulled his hand away. A spark jumped the gap from skin to skin and the Doctor stepped back, rubbing his palm.

"Can I help you, sir?"

The Doctor bowed. "You've helped me quite enough, young man."

He hurried away, glad to have been able to help. Or rather, glad to have hindered the Bride's plan in yet another way, albeit a small one. In his own way, Omega was as remorseless and unbending as she; they were on opposite ends of the spectrum, perhaps, but their shades complemented each other, the various lights and darks blending to an all-encompassing shade of grey.

As he hurried up to the fourteenth floor, he pushed that thought out of his mind. He would need all his focus for what was to come.

At the door to 1408, Doctor Omega inserted the key and wrenched the door open. The room was grand with a view of Chicago most likely unrivalled in any other hotel. One thing never changed about the Bride, she was addicted to opulence. Never would any time go by that Eve did not surround herself with the best of everything, as she saw herself as the best of everyone, even unfinished as she was. And she had a point . . . to what might she aspire if she were ever to become whole, the Doctor shuddered to think. Eve <u>was</u> ambition.

Carefully, he searched the room. He knew from prior experience (and from the one-time contact with her mind) that the Bride kept a diary, or journal of sorts. What was in it, he did not know.

Sometime later, he came up with a cry of joy. He'd found the book! It was an old thing, bound in leather and iron, with a lock and hasp that looked sturdy, indeed. The book was thick, its spine creased with age and use, the pages yellowed and feathered. With a glitter in his eye, Doctor Omega turned to leave.

He stopped. There, in the room, something brushed his mind.

"Are you there?" he asked the empty room.

You know I am everywhere, Exile, spoke the Bride into his mind. *You know that when I am in this state, I am free to travel where I would.*

The Doctor made a face, almost a look of sympathy. "Then why don't you leave here, Eve? Send your mind out to the stars, where there are countless planets and species to learn of, and learn from. Why must you insist on this course of action? It will only lead to doom and despair."

But for whom, Exile? Despair for me? I think not. After I have reconstituted my form, Doctor Omega, I will have Tesla and his wild imagination for myself, and he will build a machine to harness the power of the Earth to bring me fully to life!

Setting the journal inside his coat, the Doctor smiled faintly. "Perhaps. But will you leave him empty in the process? Will you discard him as you have so many others once he has fulfilled your dreams for you?"

What will be will be.

The Doctor straightened. "I cannot accept that. And I will stop you, unless you give me a guarantee that Tesla, and every other inventor after him, will be safe."

There was a stillness in the room. The presence of the Bride had left.

"Very well," said the Doctor. "Let us forth, and arm ourselves!"

Returning to the exhibit, Doctor Omega picked the lock on the diary and opened the book, seeing immediately the initial entry: her very first thoughts and impressions of the world, her first memories and how she knew what she did about her surroundings, filtered by the mind of the original Creature.

How that must have damaged her, the Doctor thought. *A mind, so fresh and pure, immediately tainted by that of a malevolent creation bent on revenge. If only there was a way to reverse that.*

With a shake of his head, he pushed that thought away, as well. He knew better than most how fruitless it was to dwell on might-have-beens. For all his ability to travel through time and the universe, the one space and time he most desired to see again was closed to him. Still, the notion wormed itself back to him: how might he turn out one day, if his exile became too much to bear?

Frowning, he perused the more recent entries of the journal, his hand and eyes flying over the pages to the astonishment of the newly-arrived Tesla.

"How can you do this? How can a human mind take in so many pages so quickly?"

"Never mind that," the Doctor muttered as he scanned the pages in front of him. "Have you finished the frequency detector?"

Tesla stood back and with a flourish displayed a crystal.

"That is a rock, young man. We don't have time for . . . for . . . frivolities!"

"This rock, Doctor, will give us what we seek. Or rather, the speed at which it vibrates will do so. This exhibit was built to my specifications to be a part of the closing ceremonies. Not even Westinghouse knows what I had planned. I have chosen the World's Fair to introduce my magnifying transmitter."

His hand no longer moving on the page, Doctor Omega looked up at the excited inventor. "Go on."

"I said earlier that she has a frequency. When the crystal picks up on Eve's Hertz-wave radiation, I will use it to set the variable frequency on the secondary of the transformer as well as adjust the resonance circuit, and the entire building will be a receiver for her thoughts."

The Doctor nodded. "That is wonderful, my boy. Now, write that down. Instructions, we will need instructions."

"Doctor, I am perfectly capable of--"

With a raised hand, Omega stopped Tesla. "You are, of course you are. But please, trust me. Write down explicit instructions, for we have another project as well."

Tesla, with a look of annoyance on his features, bowed to the Doctor's wishes and made for his desk. And Doctor Omega, heedless of this, returned to the journal.

An hour later, the Doctor sprang from his seat with a cry. "Yes!" he said, jubilant. "Of course, why didn't I see it before?"

Tesla rushed over. "You've found something?"

Shaking the journal, Doctor Omega slapped the pages. "It's all in here, only spread over the years. She's only recently herself discovered what it is she needs. And--are those the instructions? Everything as you visualized it?"

Brandishing the papers at the Doctor, the inventor nodded. "They are. Instructions, drawings, underlying theory." He handed the stack over. "Shall we put it in motion?"

Doctor Omega looked the papers over, murmuring to himself. "Yes. Yes, I see that. Brilliant!" He stood straight, looking at Tesla. "Bring me a pencil! Er, and hat."

Doubtfully, the man turned to do as he was asked. Handing the pencil and hat to the older man, Tesla cocked his head. "You are going to change it, yes?"

"Yes," the Doctor said, scribbling. "Just so . . . and here we are." He turned to Tesla and put the pencil down. "Do you, Nikola Tesla, trust me?"

The inventor straightened. "I caught a feeling of the Bride, as you call her, Doctor. She is malice personified. And yet, she fears you. So yes, Doctor Omega. I trust you."

The Doctor smiled. "Excellent," he said, placing one hand on Tesla's forehead. "Now, look into my eyes."

The Bride, newly reconstituted and fully-formed, strode haughtily into the Wes-

52

tinghouse exhibit, flinging the door open before her as if daring Doctor Omega to try to stop her. She raised her voice as high as she could, and it still came out as a harsh whisper.

"I am here, Exile! Bring the inventor to me, and play no games this time. You know you cannot stop me by destroying my physical form."

Doctor Omega strode into a spotlight, bearing a gem-topped cane and wearing a hat. He smiled at the Bride and swept the hat off his head with a bow.

"No games, madam," he said, replacing the hat. "But perhaps a proposal?"

Sneering, the Bride put out one pale hand and advanced on the elderly man. "I have no need to listen to your proposals, Exile. At a whim, I will . . . I will . . ."

She faltered and stopped in her advance.

With the end of his cane, the Doctor lightly tapped the top of his hat. "Interference. I don't know why I never thought of it before. You'll have to try harder."

Snarling, the Bride stuck her head forward, clenching her fists behind her and giving all she had towards projecting her mind at the Doctor as a weapon. Then, panting, she stopped, all her effort to no avail.

"You've given me several hours to prepare, Eve, so why don't you at least listen to what I have to say?"

Dropping her hands to her waist, she lifted her chin and looked daggers at the Doctor. "Speak," she hissed.

He clapped his hands once. "Excellent! Now, listen to me. The building you are in is actually an invention of young Tesla. Something new. He calls it his magnifying transmitter. You, my dear," he said, producing the journal, "might call it your salvation."

"Exile . . ."

"Stay your wrath. I know what it is you seek, Eve. When you are complete, I believe that you will be able to travel bodily as you do astrally. Instant movement from one place to another. Possibly from one time to another? I cannot say. But I can give it to you, but you must promise me that this will be the end.

"No more destruction, Eve. No more empty men in your wake. If you will but take this gift and leave here, leave the men and women of this planet in peace. You can have peace, yourself."

Slowly, the sneer left the face of the Bride. Muscle by muscle, her face lost its lofty look, her attitude draining away as water runs from a sieve.

"Peace?" she asked.

"Peace," the Doctor said.

With a nod, the Bride acquiesced. "I know you've no reason to trust me, Ex . . . Doctor Omega. But the prospect of peace . . ."

"I know," he said, one hand on her journal. "I have read your heart, Eve, and know you. Peace, rest from your half-existence is all you seek. Of all the cruel things your creator has done in this world, inflicting this half-life upon you was the worst."

Wiping her face, the Bride strode forward. "What must I do?"

Smiling, the Doctor indicated a spot on the floor. "Just stand here, my dear. Our man Tesla will take care of you."

With that, the young inventor strode from the shadows and began his machinery. "Please bear with me," he said. "It'll be a minute for the generators and transformers to warm up, and then we will begin."

His back to her, Tesla did not see the momentary look cross the Bride's face, that of a predator. She narrowed her eyes and focused on Tesla, he savior.

"Yes," she whispered. "This *is* what I need."

The Doctor, behind her, frowned. He'd been afraid of this. He cleared his throat.

"You must know, madam, that once Tesla begins the work, he cannot stop it. You must absorb all he has to give to you for the process to take effect."

"Oh," she said with a grin, "that won't be a problem at all, Doctor Omega. I intend to take every bit of this."

I tried, the Doctor thought.

"Nikola," he said, "begin the process."

With the turning of a great switch, the air of the exhibit hall began to hum with the typical sound of Tesla's high-frequency equipment. From all corners of the room, there came a blue nimbus of power, gathering itself before leaping from protrusion to protrusion in arcs of bright, electric blue. Soon the entire building was shaking and humming along, every corner and metal bit shooting off arcs of lightning.

The Bride extended her arms.

"Yes!" she shouted in that horrible whisper. "I can feel it working. This day shall not be forgotten, Exile!"

With a sigh, the elderly man leaned on his cane. "What happened to 'Doctor'?"

"The process cannot be stopped! It feeds on itself as it feeds me. I saw that in your young inventor's brilliant mind. And what a mind it is, Exile. And it shall be mine. It shall *all* be mine!"

Standing tall, the Doctor moved towards the control panel. "I wish you had been sincere in your quest for peace, Eve. I could have helped you."

Laughing, she raised her hands and floated into the air. "You have done well enough, Exile! The people of this world will remember forever that it was *you* that placed me upon my throne!"

The Doctor twirled his cane. The glittering crystal at the top caught and sparkled with all the blue light in the room. "No, Eve. They will not. Nor will they know of you."

Saying so, Doctor Omega thrust the tip of the cane into a slot on the control panel, dislodging the crystal from the cane-top and setting it in place on the machine. Abruptly, the throb of the magnifying transmitter changed and the air

54

took on a pungent tang.

"*You!* What have you done?"

With that cry, the Bride pushed her hand out towards the Doctor. A blue pulse of lightning shot from her hand, knocking him away from the control panel and the switch he was about to throw. He landed several feet away, the hat flying from his head. A stray bit of electricity caught it and sparks flew and danced in the hat.

"How dare you?" the Bride continued, holding out both hands towards the Doctor. An arc started at her shoulders and jumped from arm to arm, forming a Jacob's ladder as it travelled to her hands, gathering energy from the surrounding electric mayhem. "I will end you, Exile!" A blue glow surrounded her hands, and the Doctor yelled once.

"Tesla!"

The inventor sprang at the panel and threw the switch. As if she was a puppet whose strings had been cut, the Bride dropped out of the air, all glow of power extinguished. She landed face-down, arms splayed out. With a herculean effort, she raised her head and looked at Tesla.

He turned from her. The machine, *his* machine, was now using the crystal to receive the Bride's intellect, her Self. And as it did so, the indomitable will that held her form together was leaving its vessel.

Eyeing a gauge, Tesla pointed. "We are almost at capacity, Doctor!"

"It will be alright," Doctor Omega said from the floor. He, too, knew what was happening to the Bride, and he could not but help to feel a pang of regret. For her nature, for his own. For a universe that would stand idly by and watch as things, horrible things, happened to its inhabitants.

With something of a smile on the mostly-ashen face, the figure of the Bride said one last word.

"Peace."

And she was gone, entrapped in the machine. Her body disintegrated, no longer able to sustain itself without the driving force of the Bride's being. All that was left was her dress, covered in dust.

October 10th, 1893

Doctor Omega and Nikola Tesla sat in the empty Westinghouse exhibit, sipping cups of tea and talking.

"What will become of her?" asked Tesla. "Is she . . . gone?"

The Doctor put down his cup. "No, no, not gone. You should know better, dear boy. Energy cannot be created or destroyed." He held up a large crystal. "Only altered in form. This, what used to be a pile of carbon, is now the repository of everything the Bride was. And I will find a fitting place for her in the galaxy, one day. But it won't be here, on Earth."

Tesla sat back in his chair. "You tampered with my memory, Doctor."

Leaning on his cane, now bereft of the crystal top, the Doctor sighed heavily. "I had to. You could retain no knowledge of the crystal, of the Faraday cage in my hat, or what I'd planned with either. Nor could you remember the alterations I'd made to your drawings or your machine. Eve was a creature of malice and treachery, Nikola. She was perhaps one of the most incisive of beings and would have sensed in an instant our trap.

"Still," he continued, standing up. "I did not have your permission to do so. And for that, I must apologize."

"Accepted," Tesla said, not looking up from his tea. "There is one other thing, Doctor. You travel in time and space. Before these last few days, I would not have accepted that, but now . . . you do, don't you?"

"I do."

"Then take me with you."

Doctor Omega turned away. "I cannot, my boy. I cannot. There is no guarantee that you would return, and this world needs you, your inventions. What you have done, and what you will do."

The Doctor picked up the large crystal and walked away from the table. He stopped by the door and half-turned back to the still-sitting inventor.

"I will send you a message, Nikola. One day. Watch the skies."

In the story that follows, Matthew Dennion, pays homage to George Franju's ground-breaking 1960 horror film, Les Yeux sans Visage [Eyes Without a Face], *staring Pierre Brasseur as the surgeon with a disfigured daughter, tragically played by Edith Scob. Based on a novel by Jean Redon, the film was scripted by those two masters of the macabre, Boileau & Narcejac, who also provided the source material for both* Diabolique *and* Vertigo. Eyes Without a Face *has been much imitated, including by notorious Spanish horrormeister Jesus Franco with* The Awful Dr. Orloff *(1962).*

Matthew Dennion: *Faces of Fear*

Paris, 1959

She was sweating profusely as she ran, not just from the exertion of sprinting at full speed but because the enormous boiler room she was in was giving off a tremendous amount of heat. What made it worse was how the sweat stung as it slowly worked its way into the cuts all over her body. *I shouldn't be here,* she thought. *How did I even get here? This whole thing is insane.* Behind her she could hear the sound of metal scraping against metal. She stopped for a second turned and could see sparks in the darkness. *I shouldn't be here. Where is here anyway?* She began to cry as she ran. Where was her father? The last thing she could remember was her father taking her to the clinic.

"The clinic!" she said aloud "I am in the clinic!"

The girl ran over the recent past in her mind to see if she could remember how she got where she was.

"I was in a terrible car accident; my face was horribly scarred and disfigured. My father took me to his clinic to treat my wounds. My face was disfigured to the extent that I was forced to wear a plastic mask to conceal it. I was having terrible dreams about becoming a monster. I began to see a horrible, burned and mutilated face every time I closed my eyes. When the dreams got worse, my father sent for Dr. Crane, from the psychiatric hospital, to see if he could help me out. He treated me with medication for a few days but the dreams only got worse. The dream was no longer just the burned face, the face started to become something more!"

She began to form the picture of the creature in her head and, as it formed, her steps seemed to get slower and slower. It was as if she was running in ankle-deep mud. The floor beneath her seemed to be changing or melting.

The scarping sound behind her got louder and closer as she screamed in terror. Her head snapped back just as someone grabbed her hair from behind and she came to a dead stop. An awful smell assaulted her like flesh burnt and decayed. Were she not so terrified, she would have vomited.

A series of blades appeared next to her masked face. Two of them slowly reached over, punctured the plastic mask and cut into her already burned cheek. As the blood fell from her, she noticed that the floor directly in front of her dropped. Suddenly, she was standing on the end of scaffold in front of long drop.

"What's going on? This can't be happening! This can't be real!" she screamed.

The girl could feel something rough next to her face, as a raspy voiced joked: "Oh, it's real Christiane, real enough to leave you scarred for life!"

She was pushed from behind and fell head-first into a chasm. It felt like three stories before she came to hard stop, hitting another steel floor.

As she hit the ground, her mask went skidding in the darkness. Shaken and bruised, she turned on her back to look up at who—or what—was after her. She could only see a silhouette of what looked like a man with a red and black stripped sweater and some kind of fedora hat. Then, she noticed his hands—or his one hand to be specific. The fingers were elongated and thin. As she was looking, the man lifted the misshapen hand and a glint of light reflected off of it. Her body went rigid as she realized that those weren't misshapen fingers but blades. The man continued to lift his gloved hand to his mouth and lick her blood off the steel.

The man cackled; he arched his body back in the throes of ecstasy. His voice echoed elation as he looked down at her.

"Your fear!" he said. "It's more powerful than all of the other children I've consumed combined! Devouring your soul will make me a virtual god!"

He laughed in a high pitched cackle as he jumped down in front of her. Yellow eyes stared at her as the demon reached down and wrapped his bladed hand around her chin.

"You know, ever since that S-Mart flunky used that dammed *Necronomicon* to send me hurtling through time, I've been so lonely trying to make my way back to my children. Lucky for me, I found you and now, look at us—don't we make quite the pretty pair!"

The monster howled at his mocking remark, while he raked her ravaged face with his knifed fingers. The girl pulled away, got to her knees, and started to run. She didn't know where to go, but she had to get away from him.

She was running again, crying, looking for any hope of salvation. In the distance, at the end of the pitch black corridor, she could see a blood red light in the darkness. She ran for it as the man—or whatever he was—behind her mocked her and chased her down and down the endless corridor.

The girl kept running toward the light, until she came to a dead end. She was now bathed in the light. She looked for somewhere to escape, to keep running, but the walls seemed to go straight up forever, with a series of pipes and bars connected to them.

She had thought that the light would save her, that she would get out, leave this torture behind, but now, she was trapped again and the creature had caught up with her.

He slowly wiggled his bladed fingers as he stalked towards her.

"Just keep telling yourself, it's only a dream," he sneered as he approached, laughing his high-pitched laugh.

She bent down and curled into a ball against the wall as the laugh echoed all around her, but, suddenly, it started to sound deeper and hollow, and come from somewhere above her.

The creature suddenly stopped in his tracks, as the deep laugh erupted again.

This time, it was no echo.

Both the monster and the girl looked around as the laugh continued. Neither seemed to know where it came from. The creature swung his bladed hand through the air and screamed:

"Who are you? What are doing here? You can't be in here—this is my world! The dream world! Only I can enter this girl's head! She's mine!"

But the eerie laugh only increased in speed and was so chilling that it gave even the creature pause. Then a deep voice answered:

"The dream world in people's minds may be yours, but I can see directly into their souls! Judex judges men by the acts they commit, and I find you to be an abomination!"

Christiane was still scared, but she could have sworn that the creature chasing her was even more terrified of the voice than she was!

The voice started again:

"This girl has suffered enough! Your suffering, however, is just beginning. You have taken your last life!"

Christiane looked up and saw a massive cloaked figure swoop down from seemingly nowhere. As it descended, she could see a man's face under a tight fitting hat. The light suddenly tightened and focused on the creature like some kind of blood-red spotlight. The creature lifted his bladed hand into the air as Judex crashed into him. Christiane watched as the two figures tumbled into the darkness…

Suddenly, she shot upright in her bed. She was back in the clinic, but her cheeks and back were still bleeding from where she had been cut in her dream.

Panting, she looked next to her and was even more terrified than she had been in her dream. The psychologist, Dr. Crane, was standing next to her bed with a maniacal look on his face. He was looking at her charts, but was smearing them with blood.

The girl became terrified as she realized the doctor had her blood all over his hands. She screamed in terror.

The lights turned on as her father came running into the room. He ran as quickly as he could over to the bed.

"Crane, what have you done?"

Two orderlies came through the door. Dr. Genessier yelled at them:

"Get him out of here!"

The orderlies quickly restrained Crane. Genessier snarled at the psychologist:

"Crane, why would you do this to my own daughter? She's your patient, for God's sake!"

"It wasn't me, Genessier," shrieked Crane. "Not me! Don't you see her fear! Her own fear did this to her! Never did I think my serum would lead to such levels of terror!"

Genessier couldn't understand what Crane meant until he looked at Christiane's I.V. bag.

"What is this? What have you been treating her with?"

The psyhologist smiled as he said: "My masterpiece, Genessier! Don't you see? Now, I can study fear at its full potential!"

As the psychologist was forcibly dragged away, Genessier shouted: "You're through in this country, Crane! I'll see you deported for this!" Then, he turned to his daughter. "Are you OK, my dear?"

Christiane was sweating as he began to treat her wounds. The girl had a stunned appearance about her.

"What happened?" she whispered. "I thought it was all a dream."

Her father sighed. "It seems Dr. Crane was experimenting on you with some kind of fear toxin; he attacked you in your sleep to increase the level of terror you were experiencing."

Genessier's eyes began to tear up as he removed Christiane's plastic mask. He fought hard to keep his reaction to a minimal when he gazed on his daughter's hideous face. Whatever Crane had done to her had caused fresh wounds to appear on her already damaged face. The previous condition would have made the healing process difficult, but with the additional damage, Genessier knew that he would have to take drastic steps to restore his daughter's beauty.

Raising his eyes toward the ceiling, he made a vow to himself that he would right these atrocities wrought on his beloved Christiane no matter what the price.

Suddenly, a red light flashed across the room, catching all of the people in the room by surprise.

In the bed next to Christiane, the hand of the wounded man sharing her room moved slightly. As it slid out from under the cover, a bright red ring could be seen on one of his fingers.

Genessier, however, was more fixated on the printouts from the electroencephalogram connected to the man. The printouts flashed a series of activity. The doctor looked at one of his assistants.

"Orloff, check that equipment. That man has been brain dead since he came in here with those gunshot wounds last night."

"But his hand—it moved from under the sheet?" Orloff stammered.

"With all of the commotion in this room," Genessier sneered, "I'm surprised it was only his hand and not his whole body that fell out of the bed! Now, please check the equipment."

As Orloff approached, the electroencephalogram the printouts went buzzing again. "Well, well, he seems to be doing much better suddenly…"

Christiane started at the man's ring and wondered:

It's the same color as the light in my dream! It was just a dream wasn't it?

With his contribution to our previous volume, Win Scott Eckert has begun to paint a broad canvas leading to the events that will eventually culminate with the fateful meeting at Wold Newton conceptualized by the incomparable Philip José Farmer. This new installment—a vignette—carries the plot further, setting up the characters in position for what is to come, like pieces on a chessboard...

Win Scott Eckert: *Nadine's Invitation*

France, November 1795

Blakeney Manor, Richmond: Thursday the 19th of November
My Dearest Countess Carody,

I do hope Paris finds you well, although Hungary must be missing its sweetest flower!

Sir Percy has gotten a bug to winter at Blakeney Hall. It's a bit out of the way, situated near some sleepy villages—Would Newton, and Thwing, if you can believe it—up in Yorkshire, but that's part of the charm, isn't it?

In fact, it's to be a rather large gathering, and Percy and Alice and I couldn't help but recall the many charming—almost mesmerizing!—evenings we spent at your townhome on the Crescent last April. You were absolutely captivating, my dear, and all of Bath was abuzz with disappointment when you decamped for the Continent.

Nadine, you simply must join us for the Christmas holidays. Come earlier, if you can, as we hope to gather all around the second week of next month. The Darcys will be there, naturally—Lizzie is dying to see you again—as well as several others you unquestionably must meet... The Duke of Holdernesse, Baron Tennington, M. and Mme. Delegardie—too many to mention, really.

Do write that you will come, my dear, and send news of Paris as well; I haven't been home for ages, for obvious reasons, and miss it so.

Believe me at all times with sincerity and respect,

I am affectionately yours,

Marguerite, Lady Blakeney

Rue des Filles du Calvaire: 21 Nov. 1795
Dear Colonel Bozzo-Corona,

All is proceeding as planned. I have responded to Lady Blakeney accepting her kind invitation to winter at Sir Percy's estate in Yorkshire.

By the way, your man Lecoq eyes me a little too appreciatively when he delivers your missives. You know my preferences, and in any event his reach exceeds the grasp of his station. Please correct him accordingly.

Yours,

Countess Nadine Carody

Rue Thérèse: 22nd November

My Dear Countess,

Splendid, just splendid. The seeds you planted last spring in Bath have borne sweet fruit, indeed. I received my own invitation today, and of course will be in attendance, although circumstances may delay me one or two days beyond the time of arrival Blakeney prescribed.

Of course, I will chastise Lecoq with all due severity. I understand, after all, your ravishment last year at the hands of the Martinovics radicals dictates your current preferences.

Taking the larger view, however, I cannot regret those unfortunate events which have shaped your new destiny and brought us into accord. These Revolutionary sentiments must be suppressed. The last several years of instability on the Continent have shown that to be the case. We are now well-positioned to exert our influence at Blakeney's conclave, and to impose the order which will surely prove to be to our mutual profit.

Yours ever,

Colonel Bozzo-Corona (ret.)

Calyx Bar: November 22

Dear Colonel,

I'll come straight to the point. There's something a bit off about the Countess Carody. Her behavior is quite odd. Her townhouse is filled with floor-to-ceiling mirrors, in which she positively revels in admiring herself at every opportunity, almost with an odd sense of triumph. She presents herself in long silky robes, and a flowing red scarf, which do little to preserve her modesty. Finally, she keeps a female servant who stands stock still and allows the Countess to manipulate her limbs and turn her head as if she were a life-size fashion doll.

Do you believe the Countess to be a reliable partner in our ventures?

Your most obed. servant, Sir,

Lecoq

Rue Thérèse: 22nd November

My son,

Your imagination runs away with you. She's a Hungarian noble. What more needs be said?

Kindly control your libido in her presence. She has taken note of your interest, and is immune.

C.

Rue Morgue: 22 Nov.
My Dear Sir Percy,

As you suspected, the Colonel and Countess Carody are in league. After shadowing Lecoq to the Calyx Bar, and thence to the Cordon Jaune brothel (he went there, apparently succumbing to his urges after delivering his master's latest note to the Countess), I took up a disguise as a customer. A few well-placed *sous* to the Madame garnered me a fast look at the contents of Lecoq's pockets. This Countess must be an alluring beauty indeed if he had to satisfy his base cravings immediately after departing her presence.

In any event, it remains to be seen if they will see things our way or constitute an obstacle. We shouldn't forget, though, that the Colonel and the Brothers of Mercy certainly came through in the de Musard matter by supplying Marguerite and Alice with the Heart of Ahriman.

Believe me, dear Sir,
Your obliged and faithful humbl. sert.,

Dr. Siger Holmes

Rue des Filles du Calvaire: 23 Nov. 1795
Dear Colonel Bozzo-Corona,

We agree, but Francis II is stirring strong opposition among other nobles. I'll attend Sir Percy's gathering to determine what the consensus is regarding French Revolutionary sentiment inflaming the rest of Europe, and what action they propose to prevent its spread.

Do you think there is any chance Blakeney suspects that the Brothers of Mercy were behind the de Musard affair, and thus you have, in essence, engineered his response to those events, this Yorkshire gathering itself?

Yours,

Countess Nadine Carody

Rue des Filles du Calvaire: 23 Nov. 1795
My Lord,

By design, I am in receipt of an invitation to England, as is Bozzo-Corona. The Colonel is pleased to believe that he and I are aligned in our reasons for attending this conclave, not understanding my service to a darker power surpassing his mortal concerns. It delights me no end that, despite this service, in other ways I am unlike you, or your so-called Brides; I am pleased to retain a modicum of my own free will. That I am able to deprive you, for an eternity, of any further impositions of the lustful behavior to which you originally subjected me, and continually remind you of this, brings me great joy.

In any event, I will of course report on the machinations discussed at this conclave, the possible influence on the political landscape across the Continent, and their potential impact to your long-term plans for expansion beyond your Transylvanian stronghold.

My destination is an estate far from the teeming centers of society such as London or Bath. The location is near the Yorkshire coast, nonetheless accessible by the ports at Bridlington or Scarborough or Whitby. One or more of these may be of suitable use for your eventual migration from the Carpathians to Albion, understanding, as only those of us can, that such event is conceivably decades away.

But I digress. I plan on entry via Whitby, but shall investigate the other ports if the opportunity avails itself, and report back soonest.

Never forget that I despise you, and what you have made me with your dark kiss.

Nonetheless I remain, my dear Count,

Your unwilling servant,

Nadine

In pulp literature, there is a respectable tradition of heroes who span multiple generations: the Phantom, the Slayers, the Eternal Champion, to name but a few. In this story, Emmanuel Gorlier delves into the Nyctalope's family tree and investigates whether Leo Saint-Clair might not have had some equally remarkable predecessors—and why...

Emmanuel Gorlier: *Fiat Lux!*

Paris, 1639, 1641

Report prepared for the Watcher's Council by Quentin Travers, Chief Librarian, June 22, 1965.

The following narrative has been translated and adapted from the diaries of Marquis Henri-Jean de Sainte Claire, who served as Lieutenant in the notorious Guard of Cardinal Armand du Plessis de Richelieu. Several events described therein might, at first glance, seem to stretch believability but I have attempted to make sense of them through logical extrapolations based on information already in our possession. This poem, allegedly composed by Cyrano de Bergerac, was found amongst the personal papers of Comte de Rochefort and, therefore, might not be authentic.

> « *Il convient de se dire, entre francs chevaliers,*
> *Tout le bien qu'on retire d'une histoire, versifiée*
> *Par une rouge Eminence à ce point inspirée,*
> *Que rien sur notre terre ne saurait l'égaler.*
> *La flamberge au vent froid met fin au long sursis,*
> *Et la face du faquin au fond du limon git.* »[1]

It was on a cold winter morning in the year of Our Lord 1639 that one might have heard those verses declaimed loudly and clearly over the sounds of sword rattling against sword, if one found oneself in a lonely clearing in the woods lining the banks of the river Seine—in an area which, three centuries later, would become the location of the fabled Avenue des Champs-Elysées.

---

[1] It is proper to speak between gentle knights / Of all the good one thinks of a lyrical play / Penned by a crimson eminence so wonderfully inspired / That nothing in this world could ever be its equal. / The rapier in the cold morning quickly decides / And the oaf's face soon lies in the mud.

If fate had indeed brought a spectator to that muddy clearing, our bystander might have beheld the sight, familiar for the times, of two gentlemen engaged in a flamboyant duel. One was dressed in the dark red livery of the Cardinal's Guards; the other wore the proud uniform of the Cadets de Gascogne.

« Mais enfin en baillant, je me suis éveillé.
A la fin de la pièce, aux vers si torturés,
Seuls les bras de Morphée avaient pu me sauver
Des affres de l'ennui où j'avais cru sombrer.
La flamberge au vent froid met fin au long sursis,
Et la face du butor au fond du limon git. »[2]

These bold verses were being recited in a stentorian voice by the Cadet. Both combatants were of equal size and stature, and they each sported a thin mustache in the fashion of the times. The poet's face, however, was unique and truly remarkable. It was dominated by a nose that was so big and pointy that he himself had, occasionally, referred to it as a promontory.

Were our hypothetical spectator acquainted with Parisian society, he would have immediately recognized the notorious Savinien Hercule Cyrano de Bergerac, rightly feared as the deadliest swordsman in France, and equally famous for his fearless conduct. One might well have asked what insanity could have compelled his adversary to challenge such a man to a duel?

Cyrano's impromptu poem might have offered a clue: listening to it, one would have understood that the swordsman had, once again, publicly mocked Cardinal de Richelieu's literary aspirations, drawing inspiration, for reasons no one suspected, from the title of his most recent play, *Roxane*.

« Aujourd'hui, à l'épée, pour l'honneur d'un Duc,
Afin de préserver toute gloire caduque,
De Sainte Claire et moi allons nous rencontrer.
Sur ce grand champ d'honneur, l'un de nous va tomber.
La flamberge au vent froid met fin au long sursis,
Et la face du cuistre au fond du limon git. »[3]

---

[2] But at long last I woke up yawning / At the end of that wretched play; / Only Morpheus' arms had saved me / From the deadly boredom engulfing me. / The rapier in the cold morning quickly decides / And the lout's face soon lies in the mud.

[3] Today with my sword, for a Duke's honor, / In order to protect dubious glory, / Sainte-Claire and I shall meet / And on the battlefield one of us will fall. / The rapier in the cold morning quickly decides / And the boor's face soon lies in the mud.

That last stanza identified Cyrano's unfortunate opponent. Equally well-known throughout Paris for his bravery, he was none other than Marquis Henri-Jean de Sainte-Claire,[4] a man loyal beyond words to his master, who was obviously seeking retribution for Cyrano's insolence, despite the Cardinal's own edict forbidding duels.

Yet, despite Sainte-Claire's obvious talent with a sword, he could not prevail against Cyrano's superior skills. Soon, the issue of the duel was no longer in doubt. The Cadet de Gascogne easily blocked all of his opponent's thrusts, while he himself managed to drive the tip of his rapier ever closer to Sainte-Claire's face. It was obvious that Cyrano, as was his wont, waited only to finish his poem before delivering the fatal strike.

The young Marquis, against almost all hope, nevertheless managed a skillful feint, parry and thrust that would surely have maimed Cyrano had he not been so light on his feet. In a bold counterstrike, the poet struck Sainte-Claire just above his left eye. The blow was so unexpected and the shock so violent that the Marquis fell face first on the ground—just as Cyrano's poem had predicted!

Sainte-Claire woke up four days later inside a dark bedroom in an inn that was patronized by the Cardinal's Guards. He heard someone come into the room.

"Rochefort—thank you for taking such good care of me," he said, recognizing his visitor at once.

"Henri! It's so dark in here! How could you tell it was me?... Well, who else would care for you, I suppose... I feared that Cyrano's blow might have left you blind, but it seems that, like the Duc de Guise and I, you're only condemned to wear an ugly scar on your face!"

"Please pour me a glass of wine! I see a jug and a glass on that table over there."

"How the Devil can you see in here! It's as dark as the Devil's bottom! Let me open the shutters first!"

Thus did Henri-Jean de Sainte-Claire become aware that Cyrano's sword had mysteriously affected his sense of sight. He was able to see in the dark as if it were daylight! He thought this new talent might prove very useful in the Cardinal's service...

Two years later, during a moonless night in December 1641, Sainte-Claire was back in the same fateful clearing where his duel with Cyrano, which had almost killed him, had instead ended up gifting him with his strange, new power.

---

[4] Historical records indicate that some members of the Sainte-Claire family later shortened their name to Saint-Clair during the French Revolution, when Louis-Jean de Sainte-Claire, a friend of the notorious Sir Percy Blakeney, helped saved numerous members of the French aristocracy from the blade of the guillotine.

Wrapped inside a long, dark cloak, the Cardinal's Guard had been discreetly following a messenger dispatched by the Marquis Henri de Cinq-Mars.

The man had often turned back to check if he was being followed, but the darkness was too obscure for him to detect Sainte-Claire's presence—and unlike the Cardinal's man, Cinq-Mars' agent was not a nyctalope!

Sainte-Claire had been following the man since he had left his master's Parisian mansion. A few days earlier, Rochefort and he had been summoned by the Cardinal, who wished to entrust them with an important mission. When they had faced the man who had secretly ruled France for so many years from behind the scenes, they had found him pale and sickly. Yet, his eyes still carried within them the cold flame of his unbending will.

"Gentlemen," said Richelieu, "I have just obtained information about a plot against the Kingdom. Some of the ringleaders belong to the highest strata of our society and are even close to the King himself. One of them is the Marquis de Cinq-Mars, who owes me everything in life, and yet, it seems, hates me deeply. I do not know the details of the plot, but it is said to be bankrolled by Spain. We have been at war with King Philip IV for six years now; no doubt, he has found a more expedient way to bring our conflict to an end. Rochefort! Sainte-Claire! I trust you above all others. I want you to keep a close eye on Cinq-Mars and report anything suspicious to me at once."

Following their orders, the two Guards had kept a close watch on the Marquis' mansion, Rochefort by day, Sainte-Claire by night. That's how the latter had spotted the mysterious messenger dispatched in the depths of night and had followed him into the woods all the way to the banks of the Seine.

Cinq-Mars' envoy reached the clearing by the river. There, two men appeared to be waiting for him. They were wrapped in long, black cloaks which, nevertheless, did not hide the swords hanging from their belts. Sainte-Claire thought that they must be gentlemen of the nobility.

A stranger sight, however, was that of a small metal embarkation in the river, which looked like no boat Sainte-Claire had ever seen. It was smooth, grey and oval in shape, and was topped by a metal turret with a door large enough for one man.

Sainte-Claire watched the three men who, normally, would have been invisible to all in the darkness and listened eagerly to their exchange.

"Gentlemen, 'tis an ill wind that blows nobody any good," the Marquis' envoy said.

Obviously a pre-arranged signal, thought Sainte-Claire.

"The windmill doesn't care for the wind that's gone past," responded one of the two newcomers with a strong Spanish accent, making a courteous salute. "Do you have the draft of the new treaty?" he added, extending his hand.

At that moment, Sainte-Claire noticed something unusual about the Spaniard's hand: his fourth finger did not move and was bent at an unnatural angle.

He looked at his companion and saw that his hand, too, presented the same, unusual characteristic.

Meanwhile, the Marquis' messenger had pulled a document from under his cloak and was handing it to the strange Spaniard.

"Here it is," he said. "My master asked me to tell you that it faithfully reflects our latest agreement, and your King should be pleased with the new territories conceded to Spain."

He then pulled back his hood and Sainte-Claire recognized François de Thou, Councillor at the Parliament and great friend of the Marquis de Cinq-Mars.

As the treaty changed hands, Sainte-Claire became concerned that such a damning proof of Cinq-Mars' guilt might be lost, so he pulled out his sword and jumped into the clearing, shouting:

"In the name of the King and the Cardinal, you are all under arrest!"

After a second during which they were struck by surprise, the three conspirators reacted—very differently.

François de Thou, his face contorted with fear, stepped back, trying to see who had sprung on them, already looking for a means of escape.

One of the two Spaniards seized the treaty and jumped aboard the metal boat. The other pulled what looked like a strange hand-held metallic weapon from beneath his cloak and peered through the darkness, trying to find his opponent.

With a swift turn of his blade, Saint-Claire disarmed him, causing the gun to fall on the grass, and stabbed him through the neck. Then something truly extraordinary happened: As soon as his foe's body touched the ground, it was surrounded by a reddish glow and disappeared, leaving only a scattering of ashes behind!

It was now Sainte-Claire's turn to be awestruck on the spot.

François de Thou took advantage of the Cardinal's man's shock to vanish into the woods, running as fast as his portly legs would carry him.

Meanwhile, the third man, the one with the treaty, had reached the door in the turret of the strange metal ship. Sainte-Claire was too far to catch him. He saw the strange gun lying on the ground, grabbed it, pointed it at the fugitive and pressed the knob on its side.

The gun made a strange high-pitched sound and the Spaniard's body became also enveloped by a red glow before it, too, disappeared. Then, the metal ship began to vibrate and disintegrate. The Seine waters bubbled up and, after a few seconds, nothing was left of the incident, except some thin grey smoke which floated above the water before the wind blew it away.

Sainte-Claire looked at the supernatural gun in his hand. "Even the treaty is gone," he muttered dejectedly. Then, he threw the accursed object in the river and went home to write his report.

Sainte-Claire's diary does not contain any more information about this strange affair, the next section being devoted to his dalliance with a young lady-in-waiting from the Court, which offers little or no interest as far as we are concerned.

A few months later, Cardinal de Richelieu was able to lay his hands on written proof of Cinq-Mars' treacherous exchange with King Philip IV of Spain, a conspiracy which also implicated the King's own brother. On September 12, 1642, Cinq-Mars and de Thou were beheaded in Lyon. It is not impossible that Sainte-Claire took some further part in those events.

The strange facts related in his diary are, as far as I have been able to ascertain, not mentioned anywhere in any other chronicles of the times. The identity of the two strange persons posing as Spaniards remains unknown. It is possible that they were Invaders from another world, who, upon seeing their plot foiled, left, never to return. It is highly uinlikely that we will ever learn the truth about this matter.

As for the remarkable powers exhibited by Marquis Henri-Jean de Sainte-Claire, it is tempting to juxtapose this information with what we know is contained in the papyrus written by Greek historian Manetho preserved in our Library.

Manetho relates that, during the reign of Pharaoh Akhenaten in 1360 BC., the High Priest of Aten, Merira, created a special caste of sacred warriors to spread the faith of Aten and defend the values of light and justice throughout Egypt. The leader of that caste, one special warrior, was endowed by the Sun God with a special power which enabled him to see in the darkness as if it were light. As we know, Manetho went on to mostly detail the story of Akhenaten's death and how the Pharaoh was buried in the Chamber of Horus located beneath the Great Pyramid, but he also noted that this warrior had the ability to transfer his power to his descendents in order for them to keep defending the values of Aten in times of great need.

Might Marquis Henri-Jean de Sainte Claire have been a descendent of this great warrior whose name has been lost in history? Certainly, the fact that his descendent, Leo Saint-Clair, a.k.a. the Nyctalope, was endowed with the same power and fought a great number of foes threatening the stability of our world leads us to speculate: as there has been a line of Slayers since time immemorial, can there also have been a line of Nyctalopes?

(English adaptation by Jean-Marc & Randy Lofficier)

71

Micah Harris has regaled us in the past with the exotic adventures of Becky Sharp, first with The Ape Gigans *in Volume 3, then with* The Scorption and the Fox *in Volume 6 (co-written with Matthew Baugh). This new chapter in the life of William Makepeace Thackeray's heroine takes a giant leap forward to 1917, when we find the indomitable Miss Sharp...*

Micah Harris: *Slouching Towards Camulodunum*
(*from an idea by Mark Schultz*)

It is probable that, upon mature consideration, after weighing the good and evil, I shall one day destroy this paper, or at least leave it under seal to my friend D., trusting his discretion, to use it or to burn it, as he may think fit.
Robert Matheson, Med. Dr.

Bath, 1917

I. The Encounter on Great Pulteney Street.

The man in the turban, with the olive complexion and a beard the texture of a tightly coiled vine, summoned images of a remote landscape, both arid and lush, and seemed to have stepped out of one of the paintings of the nearby Victoria Museum, inspired by *The Rubaiyat of Omar Khayyam*.

As with the *Rubaiyat*, Sâr Dubnotal might well have come from a Platonic overrealm of unchanging forms. His turban, puffy white trousers, and gold embroidered sash gave his countenance an antiquity that was belied only by his fashionable Edwardian frock coat and cravat.

El Tebib—as he was known in the East—and his massive Hindu manservant Naïni sat in an enclosed black carriage drawn by horses dark as pitch and driven by a soberly dressed man in a black top hat. Like a preternatural shadow without a source, the somber conveyance loomed in the midday sunlight that brightened Bath's Great Pulteney Street.

The carriage sat by a row of homogeneously designed Georgian homes, which, along with the series of similar houses across the street, gave the impression of a single image repeated infinitely in a vast, open corridor of mirrors. The object of Sâr Dubnotal's quest had thought herself hidden among these residences indistinguishable from each other.

But little in this terrestrial sphere was hidden from the Great Psychagogue.

"Look, Naïni." Sâr Dubnotal did not break his austere emerald gaze, nor move other than to slightly peel his forefinger up and then smoothly lower it. His manservant's powerful frame was cloaked in even more conservative Edwardian attire than his master: charcoal frock coat and trousers and black Stetson hat. Naïni nodded, his hand already on the carriage door's handle, awaiting the next command.

They watched a petite, shapely Gibson girl tentatively making her way down the row of houses on the opposite side of the street. An abundance of strawberry blond hair spilled from beneath a broad brimmed hat, the shadow of which veiled her eyes. Under a dark vest, she wore a high, white collared blouse clasped at the throat by a thin tie. Her full-length skirt was the cut favored by the "new woman": straight and sensible.

Sâr Dubnotal, still without breaking his stare, raised five fingers to signal Naïni to hold. The woman answered the physical description of their quarry, but she seemed not to know where her home was. But, of course, the similarity of a row of houses could disorient even those most familiar with the street.

Then the woman's chin raised alertly at a melodious chanting in the air. Sâr Dubnotal recognized the words, but he was compelled to keep his attention riveted on the woman herself and so let the chant recede into the background. She was now heading briskly towards the specific house they were watching. With the stakes so high, they could ill-afford to hesitate any longer.

Sâr Dubnotal flicked his wrist in the woman's direction and Naïni went into action. The pair expected no resistance for *El Tebib* had planned the abduction for the heat of the day, when the wealthy would be seeking fashionable salons indoors. Still, speed was paramount, as well as stealth. To that end, the giant was both quick and strangely ephemeral, as though carried along on the summer breeze stirring in the heat of the brick and mortar canyon that was Great Pulteney Street. His stealth was aided by the woman hesitating uncertainly before the house. She looked up at an open window from which the chanting came.

As she was about to mount the front steps, Naïni moved in behind her, one muscular arm lashing out about her waist and pulling her to him while his other hand pressed a cloth dabbed with chloroform over her nose and mouth.

The woman immediately went limp. The coachman cracked the whip and the carriage lunged forward to meet the Hindu. In the next moment, Naïni was lifting the woman into the carriage and the receiving arms of Sâr Dubnotal. Then, before the door was closed behind him, the coach was already bolting down Pulteney Street towards the bridge.

"It is her, master?" Naïni asked.

"I have never seen Helen Vaughan before," Sâr Dubnotal said, looking down into the beautiful, creamy face. He began to search her pockets.

From there, he produced a small packet of papers bound by twine which ran through a ring. *El Tebib* loosened the string and examined the jewelry. It was an ancient bit of Roman work. He found it significant that the front of the ring was shaped into a satyr's head. On the inner side of the band, his keen eye could make out a script in Latin: *DEVOMNODENT-MAVORS CAMVLOS.*

He cupped the ring, feeling strange eddies in the mystic fluids. Turning his attention to, and shuffling through, the papers, he came at last to a document of identification. He gave a sigh of accomplishment—together with the ring, there was little room for doubt as to the woman's identity.

Yet Sâr Dubnotal could not completely relax, for a spur of uncertainty remained lodged in his mind. His keen ear, which retained detailed information from even ambient noise, allowed him to recall the words to the song he had heard on the street:

Old King Cole was a merry old soul,

And a merry old soul was he,

He called for his pipe, and he called for his bowl

And he called for his fiddlers three.

Sâr Dubnotal initially had thought that the voice belonged to someone who shared Helen's dwelling, and that it had helped her recognize her own house, after a brief moment of disorientation. Yet, she had hesitated on the front steps, looking up at that open window instead of striding into her rightful home.

They crossed the bridge and soon were at the rear entrance of the Psycha-gogue's temporary lodgings near the Victoria Museum. Naïni swept the woman into his arms, then effortlessly carried her up the back flight of stairs to their flat.

The driver dismounted, removing his black hat to reveal blond hair. His face, though now in early middle age, seemed, over their long association, to have partaken of the effulgence of Sâr Dubnotal's own timelessness.

"You look troubled, master," he said. "Why?"

"Rudolph," said the Psychagogue, "I am no longer sure that this woman is Helen Vaughan. In our haste, we may have taken an innocent. Or much worse—Helen Vaughan knew we were in Bath searching for her, and is now long gone, while we have wasted time stalking an impostor...

"Let us ascend," he continued. "Naïni should have her well restrained by now. We will come to the truth of this matter by whatever means necessary."

Upon reaching their floor, their ears were assaulted by shrill screaming that would soon summon the local constabulary if allowed to continue. Sâr Dubnotal raced down the hall: one thing they did *not* need was a red blooded English bobby bursting upon the scene to rescue this lovely flower of British womanhood, bound and at the mercy of him and Naïni—"dark heathens" both.

Now he heard Naïni screaming along with the woman. Reaching the still open doorway, the Great Psychagogue and Rudolph saw the Hindu standing beside the woman, whom he had successfully bound in a wooden chair, holding a bleeding hand. The same blood smeared the woman's mouth, open wide in wailing.

"Rudolph! See to Naïni's wound! Take him to his room, then summon our new friends with haste," *El Tebib* ordered as he crossed the room, plucking away the skull ornament that pinned his cravat. He stuffed the freed article of clothing into the woman's mouth as she desperately turned her head from side to side, all the time bellowing. Then, Sâr Dubnotal tore asunder her high collar, undid her tie, and tied it around her head, securing the gag.

The woman was now looking up at him, her eyes widening as she fully took in his strange, austere appearance for the first time. This initiated a new round of bellowing, but, this time, it lodged and rumbled in her throat.

When she was spent, the Great Psychagogue asked, "If you are through screaming, Miss Vaughan, might we talk now?"

Still eyeing him dubiously, she nodded "yes." He began to remove the gag, and, before he could pull his cravat from her mouth, she had regurgitated it into her lap. Gasping for air and vehemently shaking her head, she shouted:

"I am *not* that *bitch* Helen Vaughan!"

"Exactly what the real Helen Vaughan would say in this position. My great tutelary, Ranijesti—blessed be he!—to whom nothing is lost in this world or the Empyrean beyond, and who is beyond reproof of error, says otherwise."

The woman's features trembled between an expression of rage and utter bafflement: "Your great Rooney-jesty—*what*?"

Sâr Dubnotal's eyes narrowed and his nose lifted in the air at this slurring of his master's name. "Ranijesti—that Bodhisattva who even now enjoys fore-tastes of Nirvana from his cell submerged in the earth of India…"

"You think I'm Helen Vaughan because a man *in a hole in the ground* on the other side of the globe told you so?" the woman responded, incredulity and contempt in her voice.

Sâr Dubnotal drew himself up and glared down ather. "Ranijesti directed us *where* to find Helen Vaughan. *This*," he produced the pack of papers bound with the ring, "says that you are the object of our quest. So, instead of bantering metaphysics, let us limit ourselves to the more mundane evidence, shall we?

"I adjure you to tell me why you are carrying these papers. If it's because you think you may have killed Helen Vaughan and taken her identity, let me disabuse you: Helen Vaughan does not die so easily and remains a present danger. On the other hand, if you are her willing accomplice, planted to misdirect us while she escapes, I will see that you will bear the full expiation for this crime—after you have told us where to find her."

"You, swarthy fool!" the woman snapped. "Your head is as brown as a hen's egg, but apparently nothing grows inside it! It was Helen Vaughan who murdered *me*—or, at least, came close—and took *my* identity. Not the other way around. *She* switched our papers! If you would ever withdraw your turbaned head from the 'Empyrean,' you might notice there's a war going on. With the Huns at the gate, I could ill afford to risk moving about England without some form of identification, and this was the only one available to me.

"I was at her home today because I have been searching for Helen Vaughan for two years to exact my own revenge on her, and to take back something that witch took from me. I did not know I was even on the right street until I heard that accursed song coming from the window…"

75

"If you are not Helen Vaughan, then who are you?" Sâr Dubnotal asked.

"My name is Rebecca Sharp!"

Sâr Dubnotal studied the woman whose initial conflagration of outrage had now cooled to simmering indignation. He was not yet certain she was not Helen Vaughan and this tale of woe but a fabrication. He could no longer wait for Rudolph to return with their colleagues who could settle the matter. If she was an impostor, the real Helen Vaughan was free—though perhaps not yet far beyond Bath. A few minutes might make all the difference in her slipping beyond their grasp.

He began to move to the back of the woman calling herself Rebecca Sharp.

"What—what are you doing? Get off!" she demanded as he took her head between his hands. She thrust her head from side to side to try to wrench it free as he pulled back her blonde locks to examine her scalp. He ran his index finger along a long groove there.

She flinched and bellowed with indignation: "How *dare* you! *Don't touch me!*"

Sâr Dubnotal did not answer, but crossed the room to open a drawer from which he took a large pair of scissors.

The woman's eyes bulged as he approached her with the sharp object. "What are you going to do?" she gasped out.

"Only the science of phrenology can quickly resolve the enigma you present, Miss Sharp—if that is who you are," the Psychagogue answered. "I have noted an irregularity in your skull—of which you seem very protective. Helen Vaughan is the Devil's child, and that may be your father's mark."

"You're mad!" she gasped.

"Even so, I have studied various specimens of human skulls in the development of my phrenology skills—skills for which, if I may say, I have demonstrated a high aptitude. Your skull shall now testify for or against you. To that end, your head must first be sheared…"

The woman screamed in face of this new humiliation and again struggled against her restraints, lifting the chair legs off the floor in her paroxysms, as the Great Psychagogue moved in to fulfill his declared purpose.

Suddenly, the door thrust inward. Sâr Dubnotal looked up to see Rudolph, Naïni, and the two men he had joined in their quest. One shouted out, "Stop! Whoever she may be—this woman is *not* Helen Vaughan!"

"Finally—someone *sane*!" Becky cried out. "Now will one of you help me rescue my child—something that this turbaned buffoon sabotaged!"

II. What Lurked Within The Artists' Gallery.

Becky Sharp delicately gnawed the broiled chicken breast and surveyed her new and exceedingly colorful surroundings. She was eager for some distraction from the bitingly disappointing report that the two men who had interrupted her head shaving had brought back from Great Pulteney Street. Helen Vaughan had once again absconded with her child. More, the condition in which she had left the house made it clear that she would not be returning.

For that, Becky hated Sâr Dubnotal. But she hated Helen Vaughan far more, and she desperately needed allies in what she had thought was a personal war with that wretched woman. The revelation that she was not a lone foot soldier in that battle gave her more hope than she had had for two years.

She was no longer in the room in which she had been bound, but in the largest one in the flat. Its dimensions were necessary to contain Sâr Dubnotal's entourage, along with a number of guests who had traveled from all over County Somerset to break bread with the renowned Psychagogue.

Becky had bathed and now wore a fresh dress from the wardrobe of *El Tebib*'s medium, Gianetti Annunciata. Frankly, the woman gave Becky the creeps: her pale visage suggested the disturbed, emaciated faces of medieval iconography. Becky did not relish wearing a gown—no matter how resplendent—that had rested against the flesh of a conduit to the dead. She couldn't help an occasional, writhing shrug of her shoulders, thinking that she had felt a residual ghost creep over her skin.

Naïni, had recovered and apologized for his role in her mistaken abduction. Becky had not apologized for the bite.

In a corner of the room, a dwarf, perched on a box atop a stool, tossed some chicken to the enormous dog that lay before him. He wiped his greasy fingers on the dog's coat and affectionately tousled the fur of its neck, saying, *"Bon Eustache. Bon chien."*

Whatever was inside the box thumped against its lid and sides, as though trying to kick through. The dwarf glared harshly at Becky when he saw her staring at this unexplained phenomenon to which no one else at this bizarre soirée was paying attention.

In the middle of the room, before a draped painting on an easel—to be debuted at Sâr Dubnotal's salon that night, before being displayed at the Victoria—two men from the Order of the Golden Dawn were attempting to engage the Great Psychagogue on a topic that was apparently paramount with them. A blond man named Rudolph stood beside *El Tebib*. Becky had noticed that he seemed to make a point of being always as close to Sâr Dubnotal as possible, never removing his adoring eyes from the pompous fakir.

"Sycophant," Becky hissed under her breath, continuing to chew her chicken, watching and listening to the conversation between Sâr Dubnotal and these men, one of whom spoke with a heavy French accent, the other with an Irish lilt.

"But what about the dream?" the Frenchman said haltingly in English. He was thin, bearded, with a long face. He wore a cabby's hat atop his head, and sloppily put together evening wear. Yet, Becky had heard some gossip that he was actually from the wealthy Toulet family of Paris.

"I have written down my impressions," the Irishman said, producing a leaf of paper from inside his coat. He was handsome in a bookish way, but his disheveled hair added a distracted quality to his appearance that didn't seem appropriate in an academic—absent-minded or not.

As Sâr Dubnotal looked at the papers with a patronizingly air, Toulet spoke again: "I, too, have shared this dream of Monsieur Yeats from across the Channel. The *same recurring dream*, between two men who had never met until recently."

Sâr Dubnotal muttered aloud the lines as he cursorily read: " '*Widening gyres*' umm-hmm. *'The rough beast... hour come round at last...'* Ah, I recognize the motif begun with the gyring falcons. Very nice."

"The dream began with me over ten years ago," Yeats said. "A figure of something half-man, half-beast. I thought of a sphinx..."

But the Great Psychagogue was no longer listening. He brusquely returned the paper to the Irishman. "I am sorry, Mr. Yeats, but the novelty of a sphinx sashaying about the deserts of Palestine must yield to a much more pressing affair of mine. But, please, if the Order of the Golden Dawn should ever need my assistance in the future, feel free to call on me again. Rudolph, before escorting these gentlemen out, make sure that they have my card."

Becky bristled at Sâr Dubnotal's approach, but her feelings were assuaged by the fact that a contingent of artists from the Victoria who were attending the soirée—and who were not part of the Psychagogue's usual crowd—had taken his cue and were also walking towards where she sat. Her father had been a painter, and though her childhood had been impoverished, it was the only time she had known a sense of security. This left her favorably disposed to men who wielded the brush.

Joining the group that was forming around her were the two men who had saved her from a head shaving: Villiers and Clarke, occult investigators who were compiling a mammoth repository of such cases, originally begun by Clarke alone, entitled *Memoirs to Prove the Existence of the Devil*. Helen Vaughan, they had learned, was not the last chapter in that book, as they had believed.

"Miss Sharp, if you have sufficiently recovered your wits after our unfortunate misunderstanding, we would like to question you about your relationship with Helen Vaughan," Sâr Dubnotal said. "All of these men with me—and little Jacques Courbé in the corner there—have seen their friends suffer catastrophe through their association with her. We have united in a single purpose: to purge this Earth of her vile stain—this time, forever."

"If that is the case, you will find a willing ally in me, gentlemen," Becky said. "Please. Be seated. All of you. I'd like to know the natures of all your grievances. Then I will tell you how my life was nearly destroyed by an ill-considered alliance with the witch."

"Introductions are in order, first," Sâr Dubnotal said. "You'll recall Messrs. Villiers and Clark..."

"Given the circumstances of our meeting," Becky said, looking *El Tebib* in the eye, "I dare say I would be hard pressed to have forgotten them."

Becky thought she could see a hint of a blush in the Psychagogue's face, but he did not deign to acknowledge her veiled rebuff and continued the introductions.

"This gentleman," he continued, "is Francis Aytown, whose own exhibit just closed at the Victoria. What was it called again, Mr. Aytown?"

"False Impressions of a Hungarian Count," Aytown said. Becky gave Aytown a slight smile and nod of the head.

"And this is Mr. Randolph, from America." Becky saw a man whose face shone with a mild fanaticism—but one of a benign, even *mirthful*, spirituality. This was no decadent *bon vivant* from the *fin de siècle*. She was intrigued.

Sâr Dubnotal, seeing her interest, seized the moment: "Mr. Randolph is conversant with the powers of good that radiate from the Empyrean void, though he and I conceive of these powers differently..."

The smiling Randolph beamed at her and said, "I see them as an electrical current..."

"...while *I* see them as currents in the fluid," Sâr Dubnotal said. "It is through the fluids that the parasitic larvae swarm, for corruption can only spread through that which is wholesome, fouling the fluids with their rot—"

"Sir, must I remind you that I am trying to eat while you prattle on about secretions and maggots?" interrupted Becky indignantly. "It's revolting!" She looked at the chicken breast she still held in her hands and set it down—loudly—on her plate. "You're about to put me off broiled chicken for life!"

The men about Sâr Dubnotal all squirmed uneasily—except for Randolph, who appeared bemused.

For a moment, *El Tebib*'s lips pressed tightly, then he relaxed and continued. "An unfortunate aside. Forgive me, Mademoiselle. Your rebuff is an appreciated reminder to stay focused on the business at hand. If you are sufficiently recovered, I will continue:

"This New Englander is Richard Upton Pickman. His current showing is entitled *Back Into the Fabulous Darkness*."

Becky coldly regarded Pickman, his evening attire immaculate except for an asymmetrically gloved hand. "I loathe the dark," she pronounced curtly.

Sâr Dubnotal knitted his brow; he understood Becky's grudge against him, but wondered what she could possibly have against Pickman.

"The man beside Mr. Pickman," he continued, "is Monsieur Pierre Rodin—whose great-grandfather Henri's canvases of graveyard tableaux were a source of inspiration to our Mr. Pickman. I trust, Messrs Pickman and Rodin, that what is on that draped canvas will not revolt the delicate Miss Sharp further?" Though addressing the men, it was Sâr Dubnotal's turn to look Becky in the eye so that she wouldn't miss the caustic sparks that shone there.

"Indeed not, sir," Rodin said. "What is on that canvas is more in the nature of a portrait. I have recovered a lost technique of great-grandfather's—you haven't visited what the locals call the Judge's House in Benchurch by any chance? Any of you? No? The eponymous judge was rendered by great-grandfather in the same manner as thispainting. It is my great pleasure to share his advance on the *trompe l'oeil* with you all tonight."

"We will look forward to it," Sâr Dubnotal said and continued the introductions: "Also from New England, though by a different route than Pickman, is Mr. Charles Delaware Tate."

Becky immediately liked the slim, handsome Tate. "And are you also showing at the Victoria, Mr. Tate?"

"I'm afraid not, Miss Sharp. "I came here on a pilgrimage, you might say: a long delayed visit to pay my respects at the empty grave of my mentor, Basil Hallward."

"Now, as to these men's grievances concerning Helen Vaughan," Sâr Dubnotal continued, "they had a peer who, when barely more than a boy, fell into the salon which she presided over in the 1880s under the alias of Mrs. Belmont. His name was Aubrey Beardsley, and, like so many to fall under her sway, his life—while still a young one—was cut short."

Pickman spoke up: "Gentlemen, let us be careful to keep our heads lest our quest degenerate into a Salem-style witch hunt. I do want to remind you all that Beardsley's consumption may have been inchoate *before* he met Helen Vaughan."

"Then she sped it on," Aytown snapped. "Many with his affliction live far past 25 years. Are you defending her, Yankee?"

"My dear Pickman," Sâr Dubnotal said, raising his hand. "Villiers and Clarke have shown you their record of the trail of death she left in London. That her association with Beardsley was concurrent can leave no room for doubt."

"I've always suspected she had a hand in poor Basil's disappearance," Aytown said. "And Dorian's fate, too. That portrait could have only been painted under such a malign influence as hers."

"Apparently Lord Henry does not share that opinion," Pickman retorted. "He was intimate with both men, yet remained Helen Vaughan's friend until her demise."

Again, Sâr Dubnotal raised his hand commandingly and aborted Aytown's retort. "Mr. Pickman, need I remind you that Beardsley's death is not the only crime laid to Helen Vaughan's charge? Her maleficence is well documented in Clarke's book. Hers is an evil truly not of this Earth. My late associate Robert Matheson was a medical doctor of sober mind who described via sealed document—which I was instructed to burn or use upon my own discretion— Helen's true ungodly form revealed at the moment of expiration.

"I believe his discovery that she had somehow managed to reincorporate was responsible for the seizure that took his life three and a half years after her death, though, of course, this can never be proven.

"And you may add to all this what she did to poor Jacques over there."

Sâr caught the mischievous gleam in Becky's eyes, the trembling of her pressed lips and the oscillating spasms of her cheeks.

"No, Miss Sharp," the Psychagogue added. "Before you ask, she did *not* shrink him.

"When he was with the circus, Jacques was in love with a perfectly proportioned midget ballerina named Minuette, who would pirouette on a specially prepared saddle atop a pony. Helen Vaughan saw her, proclaimed her adorable, and Minuette was accepted for the first time into the society of 'big people.' Helen would even buy matching outfits for the two of them and have her sit on her lap during her soirées. Minuette resented Jacques's warnings as an attempt to keep her within the fringe society of the circus freaks.

"Of course, by the time Helen was through with her, Minuette was destroyed. Brave Jacques stormed Helen's home in the midst of one of her decadent gatherings atop his previous Eustache, who, like the current one, could be most vicious when his master requireed it. Jacques himself was armed with a sword, and did not wield it in vain. What followed was…. the epitome of 'too horrible to tell.' Let us leave it at that for the nonce.

"Now, Miss Sharp, you know all our grievances. If you will, please tell us yours."

"I shall gentlemen, but before I divulge my story, I think it expedient that we eliminate the traitor sitting here with us."

An almost audible muteness struck the men around the table. Their eyes darted reflexively from side to side despite the restraint they were exercising to not look from face to face.

Becky slammed one hand on the table and pointed with the other: "*J'accuse!* Pickman is Helen Vaughan's spy!"

"What? This is extraordinary!" a clearly stunned Pickman blurted out.

Only Aytown smiled at her revelation. Randolph appeared to be trying to keep an open mind while Charles Delaware Tate, with a slight nodding of his head, seemed to already find her charge plausible. Only Pierre Rodin joined Pickman in protesting his innocence:

"Why—this is an outrage! You've never even met the man before tonight, have you?" Rodin said.

"I do not require a prior acquaintance," Becky said, looking Pickman in the eye. "Pickman knows I'm telling the truth, and if you wish to succeed in your quest to destroy Helen Vaughan, I suggest you see that he never leave this room alive."

Pickman's face twisted with outrage and he stood to his feet, Rodin following his lead: "Clearly, I'm not safe in the same room as this woman! Don't anyone attempt to stop—"

Sâr Dubnotal, who had risen with Pickman, clamped his hand to his shoulder and exuded an inexorable pressure which returned the New Englander to his chair. The Psychagogue then relaxed his grip, and Pickman shrugged off his hand, looking up angrily at him.

"Never touch me again, sir!" he said.

"Believe me, Sâr, you will soon feel that once was enough," Becky said. "In fact, once you hear what I have to say, you'll want to make for the nearest W.C. and *wash* that hand."

"Why you revolting minx!" Pickman sprang across the table at Becky, hands spread and grasping toward her throat. Immediately, Aytown and Tate were on top of him.

Becky did not flinch but smiled, "Oh, dear, now you'll *all* want to make for the water closet. Queue starts on the right…"

They dragged Pickman back across the table, pulling with him the cloth that he clawed into and sending the dishes, cups and cutlery clanging to the floor.

"You're losing your touch, Sâr," Becky said gleefully. "I thought the first trick you magical chaps learned was pulling a table cloth free *without* dislodging the china."

Meanwhile, Naïni had bolted across the room and his strength decided the struggle. The Hindu slammed Pickman back into his chair and held him by his shoulders as the Psychagogue pointed at Becky:

"Woman, shut your mocking mouth—unless you're ready to tell us the basis of your accusation. As far as any of us still know, your 'child' is a fabrication. Perhaps it is you who are in league with Helen Vaughan. Do not make me regret having risen to your defense—if you have played me false…"

Rodin, who had stood by during all this, helped straighten his friend's disheveled, evening clothes. The skirmish had, of course, captured the attention of the whole group. Eustache the hound growled in the corner and the hair on his back rose. Jacques snapped at him while grasping the back of his neck.

Sâr Dubnotal turned to the others who were moving tentatively from across the room toward the site of the altercation and commanded in a voice that none dared resist: "All of you, stay back. Return to enjoying your meal."

The Psychagogue then saw Rudolph, who had sent Yeats and Toulet on their way, standing in the doorway, eager to hear whatever his master's orders might be.

Sâr Dubnotal made a quick, slight shake of his head. "Rudolph, please close the door on the other side and lock it until you hear expressly from me to the contrary. Naïni, stand before the door on our side.

82

"Miss Sharp, as you have ruined my soirée, and, I am certain, reduced cook to tears, you had better have evidence to support your charges, or it will not go well with you."

"I think I know what you're capable of, Sâr," Becky said.

The Psychagogue expelled his breath from bloated cheeks. "Your evidence, Miss Sharp—*s'il vous plait*."

Becky sat back in her chair and dropped her hands into her lap, clasping them together and giving them all a demure look as she said, "Why, I don't exactly have it on my person…"

"Then why do you continue to look so revoltingly pleased with yourself?" Sâr Dubnotal thundered.

"It's on his!"

Now it was Becky's turn to rise suddenly from her chairand stretch across the table. She seized Pickman's gloved hand. He shouted indignantly at this new affront, grabbingat and then repeatedly and painfully striking Becky's hand with his other one.

But Becky refused to yield, continuing to wrench the glove from Pickman Fortunately, Sâr Dubnotal once again came to her aid and grabbed Pickman's assaulting hand. A few more tugs and Becky pulled the glove free. She fell back into her chair and waved the glove over her head, shouting: "*Vive la France! Vive l'Empereur!*"

Pickman quickly clasped his hand over the other to cover an exposed claw, scaly as a rat's tail. Sâr Dubnotal grabbed the covering hand, but Rodin sprung to his friend's defense. The Psychagogue drew up and expanded his shoulders, sending the effete Frenchman falling backwards and tottering.

Then he returned to yanking Pickman's covering hand free, while speaking to Rodin behind him, "Do not attack me again, sir. Your actions make clear you have taken Pickman's part in this affair—pray, do not make your position even more fragile than it already is."

Rodin stayed put, but struck out verbally: "You condemn him for a deformity he cannot help!"

"No," Tate said, looking down at the claw with his discerning blue eyes. "I was surprised to learn that Pickman was showing at the Victoria—or anywhere—since he vanished from the States without a trace a year ago. I do not know what his choice of subject has been since arriving here, but his paintings back in New England are full of rat-like, man-size creatures. A photograph taken from his studio the night he disappeared showed that he was working from models!"

"What? Impossible!" both Randolph and Aytown exclaimed.

"I tell you… *it was a photograph from life*!" Tate said, his teeth clinched. He then looked at Sâr Dubnotal. "A motif of his paintings was that of the Changeling. Ghoul spawns who become human cuckoos, while the ghouls take the human infants to raise as their own."

"Yes! Changelings! You're intimately familiar with the practice, eh, Pickman?" Becky said triumphantly. "Was that why you hit it off so well with Helen Vaughan, another Hell-spawn bastard like yourself who took *my* child for her own?"

Pickman remained silent, but kept his defiant expression, registering no remorse, though he no longer denied the accusations.

"You will, of course, tell Miss Sharp where we can find Helen Vaughan and her child," Sâr Dubnotal said, his tone making it clear that he was implacable in this regard.

A woman's shriek trilled through the room, and all attention immediately riveted on Gianetti Annunciata who stood, pointing at the draped painting.

Becky smiled at the defeated Rodin while pointing at the Psychagogue: "It would appear *his* medium doesn't care for *your* medium."

"There's blood seeping through the covering!" Annunciata shouted.

"Yes, but in the final analysis…" Becky said with an inquisitive cock of her head and a mocking sideways stare at Rodin, "…is it *art*?"

"Will you ever stop your mocking mouth, woman?" Sâr Dubnotal said, as he made his way to the painting. "Must I remind you how grave is the situation for your own child?"

"You scarcely need to remind me of that, sir! My situation has been grave for two years! If I appear giddy—hysterically so—it's because, for the first time since she was taken from me, I have real hope that I might reclaim my daughter!"

Sâr Dubnotal now approached the veiled painting and carefully touched the red fluid on the canvas's drapery. Examining his wet fingertips to make certain that it wasn't merely wet oils, he then pronounced: "It *is* blood."

He took the drapery over the canvas and swept it away, discarding the stained material as eloquently as a matador does his cape. A collective intake of breath was heard around the room.

Perched on the easel like a vulture biding its time, piteously looking down on its prey, was the medieval representation of Death: a robed and hooded skull, a scythe grasped at the ready in skeletal hands. From the edge of its blade, the blood seeped.

Sâr Dubnotal indignantly turned on his heel to face Pickman and the blanching Rodin over whose now pale face a sickly glaze of perspiration glistened.

"Pickman!" Rodin shouted. "The painting has betrayed us!" In the next instant, he was bolting for the door, but the giant Hindu caught him. He beat and struck at him heedlessly—and futilely.

"Bring him here, Naïni!" Sâr Dubnotal ordered.

Rodin's heels scraped the floor as the Hindu pushed the artist along, then planted him before the Great Psychagogue.

"Is *this* that advance on the *trompe l'oeil* you promised us this evening, Monsieur Rodin?" *El Tebib* demanded. "Or is it merely harbinger of something else to follow? Why were you so adamant about leaving the room? There is something more, is there not? A fate that you and Pickman have planned for all of us here, but which you do not wish to share?"

Rodin slapped moist palms over his face, his nails clawing wretchedly into his flesh. "Yes!" he shouted. "Yes! I beg of you—it is not too late, we can *all* still flee."

"But at least *someone* must die, yes? No matter where we scatter. Once begun, I dare say the Grim Reaper's work cannot be turned back." Sâr Dubnotal surveyed the room: "You have all heard his confession. Will any of you dare come between me and the administration upon this person of the same judgment he would have dealt us all?"

Mutely, all shook their heads, though there was a sick horror in their eyes at the bleeding scythe and the contemplation of what must now follow.

"Rudolph," Sâr Dubnotal shouted so that he would be heard through the door, "come to me. Naïni, quickly take Monsieur Rodin to the walk-in closet—no, the small room that connects with the W.C. I suspect that arrangement will facilitate leaving the facilities as clean as we found them when we remove hence. Ah, Rudolph, here you are... Take the canvas and go with Naïni. Lock in both artist and painting, Naïni. I suspect you will know when it's time to open the door again."

Rodin sagged toward the floor. Naïni caught him in his arms. Rudolph came forward, balking at his first reach for the canvas. Then, grasping it by the edges, he walked briskly behind the Hindu, careful that the side with the image of the Grim Reaper was not against him.

"Rudolph, when your part is done, return and again lock our door on the other side until you hear from me."

Now Sâr Dubnotal approached Pickman who glowered defiantly at him. The Psychagogue, in turn, held Pickman in his own, commanding stare. Invisible to the others, inexorable currents of mesmerism from the Sâr were assaulting Pickman's psyche with magnetic waves of force.

"I adjure, you, Pickman, to tell us where we will find Helen Vaughan. You *will* tell me. I sense your resistance, the awakening of defenses buried in your brain in so deep a strata of tissue that you yourself have forgotten that they sleep there... Sleep to be awakened for just such a moment as this."

Becky noticed that the hair on Pickman's head was rising as though from a static charge. Then the cutlery began to tremble and Becky saw that his other hand—the "human" hand—was now drawing up into a claw with the same scaling beginning to manifest like a vile stigmata.

Pickman bellowed, leaping to his feet, and Sâr Dubnotal fell back, as Becky and everyone else retreated.

Pickman's body was warping, bursting the seams of his coat, sleeves and pants. His chest expanded, firing buttons like shrapnel from his shirt—and exposing a breast of scabrous flesh.

A snout thrust out from Pickman's face; his jaw seemed to have dislocated, and fangs jutted out from his lower gums and over his upper lip. His face and body had grown increasingly hirsute, sickly gray shoots spreading into tangled brambles of hair.

Now he stood completely revealed: Pickman—the Ghoul!

Eustache tore free from Jacques's grasp, leaving hair in his master's tiny clutching fingers. The dog hurled itself at the Ghoul, the weight of its body slamming into Pickman like a catapulted frozen side of beef. Yet the monstrosity did not stagger, but grappled at the exposed fangs frenziedly ferreting at its throat.

The Ghoul sank its claws into the hound's sides, causing it to yelp in high pitches of pain, and cease its gnawing. Pickman raised Eustache over his head and hurled him at the crowd huddling on the far side of the room. They scattered as the hound flew towards them. But Eustache fell short, landing on his side in a slide. Still skidding, he righted himself, nails tapping a frantic staccato in an attempt to regain traction.

Jacques was already running toward the Ghoul, his short sword drawn. The rest of the group were surging against the door, shouting and beating on it. But Rudolph remained on the other side, holding the key, unyielding in his word to his master.

"Back, Jacques!" Sâr Dubnotal commanded, and the angered dwarf, while simmering with displeasure, obediently turned to see to his dog.

Only Becky and Annuciata had not run for the door—Annuciata lay in a fainted heap by Rodin'sbare easel, and Becky had retreated to a corner, brandishing a steak knife.

"Pickman!" Sâr Dubnotal's voice resonated powerfully as he gestured at the hissing, screeching Ghoul. "Your true self is revealed. You can no longer remain here, for the light has revealed the darkness. Hear me, Pickman! Depart hence! Go to your own place! I bind you to the plane of Leng, into the region of unknown Kadath—there to perform expiation if it may be that something human remains within you!"

The Ghoul screeched in indignant agony at its humiliation, the screech rising into the unbearable pitch of nails dragging across slate as the room's lights began to drop. Pickman seemed to be drawing the darkness to him in a desperate attempt for succor. Up went a group cry from fear that they would be plunged into the darkness, locked in the room with that thing. But even more quickly than the lights had begun to dim, they rose—into a brighter splendor than they had cast over the chamber before.

And Pickman, the door still locked, was gone.

Sighs of relief were expelled over the room, ending in a moment of silence, pierced immediately by a shrill scream from the corner. Becky charged at Sâr Dubnotal with her knife, shouting:

"What have you done? You took him from me—the one man who could have told me where to find my child!"

She collided into him, knife raised. Sâr Dubnotal grabbed her thin, delicate wrist, easily disarming her and sending the knife clanking to the floor.

He now grasped both wrists together as Becky writhed in violent spasms: "You're as much a beast as that thing! You have just handed my child over to Helen Vaughan's corruption that will surely transform her into the same bitch of Hell as she is! This is on *your* head, Sâr Dubnotal! Do you hear me? I'll never forgive…"

"*Miss Sharp!*" Sâr Dubnotal's voice resonated like the sharp crack of a frozen river breaking at first thaw; it struck her like a slap. At once, she ceased her struggles and fell limp, sobbing. She would have collapsed to the floor, but the Great Psychagogue caught her up and cradled her.

"I did not mean to see it; I did not *mean* to see it. I had no choice…" she mumbled lowly over and over as though in a fever.

"Miss Sharp," the Psychagogue said gently. "I understand that I have given you little reason to trust me. But I do know that your burden is great, that you are in maternal agonies that I cannot begin to fathom. I am your friend, Miss Sharp, though I have not seemed like it. And apart from destroying Helen Vaughan, I wish nothing more than to reunite you with your child.

"But even I, the greatest of Psychagogues, cannot foresee all things. My desire to wrest the truth from Pickman, the unwise use of the magnetism as coercion, blew out what I thought were defenses, but were instead psychic barricades he had set up to restrain the beast within. I could not open the door and unleash the Ghoul upon the city, which meant I was jeopardizing the lives of everyone in this room—including yours. If anyone was to be left to save your baby, Pickman had to be dispatched immediately. Your burden is already too great; I am so sorry for any additional grief I have caused you."

Becky raised her tear-streaked face up at this great man who cradled her, and for the first time, her expression softened as she looked at him.

"Now, dry your eyes," *El Tebib* said as he gently sat her down next to the recovered Annunciata. Distraught as she was, Becky maintained enough of her wits to immediately slide down the couch away from her. "And when you have sufficiently regained your composure, we all still earnestly desire to hear the circumstances of your relationship with Helen Vaughan."

END OF PART I

(to be continued in Volume 8)

Fritz Lang and Thea von Harbou's 1927 classic Metropolis *has inspired a trio of* Elseworld *graphic novels at DC written by the undersigned and illustrated by Ted McKeever.* Metropolis *made a return appearance in our contribution to Volume 6 of* Tales of the Shadowmen, *"J.C. in Alphaville." The torch is now passed to Travis Hiltz who brings Arnould Galopin's remarkable Doctor Omega into the mix and imagines one more sequel entitled...*

Travis Hiltz: *The Robots of Metropolis*

Metropolis, The Future

The city stretched to the horizon. Called a city, it was in fact the size of a continent, a vast landscape of concrete, steel, glass and plastic. Mountainous towers stretched to the heavens and its valleys sank deep into the very depths of the Earth.

Armies of citizenry made their way through the miles of monorail tracks, moving walkways, roads and even air vehicles. The lights were never dim in Metropolis and no moment silent of the hum of activity.

The lowest level of Metropolis was a labyrinth of alleyways, service tunnels, power stations and storage bays. With a screech of metal, a bulkhead opened and a most unusual trio stumbled out.

A young man wearing a suit that had last been in fashion in 1910, his dark hair disheveled, was half supporting, half dragging a robot.

It had blank metal features, but its body shape was obviously meant to resemble a woman.

On the other side of the robot, attempting to help support her as they stumbled along, was a small being with a large, pumpkin-sized head that seemed too big for its child-like body. It was dressed in an old fashioned striped, one piece bathing suit and had a towel draped over its neck. As they ran, it muttered to itself in its native tongue.

"No point sniping at me," the young man said. "As you'll recall, it was my idea to see the opening of the Brighton Beach Pavilion. It was our learned host that decided to come here. 'Denis, my boy, none of that lounging about on the beach for us! We'll visit one of the golden ages of mankind!' We never even got to have coffee…!"

As they ran, the robot flickered and for several seconds took on the appearance of a young woman dressed in coveralls. She then returned to her original metal form.

The alien grumbled some more.

"Why do you keep asking me, Tiziraou?" Denis Borel snapped. "Before today, I'd never even heard of an 'electronic imager,' let alone how it works or why hers doesn't. Believe me, if I'd known this society would react so violently to a robot in their midst, I'd have asked Doctor Omega to repair the imager before we agreed to 'escort' this young lady back to the *Cosmos*. Though, I suppose the public square with that robot tied to a stake that appeared to have been set fire to should have served as a hint."

The alien Tiziraou muttered some more.

"Well, I think by the time we realized that mob was coming after us, it was a bit late to rethink our strategy," Denis replied.

More alien mutterings.

"Yes, I supposed it is somewhat comforting that nothing else can go wrong," Denis mused, right before the earthquake hit.

It was a very brief earthquake; Metropolis was able to ride it out with minor damage. People stumbled, a few items fell off of shelves and dust was shaken lose from the older buildings.

Doctor Omega, that learned savant and mysterious traveler in space and time, brushed a bit of dust off the lapel of his black, Edwardian suit and glared up at his host. He was seated in a utilitarian metal chair, bookended by claw-handed robots. Unlike the robot accompanying his companions, these were crude and bulky machines, resembling water heaters on legs. Disguising them as attractive young women would be a near impossible feat.

The Doctor smoothed back a rebellious lock of his receding white hair and peered sternly down the length of his beaky nose at the man across the table from him.

"Are these earthquakes your doing as well, Rotwang?" he asked, "or merely another 'unfortunate effect' of your latest scientific endeavor?"

Rotwang glared back from his chair at the other end of the table.

The two men shared many similarities, but at the same time seemed to be opposites or distorted versions of one another.

Like Omega, Rotwang was an older man, a man of learning. His white hair was coarse and matted. His eyes burned with equal parts genius and anger. He wore an older suit, made of a rough, plain cloth. Acid burns and various chemical stains decorated his long coat. Encircling his neck was a wide metal collar, which sprouted several wires that snaked down under his shirt and seemed to plug into his skin. This caused his head to crook slightly to one side, and as he moved, the muffled sounds of machinery issued from beneath his clothing.

"Omega!" Rotwang growled, tapping upon the table top with his artificial hand. "I should have known, as I am on the cusp of success, you would return to keep me from accomplishing my goals. You are yet another that cannot stand to allow my genius to shine."

"Really, Rotwang? Am I to believe you are still attempting to play the martyr?" the Doctor asked. "I discovered one of your robots attempting to tap into the city power grid and shortly afterward these tremors occur. No sooner do I arrive at your palatial manor, that I'm set upon by your tin bullyboys!" he gestured over his shoulder, dismissively at his clunky guards. "Though, I must say, they don't appear to be up to your usual standards. Rush job, were they, Professor?"

Rotwang leaned forward and smiled disdainfully at the jibe.

"No, I cannot take credit for the Volkites. I was not their creator, rather just their discoverer. Following my... fall from grace," Rotwang said, running his flesh hand across his metal collar, "I took refugee in the tunnels beneath the City. To avoid my pursuers, I was forced to travel ever deeper below the Earth's surface. I became lost, and delirious from my injuries, wandered off the secured routes. It was then that I stumbled upon the remains of an ancient city containing stockpiles of amazing devices. Metropolis is built upon the bones of Atlantis!"

"Really?" Omega asked. "When you speak of your injuries, would that list include some form of head trauma, perhaps?"

"You mock!" Rotwang shouted, slamming his artificial fist against the table. "But you have witnessed with your own eyes what I have accomplished using the devices I salvaged from beneath the city. The Volkites, though crude, are sturdy and capable automatons and while the earthquake ray was conceived as a weapon, the thermal energy it generates is adequate for my purposes..."

"Yes, of course!" the Doctor exclaimed, with a snap of his fingers. "I knew I'd seen your Volkites before! They and the earthquake ray—quaint little name—were some of Unga Khan's toys. There are so many places that claim to be Atlantis it's sometimes hard to keep track of all of them. If I hadn't been there when the original sank, I'd have my doubts that there ever was a true Atlantis."

He smiled at Rotwang, obviously proud of himself.

"You are using the Earthquake ray to generate low-level tremors and then siphoning the thermal energy from the tectonic activity. If you weren't always wasting your efforts on these bits of petty revenge, I would almost find myself in awe of the brilliance of your creativity."

The two men glared at each other across the table, a sneer further marring Rotwang's haggard features, as his fingers tapped against the table's surface. Doctor Omega sat statue still, his expression unfathomable, as though he was attempting to force his opponent's surrender with the sheer power of his gaze.

For several seconds, all that could be heard was the hum of distant machinery, as the two men locked gazes.

It was as though they were playing a game of chess, in which only they could see the pieces or the board.

"This is no vendetta, Omega," Rotwang said, standing up. "I have turned my back on the City, as they so long ago turned their backs upon me. My current project is not to punish Metropolis, but rather to escape it."

He limped across the room, to where a large square object was covered with a grimy tarp. Tubes and wires snaked out from beneath it and connected to various devices scattered about the room. Grabbing hold of a corner of the tarp, Rotwang pulled it down, revealing a featureless grey, metal cube. It hummed and had a vaguely indistinct quality, as though seen through heat haze.

"Oh, Rotwang," Doctor Omega breathed, his stern expression faltering for a second. "What have you done?"

"You should be proud, Omega," Rotwang announced, turning back to face his guest. "You were my inspiration. After your first visit, and then hearing your lectures at the university about the science of the continuum, I was able to piece together my own, humbler version of your craft. If Metropolis feels it has no more use for Rotwang, I now have all of history in which to find a place that will appreciate my genius!"

"Rotwang, this is a dangerous game you are playing. You truly cannot understand the forces…!"

"Yes, yes," Rotwang interrupted with a disdainful gesture, "the forces that I have already released! This is not some quaint old novel, my dear Omega. My device has been tested. I sent one of my robots on a journey, a quite successful one, I may inform you, to the early decades of the 20th century. I have had a decade to build and plan. My army is in place, theories and equipment tested and perfected. You have arrived years past the time when you could have stopped me. "

He began to pace as he talked, giving the appearance of a deranged, disheveled university professor.

"I realized that despite my efforts, and the years I devoted to this City, the sacrifices I have made, that I was never to be appreciated…rewarded. It is time Metropolis and I parted ways. The devices I am employing, the earthquake ray, the Volkites and my own robots, are merely in order that I may power my ship and be free of this City at last."

Doctor Omega stroked his chin, thoughtfully studying the other scientist.

"Rotwang, I must say you are a genius," he said, with quiet intensity. "Your work in robotics is brilliant. Quite brilliant. Beyond anything I could hope to accomplish. The machinery and systems you helped to put in place will be serving this City for centuries to come."

He leaned forward slightly, his elbows resting upon the table's edge, but never taking his eyes off of Rotwang.

"What such a mind as yours could accomplish once free of this petty and destructive need for recognition. How much more could you create if you gave up on this feud with the Fredersons? Yes, truly, a brilliant mind. Brilliant enough to know that in order to generate enough power to launch your time cube, the ray could easily generate an earthquake beyond your ability to control. You would put all of Metropolis at risk in your escape attempt."

"What would you have me do?" Rotwang asked, in a quiet voice.

"Come with me. Walk away from all this. The *Cosmos* has more than enough room to take on another passenger. It would be a pleasure to have you join us, to show you the length and breadth of time and space. The sights we would see…the wonder… and to have someone of equal intellect to discuss it with. You would understand why once you've seen what the universe can offer there is no need to feel that you should have ownership of any part of it."

Rotwang took a step towards Doctor Omega, and then hesitated. His artificial hand stroked his chin in thought. He looked about his lab and then back at the other man.

"Well?" the Doctor asked, with a smile. "What do you say?"

"What do I say…?" Rotwang repeated, quietly. He then glared at Omega. "What do I say to such a generous offer to gain a nurse maid? Rather than freeing myself by my own abilities, I can abandon my work in order to gain a comfy chair in a corner of your drawing room! Have you take me by the hand and show me the points of interest like I was some simple-minded child on a day outing to the museum! I am Rotwang! I will pull myself out from the mire of obscurity, the City fathers wish me to sink into, by the skill of my own hands and the brilliance of my own mind!"

Doctor Omega sat back in his chair, shoulders slumped, one hand tugging at his lapel anxiously.

Rotwang began to pace. As he spoke, his voice grew louder and angrier.

"You, like all the others, hope that your pretty words…your empty gestures, will turn me from my path, my plans…my destiny! I will be free of this City and if it suffers in the process than it is no more than it deserves."

"There is no need for this," Doctor Omega protested, leaning forward. The Volkites reached down and using their clamp-like hands, pushed him back into his chair. He scowled at the robots, and then back at Rotwang. "Are you sunk so deep in bitterness that you cannot see an offer of friendship or have you so little human feeling left to think twice about the death and destruction you may cause to the City? Have you become no more emotional than one of your robots?"

"I have given too much to this City!" Rotwang roared, holding up his artificial hand. "While you helped the founding fathers and then went on your way, I was here! Toiling for decades to make their lofty dreams a solid, workable reality! No more! Metropolis has decided it no longer needs or wants me, then so be it! Whatever occurs next is not my concern!"

Rotwang limped over to his chair and leaned his hands upon the back to steady himself. His breathing was ragged and his eyes wide and over flowing with hate and madness.

Doctor Omega pursed his lips in thought and then nodded to himself.

"If that is your final word, then so be it," he said, with a tone of sad finality. "How shall we pass the time before your departure? Can I at least see what you have accomplished with Unga Khan's toys?"

Rotwang peered at him for several moments, than gave a curt nod.

"Come," he grumbled, gesturing at the Volkites to allow Omega to stand.

The Doctor strolled over towards the earthquake ray casually, looking about the laboratory at Rotwang's other devices with a vague interest and occasional nod of approval.

The control devices for the ray resembled a round altar that had been melded onto some primitive, over-sized computer. Several other bulky devices were wired onto it.

"Interesting additions you've made," Omega mused, as he strolled around the device, closely followed by the Volkites. "Replacing the radium core with Lunarium. Ah, you're using oscillation overthruster circuitry as part of the targeting mechanism…"

He looked up at Rotwang and gave him a small smile.

Rotwangs' glare began to falter, as he was unsure if he was still in conflict with the other man. He suddenly felt more like a student who was being appraised by a teacher.

"Amazing how you've taken technological devices that were built centuries apart and been able to adapt them to each other," Omega nodded. He reached into his coat pocket, only to have one of the Volkites seize his arm. He slowly drew out his hand to reveal a pair of pince-nez glasses. Rotwang waved his mechanical minion away and Omega, with a nod of thanks held the glasses up to his eyes and continued to study the machine.

"Hmmm, well, as I've said before, your genius is admirable, while at the same time it saddens me that you've wasted it. Is there nothing I can say that would dissuade you from this course of action?"

"Nothing. I have made my choice and the City will have to live with it."

"As will you, my friend, as will you. Then, may I offer one last bit of advice? Something that I think will aid you in future creations."

"As you will," Rotwang replied, arms crossed.

"When dealing with a complicated bit of machinery," Doctor Omega said, leaning forward, pince-nez held up to his eyes, to look at an open panel, out of which several cables were snaking out of, "it takes but the simplest thing to disrupt its workings."

With that prouncement, he opened his hand and the shilling piece he had palmed when he had fetched his glasses fell into the opening and plinked its way down into the depths of the earthquake ray device.

"No!" Rotwang shouted, hobbling frantically over to the machine.

The Volkites each grabbed hold of one of Doctor Omega's arms. The savant paid them no attention. He stood, tapping his glasses absently against his chin, as he listened to the various clinks and tonks the coin made as it wandered through the great devices' guts, as though he was enjoying a piece of music.

Rotwang adjusted controls and then moved the cables, so as to allow him to peer into the open panel, seeking some hint of where the shilling piece had come to rest.

There was a final plink and then a grating noise.

Rotwang gestured at the Volkites to release Omega, so they could help him pry open a large panel in the base of the machine.

"Unless I miss my guess," Doctor Omega said, his expression changing from that of a stern teacher to a mischievous child "that noise can mean only one thing…"

"What?" Rotwang demanded.

"We should duck."

With a nimbleness that seemed beyond his years, he ducked behind the nearest Volkite, just as the grating became a groan, and then the building began to shake. Sputtering and cursing, Rotwang lurched away from the earthquake ray. He stumbled, then crawled beneath the heavy wooden table, only seconds before the device began to smoke and spark. The building trembled and a blizzard of dust and debris filled the over-sized room.

Both men scrambled towards opposite ends of the house in a dash for safety, as a column of energy geysered up from the top of the ray machine and the old building began to collapse…

Back at the *Cosmos*, Denis Borel and Tiziraou were slumped on the sofa in the common room. They were explaining to Fred, the ship's bearded handyman, what had caused the current appearance of their clothes and where they had acquired the battered robot. Fred sat at a nearby table, tools and the various bits of the robot scattered across it.

"That was when they tore the sleeve off my jacket," Denis said, holding some ice to his bruised forehead. "These people really do not like robots."

"Well," Fred said, not looking up from the robot arm he was tinkering with. "If you knew this place's history, you'd understand…"

The door opened and Doctor Omega entered, leaning heavily on his cane and seemingly unaware of his surroundings. He sat in a corner chair with a heavy sigh.

Fred looked up from his work and tapped at the nearest robot part with a screwdriver. Doctor Omega glanced up, and met Fred's questioning raised eyebrow with a wan smile and a shake of his head. With an effort, he rose from his chair and strolled over to the table.

"I see the boys brought you back a new toy to play with," he said, hanging his cane on the crook of his arm and picking up the robot's head and peering into its blank, metal eyes. He tapped it and the eyes flickered to life.

"The workers musssst…rise up! They are…zzztt… but pu-puppets, danc-
ing on the elite's string…!"

"Hmmm, and what might you become, now that your own strings have
been cut, I wonder…?" the Doctor mused and returned the head to the table. He
turned and seemed to suddenly realize Denis and the small Martian were also in
the room. He took in their bruised and disheveled condition with a quick up and
down glance.

"Oh, dear! I leave you two alone for the afternoon and you come back
looking like you've been playing rugby with apes…!"

He walked away before they could turn the full force of their glare upon
the old traveler, and went back to Fred, patting the burly handy man on the
shoulder.

"Leave that for later, Fred, I'd just as soon be on our way. Nothing more to
be done here."

"I take it things did not go as hoped for?" Fred asked, standing up.

"The City was saved, the madman vanquished," Doctor Omega shrugged,
"but, I had hoped for more…yes, I had hoped…well, no point dwelling on what
might have been."

He clapped Fred on the shoulder again, and gave a brief, sad smile.

"Let's be on our way. So much still to see," he mused. "You know, I've
been meaning to visit the opening of the Brighton Beach Pavilion…"

The rest of his plans faded, as he and Fred wandered off to the *Cosmos'*
control room. Denis and Tizarou shared a worried look and then slumped deeper
into the sofa.

The robots came, marching through Metropolis. Of the many that had been sent
out, only a few had survived the wrath of the mob and the earthquake rays energy surge. Their human disguises flickering on and off, they walked back to the
wreckage of the creator's home. With bare hands they dug through the rubble. It
took hours, and the loss of two more of their number, but eventually they
reached their goal.

Rotwang was huddled up beneath the twisted remains of a Volkite. His
clothes and hair were stiff and matted with dirt and blood.

"There," he rasped, gesturing weakly at the corner where the grey time
cube nestled among the wreckage. "En-energy enough…for one… journey. I
will be…free…of…city…I will see…universe and… discuss what I've
seen…with Omega on…my… own terms…!"

There is nothing like another good Egyptian yarn to evoke images of pyramids, animal-headed gods, desert-lost tombs and ancient curses... Following in the footsteps of Talbot Mundy, Sax Rohmer and others, and echoing some of the re- velations contained in Emmanuel Gorlier's tale, Paul Hugli takes us to the mag- ical land of the Pharaohs in...

Paul Hugli: *Death to the Heretic!*

Egypt, October 1929

> *He's fond of enigmas, of conundrums, of hieroglyphs...*
> Edgar Allen Poe
> *The Murders in the Rue Morgue*

Ra's Solar Barge had barely begun its journey from the East to the West and, already, the heat was oppressive. Yet that was expected at 8 a.m. just a score miles south of Cairo. Removing his broad-beamed straw hat, Bruce Wayne fanned his face, hoping to cool himself, to shoo away the sandy dust which had caked his sweaty face. He stared at his manic driver, Alfred Pennyworth, man- servant, guardian and oldest friend. The butler was taking the ride all in stride, dressed in an *abayyah*, cloth face mask, goggles and aviator cap. The 1907 Daimler bumped and groaned as it traversed a barely utilitarian desert road. Having spent time in Egypt during the Great War, he knew the proper attire for surviving a motorized jaunt through the desert in an open touring motor-car, al- though Bruce doubted Alfred had driven such a sporty motor-car during the War to End All Wars.

"Long ways from Gotham, eh, Alfred?" Bruce said, a bit green around the gills, replacing his hat, covering his now dusty jet-black hair, wishing he had listened to his friend: a blue-blazer and white trousers were not proper attire for the open desert. The straw hat was acceptable, but a *kuffryah* was more practical. Next time he would listen to Alfred

Maybe...

"Yes, Master Bruce, a long way from Gotham. A long way from any- where... civilized, if I may say so," remarked Alfred, as he skirted the motorcar around a flock of sheep and goats without slowing one iota. "It was kind of Mrs. Emerson to loan us his Daimler."

"Yes, kind," Bruce echoed unconvincingly. He had given up trying to read the Cairo daily about reported incidents of "fire-stick robberies" having set it aside to get a better grip on the dashboard—and his nerves. He swore to himself: *When I get back to Gotham, I'm going to sell my Stutz, Ballot, Grand Prix, Hotchkiss, Indian, and DKW, and get a Model A—no a Model T.* His need for speed was sated, thanks to Alfred. Ford used to brag that you could get a Model T in any color—as long as that color was black. *Yes, a black motorcar... nice and safe.*

His thoughts were interrupted when the Daimler hit a pot-hole and bounced. A "Sorry, Sir," from Alfred did nothing for Bruce's nerves.

They came to a rise, and Alfred stopped. In the morning haze—almost mirage-inducing—was the splendor of the Sakkara plain, stretching out before them, majestically littered with ancient burial ruins of rulers and couriers of Egypt's Old Kingdom, dominated by the Step Pyramid of King Djoser, over 4500-years-old, consisting of a series of unequal mastabas stacked atop one another, the world's first large stone structure ever built.

Shifting the Daimler back into gear, Alfred followed the dusty trail into the Saqqara plain and passed the mastabas of brick-sized stones and stone slab ceilings. Bruce pointed out an encampment of tents. Alfred nodded and slowed the motorcar to a reasonable speed, skirting around workers carrying dirt and stone in baskets upon their heads, avoiding scattering geese and chickens, and downshifting to a safe and successful halt just a few meters from the largest tent, which Bruce surmised was the dig's headquarters.

Exiting the Daimler, the Gothamites adjusted themselves to Terra Firma. Bruce used his hat to swipe the dust from his suit as Alfred removed his scarf and goggles, placing them in his up-turned helmet before tucking it under his arm.

About to make a remark, Bruce was interrupted when a *kuffryah*-covered head popped up out an ancient walkway buried beneath the ground and said: "Thomas?"

"No," Bruce said as the lanky man climbed out of the tunnel.

"Of course, your father, ah..."

"Yes," said Bruce, his face a blank mask.

"Then you must be Bruce," the blue-eyed man said, offering him his hand. "I was sorry to hear of your parents' death. You father was quite generous in funding my research."

"Yes, Doctor Jones. And Wayne Enterprises will continue to contribute to you excavations."

"As long as I get results?" he said with a crooked smile.

Allowing himself a reflective smile Bruce said: "Dr. Jones... Henry, if I may... I read your proposal..."

"Indiana," he interrupted.

"Excuse me..."

"I prefer 'Indiana' or 'Indy.' Dr. Henry Jones *is* my father's name. We are two different persons."

"No doubt, er, Indiana. As I was saying, I read your proposal. A search for the tomb of the legendary—I believe you wrote 'mythical'—Imhotep…" Bruce said with a sweep of his hand, indicating the entire burial complex around them, "the vizier and chief architect of the Djoser Pyramid. If I recall, correctly, he became the patron saint of scribes in Greece, while other cultures consider him the world's first physician. Quite an achievement for one man."

"Yes, indeed," Jones concurred, absently brushing the dust from his *galabeeyah*. "People have fanciful goals and beliefs, searching the world, hoping to verify myths: Noah's Ark, the Ark of the Covenant… or like my father, right now in Alexandria, pouring over Coptic records, believing they will lead him to—of all things!—the Silver Chalice of Christ. As I said: fanciful."

"And you are being more factual, searching for Imhotep's Tomb?"

"Actually," Indy smiled, "that and his Ibis Stick. Empowered by Thoth, himself, it is said."

"Empowered to do what?"

"According to legend, the Stick possesses the power to levitate gigantic building stones, like those used here and later at Gizah… that the wane could create city-wide force-fields, and cause images to appear and disappear at will."

"I see. Nothing fanciful."

"No," Indy answered with a straight face.

"Master Bruce," Alfred voice filtered into Bruce's consciousness before the latter could ask a follow-up question relating to Jones' quest, and turned to his friend, who added: "If you are not presently occupied, I have a gentleman who wishes to meet you."

"I shall be there momentarily," Bruce said, turning back to Indy to say they would talk later.

Entering the excavation's main tent, he spotted Alfred standing next to a tall, handsome man, with a timeless quality about him. "Master Bruce, may I introduce you to Monsieur Leo Saint-Clair."

"It's an honor, Monsieur," Bruce said in stilted school-book French.

Saint-Clair smiled, wondering again why Americans always felt it necessary to tell a person they are honored to merely meet him? He shrugged it off; he should be used to it by now.

"Leo and I have been chatting-up old times, and I am at liberty to inform you of his true identity and work," Alfred stated as he poured tea. The three men had settled in canvas camp chairs. The butler filled his employer in on some of his adventures during the Great War, dealing with a score of espionage missions with the Frenchman. Bruce was amazed, but not surprised.

The whole time, he studied Saint-Clair: medium-height, quite broad-shouldered and thick-chested, a handsome man with striking, penetrating greenish-blue eyes which reminded him of the almost hypnotic eyes of a pilot named Allard he had met once. Bruce had to break his glance; the man seemed to have the ability to force his personality on others…

"Are you aware of a Doctor Hugo Strange," Saint-Clair began, after a sip of tea, "formerly employed by Wayne Enterprises? And a Professor William Omaha McElroy, who is funded through the Wayne Foundation's Oriental Studies Museum?"

"Yes, of course," Bruce replied cautiously. Even before reaching his majority—and inheriting 51% of the vast Wayne holdings—he has tried to keep current with the running of the vast empire. With the help of advisors and, of course, Alfred Pennyworth.

Wayne Enterprises, in conjunction with Wentworth Works, sponsored Hugo Strange's experimental research into the practical applications of "concentrated light," based on work theorized by Nikola Tesla. The goal: a polyphase system to power and direct an elevated monorail through Gotham City. By the end of the project's first year, the outlook had been promising. Yet, clandestinely, Strange had adapted the polyphase system into a primitive "ray gun"—like something out of *Amazing Stories*—and embarked on a crime spree. He was eventually defeated and imprisoned, but his invention and research papers had been destroyed in the process.

"Yes," Bruce repeated, studying the Frenchman: there was something about his eyes... something he couldn't put his finger on... "Yet, how does Strange tie-in with Professor McElroy? Sure, he's a little eccentric..."

McElroy had recently been referred as the "Tut Nut," due to his almost fanaticism over the Boy King—especially since Howard Carter's discovery of the almost intact tomb of Tutankhamun seven year before—and total antipathy toward his predecessor, King Akhenaten, the "Heretic." A dreamer or a madman, Akhenaten had erected his capital city half-way between Memphis and Thebes, and upset the *ma'at* (The Divine Order of Things) by elevating his personal God, the formally obscure solar disc Aten, to the One and Only, outlawing the worship of *all* other gods and goddesses. And the Glory which was Egypt was in jeopardy. The "renegade" king was disposed of, Tutankhamun was elevated to Pharaoh, and the priesthood was restored. Alas, the damage was done and—except for the reigns of Seti I and Ramses II forty years later—Egyptian known-world domination had ebbed, soon to be over-run by a succession of foreign powers.

This much Bruce had learned from reading abstracts from papers presented to Wayne's Oriental Studies Museum, and also that—even though he felt antipathy toward the "heretic"—McElroy was preparing to resume digging at Tell el Amarna, looking for evidence that Tutankhamun had resided there before becoming king and returning the capital to Thebes. Bruce believed that the professor was a professional, and that he put his science before his personal beliefs.

Leo Saint-Clair listened, nodding, noting a slight hesitancy when the young American mentioned Howard Carter. A look from Alfred confirmed the Frenchman's thoughts of Bruce's parents' relationship with the Carter dig and their...

"In fact," Bruce said, "my next planned stop is Amarna. I still don't see how Professor McElroy figures in your scheme of thing… with Dr. Strange."

Leo smiled at the American's naiveté, his inability to connect the dots. He had found that most, if not all, opinionated intellectuals are blinded by their own brilliance, failing to see any other interpretation or even consider other facts, even to the point of falsification and open hostility to any opposition. And the Frenchman's file on McElroy had been getting thicker by the day, especially his rants since the opening of the Boy King's tomb, and his questionable activities. This young man Wayne didn't realize how much in the dark he was… as blind as a bat…

"You will not find Professor McElroy at Amarna, nor anywhere near," Leo said matter-of-factly.

"What?" Bruce said incredulously. "But I received a cable from him… just before we set sail from America."

"Perhaps…"

"A forgery?" Alfred offered.

"Or a ruse," the Frenchman replied.

"But why?" Bruce was confused.

"To deceive you. To make you believe he was going to the dig, so you wouldn't become suspicious of his actions. He didn't figure on your trip to Egypt."

"Why? What's he hiding?"

"For one thing, we believe he's trafficking in illegal antiquities. Most notably, a suspicious group of pillow-shaped clay tablets from the razed administration office of King Akhenaten at Amarna have appeared on the market. Also, a brown quartzite bust of Nefertiti… not as fine as the limestone bust in the Berlin Museum, but valuable, nevertheless. Your McElroy has been raising a great deal of money."

"For what? He never struck me as a greedy man. Oh, of course, in a scholarly way… always promoting himself. For the fame. But never for financial gain."

"It's always about money," Leo said to Bruce, a young man who never had to worry about where his next meal—or million—would come from; in fact, the whole Tut-mania and talk of a curse was nothing more than greed. "In answer to your question, I believe that McElroy has been trafficking in antiquities to finance the construction of a polyphase weapon based on Dr. Strange's designs. That, in some manner, he has obtained copies of Strange's supposedly destroyed blue-prints."

Bruce's head was swimming. "You believe McElroy has perfected Strange's device, and that he's using it here, in Egypt?"

"Threre has been *fahddling*—rumors—of 'fire-sticks' in the outlining villages, of the Fire of the Prophet."

"Yes," Bruce said with a glance at Alfred, who just lightly traced the edge of his mustache. "On the way out here, I saw a mention of this in the newspaper. An Anubis Gang, if I'm not mistaken... Strange's polyphase device?"

"It would appear." Leo paused for a sip of tea. "And we have a lead."

"I want in," Bruce said without thought.

Getting a glance from Leo, Alfred said: "Just as I told you: If you tell Master Bruce the whole story, he will want to take part."

"So you did."

They made plans.

Sipping tea, Bruce watched the Great War veterans discuss old times, old adventures. Yet, he couldn't help thinking that, at the turn of the last century, the British (especially under Admiral Horatio Nelson at the misnomer "Battle of the Nile") had defeated Napoleon's forces. Not too far from where Bruce sat, a treaty was signed, in which the 167 French *Savants* were forced to cede to the British their collection of antiquities, including the Rosetta Stone; though the British had showed some magnanimity: they had allowed the French to keep their animal collection and plant pressings.

The world has come a long way, but in other ways, it was drifting apart...

Ra's Solar Barge had settled in the West long ago as the trio made their way pass the Giant Sphinx, beyond the Great Pyramid of Khufu, and in amongst the tombs of pre-Empire Egypt. Leo Saint-Clair and Bruce Wayne were dressed entirely in black, and as point-guard was Indiana Jones, dressed in tan slacks, bomber jack and brown fedora. Coiled on his belt was a bull-whip; holstered on his hip a Welby Mark VI .455 pistol.

"You appear prepared, Indy," Bruce whispered, nodding at Indy's bull-whip and pistol.

"I was a boy scout."

"I never had the time."

Indy nodded. "Plus, the tomb might have snakes. I hate snakes."

"I feel the same about bats."

"Great, kid. Snakes and bats just love dark, warm places. Like tombs." He shrugged. "We're OK on scorpions, right?"

Though Bruce hated being called "kid," he had to grin at Indy's obviously sardonic remark and turned his attention to Saint-Clair, who led in only the ambient light of a waxing moon, without the benefit of a map or of an electric torch (almost as if he could see in the dark), appearing to know where he was going, even if he and Indy were constantly tripping over every tiny rock or stone in their path.

Perhaps what Alfred had told Bruce was true. He was The Nyctalope, the champion of the French Republic and its waning Colonial powers. The reality of the man was fantastic enough, but then, there were the rumors that he could see in the dark, that he had an artifical heart, was perhaps immortal... Yet, the man leading them looked no more than 30, at the most, and, save for his uncanny eyes and obvious strength, there was nothing to suggest he was any sort of *ubermensch*. No doubt, like Lawrence of Arabia, there was some exaggeration at play. The public did love to embody its mystery men with almost superhuman abilities, and no doubt Saint-Clair used that to his advantage. Then, again, Alfred himself had been known to exaggerate, especially over late-night milk and cookies in the kitchen when his master was younger.

"We're here," Saint-Clair said *sotto*, coming to a stop. His intrepid companions managed not to bump into him.

"You sure?" Indy asked, studying the structure as best as he could in the dim light. It was an offering niche with a statue of the deceased. "Doesn't look like much. In fact, it looks just like all the others we've passed."

Without comment, the Frenchman pushed against a stone slab and it swung inward on silent hinges, revealing nothing. Just blackness. Or so it seemed to the Americans. The Nyctalope's eyes adjusted to shifting shadows, the lights and darks and grays, searching the heat emulations for any hidden traps, literal pitfalls. His intelligence had been accurate: there were none.

Satisfied it was safe to proceed, Leo motioned for his companions to follow, switching on a mini-torch to lead the way.

"Let us proceed... vigilantly," he said.

The passageway was of claustrophobic granite. Yet, the two older men proceeded unfettered as if it was a walk in the park. *Perhaps it was, to them*, Bruce thought. Fortunately, his fear of enclosed space was cured some years back, after a fall into a cave on the manor's back lot. He noted that there were no bats here, or snakes... with probably put Indy at ease.

The Nyctalope's eyes detected heat registers and followed them south, which brought him to a chamber, the interior naked light flickering on the passageway's stone walls. He motioned for his companions to halt. A quick glance revealed a long, rectangular altar, piled high with a cornucopia of electrical and mechanical parts, dominating the chamber. Also he saw the backs of three burnoosed men hunched over what appeared to be a set of blue-prints. Turning to warn his companions, he realized it was too late, even before Indy whispered: "What do you see?"

The answer to his question was obvious when the three burnoosed men turned and ran at the intruders, screaming: "*W'Allah*! *Ferenghi*!" [By God! Foreigners!]

The *ferenghi* reacted.

Quickly, Leo stepped to the side and brought down his hand against a man's carotid, dropping him to his knees. Bruce was backed up against a wall, his fists balled at his sides, trying to remember everything boxing champ Ted Grant had taught him in the sparring ring. His fist shot out, landing a haymaker across his attacker's jaw. But the man did not go down. He just grinned at the young American, trying to shake the sting from his bruised knuckles. Gloves were preferable to bare knuckles, but he had to make due with what God had given him. Still shaking his fist as the man grinned and inched forward in a hunch, Bruce forcefully brought up his steel-toed booth and rammed it into his attacker's jaw, sending him into a back flip.

Indy was making headway with his attacker until Bruce's henchman slammed into the back of the archeologist's opponent, propelling both men into Jones, sending them all to the hard stone floor, in a snarl of arms and legs. In the entanglement, a hoodlum got the upper-hand on Indy, grabbing his Mark VI and waving it from one intruder to the next. When he turned to make his escape, a *crack!* echoed through the chamber and the tip of Indy's bull-whip lashed around the man's ankles, crashing him to the floor, dragging the struggling man toward him.

"Here, kid, hold this," Indy said, retrieving his pistol and handing it to Bruce, who wasn't sure what to do with it. Indy hauled the man to his feet and stared into his eyes. "I don't like your looks." Then landed a haymaker across the captive's jaw. As he fell unconscious to the stone floor, Indy shook his pained fist. "Ouch! That hurts."

""I could've told you that," Bruce said, grinning.

"Thanks, kid," Indy replied without conviction.

The three burnoosed goons were bounded and gagged; later to be picked up by the proper authorities.

"Hey, kid," Indy said, removing the tarp off an object on the altar, "remember what we said about snakes and bats?" Bruce nodded as Indy continued: "Well, here's the scorpion. I wonder if it has a sting."

"I would say, yes," Saint-Clair said, studying the three-foot long pewter sculpture of a scorpion, with eight-segmented and flexible legs ending in semi-circular claws, which when brought together formed four in-lined lens-holders of diminishing sizes. "No doubt a prototype for a polyphase device. Too bulky for practical use."

"Why the scorpion motif?" Bruce asked, "It seems rather bulky... impractical."

"Who can truly understand the working of the criminal mind?" Saint-Clair said, adding: "Criminals are a superstitious and cowardly lot."

"Perhaps to strike fear into the hearts of men?" Bruce offered.

"I think I'll stick to this," Indy opined, patting his Welby.

"Obviously," the Frenchman continued, pointing, "when the claws are brought together and the lens in place, an energy harvester is created."

"Like the Ark of the Covenant is alleged to have been?" Indy asked as he dusted away the dirt and soot from the wall hieroglyphs, studying them.

"Yes, but impractical," the Nyctalope stated as he unrolled a set of blue-prints. "Now, this is more practical. It explains the 'fire-stick' rumors."

Gracing over his shoulder at the blue-prints, Indiana Jones decided they had no archeological value and went back to the wall. But Bruce was interested in the schematics. He had studied many just like these as he had busied himself over the last few years with the workings of the varied Wayne enterprises, including trying to grasp the scientific implications of a myriad of details. He listened as Saint-Clair indicated the drawing of a long tube, with two trailing wires, labeled "R" (red) and "W" (white) to a bulky metal "nap-sack." A cutaway of the "nap-sack" revealed a series of vacuum tubes, wires and piezoelectric quartz arranged in a zigzag configuration. Flipping through a few more blueprints, the Frenchman said: "Yes, this design is a polyphase arrangement of non-centrally symmetric crystals."

"And this," Bruce said, jabbing a finger on the diagram, "is based on the work of Dr. Hugo Strange? It doesn't look the same."

"No. It's been adapted, adjusted from linear oscillation. It's an energy harvester similar to the one employed by the Martians, except that those manipulated heat, while this instrument converts mechanical stress into a potential current of electroplasmicized concentrated energy."

"A ray-gun?" Bruce asked, which got Indy's attention.

"A crude analogy, yet correct."

Saint-Clair returned to studying the blue-prints, while Bruce turned to a tap on his shoulder. Indy asked: "Did he say Martians?"

Bruce smiled. "I think he was referring to *The War of the Worlds*. That these 'fire-sticks' or 'ray-guns' are different than the ones in Wells' novel."

"Good. Because I don't want to wake up 30 years from now and find out the Earth has become the playground for space aliens."

"Perhaps they will be benign."

"More likely some super-race with powers and abilities beyond those of mortal men."

"No such thing," Bruce stated plainly, turning back to the altar as the Frenchman ran his finger under the lip of the slab top, an amused look on his face in relation to the Americans' talk of Martians.

Indy returned to studying the tomb's walls, running his fingers along a groove, noting dust and plaster falling away. Removing a knife from his pocket, he opened it, inserted the blade into the cracks and wiggled it back and forth, mostly chipping away ancient dust and plaster. After a bit of work, he was able to dislodge the a two-foot long dried mud-brick, hoping some treasure was hidden behind it—perhaps the Lost Treasure of Khufu.

"Ooophs," Indy said as the brick fell, shattering on the stone floor, alerting Bruce and Saint-Clair, who watched as their colleague bent down, and noted a collection of brownish bones. "What the …?"

"Frogs," Saint-Clair said, "probably *Bufo regularis*, the common African frog. Thousands of their remains have been found in the ruins of the tombs in this necropolis."

"But blood makes poor mortar," Indy said, shifting through the remains with his forefinger.

"True," Saint-Clair agreed, "but when you had a tight time-table, you just dug in the Nile mud and mixed your mortar with whatever was available."

"So, there *are* skeltons in the old man's closet?"

Saint-Clair remained silent as he turned back to the slab, clicking a button on the underside of the slab. It slid open, revealing a hidden compartment in the base of the altar. On a bed of excelsior were three working models of the polyphase tube devices amongst a dozen six-inch long duo-tapered crystals.

"The polyphase devices," Saint-Clair stated.

"Polyphasers?" Bruce pondered.

"Or, simply, phasers," Indy two-cented.

Bruce was antsy—all but twirling his thumbs—sitting in the relatively posh suite at the Sheperard's Hotel, waiting for information—any information!—dealing with their mid-night jaunt two days ago. Saint-Clair had told him to hold tight, while Indy had added: "Just wait, kid. Don't get cocky." But that was easier said than done. The residue of the adrenaline rush was only now subsiding. It was a feeling like none other. He doubted if he would want to make a career of adrenaline-rushes. Yet, when a resolution was too slow, action was called for…

No, that wasn't for him…

….too much night work.

Yet… the waiting….

He picked up his letter of introduction to the Egyptian Minister of Antiquities, written by a colleague of his late father, a Doctor Francis Ardan. But it all became a blur; he couldn't concentrate on the actual reason he was in Egypt: to visit various digs sponsored by the Wayne Foundation's Oriental Studies Museum and to scope out a few sites—the Gizah Pyramids, Deir de Medina, Luxor, Karnak, the Valley of the Kings, and points in between—the itinerary for the Grand Prize Winner of the Foundation's "See the Pyramids Along the Nile" contest celebrating the opening of a new wing to the OSM.

Just being in Egypt had taken a great deal of courage on Bruce's part. Seven years ago, he had been there with his parents, right after Howard Carter had revealed the "wonderful things" contained within the tomb of Tutankhamun. As wealthy Patrons of the Arts, his parents had toured the cramped chambers of the Boy King. Bruce was denied entrance. Carter explained that he was too young—just passed his 13th birthday—even though many of the *fellahin*, the workers, were barely out of their nappies themselves. What happened a few months later still sent a chill up his spine…

Yet he wouldn't—couldn't—just sit around and wait for something to happen; he had to get out in the world and hopefully make it happen. Was that being cocky?

"I'm going out, Alfred." Bruce decided. "Sit by the telephone… in case we get a call."

"Very well, Sir," Alfred replied, helping the young man into the jacket of his European white silk business suit, dusting off his broad shoulders with a whiskbroom. "Mustn't have you appear untidy in public."

"Yes, Alfred. Though I doubt my shoulders will be clean once I step outside the hotel," he said, pulling on his cuffs,

"Alas..."

Bruce eschewed the easy walk to the Red Light District, proceeding to the Khan el Khakili, dodging the hectic traffic of motorcars, camels and mules, carts, and carriages of various shapes and sizes. The smog and stink of dung blended soothingly with the pleasant aroma of freshly-baked bread, which greeted him from all directions as he strolled through the *souk*, causally stopping here-and-there to take in the multitudes of shops selling fabrics and rugs, *autika*, drinks and fruits, geese and ducks. Historic mosques, facades and fountains surrounded the young American, the enormousness of it all made it difficult to concentrate.

A few steps further down the mall, Bruce picked up a cat figurine of the goddess Bastet when he felt a tug on his sleeve. Turning he saw a raggedly boy's face as dirty as his linens, who he figures was just asking—begging?—for *baksheesh*.

"Many pardons, *sahib*, you are Master Wayne?" the boy said politely. Bruce nodded and the boy handed him a note. Unfolding the note Bruce read:

Mr. Wayne,

You were not at the hotel so I sent this runner to find you and deliver this message. We have found a clue to the problem facing us. Meet us in the Abbasia Quarter. The boy will lead you.

Dr. Jones.

"Lead away," Bruce said with a sweep of his hand. Tucking the note in his pocket, he followed the boy weaving in and out, ducking under, almost losing him here and there, but managed to keep up, even though something was nagging in the back of his brain. What was in the Abbasia Quarter indeed? Only military barracks and an insane asylum, if he remembered his *Baedeker* guide correctly. Like Arkham back home?

While in his thoughts, Bruce lost the boy and stopped, looked around. Then the boy popped up and waved. "Over here, *sahib*. This way."

Rounding the corner he found himself in a long, narrow alley way—or was it a street? Alone. The boy was nowhere in sight. The hairs on the back of his neck began to tingle. That was what had been bugging him: he had been set up, sent on a wild goose chase, but by whom? And why?

Turning back Bruce froze.

Blocking the entry to the street were two large men, muscles upon muscles, dressed in priest kilts, sandals and colorful papier-mâché masks: hawk-headed Horus and ibis-headed Thoth. Each hefted an apparently hollow six-foot long tube, attached to wires leading to a metal case on the backs. But—of more direct importance to Bruce—the tubes were aimed at him.

It had been a trap. The note from Indy, a fake. If truly from Indiana Jones, it would've be addressed to "kid," nor "Mr. Wayne," and signed "Indy," not Dr. Jones. First, the false telegram from Professor McElroy before leaving Gotham, and now...

Too late...

Turning round, Bruce dashed down the alley, weaving to and fro, stopping and starting as best he could through the narrowness, as beams of concentrated light flashed, tearing chunk of debris from the mud-brick walls, vaporizing the chips into exploding dust, to rain down upon the fleeing American.

Zig... Zag...

His legs pumped. His muscles burned up lactic acid, fatiguing them. Breathing came fast, in huffs and puffs. Primitive instincts had reacted to the influx of adrenaline, and he unconsciously took the "L" passageway.

A mistake. It was a dead end...

All that flashed through his mind as he turned, his back to the wall, was Indy's reprimand: *Don't get cocky, kid!* And this was way pass being cocky...

His feet spread. His fist balled. He waited tensely as the two "demi-gods" leisurely walked towards him. They had been playing with him like a cat with a mouse, knowing his prey was trapped, just waiting to be tortured to death. And they just stood there, holding out their power-sticks. What had Indy called them? Polyphasers? No: *phasers*. That tidbit helped him not at all as the ends of the tubes neared him. Should he charge them? Try his best to make Ted Grant proud? Then, suddenly, Horus and Thoth stopped and parted like the Red Sea, allowing a jackal-headed Anibus to step between them, his phaser tube held aloft like Moses' staff. He stepped forward.

Bruce held his ground.

"Well, if it isn't Young Master Bruce," Anubis said, his sarcasm evident as it echoed in the hollow of the mask.

"What's your game, Professor McElroy?" Bruce bravely and boldly said.

"No games."

"But dressing up like a tin-plated god? Why? You had prestige. You were in charge of the Amarna dig. You were..."

"...Nothing!" Anibus/McElroy exclaimed, stamping a gold-gilded sandal on the stone path. "People laughed behind my back! Hell, they laughed to my face!" Bruce knew this was accurate, to a degree, and he understood some of the Professor's anguish, but not his fanaticism: his anti-Akhenaten rants, allowing not a quarter for opposing views. His "my way or the highway" obsession had cracked him. Bruce could see that now. "But..."

"No buts, Mr. Wayne. I will determine what is to be done. And that is the complete annihilation of Akhetaten... of Tel el Amarna."

"It's already in ruins." Bruce tried to reason with this... madman.

"Not completely…yet," McElroy's voiced boomed from beneath the mask.

"What do you mean? Can't we reason…?"

"Shut up!" Bruce could hear Elroy breathing beneath the mask as he continued: "You and your meddling friends have already costed me dearly, robbing me of my only supply of back-up crystals. But not to worry… much. Ha!" He waved his phaser tube. "I can always get more dough… more crystals…"

So, we did get his back-up supply of crystals, Bruce thought. Not that that did him any good in his present predicament. Aloud, he tried calmly to ask: "And what do you want with me?"

"Well, I expect you to die, Mr. Wayne."

With that, Anubis drew a pistol from beneath his kilt and fired. A noisome gas sprayed out, engulfing the young American, dropping him coughing to his knees. Before losing full consciousness, he heard Elroy laugh: "But not just yet."

Bats. It had to be bats! These were Bruce's first conscious thought when awakening from the knock-out gas from Professor McElroy's pistol.

Bats.

They seemed to have been his constant companions since childhood. And here the flying mammals—these "overgrown mice"—hung overhead as Bruce's meandering thoughts were suddenly interrupted by the full realization of his predicament, like being rapped on the knuckles by the teacher's ruler when she caught you daydreaming. Not that it had ever happened to him. Not the Kid Genius. The Boy Wonder. Bruce Wayne.

Yeah, sure…

His wrists were bound together, the joining leather strap hung over a hook driven into the stone wall above his head, the toes of his boots barely scraping the limestone floor of the cold, damp, swarthy chamber, illuminated by only a burning torch in a sconce. The only sound was that of a ticking clock.

A ticking clock?

The flickering flame's light revealed the clock: the hour hand was near 12 as the second hand sweep past it and the minute hand jumped a notch towards denotation time. High noon? High midnight? The clock mechanism was attached to a blasting cap wired to a small stick of dynamite atop a large wooden barrow, with fading red letter: NH_4NO_3. Fertilizer, ammonium nitrate. With the added phosphorus and nitrogen in the bat guano when ignited the tomb would go up like Krakatoa…

Tick…Tock…Tick…Tock…

"Monsieur Saint-Clair… Leo," Alfred said anguishly into the telephone, "I am worried about Master Bruce…"

"Did you manage to plant…," Saint-Clair said, his last words indecipherable due to the poor connection.

"Yes," Alfred replied, guessing the answer to the Nyctalope's unheard question.

"Fine. Then, don't worry, Pennyworth. We'll find him."

"I'm coming with you."

"Of course."

The minute hand clicked nearer 12 as the second hand continued to sweep.

Breathing in deeply and slowly, Bruce pressed his shoulders against the damp stone wall, bracing himself, willing his legs up to a "L" with the wall. His hands gripped around the hook nailed into the wall, his biceps bulging. Steadily, he commanded his stressed, spasmodic, oxygen-starved muscles to perform beyond impossibility as his legs inched higher, until the toes of his boots where over his head.

He allowed himself a brief second rest…

Tick…

…then, with all his fortitude, the toes of his boots pushed up and off the wall. The leather strap binding him wiggled, pushed up…

Tock…

…and off the hook. He came crashing down.

Tick… Tock… Tick…

Though dazed, Bruce managed to stumble to his feet and rush towards the barrel of nitrate, grabbing for the clock, and tripped…

An elderly—but spry—couple, dressed for the desert heat, walked around a couple huge boulders, a destination in mind.

"It has been a while since we visited *his* tomb," she said.

"Yes," he said, his voice booming. "It's about time we paid our respects, though one wonders where the old boy *himself* may be."

"An enigma in his own time, and still remains one."

"You and your romantic novels."

Stumbling over a discarded piece of masonry Bruce managed to catch himself before falling. He closed his eyes and inhaled and exhaled a couple time, calming himself, and finally…

Tick… Toc—

…grabbed the clock and ripped it from the blasting cap in mid-tock. The explosion had been averted. Sinking to the cool stone floor, Bruce stared at the clock in his shaking hand. He had 15 seconds to spare. Hardly exciting…

Then the flickering torch went out.

"We're here," the lady archeologist said to her husband, from under her parasol.

"Let's see if anyone's home," the man said with his trademarked riotous laugh, flicking on his electric torch.

Then—as if in direct action to the light—a thundering bawl of high-pitch screeches pieced the air.

A dozen... a score... a hundred bats shot out of a hole in the hill. Flying, flapping at the archeologists, forcing them to duck, to hold their hats down, to protect their hair. When they looked up they saw a... mirage? A scene from Dante's *Inferno*? No... it was real.

The last of the bats had flown the coop and a man stepped out, his clothes in tatters, his hand groping, finding the side of the tomb's entrance for support. He looked up, smiled.

"Hello, Professor and Mrs. Emerson," he said.

"Ramses... Walter...?" Amelia Peabody Emerson gasped, thinking Bruce was her son.

"Good Gad, Peabody," Radcliffe Emerson exclaimed, calling his wife by her maiden name as he was wont to do.

"This is Akhenaten's tomb?" Bruce asked, rubbing his bruised wrists, brushing bat-ticks off his shoulders. Bruce had read Emerson's definitive work on the subject: *Excavation at the City of Akhetaten.*

"Yes, my boy," replied Emerson, slapping the young man on the back, almost wounding Bruce further. "Yes, indeed."

As the Emersons and Bruce trudged through the arid, barren and crack-potted wasteland towards the ruins of Akhetaten—el Amarna—the American filled them in on the activities of Professor McElroy--"crackpot" was the kindest thing Emerson had to say about his fellow colleague—the Anubis Gang, the bomb and his escape from the former tomb of King Akhenaten.

When the light had flickered out, he had followed the fleeing bats through the tomb complex as they were activated by the blowing of his Galton or Dog Whistle. The supersonic sound had driven them... "batty," as Peabody joked.

Coming out of the desert, they walked along the ledge running in front of the series of tombs hewed into the cliff wall for the wealthy and courtier of the ancient capital of the 18th Dynasty's so-called "heretic."

Passing one tomb, Bruce saw a man and he froze. Then he chided himself. It was only his own reflection in two highly-polished dressing mirrors, each six-foot tall and three wide, set on bass rollers. Emerson explained he used the mirrors as light sources while working in the tombs, to eliminate the damage caused by the pollutants released by magnesium flares and common fire torches, which further contributed to the deterioration of already fragile artworks. Bruce learned, also, that even human breathing could harm the delicate balance of ancient pigments. Though, these days, archeologists used flashlights and portable battery-powered lanterns, the Emersons still had a fond preference for the old methods, the ones used when they had first met and fell in love.

At the bottom of the ramp leading down from the cliff tombs, they settled under the shade of a canvas umbrella, where Amelia tended to Bruce scraps and scratches, after a drop or two of "medicinal" brandy from the flash attached to her "belt of tools." Bruce admired her belt, how utilitarian it was with its many items: sewing kit, pen and paper, first-aid kit, and other practice items needed on a dig.

As Amelia mumbled something about "another ruined shirt" and made use of cotton swabs, iodine and more traditional alcohol to treat Bruce's wounds, he explained about his adventures during the last three days. The Emersons were especially rattled to learn of McElroy's poaching from the Amarna dig; they believed the past belongs to the present... to Egypt.

Neither of the Emersons mentioned the death of Bruce's parents—seven years back—but since then the Emersons and the Wayne Foundation had been in constant communications, both on a personal and an academic basis, there was no need to go over old ground. Emerson has always "hmph'ed" at the notion of the "Curse of King Tut," claiming that it had nothing to do with his parent's death by a street thug, within months of the Waynes tour of Tut's tomb; that Carter, himself, the Emersons and scores of others were still among the living. That there was no inscribed curse on the entrance to Tut's tomb, but a piece of fiction created by a popular romance novelist: "The kind Peabody reads," he added slyly. Amelia "shushed" her husband, ever if it was true. Bruce, himself, didn't believe in the Curse of King Tut either. Yet...

The mending done, Bruce and the Emersons settled in under the umbrella for tea and scones, perhaps a couple whiskey sours...

Sizzzzzzzzzzzzzzzzzzzzzzzzzzzzzzzzzzzzzzzz

The ground at their feet erupted, turning to dusty powder as a ruby-red beam ripped a long, razor-thin trench across the desert floor.

"Hell and Damnation!" Emerson exclaimed, jumping to his feet, knocking over the table in the process.

But ever the "Greatest Egyptologist Who Ever Lived"—in Peabody unbiased opinion—Emerson had to pause, to stop haltingly in his tracks, his face red with anger, his ham-sized fists balled antsily at his waist as he stared at the scene before him.

Anubis stood there like a monolith; his right hand out-stretched, gripping the seemingly hollow-tube—the phaser—the business end pointed at Bruce and the Emersons. On either size of him, properly attired in costumes and masked, were Thoth, Horus, Seth and Sobek, each wielding a phaser and power pack.

"I am the Judge," Anubis declared, "and you have all been found guilty of heresy."

"Good Gad," Emerson exclaimed. "Is that you, McElroy? Why the costume? This isn't All Hallow Eve!"

"It *is* the end of October," Peabody offered.

"Hmph," was her husband's reply as he ventured a foot forward. A sizzling swatch across the ground had him rethinking his action.

"Have you nothing better to do than act the fool, Professor?" Bruce chimed in, standing his own ground.

"I thought I might find you here," Anubis/McElroy spat out, "since the destruction of the Heretic's tomb failed realization. I should've killed you before."

Then, a rumbling noise saturated the air. Everyone turned and saw what appeared to be a *simoon*, a desert sand twister, coming straight at them. Closer and faster it came... the dust dissipating... frittering away to reveal:

"That's my Daimler," Emerson huffed out. "And a maniac is driving it!"

The "maniac" was Alfred Pennyworth, decked out in his "touring gear," trying his best to keep the wheels on the ground as Indiana Jones stood haphazardly on the back seat, trying to level his Welby at one—at any!—of the demigods. He quickly gave up, holstering the pistol, grabbing his bull-whip.

The recovered demi-gods swung into action, their phaser-tubes buzzing, zapping, streaming beams of lights flashing through the air like an angry Zeus, but without the accuracy of that god, coming close but missing the zig-zagging Daimler.

The Nyctalope, wearing shaded goggles, stood balanced in the passenger seat, waiting, squaring himself. Then he leapt across the span, ploughing into the bodies of Thoth and Horus, crashing them all to the hard dirt in a jumbo of electronics and humanity.

Indy's bull-whip lashed out, wrapping it around Seth's phaser-tube, yanking it out of the hood's hands, sparks flying, as Alfred swerved. Then, a lucky blast of energy hit, evaporating the left front tire, crashing the motorcar to a screeching, dusty halt, jettisoning a unbalanced Indy jetting into the arms of an unsuspecting Seth.

Anubis turned his attention back to his equally stunned captives just in time to see Emerson about to make a jump at him. "None of that, Emerson!"

Stepping back, Emerson snaked a comforting arm around his wife's shoulder, holding her close, though she was itching to bash the Lord of the Underworld wannabe over the head with her parasol, but it had fallen somewhere in the shuffle. Only at a five-foot stature and her Golden Years, Amelia Peabody was a formidable foe... given the right situation and her trusty parasol. Her husband was ever more formidable, given the edge. Yet, now, the phaser-tube was pointed menacingly at them there was little they could do... but bide their time.

In the confusion, Bruce Wayne had disappeared. Anubis almost laughed. He'd always figure Young Wayne a coward at heart. All talk, all hot air. Alas, with all his money Wayne could be anything, anyone he wanted to be.

"Hey, Jackal-Head," a voice bellowed, almost echoing.

Anubis head jerked up, to the source of the voice. High on the ledge fronting the tombs, before one stood Bruce Wayne akimbo. Anubis hissed: "Wayne... you fool... you coward! You think you can escape my wrath... your destiny! By running away?"

"If you want me, you're going to have to come up here," the Gothamite yelled back tauntingly.

Laughter echoed from the hollow of Anubis' Jackal mask. "You fool! I don't have to come up there!" Almost nonchalantly he leveled his phaser-tube at Bruce. "I failed the first time to bury you alive. Another heretic... another Criminal of Akhetaten. This time I will not fail!"

And without further fanfare the megalomaniac fired his weapon at Bruce. A razor-thin ruby-red beam of highly-intense photo-electromagnetism zapped out...

...and almost instantaneously an identical ruby-red razor-thin beam issued from the tomb, sizzling into Anubis' phaser tube, frying, exploding in his hand. In a cry of agony the former demi-god stared at his fried hand, unbelieving, disbelieving.

"How...?" he mumbled.

Emerson answered with a right cross across McElroy's chin, sending his former colleague to his knees; which was fortunate for McElroy because Peabody had found her parasol and had it raised about her head, ready for action.

From the tomb's ledge, Bruce briefly scanned the scene before scrambling down and across the ancient ruins.

Saint-Clair and Indy had been backed into each other as Seth and Horus approached them from either side, their phaser-tube inching toward them. There was no room to use the bull-whip. With their backs together, the Frenchman and the American acted as if they had practiced gymnastic routines together for years as the Nyctalope hooked his elbows into those of Indy and bent forcefully forward, propelling the archeologist up and over the menacing Seth, landing flat on his feet, his whip lashing out, wrapping around the neck of the demi-god, yanking him off his feet. While Saint-Clair, from his bent position, swept a leg around, toppling Horus.

Alfred had scooped up a fallen phaser-tube, twirling it, then stepping forward toward Sobek with an: *en garde!* He stepped forward, lunged, his tube "sword" crashing against his foe's equally unpowered tube with the sounding ring of metal against metal, the *ting* echoing through the air. Parley after parley, the butler countered his opponent and then went on the offensive, wracking Sobek across the knees, crumbling him to the ground. Alfred stepped back. Waited. As Sobek began to rise, Alfred lunged in for the "kill," dropping to one knee, planting the end of the tube into the man's stomach and the other in the ground, pulling backward, lifting up Anubis' hench-god, yanking, tossing him over his shoulder, to crash into the back of Thoth, sending them both into a thud on the ground.

Bruce had rejoined the Emersons and was looking down at the defeated, pitiful McElroy, moaning in agonizing pain. A glance at the Emersons told him they were OK, though Bruce wondered why, after the haymaker punch he had delivered to McElroy's chin, Radcliffe Emerson wasn't tending to bruised knuckles.

"How...?" McElroy mumbled though he pain.

"Something I learned from Houdini," Bruce grinned. "It was done with mirrors."

"The mirrors in the tomb!" Emerson exclaimed, slamming his knee. "Good Gad, Lad! Good work! My boy, Ramses, couldn't have done better."

Bruce acknowledged the praise, then explained. Once McElroy had turned his back on him, he had dashed up to the tomb and swiftly arranged the two tall mirrors at the correct angle, just as if performing a physics experiment at the university. Standing back a half-meter from the left-hand mirror Bruce was reflected into the right-hand mirror, egging on McElroy, giving the illusion that that was where he was standing. When the beam had been fired at that spot, at the "illusory" Bruce, it had hit the first mirror, reflected to the other, then turned back to its original source: McElroy's phaser tube.

Emerson yanked his horrified "colleague" to his feet, shaking him, not caring a wit about the man's injuries, considering the harm he might have caused Amelia. At a lost for words—definitely not a common occurrence for the "Father of Curses"—Emerson shoved McElroy into the waiting hands of Leo Saint-Clair and Indiana Jones, as Alfred finished tying-up the fallen once-but-not future demi-gods.

McElroy hissed: "You haven't heard the last of Professor William Omaha McElroy! No! No! You will—you all will! Bow down to my royal feet! No, you have not heard the last of... King Tut!"

"Hmph," Emerson huffed out.

"I couldn't have said it better," Bruce Wayne said.

"Indeed, my boy," Emerson said, slapping the American on the back and came away with a small metallic rectangle. "What's this?"

"Not a bat-mite, I hope."

"Your post, Sir," Alfred said, setting a silver tray on the desk where Bruce Wayne was trying to put together the finishing touches on the mundane details of his business, here, in Egypt; his *Baedeker* guide book-marked at various entries and fold-out maps. He noticed thar, with the mail, was a glass of a clear liquid, ice-floating in the effervescence; he wasn't about to ask Alfred where he obtained the ice cubes.

"What is it?" Bruce asked, picking up the glass.

"A new product, from the States, called Seven-Up."

Bruce tasted the lemony-lime soda, liked it. "This would go well with bourbon."

"I wouldn't know, Sir," Alfred said with the slightest hint of a smile at the corner of his mouth. "With the Prohibition and all."

Bruce grinned and tried to return to his chore, but the adventures of the last three days still jabbed at him. The rush of adrenaline, the "fright, flight or fight" complex, had evaporated. He wondered if he'd ever feel that rush in just that way ever again. Probably not. Just boardrooms and meetings: migraines and ulcers. Plus such adrenaline rushes required too much night work...

Still he considered the people he had met. The Nyctalope had provided Alfred with a tracking device—the "bat-mite" which he had planted on his Master when he had "brushed-off" his shoulders before Bruce went into the Cairo street.

Professor McElroy had been turned over to the Egyptians for questioning in relation to the stolen artifacts; then the "Tut-Nut" would probably be deported to America, for "rehabilitation" at Arkham Asylum.

Dr. Henry "Indiana" Jones, Jr. had decided to leave the Saqqara dig, having received information about the location of something known as the Cross of Coronado, an artifact he has been searching for since he was a youth.

The Emersons continued their vacation at Tel el Amarna, celebrating at the place they had first meet 40 years earlier. Though Radcliffe Emerson was a tad "peeved" at Alfred and Bruce in connection to his damaged Daimler, he promised that he and Peabody would be on hand to help promote the Wayne Foundation's "See the Pyramids Along the Nile" contest tour.

Bruce willed himself back to the task at hand, glancing through the various pieces of mail, all indicating the various subsidiaries of Wayne Enterprises were financially sound, and looking forward to a prosperous new decade.

There was a knock at the door. Alfred answered the call and then appeared before Bruce with another sliver tray, a single telegram rested upon it. "A telegram from home, Sir."

"Thank you, Alfred." Opening the telegram he noted it was dated the day before—October 29, 1929—from his CFO. It read:

Return home, immediately. Stop. The stock market has crashed. Stop.

Bruce reread the cable, shrugged and set it aside. Probably just a minor dip in the market, a glitch. The man was constantly over-reacting, creating worse-case scenarios, horror stories out of the most mundane of Wall Street indicators.

Out of the corner of his eye, beneath the window, he saw some movement. A little gray and black mouse. The mouse stopped, seemingly startled by Bruce, then ambled away. Bruce smiled. Perhaps the mice—the meek—would inherit the Earth. But, if so, they were going to need some help... A protector...

Suddenly, his mind flashed back to the tomb, to the bats. Were not bats and mice cousins?

Bats... An omen?

Naw.

Rick Lai delves here into the secret history of the criminal conspiracy known as the Black Coats, going well beyond their original appearance in Paul Féval's ground-breaking, seven-volume saga. The following story prominently features the enigmatic and seemingly ageless Colonel Bozzo-Corona, il padre d'ogni, *the All-Father of the Black Coats, surrounded by a coterie of high class villains torn from the pages of Doc Savage, The Shadow and Bulldog Drummond. Double- and triple-crosses abound in this nefarious tale, the title of which echoes the sinister brotherhood's legendary password...*

Rick Lai: *Will There Be Sunlight?*

Paris and Moscow, 1934-35

"*The legends surrounding the longevity of the All-Father are multiple and contradictory. One myth claims that he received an immortality elixir from Count Cagliostro. Another story portrays him as Mammon, the Demon of Gold, who visits the Earth at various intervals to assume human form. Like Mabuse, the All-Father has been rumored to possess the ability to project his soul into another body. A more mundane explanation exists for the sightings of the All-Father throughout history. The identity of the original Colonel Michele Bozzo-Corona, the first All-Father of the Black Coats, has been assumed by multiple impostors over the last century.*"

Reverend H. Briefenstein (D.D),
The Devil's Anatomy: Criminal Instinct of Men (1960).

The most dangerous secret society in Europe has long been the Black Coats. During the first half of the 19th century, that criminal brotherhood had mostly concerned itself with robberies and swindles. But by the 1930s, the world itself had changed. The rise of Communism and Fascism had altered the global landscape significantly. So the organization was forced to move with the times and became heavily entrenched in munitions, espionage and narcotics. The Black Coats ultimately emerged as a covert force affecting the destinies of nations.

In August 1934, 12 individuals were seated around a large table in the corporate headquarters of Nemirovitch Beauty Salons. Ostensibly, they were the board members of a company founded in 1922. In reality, they constituted the High Council of the Black Coats. At the head of the table was a thin, elderly man, the reigning All-Father of the Black Coats. Defying all belief, he claimed to be, and certainly bore a striking physical resemblance to, Colonel Bozzo-Corona, the man who had founded the society in 1807.

The Colonel was addressing a young, blond American:

"When Mussolini begins his inevitable aggression against Ethiopia, I want to be positioned to offer him a deal. We will prevent the British from interfering by generating unrest in their colonies. So you must create saboteur rings in India and Palestine, Robert."

"Thy will be done, All-Father," said Robert Thomas.

The next speaker was a foppish Peruvian. His handsome face was marked with freckles. His nickname was El Pecoso—the Freckled One. In 1919, El Pecoso had engineered the coup that brought the authoritarian Augustino Leguia to power. Leguia had repaid El Pecoso by exiling him from Peru. Joining the Black Coats, El Pecoso had mastered the munitions trade.

"On your orders, Colonel, I have been helping Germany break the armament restrictions imposed by the Treaty of Versailles. So doing, I've discovered a closely guarded secret of the Nazi Party. Its top men all have doubles impersonating them at public functions. Hess uses a distant cousin with the surname of Hest. Goering's double is an obese Russian. Goebbels has a Viennese doppelganger, who looks remarkably like him, despite lacking a clubfoot."

"What about Hitler's double?"

"He's still unknown to me."

"Concentrate on the three doubles that you've identified. Recruit one of them into our Brotherhood, if you can." The Colonel added with a deceptively senile smile: "He will be truly a double agent, my children."

"*Père*, I have come across a monetary miracle which defies all laws of commerce, said Baron Vardon, a French nobleman who managed the finances of the Black Coats. "Three years ago, Guatemala was on the verge of economic collapse. Now, its President, Jorge Ubico, has balanced the budget. It is today the most financially sound country in Central America. Ubico has also been far from frugal. He's spending money on huge construction projects. He must have a secret source of wealth."

"What is Ubico's strongest base of support in Guatemala, *mon fils*?"

"The Mayan Indians. But they're dirt poor."

The Colonel looked pensive for a few moments before responding:

"The Golden City of the Very Highest! The legend must be true! Central America has long harbored rumors about a Mayan citadel in a secluded valley, where they hid their wealth from the conquistadors. The rulers of that valley must be funneling gold to Ubico. We must locate this hoard and plunder it!"

"It will be delivered into your hands, *Père*," pledged the Baron.

The next man to address the Colonel was missing the third finger of his left hand.

"A seductress in the NKVD has defected to us, Monsieur. Her name is Natasha Malakoff. She paid an exceptional fee for sanctuary—she brought us the Black Pearl of the Borgias!"

"Don't jest with me, Gaspard, my son!" said the Colonel, shaking his finger as if he was berating a naughty child. "I know the history of that bauble all too well. It was stolen two years ago from the Colonna family. A notorious international jewel thief, the Strangler, committed the theft, not the Soviets."

"Indeed, *papa*. Natasha *is* the Strangler. She lived a dual existence as a Soviet operative and a self-employed burglar. A Marxist version of Raffles. When the NKVD learned of her robberies, she fled Russia."

Gaspard Zemba handed a box to the Colonel, who greedily opened it.

"The Borgia Pearl! I'm delighted, Gaspard!"

Having secured their master's favor, Zemba decided to settle a personal score.

"I regret to report, *papa*, that someone in our Council has been withholding valuable information. You heard earlier Irma Caber's report on her father's narcotics research, but she neglected to mention his latest discovery..."

"My father's invention was ludicrous," dryly commented a dark-haired woman of 33 years. She was slender, with black eyes and an aquiline nose. "Zemba is wasting our time by bringing up my father's foolish notions."

"But it isn't your role to make such decisions," interjected another woman. "It's the Master's prerogative."

Irma was handsome, but this other woman was stunningly beautiful. She was Dolores Valencia, a haughty Spaniard in her mid-20s. Possessing eyes and hair just as black as Irma's, the younger Dolores was also gifted with a remarkably exotic olive complexion. She and Irma were the only two female members of the High Council and there was a fierce rivalry between them. Irma was the *prima donna* being challenged by a youthful newcomer.

"You have no right to question my judgment, Dolores!" protested Irma.

"I have every right. My family is one of the most prominent in Spain. Your background is far less distinguished."

"How dare you! The Black Coats would have vanished decades ago if not for my great-grandfather!'

The Colonel stepped in.

"Irma, don't you forget that the late, lamented Professor Moriarty was but my subordinate," he said, scolding the woman. "He would have accomplished nothing without my direction. Our precious Dolores is correct."

The Colonel paused briefly to gently stroke the Spaniard's hair. All the members present knew that she was his mistress.

"Let me remind you of an incident of the past, my dove," continued the Colonel, still addressing Irma. "You once dismissed another of your father's inventions as foolhardy. He'd developed an addictive that tested positive on dogs, but proved ineffective on humans. You wanted to junk it, but I suggested we market it as dog food. It's now the extremely popular Peterson's Pup-Food, one of our most profitable sources of income."

Irma Caber bowed her head in submission. "Forgive my trespass, All-Father."

"You're forgiven, my sweet. Now, tell us about Dr. Caber's latest invention."

"It's an age-accelerator. It can increase a human being's biological age by 20 years. My father hoped to sell it to wanted criminals in their 20s. The police wouldn't be able to recognize them."

"What a ridiculous concept!" declared the Colonel. "Only a lunatic would want to add two decades to his life! Plastic surgery is far more practical to alter one's appearance. I fully understand your reluctance to bring it up."

Gaspard Zemba was annoyed. The Colonel was being unexpectedly merciful. He had his own, private reasons for wishing Irma Caber ill. He decided to launch a new line of attack against her.

"There is another matter, *papa*," he said. "Ever since Darvin Rochelle's death last year in Washington, there's been a vacancy on the Council. I think it's time to add a new member, and I'd like to nominate Jean Lumière. Irma knows him well. He was her most profitable narcotics salesman, until she recently reassigned him as her liaison to El Pecoso."

"And I'm glad that she did!" added the dapper Peruvian. "Lumière's an extraordinary man. He sold weapons to both the Regent of Hungary and the King of Rumania. Those will prove valuable clients as we fuel their rivalry."

"I noticed a slight drop in narcotics sales this year," observed the Colonel. "Your reassignment of Lumière may be the cause, Irma. Why did you do it?"

"It was for his own good, All-Father. He'd started to use drugs. It was affecting his performance."

"There's no need to be shy, Irma," snapped Dolores. "I've heard the rumors. You're not talking about his job performance—you're talking about his performance in bed!"

Irma Caber silently rose in anger.

"Sit down, Irma!" ordered the Colonel. "Dolores, my dove, I must ask you to apologize to Irma."

The proud Spaniard complied.

"I haven't yet met this illustrious fellow," continued the Colonel. "Irma, sweetheart, please bring Lumière to see me here tomorrow. If I approve of him, he'll take a seat on the Council."

"This is a mistake, All-Father," objected Irma. "Jean's too inexperienced for such a position."

"Your role is not to question but to obey!" commanded the Colonel. "I said: Tomorrow. Here."

After the meeting had concluded, the Colonel rode back to his private mansion. Accompanying him in the private limousine was Dolores.

"Are you still angry with me for insulting Irma, my darling?" she asked.

"No, I could never be angry at anyone for attacking that bitch. My asking you to apologize was only for show."

"You never told me why you hate her so much."

"Irma's the last of the Moriarty blood line. The Professor constantly defied my authority, and so have his relatives. His brother and nephew conspired against me, but they're both dead now. His daughter, Urania Caber, had two sons: James and Claud. James, Irma's father, is no threat to me. He's a scientific genius with his head in the clouds. Claud was a different bird, a brilliant actor like his father, John Clay."

"Didn't Claud feud with Zemba at one time?"

"Yes. Despite being a master of disguise, he had the nervous habit of tapping his finger. One day, Gaspard boasted of superior talents because his fingers never acted unconsciously. Claud challenged him to a duel with knives. I allowed the battle to take place hoping that Gaspard would rid me of Claud, but to my dismay, he triumphed. Rather than take Gaspard's life, Claud chopped off one of his fingers. It was Irma who suggested it."

"Claud was also Irma's lover, wasn't it?"

"Until his death in 1922," said the Colonel, dryly. "They were passionate partners."

"That's disgusting. He was her uncle."

"It's not incest according to the Napoleonic Code. Blood uncles and nieces can marry. I don't know the current marriage laws of your native country, but it was common practice for Spanish kings to wed their nieces centuries ago."

"Did they have any children?"

"Not as far as I know. But Claud was quite capable of fathering a child. Earlier on, he had allied himself with one of my greatest rivals, who at the time called himself Dr. Stewart, by wooing one of his three daughters. He and Karah Stewart were joined together according to the rites of her religion and, in 1908, she gave birth to Claud's son."

"What happened to the child?" asked Dolores

"His own mother strangled him in the crib."

"What?!"

"You see, my dove, Professor Moriarty always saw 'Dr. Stewart' and his cunning wife as a major threat. In 1887, Moriartu ordered Mrs. Stewart killed. Karah was still a child and never suspected the Professor. As always, the Black Coats made someone else *pay the law* by planting evidence implicating another of Stewart's foes... When she reached adulthood, I told Karah the truth. She went mad. She couldn't accept having given birth to a descendent of her mother's slayer, so she killed the child, left her husband and returned to live with her father. She died a few years later in Asia. The Moriarty family was always troublesome... But after Claud's death, I tolerated Irma back. Alone, she'll never defy me."

"And having her close also lets you torment her on a regular basis."

"You know me too well, my dove," said the Colonel with a dry chuckle.

Back at his Parisian apartment, Gaspard Zemba was greeted by a young, dark-haired beauty, dressed in a provocative black negligee. Wrapping her arms around the master thief, she kissed him fully on the lips.

"Did the Colonel appreciate my gift?"

"Yes, Natasha."

"Did you tell him about my collection of photos and other memorabilia?"

"Not yet. I'll reveal those assets at the proper time, *ma chérie*."

"When will I join the High Council?"

"That will take time. The Colonel's natural instinct is to allow only two women on the Council. When he permitted three in the 1890s, the male members felt threatened by a feminist revolt. One of our current ladies must therefore be eliminated."

"You mean Irma."

"Her downfall is preferable to the Spaniard's. If my new ploy works, you will succeed her."

"As a chess player, I enjoy intricate moves. How do you intend to checkmate her?"

"If the gossip I heard is true, Irma's trapped in an abusive relationship with Lumière. I've just recommended him for a Council seat. His manipulations are bound to drive Irma into a fatal collision with Dolores, one she will inevitably lose..."

The next afternoon, the Colonel interviewed Jean Lumière in a private office at Nemirovitch Beauty Salons. Lumière had the lean, gentle face of a poet. A great shock of black hair sprouted above his high forehead. His eyes burned with unusual intensity. His body was extremely long and thin. Some of his fingers were almost the length of a normal man's hand. He was dressed all in red, his shirt, tie, handkerchief, socks, shoes and suit being of the same crimson hue.

The Colonel judged Lumière to be in his mid-forties. He scrutinized the newcomer's face. There were no signs of makeup or facial surgery. He seemed to be just who he claimed to be. Still, something nagged at him...

"There's something familiar about you," he muttered. "You remind me somehow of Claud Caber..."

"We shared the same father—John Clay. In fact, I'm named after him—Jean."

"That's impossible. I would have known if Urania Caber had had a third child."

"But she wasn't my mother. My mother was a French woman named Césarine."

"Ah yes, I remember now. Years after the Professor's death, John Clay was arrested for a series of swindles. The investigation revealed that he had had a French paramour..."

"You understand why my birth was kept a secret. To what extremes the Professor Moriarty might have gone to avenge his family honor if he'd learned that my father had had a child with another woman?"

"I see. You're much taller than your father," observed the Colonel.

"My maternal grandfather is also tall, I understand."

"Irma seems reluctant to have you promoted."

"Our relationship has been stormy. She always wants to be the dominant partner in our relationship, and always flaunts her Council seat."

The Colonel reflected on what he had learned. Lumière's story explained Irma's behavior. She had already made love to one uncle, so why not another? But she wanted him to remain dependent on her. By making Lumière Irma's equal on the Council, the Colonel would be frustrating her. The idea appealed to him.

So at their next meeting, Jean Lumière was formally inducted into the High Council of the Black Coats.

That September, Dolores Valencia presented a daring plan before the Council.

"Spain has become politically polarized," she explained. "Within the next two years, the military will certainly rebel. The leftist coalition is planning to transfer a certain general whom it fears, Francisco Franco, far away from Madrid, to the Canary Islands. We need to have one of our own there to greet him. When the inevitable coup starts, Franco will have too few troops under his command. He'll be in a poor bargaining position with the other military leaders. We can enhance his prestige by offering unlimited access to guns and munitions. If we make him our puppet, we'll have a unique opportunity to control the Iberian Peninsula."

"Who among us would be best suited to carry out this mission, my dove?" queried the Colonel. He already knew the answer because Dolores had discussed her plan with him beforehand, but he had to pretend otherwise.

"Spanish officers are highly susceptible to feminine charms. A woman would make the best candidate."

"Then our representative should be Irma. After all, she is the Council's most experienced female member—and the epitome of feminine charm itself," volunteered Jean Lumière. Today, he was outfitted completely in blue.

"Jean, there's no need for this," asserted Irma.

"Lumière! How dare you?" said an infuriated Dolores ignoring her rival. "You seek to elevate your whore over me?"

"I ask that you apologize to Irma and me," Lumière coolly replied.

"You and that bitch are degenerate perverts! What you do may be legal in France, but it's still incest all the same."

"Your conduct mere proves my point," countered Lumière "You could have easily deflected my advocacy of Irma by citing your own qualifications as a native Spaniard with a prestigious family background. Instead, your immaturity prompted you to resort to bourgeois moralistic insults. By contrast, Irma has resisted the urge to retaliate. You're too young and inexperienced for this mission."

"I will not be shoved aside for this gutter trash! Valencia is one of the most respected names in Spain. The Canary Islands mission is rightfully mine."

Irma finally found her voice. She turned towards the Colonel.

"Master, I appeal to you. My honor has been besmirched. There is an ample precedent for a dispute of this nature. Gaspard Zemba once offended a former Council member. The matter was settled by a knife fight."

"You fool!' taunted Dolores. "You have no chance of defeating me! I'm younger! Faster! I'll carve my initials in your stomach!"

The Colonel finally intervened.

"I'll allow this duel under the following terms. No one in the Council must seek retaliation against the victor. Let us agree on the stakes. More than the Canary Islands assignment is at risk here. If Irma wins, she assumes all of Dolores' current duties. If Dolores wins, she takes over Irma's drug trafficking."

Both women agreed to the All-Father's stipulations. So did Lumière and the others. The Council reassembled into a large empty basement room of their headquarters

A large circle on the ground was drawn with chalk by the All-Father. The two women removed their high heels. Both combatants tore off their skirts. Strapped to each of their right legs was a sheath containing a knife. Drawing their weapons out, they walked to opposite sides of the circle. Dolores wielded a large Spanish dagger. Irma's blade resembled an ice pick. The aluminum handle was four spools fitted together.

Irma held her blade for all to see. "I call my knife Nina. It was my mother's name."

"Your weapon suits you," observed Dolores. "It's thin and scrawny. Just like you and your mother."

"Enough insults!" shouted the Colonel. "Begin!"

Dolores ran towards Irma and slashed with her knife. Irma ducked. She kicked Dolores in the ankle. The Spaniard fell backwards. As she was sprawled on the ground, Irma's left foot slammed downward on her right wrist. Dolores unclenched her knife. Irma quickly kicked the blade away. Bending downward, she then triumphantly planted her knee in the stomach of the defeated Dolores. Irma pressed her knife against the Spaniard's throat.

"What a pathetic duelist!" goaded Irma. "I could have beaten you blindfolded."

"Mercy!" pleaded Dolores. "I'll give you anything!"

"You have nothing to give. The only question is, what I should take. Your life is worthless. You value your family name more than anything else. Surrender it to me! I will need a false identity in the Canaries. Henceforth, you will no longer call yourself Valencia. Do you agree to my terms?"

"Yes," whimpered Dolores.

"Swear!" insisted Irma

"I swear by all that is holy!"

"Have you forgotten where you are? Swear by what is unholy! Swear by the one thing we all worship."

"I swear on the Scapulary of La Merci... I swear by the Treasure!"

Irma withdrew. Dolores rolled on her side and gasped for breath. The Colonel walked toward her. He looked down at his humiliated lover.

"You're a disgrace. You're no longer a Council member, but your servitude to our Brotherhood remains. You're now the property of Baron Vardon. Perhaps he'll find some role for your limited abilities.'

The Colonel turned away. He motioned Lumière to approach him.

"Jean, we need to confer in private."

In his office, the Colonel confronted Lumière.

"I must commend you, Jean. You've just shown extraordinary cunning. Your little ploy was worthy of our late, lamented Lecoq. You gauged Señorita Valencia quite accurately. You instigated that whole squabble to gain control of her territory."

"Irma owns that territory, not I."

"Don't treat me like a dunce. I see the way she looks at you. Irma was your slave—but not anymore."

"I don't understand, All-Father."

"Didn't you realize the terms of our agreement in the Council chamber? Irma must assume all of her adversary's duties. Dolores shared my bed. I expect Irma to do no less. Explain the situation to her and send her to my mansion tonight."

The Colonel was very happy that evening. This was his crowning victory over the Moriarty clan. He had humbled the Professor's great-granddaughter.

He imagined that Lumière would be rendered desolate by the loss of his lover, but he was wrong. Lumière had secretly found solace in the embrace of a gorgeous brunette named Antonia Lashley.

In October, the High Council held another meeting in Paris. The Colonel delayed Irma's departure for the Canary Islands in order to continue to enjoy their liaison. He listened intensely as Baron Vardon briefed everyone on his Mayan investigation:

"The leading crime syndicate in Mexico and Central America may prove invaluable in our quest for the Golden City. I have dispatched Dolores to negotiate an alliance with Quetzalcoatl, leader of the Sons of the Feathered Serpent."

Then, the Baron surrendered the floor to Lumière. That day, the charismatic criminal was attired in a purple ensemble.

"The late Claud Caber had strong connections inside the Soviet Union. I've located his files on several Bolshevik leaders. An interesting fact has emerged. Has anyone heard of Moisei Uritsky?"

"Wasn't he the head of the Petrograd secret police for Lenin in the early days of the Bolshevik regime?" asked the Colonel.

"Yes, I remember him now. He was assassinated in August 1918 by a student," added Zemba, snapping his fingers. "The Bolsheviks used the killing to justify a vicious crackdown on their opposition."

"That's the official version," said Lumière. "In reality, Uritsky was killed by the Red Knife, the personal assassin of a rival Bolshevik leader, who was then People's Commissar for Nationalities…"

"Josef Stalin!' exclaimed the Colonel. "I was at his wedding in 1906. He was raising money for the Bolsheviks through bank robberies. I offered him to join our Brotherhood, but he turned me down. Do you intend to blackmail him?"

"Extortion figures in my plan, but in a different way," said Lumière. "Let me invoke an historical analogy, *Père*. Why did Robespierre fall from power?"

"I knew the fellow rather well," said the Colonel, causing a slight shiver among his assistants. "He made the mistake of extending his Reign of Terror to his own party. Once he started persecuting other Jacobins, no one felt safe, and they turned on him like a rat pack. Of course, the new leaders were soon discredited because of their prior association with him, and also fell from power. They were merely warming the seat of power for Napoleon—as was ever our plan."

"Well, there's a man in the Soviet leadership named Serge Kirov who's recently been elected to the Central Committee," continued Lumière. "Stalin views him with distrust. I intend to go to Moscow and advise him to get rid of Kirov, just as he got rid of Uritsky. Others will naturally be blamed for the murder."

"*Pay the law* Russian style," quipped the Colonel. "I like it. But why should Stalin take your advice, *mon fils*?"

"Who do you think counseled him to have Uritsky killed?"

"Of course! Claud Caber."

"And I'm his half-brother. Stalin trusted Claud. He'll do the same with me."

"Do not overestimate your abilities, Jean!" said the Colonel.

"I, for one, have full confidence in Lumiere's diplomatic skills," said El Pecoso. "He charmed the leaders of Hungary and Rumania."

"Thank you, my friend," said Lumière. "Just as we have always framed others for our misdeeds, Stalin will find convenient scapegoats to *pay the law.* All his rivals in the Communist Party will be arrested."

"But Stalin won't be overthrown as easily as Robespierre," professed the Colonel. "Jacobin fanatics like Chauvelin pale before the NKVD. They'll successfully slaughter any opposition."

"There's one group inside Russia that even Stalin can't afford to attack, *Père*. The Red Army. As long as Russia threatened by both Germany and Japan, Stalin won't dare purge the military. We'll bypass the middle stage of my French analogy. No transitional rule by discredited bureaucrats. Stalin will be replaced directly by a Soviet Napoleon. Putting an end to the purges will make him extremely popular with the Russian people."

"I still fear that your Napoleonic analogy is fundamentally flawed, *mon fils*. Stalin is well aware of the danger. Trotsky was exiled because he saw him as a potential Napoleon."

"I'll deceive Stalin into fostering the Napoleonic usurper like a cuckoo. I'll recommend that he plants a spy in the military beholden only to him. This man will be someone whom Stalin could never imagine as the organizer of a coup. A foreigner…"

"…Named Jean Lumière, I see," said the Colonel, his eyes sparkling with an evil flame. "What a scheme! Why, this may well turn out to be my last affair, after all!"

"I'm actually considering using an English variation of my name. The future Napoleon of Russia needs a more colorful sobriquet."

"A minor detail. You remind me of Professor Moriarty, Jean. He too harbored Napoleonic delusions, but in the end, Sherlock Holmes checkmated him."

"I'll never have an adversary equal to Holmes."

"A dangerous assumption. You're making several such assumptions. Why would the Red Army follow you?"

"I'll blackmail its top officers."

"Now I understand. You've found Claud Caber's files and are intent on putting them to good use, but I warn you: They haven't been updated for 12 years. They're inadequate for an extortion campaign of such magnitude. Officers who weren't prominent in 1922 have since arisen."

"Caber's files were easily updated," intervened Gaspard Zemba. "Remember my NKVD defector, Natasha Malakoff? The secret police used her to romance high-ranking Red Army officers. She also had more than one noteworthy lover in the secret police. She's kept fascinating mementoes of her liaisons and passed on all her incriminating materials to Jean."

"Natasha's a phenomenal woman, All-Father," stated Lumière. "I nominate her for the Council seat vacated by Dolores."

This unexpected development disturbed the Colonel. He governed by a policy of divide and rule, encouraging rivalries among his minions in order to prevent them from uniting against him. Zemba and Lumière had obviously struck a bargain, as Natasha was Gaspard's lover. Obviously, Lumière had agreed to sponsor her for the Council in exchange for her information on the Soviet leadership.

Lumière was starting to garner too much support. The Colonel could not afford to enhance his prestige further.

"I'll consider the Malakoff candidacy later. Let's return to the matter at hand. Jean's scheme has too many contingencies, I fear. Only I decide how to commit our resources. The project is shelved."

"But, *papa*, if Jean succeeds, the Black Coats will control a military power that straddles Europe and Asia," said Zemba, urging the Colonel to reconsider Lumière's plan.

"A country vulnerable from attack on two fronts," countered the Colonel.

"Both Germany and Japan will sign Non-aggression Pacts with Russia under the right circumstances," predicted the Baron.

But the Colonel remained adamant and refused to reverse his decree. Irked at Gaspard for supporting Lumière, he also denied the petition for Natasha's Council membership.

That night, the Colonel suddenly awoke. He had heard a noise outside his private chamber. He turned to locate Irma, but she was absent from the bed.

The door burst opened. Jean Lumière and the other Council members entered. They all pointed pistols at him.

"Colonel Bozzo-Corona," proclaimed Lumière, "you should never have opposed my plan. The others have elected me the new All-Father."

The Colonel's hands and feet were tied. He laid bound in a room in total darkness. Suddenly, he heard the door open and close. Lumière entered, moving around the room with ease. .

"Yes, I can see in the dark. A trait inherited from my mother's father."

The Colonel heard a pistol's chambers open. Then, the noise of the same chambers closing filled the air. A twirling sound followed next.

"Irma poisoned the food of all your guards and disconnected the alarms," explained Lumière. "Since I'm going to Russia, Colonel, we're going to play a form of roulette associated with that nation. My gun contains only one bullet. For every wrong answer, I will press the trigger."

Lumière pressed the gun against the Colonel's right temple.

"Why did I overthrow you?"

"Because I vetoed your Russian project."

"Wrong." Lumière pulled the trigger. *Click!* The chamber was empty. "My real motive stems from your feud with the Moriarty family. Explicitly describe your relationship with the late Professor."

"Moriarty launched an insurrection against me. He was captured and brought before me. I offered him a choice: serve me faithfully or die. He cravenly chose the former. But despite that oath, he and his family have constantly sought to undermine me."

"Liar!" The trigger was pulled once again. The only noise in the room was a soft *click!* "The real story is exactly the opposite. The Professor succeeded in his revolt. He spared your life only because you still had powerful associates on the continent loyal only to you. You were stripped of your power and made a mere figurehead, but for all intents and purposes, the Moriartys ruled the High Council until your restoration in 1921. What's the year of my birth?"

"You must be about 45 or 46. You were born in either 1887 or 1888."

The gun clicked once more on an empty chamber.

"I was born in 1908. Explain the discrepancy."

"Dr. Caber's age-accelerator! You took it!"

'The truth is dawning on you, Colonel. "

''You're not Claud Caber's brother—but his son! So your mother failed to strangle you in the cradle after all!"

"That is correct. I was lucky to be treated by my uncle James. Fearing that Karah might make further attempts, my family circulated the false story of my demise and raised me in secrecy. My mother was very distraught after her attempted infanticide. She never knew that I still lived. My relatives suspected that you were behind her murderous assault. Is this true?"

The Colonel saw no reason to lie. "Yes. I told Karah about the Professor's role in her mother's death."

"Since then, I have lived solely for revenge—and power. I knew that my resemblance to Claud Caber would be immediately noticed, and if you, of all people, recognized me as his son, I would never get a seat on the Council. Why, my own life might even be forfeit! Makeup or plastic surgery wouldn't have hidden my true features from your eyes, so the only option left was to take my uncle's age-accelerator drug. But 20 years was an acceptable price to achieve my ambitions. Can you guess what is my plan now?"

"Your goal was to replace me. I now see how you achieved it. It was very clever. You leaked out news of your romantic quarrel with Irma to Gaspard, her implacable enemy. You reasoned that he would seek to irritate her by sponsoring you for the Council, which is exactly what happened. After I endorsed you, you provoked a quarrel between Irma and Dolores and tricked me into taking Irma as my new mistress. With her as a Trojan horse, you were able to overcome my defenses. The only thing left was to maneuver me into opposing a scheme that would unite the Council members behind you. But now I suspect that our lovely Irma was never a full and willing participant in your plan..."

"You're right," said Lumière. "She was reluctant. She never wanted me to take that drug. She even tried to block my accession to the High Council, and would never have become your mistress if I hadn't forced her."

"You seem to have quite a hold on her. Perhaps she genuinely loved you once, but now I think she's afraid of you."

"Enough about me, Colonel. Let's talk about you now. Who are you really? You might be the same man from the late Victorian era, but surely you can't have been born in 1722 or 1739... I suspect that you're a descendent of the original Colonel Bozzo-Corona—his great-great-grandson, if my count is right. I researched your family history. *The Brigand's Painting* and all that. Children kill their fathers in order to adopt their identity and use makeup to make themselves look older until age catches up with then and they no longer need false wrinkles and dyed hair. Am I correct?"

"I am Michele Bozzo-Corona. I was born in 1739."

"Liar!" *Click!* Another empty chamber was discharged. "Who are you?"

"I am Fra Diavolo. History inaccurately records my execution in Naples in 1806. I can never die!"

"Only a child would believe that!" *Click!* Another pull of the trigger, another empty chamber. "This is your last chance. Who are you?"

"I am one of the two greatest forces in the universe. One is God. He is good. I am the other. I am Evil."

Lumière pulled the trigger for the last time. No gunshot occurred. Surprised, he examined the gun. The chamber was empty. He must have mistakenly removed all the bullets.

"I can never die!" reiterated the prisoner.

"Your luck holds for now, Colonel. Let's try a little experiment. I want to see how long a man of your age can live without food and water. You know the old saying about those who outlive their usefulness? They're only branches to be cut."

Lumière departed the next day for Moscow. The deposed Colonel was placed in the custody of El Pecoso.

On December 1, 1934, Serge Kirov was fatally shot outside his Leningrad office. The assassin was Jean Lumière, but the NKVD instead arrested Leonid Nikolaev, a minor Communist functionary. Accused by Stalin of being part of a vast conspiracy, Nikolaev was executed by firing squad. All of his relatives were apprehended and sentenced to death. A true Reign of Terror then took over Russia, with many more arrests and executions taking place. The secret architect of these massacres, Jean Lumière, remained under Stalin's protection.

Six months later, Lumière was once more in Paris on a diplomatic mission to France. He now wore the uniform of a Red Army captain. The heir of Professor Moriarty presided over a High Council meeting held at the Nemirovitch Beauty Salons.

Among those present was Irma Caber. Using her alias as a member of the Valencia family, she had constructed a secure base in the Canaries, but had suspended her activities to attend the conference.

Also serving on the Council was Natasha Malakoff. Sporting a fashionable black coat with square shoulders, the Russian siren wore a magnificent signet ring with sharp curves.

"How long did the Colonel take to die?" asked Lumière.

"He still lives," replied El Pecoso. "We have kept him imprisoned in his mansion. Somehow he survives even though all food has been denied him."

"Someone must be secretly smuggling him food. We must find this traitor and punish him."

"The traitor is inconsequential," said Natasha. "The Colonel should be liquidated." The Russian squeezed her ring hand around an imaginary throat. "My signet can tear open his throat!"

"Let me kill the Colonel!" begged Irma. "Please! Let me introduce him to my Nina. Let me be the one to *cut the branch!*"

"As a reward for your faithful service, Irma, your petition is granted," said Lumière. *"Will there be sunligh*t?" he added, performing a variation on an old Black Coat ritual.

"It will be sunlight from midnight to noon if it is the will of the Father," answered Irma.

Lumière's duties in Moscow required his immediate return to Russia. As he boarded his plane, he was confident that the Colonel would not last another day.

The Colonel was strapped by leather cords to an upright circular frame. He was bound in a spread-eagle fashion. His arms and legs were extended. The wheel was screwed into a stationary pole.

With Irma was a man with a lurid red scar down one cheek. He was Julius Freyder, her confidential secretary. He tied a blindfold over Irma's eyes. She held ten blades, all identical to the knife she had used against Dolores.

"Once Freyder turns the switch on the wheel, it will revolve counter-clockwise. I propose to give you a demonstration in knife-throwing. As you spin, I'll throw the knives close to your body. I'll avoid hitting you until the last two knives. One will pierce your heart. The other will be aimed at a lower portion of your anatomy."

"You'll kill me long before that! You won't be able to see me!"

"If you continually talk, I'll have an excellent idea of your current position."

Freyder pressed the switch. As the wheel spun, the Colonel spoke:

"You can't trust Lumière. I know you fear him." A knife narrowly missed his left arm. "He's already betrayed you. My agents have pictures of him making love to Antonia Lashley." The next blade struck near the Colonel's left knee. "You must know her. She's younger than you." The third knife landed very close to the Colonel's femoral artery. "Free me and we can make a deal." The fourth blade was to the left side of the Colonel's head. "I'll grant you total au-

130

tonomy." The fifth knife imbedded itself near the Colonel's right ear. "You and your father will never be bothered again." This sixth knife rubbed against the top of his head. A slight cut caused blood to drip down his forehead. "You're thinking you can't trust me." The seventh blade was next to the Colonel's right side. "But I made a similar bargain with Fantômas!" The eighth knife landed near his left ear. "And I've never broken it!"

"Stop the wheel!" ordered Irma.

Freyder hit the switch. The revolving movement stopped. The Colonel's body was upright, but tilted slightly toward the right. Irma held the tip of a knife in each hand.

"Do we have a deal?" asked the Colonel.

Without removing her blindfold, Irma threw her final two knives. They cut the bonds on the Colonel's wrists.

In his Moscow apartment in July 1935, Jean Lumière was conferring with an orange-haired woman in an NKVD uniform. She was about to depart for Spain to infiltrate a Trotskyite organization.

"Once you reach Spain, Rosa, you will send detailed reports of all your activities to this address in the Canaries," directed Lumière.

"I refuse!" screamed the woman. "I'll have you shot for treason!"

"Do you recall Natasha Malakoff? You were very friendly with her before she left the country."

"We merely played chess together a few times!"

"Here's a photo of such a chess session. As you can see, the opposing queens assumed innovative positions."

Suddenly, there was a knock on the door. Grabbing the photo, the woman hid it in her blouse. When Lumière opened the door, he was facing a Soviet Prosecutor and a squad of NKVD agents.

"Captain, I'm arresting you on the charge of blackmail," pronounced the Prosecutor.

Inside his cell in Lubyanka Prison, Lumière awaited his trial. The door of the cell was opened. The Prosecutor entered.

"Captain, let me introduce you to the informant who exposed your crimes to General Secretary Stalin."

Colonel Bozzo-Corona stepped in to the cell.

"You tricked Irma into releasing you," concluded Lumière. "She will regret her decision."

"Actually, she proved to be a competent negotiator. She even secured exclusive rights to her father's inventions. With your ambitions squashed, I'll soon be restored as the All-Father."

"You're wrong, Colonel, the Black Coats will splinter into different gangs without me to lead them."

"We shall see." The Colonel turned to his escort. "Comrade Prosecutor, will you please leave us alone. Lock the door. I'll call you when I'm finished."

The Soviet bureaucrat followed the Colonel's instructions.

Lumière advanced defiantly.

"There's no one here to protect you, Colonel."

"When last we met, my limbs were tied. They aren't now."

Lumière suppressed a laugh. "You can't be serious, old man. I'm younger. Stronger. With one hand alone, I could throttle you in seconds."

"You're as overconfident as Dolores Valencia. She couldn't kill Irma. Kill me if you can."

Outside the cell, the Prosecutor heard the sounds of a violent struggle, but he had been personally instructed by Stalin not to interfere.

Inside the cell, a battered Lumière laid on the ground.

"I could take your life, Jean Lumière, but another fate beckons you," promised a victorious Colonel.

"You're going to have me shot after the trial."

"The Prosecutor will demand that punishment, but Stalin has acted on my advice. He has told the judges that you're only guilty of misdirected ambition. They incorrectly believe that you merely sought rapid promotion. You'll be sentenced to a Siberian labor camp."

"Why are you being so merciful?"

"I'm not merciful at all. Life will be unendurable in that Gulag prison. Let's try a little experiment. I want to see how long a man of your extended years will survive in the Siberian waste. A fellow physically 27 would have stood a better chance than one who's 47."

The prison cell secretly contained a listening device. In another area of the prison, a man with a wire-brush mustache was following the conversation through a set of earphones. He was Stalin's most trusted assistant. Seated in a cramped room, Stalin's aide removed his shoes to be more comfortable. Inexplicable static filled the air waves. The shoeless man no longer heard anything. Had the Colonel activated a jamming device?

"I have a little bedtime story for you, my fallen Napoleon," said the Colonel to Lumière.

Inside the darkened prison cell, the entity known to men as Colonel Bozzo-Corona told the story of his life. This tale was not a fabrication. It was the unvarnished truth. When he finished, the Colonel summoned the Prosecutor and left.

Jean Lumière finally knew the nature of the weird and terrible being that had plagued him since birth. The Colonel could only have been put on this Earth for men to dread him. The obscene revelations made the bruised Lumière shudder.

Outside the prison, the Colonel was escorted to a limousine by the Prosecutor. The Soviet official was a naïve idealist. He sincerely imagined Stalin to be a benign utopian whose violent actions were solely retaliatory measures. The Prosecutor knew nothing of Lumière's true role in Stalin's purges.

"Comrade Colonel, you've done a great service for humanity. Your actions exposed a great criminal. You're a true hero."

"There are no heroes, Comrade Prosecutor. Every man is either a fool or a knave. Which one are you?"

Like many French aficionados of my generation, I did not discover Fantômas through the original novels of Pierre Souveste & Marcel Allain (although these were still widely available in the 1960s), but through the somewhat cheesy but colorful, extravagant and humorous trilogy of films directed by André Hune-belle, starring the legendary Jean Marais (from Beauty *and the Beast) in the twin roles of Fantômas and journalist Fandor, and the comedic superstar Louis de Funès as the bumbling policeman Juve. While a parodic travesty of the original stories, those films still managed to preserve the myth of Fantômas and instill awe and fear at the sight of the green-masked villain, who was certainly anything but funny. It is to them that this story is dedicated...*

Jean-Marc Lofficier: *The Sincerest Form of Flattery*

Monaco, 1964

The man woke up.

He blinked. Twice. He could barely make out his surroundings beyond the simple fact that he was in a bed, in a white room. It was sparsely furnished, with only functional furniture: a chair, a formica table, a small sink and the narrow bed in which he lay. *A medical room*, he thought. There was a small, slit-like window. He noticed at once that the glass was reinforced.

He got out of bed and walked to the window in his pajamas. Outside was a park. *Not much to be learned from that.*

Then, he went to the door, which of course was locked. There was a square window, also of reinforced glass. He could see a corridor, white walls, green linoleum floors, and, just at the edge of his field of vision, a wheelchair parked against a wall. *A private clinic*, he guessed.

He sat on the chair and performed the set of mental and physical exercises he did on a daily basis to remain at his best. He felt oddly tired, as if he had just been running a marathon. *How long have I been here?* he thought. *And where is "here?" Have I been injured?*

His neck hurt. *Maybe I have whiplash.*

The man looked at his reflection in the small mirror above the sink and suddenly remembered who he was.

He was Diabolik.

Diabolik's last memory was of the accident.

He reran the events through his head, as if he was running a film in reverse. The casino. The corniche overlooking the Mediterranean. The sparkling lights of Nice behind him. A king's ransom in diamonds safely stored in the Ja-

134

guar's glove compartment. The car, hugging every bend in the road, obeying its driver like a tame panther. And, at the end of the road, Eva, waiting for him in their getaway plane...

The black helicopter had come out of nowhere, oddly silent (*a new model? to be checked later*), spitting a hail of bullets from its twin machine guns. Diabolik had swerved, managing to avoid the enemy's fire, but a stray bullet had shredded a tire, causing the car to careen out of control, running over the edge of the cliff and falling straight into the sea.

That was all he remembered. Nothing more.

He returned to the door and banged on it several times, calling out. Almost at once, he heard a voice saying: "Doctor Garrick! Monsieur Valmont is awake!"

There was a flurry of steps and a man dressed in a white coat unlocked the door and entered. He was somewhat portly and Diabolik thought that, with his jowls and kindly eyes, he looked like the French actor Michel Simon.

"Good afternoon, Monsieur Valmont," said the man, extending his hand. "I'm Doctor Garrick. You have caused us a lot of worry, you know..."

Diabolik shook the doctor's hand. It was oily, almost greasy, but deceptively firm underneath.

"Where am I?" he asked.

The Doctor shook his head.

"Yes, yes... The neurologist said you might suffer from some memory lapses, after your... your... er..."

Somehow, Eva must have rescued me and left me in the care of these people, thought Diabolik. *Obviously, she can't have told them the truth. They must think the car went over the cliff in an accident. Better play along until she shows up...*

"My accident?"

The doctor's eyes grew wider while his face suddenly expressed deep concern.

"No, no, Monsieur Valmont," he said, very softly. "Facing up to the truth is the first step towards your recovery. There was no accident. You tried to commit suicide... To hang yourself."

Automatically, Diabolik reached for his throat with his hand, *and he felt the bruises on his neck.*

"If your son hadn't come home unexpectedly, you would have died," continued the kindly Doctor. "Now let me examine you." He pulled an ophthalmoscope from his pocket.

Diabolik grabbed the man's wrist and saw him wince, so strong was his grip.

"What do you mean, *my son?*"

The doctor's face looked increasingly concerned.

"Your son Carlo, Monsieur Valmont... Don't you remember?" Then he added to himself, muttering under his breath, "Heavens! This is bad!"

Diabolik let go of the Doctor and forced himself to count down slowly from ten to zero. *I don't understand what's happening. Is this man playing some kind of game? I have to find out more...*

"You're right, Doctor," he said with what he hoped was a sincere smile. "My memory is still playing tricks on me. Tell me what you know. I'm sure it will help me remember."

The Doctor smiled again, although Diabolik could tell that he didn't totally believe him, but probably saw no harm in doing what his patient requested. While he performed the eye exam, he said:

"You're Horace Ralph Valmont; you're married to Anna and you have two children, Carlo, 18, and Francesca, 16. You work at the Depository Bank of Zurich here in Monaco. Something to do with Mergers & Acquisitions, I believe... Now, what I'm going to tell you next is very hush-hush... Your wife was terribly concerned about your safety, which is why she booked you into my private clinic... Apparently, your son..."

"Carlo?"

"Yes, Carlo, owed money to the Mafia... A pretty large sum, I understand... You were working on an important deal, with several bidders, including one connected to the Sicilians... They blackmailed you to push things though in exchange for forgiving Carlo's debts... You did it, because you had no choice... But your boss, Signore Ginko, who hates you, found out about it... He was going to report you, have you arrested and sent to jail... The Sicilians, of course, wouldn't like that... So, understandably, you chose the quickest way out... I'm sorry."

"You mean, I hung myself?"

"Yes, but Carlo, who was supposed to be away with friends, came home early and found you. He saved your life, Monsieur Valmont. Your wife immediately had you transported here. You remained nearly comatose for three weeks. Frankly, some of my colleagues were starting to give up on you, but I said, wait, he'll pull through, you see..."

This isn't possible. I'm not Horace Valmont. I'm... Diabolik.

"Now that you're better, we're going to move you to a more comfortable room. And I'll call Anna to tell her that you're awake. No doubt she'll want to visit you soon... But you must take it easy, you understand?"

In the course of the next five days, Doctor Garrick introduced Diabolik to his wife, Anna, a middle-aged, mousy-looking brown-haired woman with a chubby face, a non-entity; Carlo, his duly contrite son, whom he could tell right away would never amount to anything and would break his mother's heart; and Francesca, his daughter, 16 going on 25, wearing clothes that made her look like the cheap tramp she was likely fated to become.

He learned that his nemesis, Ginko, his boss at the Monaco branch of the Depository Bank of Zurich, had hounded him ceaselessly, denied him a promotion and purposefully kept him under his thumb to do all the drudge work—that is, until the day of the scandal.

Diabolik asked to spend time in the clinic's library and combed through the newspapers and old magazines kept there, searching for a trace of his criminal exploits—anywhere, but none were to be found. On the other hand, there was a small press article in the bank's internal reporting that the trusted and reliable Horace Velmont had fallen victim to a domestic accident (*fallen off a ladder while changing a light bulb! Even that cover story was transparently lame—like the rest of his presumed life*)

Could it all be true? Could he be this mediocre bank employee, frustrated in a dead end job, with an utterly dreary family, who, in what he thought would be the last moments of his life, had constructed a glamorous scenario—one where he was strong, free, rich and powerful, bold and handsome, with the stunning Eva Kent for his lover, always triumphing over the plodding Ginko, his natural inferior?

Or was "Horace Velmont" the fictional scenario, an elaborate conspiracy meant to drive him out of his mind?

There was only one way to find out.

Diabolik took his wallet from the inside pocket of his jacket, hanging in the closet, and fished out an electronic pass in the name Horace Valmont from the Monaco branch of the Depository Bank of Zurich.

There he would find the answer.

Doctor Garrick had not objected to the visit. On the contrary, he told Diabolik—Horace Valmont—that finding himself back in familiar surroundings might stir his memories. As far as the good doctor knew, Diabolik was still suffering from a bout of amnesia.

Once inside the building, Diabolik had gone straight to the elevator that would take him down to the vault. His electronic pass had sent the cabin down, and enabled him to open the several gates of titanium bars that stood between him and his goal.

Safe deposit box number 9.

At last, he stood before the blank metal wall, with ten indentations.

The box could only be opened with his retinal pattern and the print of his ring finger.

Diabolik stared at the tiny scanner while applying the surface of the fourth digit of his right hand to the ultrasensitive plate.

If he was really Diabolik, and not the insipid Horace Valmont, the vault would release the box and, inside, he would find what he remembered storing there: a small gun, ten passports in various names and countries, and 20 bearers bond drawn on a Liechtenstein bank for an amount totaling $100 million—one fifth of his treasure, the rest kept in other safety deposit boxes in other banks known to him alone.

He heard a discreet whirring sound. *Excellent!* he thought. The silver metal box slowly slid out on invisible railing. Diabolik breathed a sigh of relief.

He grabbed the box and opened it. The gun was there; so were the passports.

The bonds were gone

Suddenly, he heard a laugh behind him, except it wasn't that exactly, but more like the low growl of a tiger—if a tiger could laugh.

He turned around and saw that the eerie laugh came from Doctor Garrick, who was presently pulling off the lifelike mask that had been his face. Diabolik couldn't help admiring the rubber-like syntheflesh which was undoubtedly superior to his own products.

Beneath it was another mask—a pale, green face, with barely sculpted features; naked, brutal, emotionless; the only thing alive in it were the two steel grey blue eyes shining with incredible intelligence and malice, and occasionally a flash of humor—the macabre wit of the torturer taking delight in his victim's pain.

"Do you know who you are now?"

"Yes; I am Diabolik."

"Excellent. My job is done then. You're cured."

"You took my money. Knowing who I am, you still dared to steal from me. Are you insane?"

"Ah, yes. I thought you might want an explanation. Very well. That gun is totally harmless by the way. Unlike mine... You'd do well to listen to me..."

"Who are you?" asked Diabolik.

"Fantômas," replied the man in the green mask.

"That's impossible. Were he still alive today, Fantômas would be almost 100!"

"And yet here I am. Because of you, one might say, you and all the others. Fantômas in Mexico, in Argentina, Kriminal, Killing, Satanik... The world today seems awash in Fantômases. At first, I planned to kill you all, one by one... You don't know how close you came to death when I shot your car on the corniche... But then, I came up with another plan... I decided to... tax my imitators."

"What do you mean?"

"I told myself: Make them pay—pay a tax on the right to be Fantômas— the right to live really. So I set up the clinic and the persona of kindly Doctor Garrick. I took your retinal pattern and fingerprints during the initial exam. After that, I needed a few days to get in here, which explains our little mind game... From my study of you, I knew you wouldn't be fooled for very long. But I wanted to have this chance to explain myself to you."

"Where do we go from here?"

"You go on being Diabolik, just as before. I still have many others of your colleagues to visit. Unless you prefer another kind of resolution?"

Diabolik looked at the man who called himself Fantômas. For the first time in his life, he truly felt that the issue of a combat would be... uncertain. It was a new sensation and he didn't like it.

"You can have this victory Fantômas—if that is who you are," he finally said. "But never cross my path again. Never touch even a hair of any of my friends. Never let your shadow fall across any of my interests, or else, I swear I will kill you, no matter how strong you are."

"I would expect no less of you, Diabolik."

And before Diabolik could utter another word, Fantômas had stepped out into the corridor, leaving behind him the mask of Doctor Garrick. When Diabolik rushed out to look for him, he was gone. The titanium bars, the electronic elevator, none of that seemed to have mattered. He had vanished like a wraith on the first ray of dawn.

Fantômas was true to his word. He and Diabolik never crossed paths again.

On the secret grapevine exclusive to the world's top criminals, Diabolik heard that others had been similarly taken in by someone claiming to be Fantômas—then no more was heard of him. It seemed that the first and greatest Lord of Terror had returned to oblivion.

But in his dark heart, Diabolik knew that, one day, Fantômas would return.

David McDonnell, former managing editor of Starlog, *and long-time friend of Black Coat Press, has not written any fiction for a long, long time, which is why we are extraordinarily pleased to welcome his return to the genre in* Tales of the Shadowmen, *with a story that unexpectedly brings together two villains from popular fiction—the kind we love to hate... No doubt, this is one of the most unusual crossovers of all times...*

David McDonnell: *Big Little Man*

Fort Bayard, NM, 1961

He loved to look at the deer grazing outside his hospital window. They fed there, nearly every night at dusk. Mostly, they were does and fawns, the occasional young buck, but he had never, as of yet, seen a well-antlered stag. Perhaps, with those magnificent horns on their heads, they had better things to do and preferred to dine around and lounge about forest glades far from the hospital lawn.

It reminded him of *Bambi*, which was his favorite moving picture, but then he had seen so few of those. To be certain, it was his favorite talkie. He had also watched *Snow White and the Seven Dwarfs* and *The Wizard of Oz*, but then he kind of had to—he was fascinated by the former and actually in the latter. When Hollywood needed Munchkins, the call had gone out to just about anybody anywhere. And he was short enough to qualify.

At first, he thought he might be too old, but he had always looked young for his age—even now, he thought ruefully, decades later as he was closing in on 125—and they gladly cast him. But they weren't crazy about his singing, that lusty baritone, so there went the chance to represent the Lollipop Guild. No, he had simply been a background Munchkin, somewhat anonymous—which was as he liked it.

Once, it was true, he had been one of the most famous short people in the world, inches lower than fabled Napoleon Bonaparte, but far, far greater. Woodrow Wilson, Shirley Temple, Tom Thumb. He towered over them all! He was a pioneering scientist, an inspired inventor, a brilliant tactician (even if he did say so himself), the finest criminal mastermind of his generation. But that was long ago.

Now, he sat in his wheelchair (which made him considerably taller) in a Veterans Administration Hospital in Fort Bayard, New Mexico, solitarily looking out the window at deer eating the lawn (and searching for the bread crumbs he had once tossed there). How James West would laugh if he could see his arch-enemy now!

It was fortunate for both of them, thought Dr. Miguelito Loveless, that West was dead, long dead, truly dead. Buried! Loveless had sent flowers (and candy) to the funeral and wept actual tears at the thought of his nemesis being no more. West's death had truly diminished him, not because he was all that involved with mankind (except as an object of possible subjugation) but because without his formidable foe, Loveless felt lost, lesser, shorter. A great hero (like him) needed a great villain (like West) to take his measure.

He smiled. Some people might favor reversing those labels, and consider Loveless unheroic. Bah! Critics! They didn't appreciate the genius it took to conquer the West (not to mention James West) with schemes involving Indian ancestry, giant toys and earthquake machines. True, they hadn't worked out (and the press had attributed the infernal device that shook the Earth to another renegade scientist, thereby annoying Loveless), but still wasn't it the thought, the idea, the sheer genius that counted? His grandiose plans might fail, often did, but nonetheless they were his. No one else could think such things up. Just Miguelito Loveless! Well, the Toyman had done the giant toys bit. And Professor Moriarty. John Sunlight. Sumuru. Jay Gould. Pretty Boy Floyd. And Macy's, the folks with that parade and all those pretty big balloons. But Loveless was first!

His brow furled. "Maybe that doesn't matter," he muttered quietly to himself and suddenly noticed the furor outside—an ivory figure among the brown deer. It was her, cape flapping. What was she doing now?

Loveless stopped smiling. The deer were upset, running from her and away, off into the night. She was spoiling it all, ruining his only pleasure. Those were his deer! And she was making them flee.

She stood outside in the chilly October air, her white cloak still flapping about her. The deer were long gone. She stared deep into the locked window, directly into his eyes as her lips curled into a hospitable smile.

His blood ran cold.

She had come to Fort Bayard a mere five weeks previously, to take charge of the long-term wards in Building C. At first, nothing changed. The eternal waiting room of Ward Six remained just what it was. No one had died lately, but you couldn't really call what they were doing living. Patients awoke after sometimes sleepless nights, ate three square meals and spent the rest of the day in time-killing pursuits (reading, napping off, playing cards, checkers or chess, listening to baseball or music on the radio, staring out into space). They waited for something new to happen, for some novelty, but most of all for comforting routines. In Loveless' case, it was the deer. He loved watching the deer.

Without any warning, the new Nurse had come, she of the baby doll face and the enormous breasts. The Big Nurse. Employee scuttlebutt overheard by Loveless pegged her as a refugee from two decades of service at a sanitarium where, among other irregularities, a troubled patient had committed suicide on her watch. There were rumors that she herself had been assaulted and after initially returning to work, had decided on a change of clime. She had traded in the madness of the Chronics and the Acutes for the lameness of the Infirm and the Old. Goodbye to the cuckoos! But both bughouse and Veterans Administration shared certain types. Generally speaking, whether insane or sane, their patients could be divided into Walkers (those still ambulatory enough to amble around on their own two feet), Wheelers (like Loveless, pretty much stuck in chairs) and Vegetables (the helpless confined to their beds longing for an ending). In short, she had switched from the mad to the sad.

And then she had proceeded to make their lives sadder, confiscating playful contraband that other nurses and orderlies had ignored, enforcing long-forgotten edicts concerning smoking and playing radios loudly and leaving no doubt she was in charge—in control—of their every waking moment, every beloved memento, every damned bowel movement.

At first, Loveless hadn't cared. She might be the Big Nurse, but she was small potatoes to him. He was Loveless! He had fought the mighty likes of Jim West, Lecoq, Paladin, Bulldog Drummond, Bat Masterson...! He had made presidents and potentates, caterers and chocolateers, tremble. Thomas Alva Edison, Buster Keaton and Fantômas dare not speak his name! What was this woman in white to him? Besides, he was tremendously old, not immortal (despite the age-expanding serum so generously provided by his alchemical colleague Count Manzeppi, which had given him long life indeed). It was utterly fantastic that he had been around for America's Civil War (gleefully selling scientific innovation to both sides) and yet here he was still breathing while the nation once divided against itself celebrated that conflict's centennial. But he couldn't last much longer. His stubby legs weren't reliable. They couldn't always support him now. That's why he mostly used the wheelchair, leaving his cane next to the bed. Loveless was not long for this Earth.

West might have laughed at that notion, too. Loveless had faked his own death so often he had simply lost track. Some of those demises were necessary. Like his friend Walter Jameson, Loveless knew it was trouble to be seen hanging around too long in one place while your friends (the giant Voltaire, the singer Antoinette, the painter Toulouse-Lautrec) grew older and passed from the scene. He had once kept a small ledger book merely to keep his aliases straight—tucked in the back was the ever-growing list of dead friends and expired enemies—and to make sure the biographical details were different and memorable. This dwarf had been born on a Nebraska farm, that Munchkin in the Mercy Hospital of Altoona, Pennsylvania, the midget at the Panama Canal Zone. To further the facade, he had carefully managed different birthdays for all, though that sometimes got confusing. Only the height remained the same—three feet, ten inches. These days, as he had been for two decades, he was Michael Donovan.

Under that name, he proudly fought in World War II. It wasn't his first. On the sidelines (and serving both sides) in the Civil War, he had skipped the Spanish-American War, but he had served with distinction as a scientist without port-folio in the Great War, even meeting U.S. General "Blackjack" Pershing. It amused Loveless that earlier in the century Pershing had been stationed here at Fort Bayard, decades before setting off in peripatetic pursuit of the Mexican bandit Pancho Villa (a Loveless amigo), years prior to leading the American Expeditionary Force in France. That was back when Fort Bayard was an Army hospital, before its transfer to Veterans Administration auspices.

As Donovan, Loveless fought for freedom in his own way in World War II, putting aside all his smart schemes and worldly plans (as he hadn't really done in the Great War) to concentrate on devising scenarios to mislead, defeat and destroy the Axis. He didn't love the Nazis one bit (was there any greater evil?), hadn't liked them from the start. His friend Karl Glocken, a dwarf like him, who had foolishly cruised to nowhere by ship, told him some of what was going on in Germany. Nazis weren't particularly nice to dwarves or madmen, Gypsies or Jews or most human beings of any stripe—so Loveless had backbur-nered his own plots to solely plot against them. He even worked for a time in London with British Intelligence alongside Lt. Commander Ewen Montagu (the actor Ivor's brother), Commander Ian Fleming, Commandant Bob Morane and Sir Dennis Nayland Smith. Loveless was the proud inventor of the Exploding Moustache Cup. Sadly, Adolf Hitler had never shaved.

This stellar service during WWII had the unexpected side benefit of ensur-ing Loveless' later life under the Donovan pseudonym. He really was a veteran so with funds running low and his patents exhausted, the Veterans Administra-tion Hospital system had become the refuge of his old, old age. Miguelito Love-less had long ceased to exist (his late, ne'er-do-well son, believing the obitu-aries, had unsuccessfully tried to revisit the family business). But as Michael Donovan, he was a true veteran, entitled to his wheelchair, a warm bed, medical care and peace of mind—marooned out here in enchanting New Mexico, just 15 miles from Silver City where Billy the Kid (an acquaintance) once walked. San Francisco, Denver, Washington D.C. boasted nicer, more modern hospitals, but those were busy locales where some loquacious greybeard might recognize Loveless by height and recall fabled escapades from long ago. Better to be ano-nymous, even denying the Munchkin gig, in New Mexican isolation.

Loveless regretted nothing! Not the schemes that went awry or the enemies unvanquished. Farewell to the friends long gone and the fame long vanished. Most of his possessions, save a few special keepsakes, were lost to time. But that didn't matter. Loveless was legend. He was someone else now. In truth, he had been Donovan for more than two decades. And Donovan was slowly dying.

That's when she came and began to whisper. "And how are we today, Mr. Donovan?" she inquired, her alabaster face gleaming; her lip hirsute and impa-tient. "My, have we gotten taller? Did we take our pills? Have we eaten our lunch? Did we pass our water?" She fussed over him, futzed with his cotton robe, fooled with his wheelchair.

Glimpsing the deer timidly approaching outside his window, she rapped noisily on the frame and sent them fearfully away. She also discovered the cache of bread crumbs, carefully husbanded from his meal plates and the cafeteria, meant to feed the deer (and whatever birds may come) and now confiscated and discarded. She had found the hole in the window screen that allowed him to dispense his crumby offerings and smirked as she had it fixed. She locked the windows and kept the key.

So, Loveless disliked her. She was a femme fatale in starched white, his lady nemesis in sensible shoes. Now, he hated her. With every bone in his 78-pound body, he hated Nurse Ratched.

The next night the deer did not come.

It was Halloween, and he could see some of the VA station's children, dressed in costumes both home-made and store-bought, on the pathways and lawns outside at dusk. There were ghosts and cowboys, monsters and princesses—even a Jolly Green Giant. They clutched the hands of fearless parents as they hurried to-and-fro from Fort Bayard's home quarters, seeking candy bars and sugary snacks, engaged in the serious vocation of trick-or-treating. Happy children made him—happy.

He waited. And still the deer did not come.

Had her wild dance frightened them away forever? Or was it the kids ambling about in Halloween costumes? Had the deer tired of his futile attempts to open the sealed windows and resume the feeding sessions? Had she salted the lawn with chili pepper, formaldehyde or grizzly bear scent? So many questions, so little deer.

Nurse Ratched had to go. To be relieved of duties (cast out of this nest of wounded), to transfer to another hospital (where she could very well torment others, both short and tall) or, best of all, to die. A femme finale! He could think of many ways to eliminate her. Using the incredible shrinking processes developed by his pen-pal Dr. Cyclops (and his own experiments along that line), he could make the Big Nurse small—and then crush the miniature life out of her with the velvet heel of his blue hospital slipper! He could let loose a deadly mechanical rattler in the Break Room and risk that it might make a mistake (or a missnake) and bite the wrong nurse (what an old softie he had become; the other nurses were kind so he wouldn't want to rattle them). He could arrange for Voltaire and Antoinette to kidnap her, force her into a coach, take her to the nearby City of Rocks and throw her off the tallest natural stone formation—but, wait, like Rosencrantz and Guildenstern, Voltaire and Antoinette were dead. He would find no assistance there.

Would no one help rid him of this troublesome nurse?

The deer. Yes, if he had the time, he could train a race of cannibal deer, carefully hand-fed and bred to dine on naughty nurse and the occasional cranky gardener. But it might take generations before Bambi got sufficiently hungry to turn carnivore and evolved to savor human flesh. No, the meat-eating deer was not a viable option; ultimately, it wouldn't work, just like his—

He had an idea.

The next morning, the Day of the Dead in Mexicos New and Old, he made his way two blocks from the ward to the Quonset hut that housed the VA Canteen, pulled out his coin purse and quietly bought a gift for his nemesis in white. The clerk laughed at the purchase when Loveless declared, "It's for my sweetheart."

He wheeled slowly back to Building C, Ward Six. The gift wrap and ribbon—fortuitously saved from a prior birthday—was hidden in his bureau, next to a pile of clean handkerchiefs. He placed the presents in a small box and, singing softly all the while, wrapped the paper and ribbon around it. He found a bright bow and a carnation and added them to the top.

Then, painfully, fingers snarled in arthritic spasm, he wrote on a card: *To Nurse Ratched, From Her Secret Saint-A, Happy All-Saints' Day.* He hid the package in his robe, careful not to smash the bow or ruin the flower, and wheeled himself out to the deserted nurses' base. He left it there for Ratched.

Later that afternoon, there was a big noise, waking Loveless from his small sleep.

A great silence came to Ward C. A fire alarm sounded. Smoke poured from the ladies' lavatory. Two younger nurses looked in and spotted Ratched everywhere. She had been relieved of duty.

Much was chaos and smoke and the smell of the battlefield. Loveless sighed and went back to his nap.

After a few days, matters returned to normal. The restroom was refurbished. Loveless destroyed the Canteen receipt for the Lady Norelco he had purchased. He had noticed, on her visits, just how hairy Ratched's lip and legs were, her white support hose scarred by some unsightly hairs pushing through. So, he had purchased the electric razor and given it to her, wrapped in the pretty box, with a special keepsake from the past, his patented Exploding Moustache Cup.

Fortunately, unlike Hitler, Nurse Ratched shaved.

Some nights later, the deer came back. And Michael Donovan, once Dr. Miguelito Loveless, watched them feed on the lawn for a long, long time.

Our resident Australian, Brad Mengel, returns with a short-short in which an older generation of heroes passes the torch to a younger one, in this case, Prince Malko Linge, a.k.a. S.A.S., initials which stands for Son Altesse Sérénissime, *or His Serene Highness. Malko is the aristocratic Austrian hero of a long-standing series of espionage novels written by Gérard de Villiers (and various ghostwriters) which began in 1965 and is still ongoing today. It was twice adapted into films, last as* Eye of the Widow *(1989) with Richard Young as Malko...*

Brad Mengel: *The Apprentice*

London, 1948

"You're Simon Templar... The Saint!"

It was a phrase that had launched a thousand adventures. Simon sometimes wondered if there was a halo above his head attracting those in distress. But, this time, instead of the standard comely damsel, the Saint had been greeted by a boy of about 12, with blond hair and golden brown eyes.

"Permit me to introduce myself: I am His Serene Highness Prince Malko Linge," said the boy, handing over a card bearing a stick figure with a crown at a rakish angle, "but you may call me Malko. I want to be your apprentice."

Simon could almost hear Chief Inspector Teal arresting him for child endangerment, but he decided to hear the boy's story. One never knew where the next adventure came from.

"My parents are dead. Father died a hero in the war and Mother just three years ago. I have a small trust fund in Switzerland and a castle in Austria; the rest was pillaged by the Nazis. I tried to stop them with Father's Luger, but I only damaged a painting's frame." A cold anger swept across the lad's face. "I'm a better shot now."

"I'm sure you're worth a battalion of SAS," Simon commented. "What do you need me for?"

"I've found the painting."

The auction house was eager to welcome Prince Shamyl of Cherkessia and his nephew. Bidding on the painting with the damaged frame was fierce after the Prince rather loudly advised his nephew that they might buy the hidden masterpiece.

The painting eventually sold for $50,000 to a wealthy American. Disappointed that he missed the painting, Prince Shamyl asked management for the seller's details in case there was another hidden masterpiece.

146

Several days later, the Nazi now calling himself Henri Dumond, went to his safe to gloat again over the unexpected profit the painting had brought him. To his surprise, he found the safe empty except for a lone card that read *"Thanks for the donation to the restoration fund"* signed with two stick figures, one with a crown at a jaunty angle, the other with a halo.

Tales of the Shadowmen *is proud to welcome into its ranks mystery writer and historian Sharan Newman with a medieval story (our first since John Shirley's Cyrano yarn in Volume 4) that brings together Sharan's 12th century heroine, Catherine Levendeur, with Bisclavret, one of the first werewolves in popular fiction, imagined by Marie de France, one of the best and most famous French poets of her days.*

Sharan Newman: *The Beast Without*

Broceliande, Autumn 1134

From the safety of the forest he watched the lady ride by.

He thought she would be wan with grief, but she was laughing with one of her friends, the two of them balancing sparrow hawks on their wrists. Servants and beaters ran alongside. He moved back into the shadows. They couldn't find him, not like this.

The bells on the jesses of the birds jingled in his ears as he slunk away through the underbrush. He would have to travel far to find his dinner tonight. His body ached with love, longing, anger and, overpowering them all, hunger.

Paris, the same day

Catherine shimmied over the side wall, scraping her palms as she fell into the garden. Her heart was still pounding in terror. She hurried to the water to try to clean herself off before her mother…

"Catherine!"

Too late. Catherine turned. Seeing the look on her mother's face, she said nothing, but followed her into the house.

The home was comfortable, showing the prosperity of its owner, the merchant Hubert Levendeur. It rose three stories on a side street near the Grève with a spacious kitchen and chicken run in the back. The walls enclosed a lawn speckled with fruit trees that sloped down to a stream. Inside the house was decorated with fine wall hangings, more chairs than family members and soft cushions of velvet. The tall girl with black braids in a tangle and a torn robe spattered with mud and blood was decidedly out of place.

Her mother certainly thought so.

"What am I to do with you, Catherine?" Madeline demanded. "You're fourteen, not a child any more. Many girls your age are already married. Look at yourself."

Catherine stared at the floor, noticing that her bare toes were also tracking mud across the rushes. Her shoes had come off when she climbed the stone wall. She had no answer. Any explanation would only increase her mother's wrath.

There was a step behind her. Madeline turned her anger on the new arrival without pausing for breath.

"This is all your fault, Hubert!" she glared at her husband. "You let her learn Latin. You laugh at her antics. You encourage her to ignore her sewing and you let her dress like a peasant. She doesn't even have shoes on!"

Catherine tried to curl her toes under her skirts.

"She's not fit for marriage," Madeline continued. "No one could provide a dowry large enough. She wouldn't last a month in a convent with all her questions. What will become of her?"

Her voice dwindled from outrage to despair.

Hubert paid no attention. He grabbed his daughter in a tight embrace. Catherine gasped at the force of it. Were there tears in his eyes?

"Papa?" She realized that he knew. "*Saint Agatha, save me from his anger!*" she prayed.

"Are you all right?" His voice was breathless. "Did they hurt you? What did they do? Tell me at once!"

Madeline stared at them both; it dawned on her that Catherine had done more than fall in the mud in the garden.

"They were students, Papa," She couldn't look in his eyes. "I took the short cut between the church and the Bishop's palace. They pushed me against a wall and tried to..." She couldn't say it. "I screamed and someone heard and chased them away."

"Oh, my dear Lord!" Madeline reached out and felt her daughter: face, arms, side, back and front, searching for signs of damage.

Hubert's panic was fading now that he knew she was safe. "Pagan, the milk peddler, heard her. He clanked the cans and shouted at them. Since this one ran, too, he thought she might have been there willingly."

"Never! I wouldn't!" Catherine swore. "I think they followed me from the lecture."

Hubert ignored her. "He came and found me immediately and I raced here, not knowing what I would find. How could you do this?" He glared at Catherine.

"That's what comes of Latin," Madeline said with a kind of triumph. "Now her reputation is ruined. No one will marry her."

Both parents considered the state of their elder daughter. Catherine considered it, herself. What was she to do? Marriage didn't seem appealing, from what she'd seen of it. A convent was probably her fate if they would let her copy books instead of sewing. She enjoyed helping her father keep the records of his trade, but didn't know what good that would be to nuns. As for curbing her tongue, she suspected that only frequent beatings would teach her that, something even her mother was too soft-hearted to administer.

She looked so apologetic and frightened that Madeline relented and hugged her, carefully, around the dirt.

"Go clean yourself," she said quietly. "Are you sure they did nothing more than grab you?"

Catherine nodded. "I'm sorry. I just wanted to hear the talk on universals. I didn't think anyone would want to hurt me."

"No, you didn't think," Hubert shook his head. "This can't go on. It's time we found a convent for you, at least to let you be educated in safety. Now go. Obey your mother for once."

Catherine escaped.

That night, as she lay curled up in bed against the warm body of her little sister, Agnes, Catherine could hear the sound of her parents' voices from the alcove on the floor below. She couldn't make out the words, but the worried tone suggested that she was the topic.

At one time, her mother's voice rose, "Not Fontevraud, it's full of whores and men."

Catherine sighed. Her future did not look promising.

Two weeks later Catherine found herself on a barge sailing down the Loire River, another parcel in her father's stock of goods to trade, along with the barrels of Cistercian wine, incense, and spices. To her parents' astonishment, she had only given token resistance to the news that they were sending her to stay with the nuns at the abbey of St. Georges in Rennes in the wilds of Brittany.

The men who had followed her into the alleyway had frightened her to the core. Paris was her home. Yes, there were dangers. She could fall into the river or be run over by some nobleman on a horse. The King's son had been thrown from his horse and killed when a loose pig had crossed his path in the Paris streets. Fires were common. But she had never before been afraid of people. She was not so naïve that she didn't understand what the men had intended to do to her. But no one had ever so much as leered at her, as far as she knew. What had changed?

She began to wonder if her mother's constant warnings might actually be worth heeding.

Catherine watched a village glide by. It was a collection of a few houses with a clearing reaching to a wooden docking place. Children were gathering sticks for the fire. Two men were sawing a log. It would be winter soon.

When they arrived at Nantes, Hubert and Catherine were given a room near the palace of Bishop Brice. The wine was rolled into the cellar to enhance the Bishop's table for the coming year. Hubert requested an audience with Brice for the following day. He not only wanted to show him some fine amber from Muscovy, but he also needed documents to allow him safe passage north to Rennes.

"We'll be hiring horses here," he told his daughter. "You can ride pillion behind me. It won't be comfortable but it's only a couple of days. I want you to stay close to me at all times. Do you understand?"

Catherine nodded.

"This isn't a stroll to St. Denis, child," He had to impress her with the danger. "There are bandits and wild animals and demons lurking everywhere. The other traders and I are bringing armed guards, but they can't protect you if you wander off."

"Yes, Papa, I promise," Catherine's eyes were round with sincerity.

Hubert had his doubts. He wondered if he could chain her to his belt, but couldn't quite bring himself to humiliate her that much. He hoped he wouldn't regret it.

The road north was little more than a track. Branches hung low over it. They slapped at the riders, dropping dry leaves into their hair and down their tunics. Catherine amused herself by catching at the leaves as she rode by. Her continual movement was driving her father to distraction.

"Can't you stay still, girl?" he complained.

She leaned against his and whispered in his ear. "I have to go to the bathroom, Papa."

Hubert sighed. "We'll stop at the next clearing. It shouldn't long."

Catherine groaned. It seemed like hours before the path widened to a clearing with a spring to water horses and men. She slid off the horse and hurried into the wood.

"Don't go far!" Hubert shouted behind her.

Catherine was certain that she couldn't go more than the few steps required for privacy. She selected a spot where she could squat in the undergrowth next to an oak tree. After checking to see which way the ground sloped, she hoisted her skirts, leaning against the tree trunk. She gave a long sigh of relief.

She was just about to stand when she heard a deep growl nearby. Catherine peered cautiously around the brush and her breath stopped.

Not ten paces from her there stood an enormous black wolf. It was staring directly at her, teeth bared. She tried not to move a muscle as it slowly approached. She wanted to scream but was too terrified.

The wolf gained speed as it came closer. Its jaws opened wide and it leapt.

"Mother Mary, save my soul," Catherine whispered. She shut her eyes tightly, steeling herself for the horrible attack.

She felt the air move as he flew past her, smelled the musk of his fur. From the other side of the tree there was a scream abruptly cut off. The wolf's growl became a howl of fury. A moment later, he appeared, no more than a hand's-breadth from her face. The fur around his mouth was dripping with blood. His golden eyes stared into her blue ones and, in that moment, fear left her.

The wolf lowered his head and vanished into the dark woods.

Catherine exhaled and tried to stand. Her limbs were shaking and she could do no more than hold on to the oak as she tried to calm her racing heart. What had happened? The expression in the wolf's eyes had been almost intelligent, overflowing with sadness. But there was blood on his muzzle.

"Catherine!" Hubert's voice rang with panic.

"Here, Papa, here!" she called back. A moment later she was wrapped in his strong arms.

"*Siwazh din!*" One of the Breton guards had followed them. "Look at this!"

Hubert turned to look and immediately tried to cover her eyes with his hand. Catherine squirmed away. There in the brush behind the tree lay the body of a man with his throat torn out. His blood ran down the dry leaves and pooled on the ground. His short tunic was of rough wool, his pantaloons made of animal skins sewn together. Next to him on the ground was a long knife.

It took a moment for Catherine to make sense of this.

"He saved my life," she said in wonder.

"The poor man!" Hubert shook his head. "He drew the wolf's attention from you. But he wasn't quick enough with the knife. I wish I knew his name. We shall have Masses said for his soul."

Catherine shook her head, too, very slowly. "Papa, I didn't mean him. I think he was hiding in wait to rob me. It was the wolf who saved me."

Hubert patted her back. "Now, now, pet. You've had a terrible shock. Let's get you back. We need to reach the town of Fougerai before dark. I won't risk a night in the open after this. Here, you! Viard!" He gestured toward the guard. "Throw the body on one of the pack mules. We need to give him a decent burial."

Viard and his friend, Guémaroc, lifted the man's body and tied him to the mule. All the time they muttered to each other in tones of disapproval. Hubert heard them but was more concerned with Catherine than disgruntled guards.

Catherine said nothing as the party moved on, more rapidly now. She was still shaking. It didn't make sense. Why should a wolf rescue her from a brigand of the forest? And what was the word the guards kept repeating, *bleiz-laveret*? A shiver ran through her as she remembered tales a neighbor used to tell of her childhood in Brittany, of monsters and sprites that lived in the forests and caves. According to her, one could never trust that the world one went to sleep in would be the same one woke to.

Was the man really a man, Catherine pondered. And was the wolf really a wolf? If only she could have looked in the man's eyes, too.

The wolf loped far into the forest before he stopped at a stream to wash out his mouth. His stomach roiled at the taste of human flesh. And yet, deep inside, he knew he could get used to it, even crave it. He drank long. If that happened, nothing could save him.

The party rode in silence and haste to the town. The guards went first to the home of the mayor to deliver the body. After asking several people who apparently spoke only Breton, Hubert finally was able to find a room for himself and his daughter. The other merchants made do at a tavern, where they regaled the local men with the story of the strange wolf, even though none of them had actually seen it.

Viard returned with the mayor and his wife, Furnez. The men retired to the tavern while Furnez saw to Catherine.

"You poor child!" she exclaimed. "What madness possessed your father to bring you on such a trip?"

"I'm to stay with the nuns at St. Georges, "Catherine explained. "To learn how to behave properly and not get into trouble."

Furnez laughed. "Well, that may not be the best place to do it, *moumoun*. The abbess is well above eighty years old and I've heard that the discipline is not the best. But time enough to face that. For now, let's get you washed and into clean robes."

She took Catherine's hand. "You're freezing, little one! Viard said you'd had a near escape from the Wolf. Hot spiced wine for you, too."

Catherine let herself be led to the mayor's house to be fed and spoiled and to play with Furnez's two small children until water had been heated for a wooden tub in the kitchen. As she scrubbed herself, Catherine listened to Furnez helping the children recite their evening prayers. They said the *Nostre Père* and an *Ave Maria*. Then they added a prayer to a saint Catherine didn't know. "Lady Ségénex, protect us this night from the korrigans and their children, the poulpiquets, from goblins and spirits and the Black Knight of the woods, amen."

When the nurse had taken them to their bed and Catherine was dry and dressed, she asked Furnez about the prayer.

"Don't you ask for protection from the evil things that fly by night?" the woman asked her.

"Yes, but mostly demons and the spirits that suck out children's souls," Catherine said. "And who is saint Ségénex?"

Furnez smiled. "The lady is the ancient guardian of our people. She was once a pagan priestess and a great magician, but was converted by Joseph of Arimathea. When she died, she refused to go to Heaven as long as her people needed her. There are so many powerful creatures that still roam this land. The poor saint may be with us until the End Times."

Catherine could well believe this. Even Nantes had a feel of being only at the edge of the Christian world. She decided to tell Furnez about her strange encounter with the wolf.

"He looked straight at me and, he seemed sorry for me," she tried to explain. "Papa says I have too much imagination. But I still don't know why he didn't attack me."

Furnez had already heard the story from Viard and Guémaroc. "Was the wolf black all over with a thick shiny coat and bright yellow eyes?"

Catherine nodded. "Gold. His eyes were golden as the Moon when it first rises."

"I thought so," Furnez refilled her wine cup, adding only a little water. "Then it's a blessing that no one tried to kill it. That is Duke Conan's tame wolf."

"Then why didn't it have a collar or a muzzle?" Catherine asked. She wasn't surprised that the duke had a pet wolf. The nobility had all sorts of peculiar habits.

"I don't know that whole story," Furnez shrugged. "But I do know that it's a particular favorite of the duke and that it is supposed to be a model of *courtoisie*. If it killed a man, you can be certain it was to protect you from him."

Catherine was so sleepy from the wine that she had to be carried back to her room. The next morning, she told Hubert what Furnez had said about the wolf.

"Papa, I believe that the wolf was once a man," she said earnestly.

Hubert rolled his eyes. "Catherine, have you been reading Ovid again?"

"No, Papa! You told the Archdeacon that he wasn't to loan me any more pagan authors." The hurt from that still festered.

"If, as they say, the wolf belongs to the duke, then perhaps he was trained to protect," Hubert explained. "That's probably what the mayor's wife meant. But no one can truly tame a beast like that. Last night, one of the men at the tavern told me that recently at the duke's court the wolf took a dislike to one of the barons and tried to attack him. You see? The animal always breaks loose."

"I suppose," Catherine didn't believe him. "But perhaps the baron was a bad man. Perhaps the wolf can smell evil."

"Catherine," Hubert warned. "Why don't you save your argument for the nuns? I'm sure they know the situation better than either of us."

The next afternoon the party passed by the hunting lodge where Duke Conan was staying. The men all agreed that they should pay their respects to him. Each mentally went through their goods searching for something that Conan would discover he was in desperate need of.

They were told that the duke would see them as soon as he could. He sent out beer and sausage to help them pass the time.

"That's a proper lord," one of the merchants said as he took a long draft. "He remembers his duty to those…"

He stopped, the cup slipping from his fingers. He pointed at the shape coming out of the lodge.

"Wolf." He grabbed at the cup and emptied it without moving any other part of his body.

Catherine was still, this time in fascination rather than terror. The wolf seemed much more doglike here. It sniffed a passing cart and rubbed its side against a rough stone wall. No one patted it as they went by, but it seemed to be more from respect than nervousness. But there was no sign in him of human sensibility. Perhaps her father was right.

At that moment a short procession approached the lodge. There were two guards, a mule laden with packages and a woman, heavily veiled.

One of the men entered the lodge to announce the visitor. As she waited, the woman pushed her veil aside in order to see better.

Suddenly, the wolf froze, hackles stiff. It growled in much the same tone Catherine had heard in the forest. Before anyone could stop him, the wolf sprang at the woman, trapping her face in his fierce jaws.

"My God!" Hubert cried, but he could barely be heard over the pandemonium. Men with swords converged on the wolf as it dropped to the ground.

The woman was shrieking, trying to soak up the blood pouring down her face. Her veil and the front of her robe were stained vermillion. "Kill him!" she screamed. "Kill him!"

Her other guard raised his sword. The wolf paid no attention. His eyes never left the woman's face. With a gagging noise, he spat something on the ground.

It was her nose.

Hubert couldn't resist. "You see, Catherine? If you take in something savage, eventually it will turn on you."

"Yes, Papa," Catherine said absently. Then she ran toward the crowd. "Don't hurt him!" she cried. "Please don't hurt him!"

Oddly, others felt the same. The guard had been restrained. Others lifted the lady down and wrapped her face in cloths. Someone carried her into the lodge. Shortly after that, the duke came out.

"What is this?" he demanded, looking at his pet. "This is the second time you have attacked my guests. I thought you were an enchanted wolf, a courtly animal. You have never even chased one of my deer." He turned to his men. "There's nothing for it; he'll have to be put down at once."

"No!" Catherine tried to throw herself between the beast and the blade. "He saved my life. I know he's not evil."

The duke was startled by her interruption. "Who are you?" he snapped. "No, never mind. Jago, kill him."

Catherine began to protest again, but it wasn't necessary. The servant sheathed his sword.

"Please, my lord," he said. "I think we should consider this a moment. This wolf has been at the court over a year and been nothing but well-behaved. His courtesy has been the wonder of us all. Why would he suddenly attack two people?"

'This lady," another man spoke up, "She's Lantilde, the wife of Brochan, who was the first victim of the wolf. Perhaps the two of them have injured the animal somehow."

Conan regarded the wolf, who gazed up at him with the calm air of a knight prepared for death. The duke paused. He had grown very fond of his pet.

"Very well," he decided. "Put the animal in a cage. When the lady is able, I shall question her. Although how she could have offended a wolf is more than I can guess."

They went inside. Catherine started to follow but Hubert caught her.

"What are you thinking of? We don't belong to the court."

"I have to know what will happen to the wolf," Catherine explained. "I know he's more than a dumb animal, whatever you say. Even Duke Conan seems to think so."

Hubert sighed. "Don't worry, none of the others here intend to leave until the matter is resolved. This is a story we can use for years to gain entrance to the courts of other nobles. But you are not to simply wander into the lodge and make yourself at home. Your mother would be horrified."

The merchants set up their tents outside the lodge. If a few trades were made that evening, it was a bonus, but even if they lost money, not one of them would regret staying.

By the next morning, Lantilde's nose had stopped bleeding, although no one could replace it. She was carried into the courtyard on a litter and placed near the cage of the wolf. It growled at her a moment and then began to whimper, as if crying.

"I beg you, my lord," she cried, her voice muffled by the bandages. "Move me away from that monster."

The servant, Jago, had appointed himself advocate for the wolf.

"My lady," he began. "I grieve for your pain and disfiguration. You are the widow of Lord Paynel, my friend and one of the duke's most faithful knights, who vanished some time ago."

"Yes. His body was never found. We think he was killed by mad heretics."

The wolf stood alert, taking in every word. Catherine had managed to wiggle her way through to a spot near the cage. At the mention of the name Paynel, the wolf began to wag his tail. Catherine nodded in satisfaction. She knew she was right. Both Ovid and the Breton stories couldn't be mistaken.

Jago had also noted the response. He looked from the woman to the wolf and back again.

"My lord," he turned to the duke. "This animal has always shown itself to be gentle and docile, totally against the nature of a beast. I believe that there is a reason he hates this woman and her husband so. Since he cannot tell us, I suggest that she be put to the torture until she says what she did to the wolf."

Lantilde screamed. "Have I not been tortured enough by this unnatural creature! Look at me!"

Conan did. "It seems strange to me, Lady, that he only bit off your nose, rather than tearing out your throat. There are many mysteries in this land. My wolf may be one of them. Yes," he nodded to Jago. "Have her tortured."

"No! No!" Lantilde tried to sit up. "No, I'll tell you. Then you may understand how I have been tricked and humiliated. That monster is Paynel! He married me knowing that he was only a man half the week. I loved him to the point of folly. But when I learned what he really was, surely the spawn of a demon, I couldn't live with him anymore."

Catherine gasped. It was one thing to have one's speculations proven true in theory. It was quite another to look at a wolf and wonder who was inside him.

"I might have denounced him to the bishop," Lantilde continued, "I could have had him slaughtered by hunters or burnt at the stake. Instead, all I did was to hide his clothes so he couldn't change back to human form. I made him live all his life as the fiend he had always been."

She lay back again, exhausted.

The duke considered her story. "Is this true?" he asked the wolf. It nodded vigorously.

There was silence as everyone tried to take in this revelation. Catherine thought of the clerics who had wanted to rape her in Paris. She wondered if at night they returned to their true forms or if they always managed to hide their demons inside. It would be easier if she could have seen their real shapes.

"There is one way to prove this," Jago told the duke. "Bring Paynel his clothes."

Lantilde seemed even more upset about that than about losing her nose, but she was finally convinced to send a servant back to her castle with instructions as to the hiding place of her husband's clothing.

While they waited, Catherine and her father sat on a bench and shared some bread a cheese. They didn't speak, but Hubert put her arm around her shoulders and hugged her. That was enough.

The servant arrived late that afternoon with a parcel that contained a rough tunic, a soft linen shirt and leather pants. In a bag, he carried Paynel's hose and boots.

The clothes were put into the cage with the wolf. Everyone waited.

Nothing happened.

The wolf sniffed at the clothes, looked at the crowd of expectant faces and huddled in one corner of the cage, his tail wrapped over his head.

Duke Conan was bewildered. "Perhaps the woman is insane," he suggested. "She may have killed her husband and made up the story in case his clothes were found."

Catherine had been watching the wolf closely. She stepped forward.

"My lord?" She bowed as low as she could without overbalancing.

He looked at her. "Who...? Oh, yes, the little girl who says my wolf saved her. What do you want?"

"Um, well," Catherine knew she was going to sound foolish, but that had never stopped her before. "I think he doesn't want to get dressed in front of everyone. He may change back naked."

Someone snickered. Conan gave the offender a sharp look.

"Paynel always was a private person," he said. "Never liked to bathe with others. Very well. Jago, take the wolf and the clothing to my bedroom. Leave him there and we'll see."

Jago opened the cage and picked up the clothing. The wolf followed him with alacrity. Jago returned a few moments later.

People milled about, not sure what to do next. But they didn't have to worry. Almost at once there was the clop of boots on the wooden steps. A man appeared, his dark beard long and tangled, his hair matted with grease. But those who had known Paynel recognized him at once. He was embraced by his friends before he came to kneel before the duke.

"My Lord," his voice cracked. "Forgive me from hiding my affliction from you. It has been a deep secret in my family for generations. Because we knew ourselves to be beasts, we have always tried to be more than human."

He stood and regarded his wife. "I trusted you with the thing most hidden in my heart and you proved unworthy. I should have known better."

Conan got up from his chair and threw his arms around Paynel. "You are my loyal servant in both your forms. How many rulers can boast of such a thing? Welcome home!"

The next morning Catherine, Hubert and the merchants continued their journey to Rennes. The Sun pierced the mist and made the air sparkle and it seemed to Catherine that korrigans and fairies were peeking out at her from behind the trees. Already the adventure was beginning to seem like a fable, something she had been told rather than experienced.

And yet, tied up in her sleeve was a small silver ring, with a rough amethyst, a gift from a knight who was grateful that she had seen the man inside the beast.

(As for Lantilde, she and her husband were exiled to Ireland. It was rumored that they had several children, all born without noses.)

If one of the protagonists of Neil Penswick's story needs no introduction, his French adversary, Captain Georges Sauvin of the Deuxième Bureau, *a.k.a. the* Poisson Chinois *(because he's as ugly as a Chinese fish) does. He is a creation of writer Jean Bommart (1894-1979), who, after being wounded in WWI and being bedridden, became a writer.* Le Poisson Chinois *made his first appearance in the eponymous 1934 novel, which was filmed twice, in France in 1937 as* La Bataille Silencieuse *[The Silent Battle] with Michel Simon well cast as Sauvin, and in 1939 as* The Silent Battle *(US release* Continental Express *in 1942), with the handsome Rex Harrison in the role. In books, the character continued to entertain well into the 1960s, when he was involved in the Cuban Missile Crisis...*

Neil Penswick: *Legacy of Evil*

England, 1935

I could feel the May sunshine, on my face, as the motorcycle hurtled faster and faster. I felt a freedom not felt for years. As I enjoyed the ride, I saw two boys ahead of me on their bicycles and, for a moment, remembered my youngest brother and I cycling the roads in Oxfordshire some 40 years ago. I thought this was my happiest time. And then I realised I could finally be rid of *him...*

France, 1925

Sir Dennis Nayland Smith sat opposite me, listening intently.

"I came across the English village in the heart of the French countryside. There was a single-track road, which crossed a river just past the village green; an oak tree that stood as if it bore witness to centuries of history; and a church with an unmoving weather vane. There were animals in the fields. And there was a traditional thatched pub called *The White Swan.* Outside sat people: the numbers always changed. I don't know whether it was important, but the top floor window of the pub was open. Every day, at the same time, there was an eerie sound of hissing. And then the dying started. And it was truly terrible. Sometimes the people screamed. Sometimes they just seemed to go mad. Sometimes the animals died as well. But she wasn't happy about this. She shouted and bawled."

Nayland Smith held up his hand, "I've heard enough. Describe this woman."

"It's been almost ten years. But I'll never forget her. She was extraordinarily beautiful. I would think that she was Egyptian. In her 20s. Eyes of a true cat green."

"Think. Think hard. The future of all you hold dear, perhaps our entire civilization, depends on your answer to this question." Nayland Smith paused. "Could she have been Chinese?"

"She could have been the daughter of an Emperor."

"Damn," Nayland Smith stood and banged on the table. He was visibly shaking, "I thought the world had seen the last of him."

'Who?"

"I need to find this village. Can you take me there?"

"The war has been over for seven years. What can you hope to find?"

Nayland Smith stared. "It seems that the war has barely begun. The Great War was merely a distraction from a conflict of unimaginable proportions. And you, Mr. Shaw, and I, may be the only people able to stop the destruction of our world. We shall travel to Paris immediately. And let us hope that we are in time."

Later that night we traveled by air to Paris. The fog-shrouded journey to the airport had conjured many bizarre and unwelcome thoughts into my mind. Strange shapes and lights seemed to follow the taxicab like some hideous monstrosity stalking the police commissioner.

Had it only been 48 hours since I saw Dr. Petrie? I had been ill and was struggling for breath, particularly when the London smog rose from the Thames and laid siege to the capital. Petrie was a respected medical practitioner with a practice mainly serving veterans of the wars of Empire. He was sympathetic and listened to my story. I told him that I had served in the Great War and that I had been exposed to poison gas on the Western front. I don't know why I told him the rest of my story. I had never told anyone. There was something about his manner. A curiosity. I told him that I had been in the trenches, we had been attacked and been ordered to retreat. With hundreds of others, pursued by a yellow ghost. A yellow ghost that, by the end of the war, had slaughtered tens of thousands. Chlorine gas. I must have run for days when I collapsed onto some grass. When I woke, there was the English village in front of me. I was about 400 yards away from everything I loved about England. But I couldn't move. I couldn't shout. And they didn't see me. I lay there for ten days. And saw this insane performance played out again and again.

I expected Dr. Petrie would tell me that this was the side effect of the poison gas. But he didn't say that. Once I mentioned the woman, he became agitated. He demanded that I describe her. Having listened, he told me that I had to see a police commissioner, Sir Dennis Nayland Smith. He sent a telegram to Scotland Yard with a message of three words:

Fah Lo Suee.

Within hours, I sat in a small nook of a public house near Clapham Common telling my story to the police commissioner. I asked why I couldn't have met him in Scotland Yard. Nayland Smith replied immediately, "I no longer know who I can trust."

The police commissioner had been in contact with the Deuxième Bureau and a Captain Sauvin joined us. He was a youngish man, quite athletic, but remarkably ugly. I had heard of him. He was a rising star in the French Intelligence Service. The Frenchman grabbed me by the hand, "I am so pleased to meet you, Monsieur."

Nayland Smith interrupted, "Captain Sauvin has the highest awards for bravery that France can bestow."

The two men spoke together in French. My knowledge of the language is poor and all I recognized were three words: *le diabolique docteur*. And, as the conversation became more agitated, I also heard repeatedly that name again, *Fah Lo Suee*.

We drove across the scarred French countryside. Although the French had done much to repair the damage to their land, everywhere we saw the ruins of the Great War. Even the wonder of the fields of red poppies growing around us merely served as a reminder of the thousands that had perished defending the freedom of the Empire.

"I don't know how I could find the village again. I stumbled on it by accident," I told the two policemen. "I can't even remember how I eventually escaped."

"What shall I call you, Monsieur?" Sauvin asked.

"Shaw."

"But what is your first name?"

"Tom. Thomas Edward."

"*Mon Dieu*. What evil...?"

I found this rudeness contemptible. "I find your manner a little short, sir."

"Tell me of your family, Monsieur."

"I have a brother. He is a university lecturer."

Nayland Smith interrupted, "Do you have a wife? Children?"

"Sir, my personal life is nothing to do with you."

"Tell me, do you have a wife?"

I thought. I don't know whether I was still suffering from the effects of the gas, but I couldn't remember. I couldn't remember!

"I don't know."

"It is tiredness," retorted Nayland Smith. He looked over to Sauvin and signaled for him to make no further comment.

We stayed overnight in guesthouses and Sauvin interviewed the owners, fellow guests and neighborhood policemen. Nayland Smith explained to me that Sauvin's unsightliness had earned him the nickname of *Le Poisson Chinois*—the

Chinese Fish. He had a certain reputation. His task was to frighten people to insure that our presence was known in the region. Smith explained, "We are not trying to find a needle in a haystack. We want our enemies to find us." He explained that this approach had worked for him many times.

"But who are we dealing with? What is this enemy that threatens our Empire?"

"And the French Republic. And the Crown Heads. Even what is left of the sick men of Europe—the Russian Bear and the German Eagle." Smith paused for a moment. "In 1911, I was a police commissioner in the Eastern part of the Empire. I was investigating a series of brutal slayings on the uncontrolled border, between Siam and Burma, and heard again and again of 'the Chinaman.' Even for this part of the world, this was bestial. I once came across an entire village, which had been massacred. By strange creatures and weapons never thought of in our science. Anyone who was thought to have cooperated with the British was attacked. I pursued this further and discovered that this was part of a much wider plan. To stand up to the King and Country, and not just in the heathen East but at the heart of the British Empire."

I listened, unable to believe that our Empire had been under attack from fanatics.

"Between 1913 and 1917, London was repeatedly attacked. By devilish fanatics prepared to sacrifice their very lives. And we kept it from the press—and thank God we did—at a time when Europe was about to be plunged into war. For four years, we fought a battle as desperate as that waged on the Western front. Poisonous insects, monsters, demons, supernatural warriors and terror threatened everything we hold dear. Through the unholy abuse of corrupt science, the denizens of Hell were unleashed on our capital. But we won. We defeated the fiends: a vast organization stretching across the length of the British Empire. They called themselves the Si-Fan or the Council of Seven. By 1917, we had killed all of those in charge. And though their leader seemed to rise again and again from a certain death, at the end of the desperate struggle, he perished."

"But who is this woman?"

"She goes by many names. But we knew her as Fah Lo Suee. She was the daughter of their leader. Lethal and more dangerous than her father."

"And do you know her plan?"

"It will be no less than slavery, inhuman cruelty and the very destruction of civilization. To unleash madness across our world. I make no exaggeration when I describe that this is a battle as desperate as the Romans fought to keep out the barbarian hordes. And if we fail a new Dark Ages will descend."

I was aghast and, dare I say, scared.

As the Sun began to set, I watched Sauvin outside the small guesthouse lighting another cigarette. From the window, I could see for miles and hear the sounds of the French countryside. Cocks were crowing, grasshoppers singing and an occasional owl hooting.

I heard a gun snap. I glanced back inside. Nayland Smith was sitting on a small chair and loading his revolver.

"What is it?"

"They're coming."

Nervously I looked back outside. *Le Poisson Chinois* was lighting another cigarette.

"Shall I call Sauvin?"

"He knows."

"How do you know they're out there?"

Smith barked his reply. "What we've been listening to, for the last 25 minutes, is the sound of the Zayait's Kiss. The call of the dacoits."

"I haven't heard anything. Just the sound of the owls."

"There aren't any owls out there. I've counted two dacoits. Murderous thugs."

"Shall I move from the window?"

"They will not attack us. The Si-Fan rely on creatures from nightmare."

Outside the window, I saw nothing untoward. I picked up a small knife from a table and slid it into my shoe.

"That'll be unnecessary," Smith said, turning on the gas for the lighting. From outside, Sauvin coughed.

Suddenly there was a loud bang from above us. The ceiling itself seemed to bend. Suddenly, I heard a crash, quickly followed by the sound of fighting. I turned and saw Smith holding his revolver towards me. He moved closer and started shooting wildly out of the window. The door burst open and a giant ape-like creature burst into the room. It resembled a Sumatran orang-utan but had the head of a man! It screamed and rushed towards us. Nayland Smith pushed me to the window. He pointed his revolver at the gaslight but was too slow and the hybrid creature caught him with a glancing blow. Baring its teeth, the creature launched at Smith who ignored the menace and focused his gun and pulled the trigger, igniting the gas. The room exploded into an inferno. As it did, Smith pushed me through the window and into the unknown darkness of the night. I fell through the air and crashed onto the ground. Looking back at the burning room, I could hear the terrifying screams of the creature. Smith, struggling for breath, grabbed my shoulders.

I stood and tried to gain my bearings. Nearby, I saw a dacoit dead. Sauvin held the other with a grip tightly around the throat.

"We must go," barked Nayland Smith.

For some miles, I drove the car deeper into the French countryside. I didn't turn on the car's lights and avoided the roads, driving through bushes and over rough terrain. Nayland Smith nervously eyed the trail behind us. After approximately 20 minutes, Smith signaled for me to pull over. We waited a few more minutes as Smith listened. Hearing nothing untoward, he pointed for Sauvin to take the dacoit into the bushes.

I couldn't avoid, hearing. Many of the sounds, I can neither describe nor identify what they were. But together I imagined that I was listening to a man being slowly torn apart. Sauvin returned, expressionless but with blood staining his shirt.

"This is not the way of the British Empire," I replied indignantly.

"If we don't change, all that we hold dear will be lost forever," replied Smith.

Sauvin spoke quietly to him.

"Why does he only talk to you?" I asked.

"Because he doesn't trust you, Mr. Shaw." He emphasized my name. "We must move on. We now know where we are going. And it is to the heart of an evil empire."

"Why doesn't he trust me?"

"Because your name isn't Shaw. And where we are going, you will find out who you are and the terrible things that a cruel and evil woman named Fah Lo Suee did to you. Sauvin is concerned that this knowledge will drive you insane. If you weren't one of the greatest heroes this empire—or any empire—has ever produced, I would agree with him."

"I don't understand. What are you saying?" I said, astonished at this revelation.

Sauvin moved to the front of the car and gently pushed me aside. He started the car, turned on the lights and started to drive.

"We met in 1913 in Syria," Nayland Smith said to me.

"I have never been to the Middle East."

"Petrie recognized you and sent you to me. I was not greatly surprised that you didn't remember me—I was but a lowly police commissioner—but that your had no memory of your contribution to the Allied win in the Great War puzzled me. Once over here, I requested that the French supply Captain Sauvin. He knew you personally in Syria."

Sauvin interrupted, "Monsieur, you are a great warrior. You once saved my life."

"Sometime, and we don't know when, you fell foul of the Si-Fan fanatics. I suspect that your presence—as a representative of the Empire—and a fighter for the Arab cause—led them to decide that you had to be eradicated. You disappeared in 1922. Fah Lo Suee must have erased your mind."

"Was I important?"

"Some say that you ensured that we won the war."

"I don't understand. Am I not even called Tom?"

"Your name is Thomas Edward."

"But not Shaw?"

"Thomas Edward Lawrence. You united the Arab peoples into a revolt in the desert. The British press called you 'Lawrence of Arabia.'"

I shook my head in disbelief, "Who?"

The monastery was framed against the Moon. Its imposing figure, perched on top of a mountain, dominated the landscape for miles around. We stopped, abandoned the car and continued the trek on foot. To approach the monastery took us several hours. We barely spoke. Smith told me that I needn't go with them and that if I wished to stay behind then he would understand. I looked at my colleagues—the Scotland Yard detective and the French secret agent—and replied that although I didn't remember living as Lawrence of Arabia, from what they had told me, I would be happy to die as him. Sauvin patted me firmly on the back, calling me *mon ami*.

Getting closer, we passed a nest of gigantic cochroachs. They had caught a rodent and were devouring it alive.

"Another experiment," said Smith.

It was about noon when we arrived at the monastery. Together, we walked to the front entrance. And not knowing what to expect, we pushed the gate open and entered. An extraordinary sight lay before us. There was a large courtyard. And it was set up like an English country scene. Large painted boards. And, in front of them, a stage set of a public house called the White Swan with tables in front and a narrow strip of road running over a trench filled with water. The upstairs window of the public house was open and creaked in the wind.

"It looks like I have been here before," I said.

Sauvin walked round and stopped at the trench. "There are dead animals. Sheep. Cows."

Smith looked at the carcasses. "Don't touch them," Smith barked. "There is something about this place. I think I have seen this before."

Sauvin shook his head. "I see nothing but an abandoned monastery."

The window creaked, too loudly.

"We must go. Now!" Smith turned and started to head quickly to the gate. "I have no time to explain. We are in deadly danger." Smith stopped.

"Sir Dennis, how good to see you again," a woman's voice echoed out.

Sauvin and I looked to the window. There stood the most beautiful woman I had ever seen. It had been over ten years since I had last seen her and she had not changed. Her eyes seemed to radiate into my soul.

"Fah Lo Suee," replied the police commissioner. He pointed his revolver in her direction and pulled the trigger. However, before the gunshot sounded out, the revolver was knocked from his hands and he was wrestled to the ground. We were surrounded by a grab bag of assorted thugs and dacoits.

"Do not hurt them. Yet," Fah Lo Suee said.

Our weapons were taken away from us and we were forced to kneel. After several minutes of being held down, the three of us were made to stand. The

Chinese woman stood in front of us. She was dressed in red robes and adorned with gold jewellery.

"The mercy of my father was a weakness. Have no fear, Sir Dennis, I will kill you and your colleagues. The Si-Fan will be reborn."

"What you are doing here is vile. The people you intend to kill are innocent."

"None are innocent. Your Empire have exploited the soul of a people and now is the time for our revenge. Do you know what it is?"

"I don't want to know."

"It is a form of cockroach plague!" Fah Lo Suee laughed. "I have adapted the virus and purified it to ensure it is lethal for human beings. I have worked on this for many years. My plan is simple—to unleash it across your Western world."

"How?" I asked.

Fah Lo Suee stared at me. "You are going to die and yet you are still curious. Through a campaign of terror like this world has never seen. You would expect us to attack your capital cities or your centres of industry. Instead we have identified 100 small villages—Louth, Bonneval, Mittenwald—across the West of Europe. We have mapped the way the disease will spread, through the hissing cockroaches, and before anyone can stop it, millions will be dead."

"You cannot do this," Smith said. 'Even your father would not have stooped so low."

"I can do as I wish," Fah Lo Suee screamed. "I am the daughter of Fu Manchu!"

Suddenly, like a man possessed, I stood, grabbed the knife from my shoe, lunged forward and stabbed Fah Lo Suee. As I did this, Nayland Smith and Sauvin launched an assault on the shocked thugs. I stood over Fah Lo Suee, repeatedly stabbing her.

"We must burn this place down, destroy any evidence of this fiendish evil," shouted Nayland Smith. Sauvin was a killing machine and continued to attack—without fear—slaughtering the thugs and the dacoits.

"Smith," whimpered Fah Lo Suee, "help me." He glanced at her and quickly moved away. Fah Lo Suee looked at me and, barely audible, asked, "Who are you?"

She didn't know me! The woman who I had believed had wiped my mind did not recognize me. If it wasn't Fah Lo Suee who had made me forget my identity, then who was it? I held the knife but didn't stab her any further.

Suddenly, an almighty explosion rocked the monastery and I found myself thrown across the courtyard and against a wall. My head felt that it had exploded in pain. I struggled to stand. I could see the Chinese woman, dying on the floor and smoke and flames billowing out of the windows of the monastery.

It was almost two days later. The French had searched the burnt out monastery. Smith had ensured that whatever had been worked on in that diabolical monastery could never be used again. He'd also found tens of thousands of the hissing cockroaches locked in cages in the dungeons. He destroyed all signs of the biological warfare experiments. Altogether the bodies of 17 men were found. There was no sign of Fah Lo Suee.

I was exhausted. I was asked again and again by Smith why I had launched the attack on Fah Lo Suee. I couldn't remember what had happened. And now, aware that many of my memories were inaccurate, and that I had an identity of which I had no knowledge, I struggled to know why I behaved as I did.

Smith, Sauvin and I were escorted to the nearest railway station. The French military wanted to ensure that we left France immediately. We boarded a train and were shown into a private carriage. I sat in the corner, staring out of the window. As the train sped away from the station, I closed my eyes and fell asleep. I don't know how long I had slept. I felt a violent shaking as the train seemed to slow down again. I opened my eyes.

Sitting in front of me, in an otherwise empty carriage, was a solitary figure. Of extraordinary age, perhaps even a thousand years old. Long yellow robes, shaven skull and cat-like green eyes. Fu Manchu!

"Mr. Lawrence. You have served me well and have taught my daughter a lesson. She will survive and, in the future, I trust will follow the true path and make her father proud." Fu Manchu paused. "If this fails, then I will need to punish her in an even more terrible manner. And this will pain me."

"It was you that kidnapped me and wiped my mind!" I screamed at him. "Why?"

"There can be no greater honor than to serve Fu Manchu." He lent forward and raised his hand in front of me. "Now sleep. I call upon my warriors again and again."

"You have morals. You prevented Fah Lo Suee unleashing her biological weapon on the West."

Fu Manchu looked puzzled. "I stopped my daughter from wasting the resources of the Si-Fan on an empire that has decayed and fallen. Your British Empire is no more. You just do not know it as yet. There are other, greater Empires growing."

I began to shout, "Smith." Fu Manchu seemed to smile and then fade away. By the time that Nayland Smith reentered the carriage, there was no sign of the devilish doctor.

"What is it?" Smith barked.

I thought for a moment. "A nightmare."

Smith looked concerned. "You are safe."

"Yes, now I am awake. I know that." I looked back out of the window. In the night sky, I thought I could see the face of Fu Manchu and in the rattle of the train, speeding to its destination, hear his voice issuing a warning to the civilizations of the world.

"The world shall hear from me again."

1935

The motorcycle had crashed. I had reacted in less than a second and now lay with broken bones by the side of the Devon road. To some the thoughts of death would have been worse than the pains of a broken body. But I was content. Happy with my life. And happy now to be free of the mind of Fu Manchu. I heard one of the boys say he had phoned for the ambulance. I muttered that he needn't do this. I begged him to leave me. I don't know how long it took but I heard the bell of the ambulance heading along the country road.

"I am free, I am free," I shouted, feeling the life draining from me. I must have been covered in blood and could barely open my eyes. "Please let me die," I begged.

"I cannot do that, Mr. Lawrence," replied a female oriental voice. I forced my eyes open. It was Fah Lo Suee! "I am taking you to the master."

"No!"

"Fu Manchu decides when you die. Not you."

I screamed.

World War I is often featured in Tales of the Shadowmen—*for example, in John Peel's "The Biggest Guns" in Volume 6 or Matthew Baugh's "What Rough Beast" in this volume—but few have depicted its horrors as boldly and viscerally as Pete Rawlik in this story, which brings together music and murder, art and science, in a unique and macabre fable entitled...*

Pete Rawlik: *The Masquerade in Exile*

Northern France, 1916-17
(written in 1922)

Much has been written of the Great War, and indeed I have set forth my own accounts of my exploits in the trenches with my constant companion and fellow Doctor Herbert West. But I have, until now, refrained from writing of one of our adventures out of respect for those who were involved. Yet, this day, the paper brings notice of disaster in the Antarctic and, with it, the sure death of the polar explorer Comte de Chagny. The report states that he died heirless, just short of his 70th birthday, and that his title will transfer to his nephew, Emile Belloq. No mention is made of his wife and son, who vanished so many years ago at the height of the war. Strange how the papers have such short memories, but I suppose that the war did its best to wipe clean the memories of newsmen, either through death or simple overload of information. Still, as I appear to be the last living participant in those strange events, I see no reason why I should not convey the tale, and let the truth be known.

Doctor Herbert West and I came to fight in the Great War in service to the Canadian forces, not as soldiers but as medical personnel, and I must admit we did not volunteer wholly out of a willingness to serve our Hippocratic Oaths. No, our motives also included a desire, an unwholesome need, to have unfettered access to a supply of both the freshly dead and the dying. With such specimens, and in such quantities we could further our experiments into the science of re-animation, and perhaps given our skills as researchers and some luck, we might have found the key to resolving the problem of death itself. If only we had realized the truth of how deluded we were. That war is no place for men of science; that war devours not just truth and innocence, but rational thought as well.

We came to the war hoping to find the cure to one of man's greatest flaws. Instead, the war corrupted us and we inevitably sunk into depravity, finding dark joy in carrying out the most twisted and amoral procedures on the mortally wounded committed to our supposed medical care. None were safe from our predations, for we experimented on allies and enemies alike, of all ranks from the lowliest private to the most highly decorated officers. Even those who knew of our secret tests were not immune from our machinations. West and I hardly hesitated from experimenting on our commanding officer and colleague Major Eric Moreland Clapham-Lee when his plane crashed during a battle in Flanders in March of 1915.

This is not to say that West and I did no good upon the field of battle. I particularly remember the Battle of the Somme, which raged from July through November of 1916 near Belloy-en Santerre. This prolonged engagement brought me wounded from around the world, including a trio of Legionnaires. Though I could do nothing to save the poet Alan Seeger from his mortal wounds, I was able to do better by his comrades Randolph Carter and Etienne-Laurent de Marigny. After several weeks of care, and with the capture of the Ancre River, conditions in the war-torn countryside and of my patients were sufficient to ship the two and others to Paris for recuperation. Both West and I had grown weary of the frontline, and when the opportunity came to rotate to a field hospital several miles back, we eagerly volunteered.

The Chateau d'Erlette was a small manor whose master had volunteered it as a staging area for injured troops to be taken to for stabilization before being moved to more competent facilities further away. Our liaison was a young American with a pale appearance and wild hair named Helman Carnby, who explained as he drove us to the house, that his lady was the wife of a well-respected member of the aristocracy who was serving overseas in some undisclosed capacity.

The war had not been kind to the landscape. The roads had been turned into paired ruts of mud and filth bordered by running mounds of debris. The refuse of years of human conflict littered the barren frozen fields of fire. Denuded trees stood like reapers, skeletal sentinels watching over the few emaciated cattle that still roamed the once lush farmlands. There was no other animal life to speak of, save for the two horses pulling the cart. The war, hunger and disease had taken their toll. What animals had survived the battles and the need to feed its soldiers had fled to less unhealthy places. Over all of this dismal landscape hung the vilest of stenches, an unhealthy blending of rot, gun smoke and the strange metallic scent of bitter deadly cold; a miasma that would have sickened weaker men, but one West and I had grown use to.

The chateau was built on a squalid grey hill overlooking fields of crop stubble and clods of frozen earth. The building itself was originally of medieval French architecture all gothic arches and flying buttresses, but it had long since become a chimera of features including heaped renaissance ornaments and baroque symmetrical facades that had long since cracked and fallen into disrepair. In the barren hellish countryside of war-torn France the Chateau d'Erlette was just another horror to inflict on the already shell-shocked populace and the men who had come to make war on their land.

The interior of the house was as bleak as the exterior, lit by meager oil lamps that did little but turn the deep shadows a murky grey. Only the flaming fireplace provided any real light and heat. Without invitation both West and I gravitated toward the comforting blaze, while Carnby went to fetch his mistress. It didn't take long before West was browsing through the various accoutrements of the room.

"Daniel, these books, this library, there are things here that not even Miskatonic has."

I wandered over to where West was perusing the shelves that lined the walls. It was a fascinating collection of volumes highlighted by the most wonderfully dark titles, some that puzzled me.

"West, I thought I had read all of the works of the Marquis de Sade, but these: *Los Reliques*, *La Cure de Prato*, and this *Tancrede*, I've never heard of these."

West nodded and pulled down a strange, green, leather-bound volume. "This is an original copy of *Cultes des Goules*, written in 1665 by the Comte d'Erlette. Most of these were burned during the Revolution. I've been trying to see the University copy for years." Just then my colleague audibly gasped and I watched as he carefully replaced the precious *Cultes de Goules* and lifted out another folio, this one heavily beaten and stained. "I thought this was a myth: *The Pretorius Commentary on the Journals of Victor Frankenstein.*" He clutched the book with two hands unable to look away from the cover, like a bird caught in the gaze of a snake.

"If you prefer, Doctor West, you may study that volume while you are here." The voice was angelic full of music and poetry but controlled. There was a trace of an accent, something Scandinavian, but the diction was perfect. We turned to face the source and did encounter such a vision that both of us were stunned into silence. Our hostess was an older woman of substance and grace. Her iron grey hair and firm figure were accented by an air of self assurance and pride. When she moved, she glided across the floor and not a hair on her head fell out of place. Had it not been for my medically trained eye, I would have thought her in her mid-forties, but certain lines around the eyes and spots on her hands suggested that she might be well into her fifth decade of life.

West stepped forward to greet the charming woman. "Lady d'Erlette, I presume? You honor us with your hospitality."

I went to make my own greeting, but was quickly silenced by our hostess. "I am sorry, Doctor West, but the House of d'Erlette is all but extinct, at least in France, put down by the Crown and the people one too many times to survive. Though I hear there may be surviving members in the Americas. These lands are now held in trust by the family of my husband, the Comte de Chagny. You may address me as Comtesse de Chagny."

With these words I recognized her immediately. "Comtesse de Chagny, your talent and fame are second only to your still radiant beauty. Your likeness still hangs in one of the halls at the Paris Opera. We are at your service."

She nodded almost imperceptibly. "You are too kind. I have prepared a meal. Afterwards, we shall show you the patient wards."

She led us out of the hall and into a once grand formal dining room, now fallen into disrepair. The table had not been polished in years, and the chairs were threadbare with signs of dry rot. But the single course that Carnby served to us, a simple roasted pig with winter vegetables, was welcome after so many months in the trenches eating nothing but rations. The meal was accompanied with a bottle of house wine, an extra dry, sweet rosé that reminded me of the days of my youth, when my parents would host lavish parties on New Year's Eve.

After the meal, the Comtesse de Chagny and Carnby took us to the wards. I was taken aback when Carnby unlocked a heavy oak door revealing a poorly lit stairway made of stone leading down into the bowels of the house. As we proceeded by torchlight, our hostess explained that the house had been built over an ancient and vast series of catacombs which were used for a variety of purposes, including storage for the vineyards and refuge in times of trouble. Under the current state of war, she had ordered them converted to a ward for injured soldiers.

As she remarked on this last usage, we rounded a corner of the descending tunnel, passed through yet another door, and found ourselves viewing the most astounding of sites. The cavern before us was a large tunnel approximately 30 feet wide, 20 feet tall and stretching a good 200 feet back. Light was provided by a series of ornate chandeliers hanging from hooks drilled into the ceiling which illuminated what I can only describe as a makeshift hospital ward. Four rows of beds ran the length of the cavern, only a few of which were occupied by soldiers in various states of injury. Six women milled about, tending to the wounded and discharging various other duties as if they were trained nurses in a city hospital. All in all it was a magnificent operation, though one could see the weaknesses that simply could not be overcome. There was a shortage of linens and of proper clothing. Many soldiers still were dressed in the tatters of their uniforms, which revealed them to be of a variety of nationalities, including French, British and Canadian. Actual medical supplies were lacking, and we could see that many of the patients were suffering from either infection or crippling pain.

Though such conditions would normally lead to a cacophony of screaming, such cries were absent, replaced instead by the sound of a viola playing the most mesmerizing of melodies. It was a tune so hypnotic that it calmed even the most seriously injured patients. As we moved into the cavern, I glanced upwards, following a wrought iron ladder set into the wall beside the entrance. There above the passageway, hidden behind a curtain, was a small alcove which was apparently the source of the music. Light from within the room cast shadows on the curtain and revealed the musician as he gracefully played his instrument. Never had I heard such music before, and I wondered aloud about the identity of the composer. The Comtesse de Chagny smiled and casually informed us that the violinist was her son, and the piece he played had been written by his father as part of an operatic masterpiece entitled *Don Juan Triumphant*.

Without hesitation, West and I began evaluating the conditions of the patients and the abilities of the ward itself. From what we could gather, the majority of the patients had come from a single skirmish that had begun not far from the vineyards. A running battle, the injured had been left where they fell and the Comtesse de Chagny, unable to tolerate the screams of the wounded, had organized the staff and pulled the survivors from the fields. There was some talk amongst the staff and amongst those who were rescued concerning the equal treatment of enemy soldiers, but that was quickly squelched. Carnby was brutal in his reprimands and stressed to the wounded and caretakers alike that the Comtesse herself was not French, and that accidents of nationality should not come to bear in determining who received aid and who was left to die. That was not to say that tensions did not run high, but all arms had been confiscated from both factions. The only things left for them to fight with were their minds, their hands, several decks of cards and a chess set.

There were 13 patients in the cavern and, while most were well on their way to recovering from minor wounds, some were not. Based on West's assessment, there were two legs and one arm that needed to be amputated as soon as possible. Additionally, there were numerous bones that needed to be set, and several infections that needed to be drained. Sadly, there were three cases that West saw no hope in wasting any effort on trying to save, including a poor soul who still had a bullet rattling around in his skull. West, with Carnby's help, had these three moved to a different room, one with a strong door and medical restraints. I knew that West had identified them as potential subjects for his reanimation experiments.

In a similar room, we constructed a surgery. Sadly, the equipment and supplies available to us were simply inadequate. Some resources had been liberated from abandoned field hospitals, but the supply of sulfa-drugs, pain killers, and proper bandages were woefully low. When he inquired about anesthesia, the matron in charge pointed to a small cask of brandy and then laughed. West cursed and then made sure that his patient had three shots of the liquor before downing one himself and cutting off two of the young man's gangrenous fingers.

"Just remember," lamented West, "this isn't Hell."

I gagged as the man I was holding down vomited under the pain of having his leg rebroken. "No," I said, "not Hell, but on a clear day I wager you can see it from here."

Working through the middle of December, West and I kept to a strict schedule of tending to the wounded. While such a routine left little time to strategize or experiment, West found a way to re-organize the make shift staff and cavern, and created a small ward for the isolation of those patients that were behind the hope of any normal medical practices. In this, we were aided by Carnby, who we found to be an able assistant and particularly skilled in translating the languages of the soldiers that made up our patients. Born and raised in Oakland California, Carnby was the minutes older of twin brothers that had decided to dedicate their lives to the study of the occult. Helman Carnby had come to France several years ago to specifically visit and study the library at the Chateau d'Erlette. When the war broke out, he found himself unable to abandon the Comtesse de Chagny, and stayed on in her service, all the while studying the vast collection of grimoires and occult treatises.

We were also assisted by one of our patients named August Dewart. This young Briton, whose bald head, flat nose and beard reminded us of a goat, had a significant amount of medical training, and despite the loss of a leg, extremely helpful as a medical and surgical assistant. Roaming around the ward on a pair of crutches, he made sure that everyone was talked to at least once a day.

As for our gracious hostess, we saw her often. Daily she would come down to the ward, climb the ladder to the curtained alcove and accompany her son's playing with her prodigious vocal talents. While such performances were beautiful to listen to, there was such an undercurrent of sadness and despair to the Comtesse de Chagny's voice and her son's violin, that I and others were often moved to tears when they performed. During this entire period, it was rare for us to catch even a glimpse of the virtuoso, and when we did see him, he always wore a matching set of a full crimson mask and gloves such that no flesh was ever seen.

The impending holiday was apparently weighing heavily on the officers in charge of the front lines, for the number of new patients we received shrunk to a mere trickle, and West and I found ourselves able to spend time in the laboratory and surgery that West had cobbled together. All three of our special patients had long since succumbed to their wounds, and all three had then been subjected to the re-animation reagent, though this was but the first stage in a new direction of research. Inspired by the Frankenstein journals and from several pieces of correspondence, we had taken it upon ourselves to pursue the possibility of using the re-animated as sources for the transplant of organs from one body to another.

Our primary inspiration for this were letters from the New Zealand surgeon Harold Gillies who had left the battlefields and was fumbling his way toward actually being able to carry out skin grafts and facial reconstruction in the British Isles. Similarly, the notes we received from Doctors Alexis Carrel and Charles Guthrie, who had pioneered vascular transplants and were kindred spirits, were just as inspiring. Carrel's transplant work had won him the Nobel Prize in 1912, and when he stopped in Arkham to lecture on the nature of cellular senescence, West and I were compelled to meet him and demonstrate our reagent. Taking a small sample with him, Carrell began a most controversial experiment, in which for more than 30 years he publicly sustained a culture of embryonic chicken cells using only a nutrient solution of his own devising. Similarly, Guthrie had also wandered down areas generally shunned by medical science. There was strong suspicion that the Nobel was awarded to Carrel over Guthrie not because he was the superior researcher, but rather because of Guthrie's rather unorthodox and successful experiments with transplanting canine heads. Photographs of his two-headed animals, while fascinating to the medical community, were considered blasphemous monstrosities by conservative and unenlightened old men who held the reins of power and money.

Yet, it was from the genius of these men that we began to formulate our own plan to resolve the problem of organ transplant. Using our reagent to inhibit rejection, we experimented in the transfer of skin tissue from one patient to another, before moving on to the actual exchange of limbs and then, finally, organs. In the end, we had no choice but to follow in Guthrie footsteps and remove one of our patient's heads and then graft it to another body. Our experiments taught us much and, soon, we were discussing the possibility of transplanting limbs and organs from one of our re-animates to a living subject, and we both agreed that young Dewart would be our first patient.

We made shadowy arrangements to carry out the experiment as soon as possible, but even as we girded ourselves for the extended surgery, we were accosted in the hall by Carnby who sent word that the Comtesse de Chagny wanted to see us immediately in the great hall. With young Dewart already prepared, we left him on the table unconscious, but secured to the table, instruments waiting.

In the house above, we were ushered into a magnificently apportioned study in which both the Comtesse de Chagny and her masked son awaited us. In her hand was our journal, the record of our experiments over the last several weeks. West started to protest, but I placed a hand on his shoulder and told him to wait.

Once we were seated, Carnby began to speak."As you may be aware, my lady, when she was much younger, vas the victim of a most obsessive admirer. It was only through the heroic efforts of her fiancé, the then Vicomte Raoul de Chagny, that she was able to escape his unwanted attentions. Sadly, while they both escaped with their lives, the Vicomte's older brother was not as lucky. Raoul became Comte de Chagny; he and Christine were married, and soon after, they welcomed a new life into the word." As Carnby continued, the Comtesse lowered her eyes. "However, it was plain at his birth that the child wasn't Raoul's, but rather that of Christine's unwelcome admirer. Devastated by this betrayal, her husband banished the Comtesse and her child from the de Chagny household, and forced her to reside here. This is where she and her son have lived for the last 34 years; it has become their home, the only one the young master has ever known. The Comtesse cannot imagine how her son will fare when he is forced from this place..."

"For what cause would the young man be forced from this house?" asked West.

The Comtesse de Chagny rose and turned her back to us. "My husband is given to moods, Doctor West. I have, over the last 30 years, been able to assuage him, but I am not long for this world. My doctors tell me that I have a cancer growing inside me, that I have little time left. And while I go to my reward without regrets, I cannot allow my son to suffer the rage that will be inflicted upon him by the Comte once I am gone." She turned toward us, eyes pleading. "He must be prepared for life outside these walls. We have been watching you for these last few weeks, and we have read your notes on your experiments. We think it may be possible that such procedures could be directed toward other kinds of conditions, congenital conditions. If my son is to survive in the world, he must be acceptable to it, his deformities must be made less pronounced. He must appear more human."

West rose, and I could see that he was prepared to reject her request. I knew his mind, and he had no reason to pursue such noble obligations as they in no way served his secret ambition. So rather than let West speak, I quickly spoke for both of us. "Comtesse, you have been most hospitable, and we have abused your trust. If it is within our power to help your son, then we shall do so."

I waited briefly for someone else to speak, but then the Comtesse motioned and her enrobed son rose up and stepped toward us. "Zann, would you show these doctors why we need their services," she said.

If the music that the man produced was hauntingly beautiful, then the musician himself was hauntingly tragic. The man that stood before us as his robe, mask and gloves fell away would have terrified any commoner on the street. Skeletally thin, with no sign of body fat and little muscle, the virtuoso's skin was yellow, translucent, and almost parchment-like. He had no nose, only two large gapped slits that sat above a slashed, lipless mouth. His eyes were red on a yellow background, and deeply sunken. On top of his head there were only a few wisps of jet black hair. Had I found this man in one of the trenches that I had so recently left, I would have thought him long dead from starvation and dehydration. That he resembled nothing so much as a walking corpse does not do justice to the tragedy of the poor creature's condition.

I overheard West ask Carnby: "His name is Zann?"

Carnby shook his head. "No, No. Zann is a pet name; it means 'ornament,' for the way he use to cling to his mother's leg as a child. His mother named him Erik, after his father."

I turned my attention back to my patient. "Erik…" I forced myself to adopt the mildest of manners with this patient. "Erik, my name is Doctor Cain, Daniel Cain; I would, with your permission, like to examine you."

The man-monster hesitated and then spoke, and his voice was deep, full of inner darkness and mystery. "Doctor Cain," each syllable was pronounced with intensity, "you will forgive me if I seem reticent. Since my birth, I have been hidden from the world, a world that would fear and despise me, and a world that, given the opportunity, would kill me as it killed my father. I think therefore a moment of caution, before exposing myself to anyone, is prudent."

I took a step forward. "Erik, I find that position to be entirely logical, even admirable, but if you let me, I may be able to find a way to change that and make it so that you never have to live in fear again."

I spent the next three hours examining the poor creature. I poked and prodded, looked in his ears and his throat, took samples of his skin and his blood. I checked his reflexes, his heart rate, and blood pressure and flashed a light in his eyes and checked pupil response. What I found surprised me. Despite all of his physical deformities, Erik's nervous system and constitution were remarkable. His strength and speed were preternatural. His senses, particularly his hearing, were highly acute. Furthermore, Erik's ability to not only repeat but perfectly mimic any sound, using either his voice or his ever-present violin, was simply uncanny. His instrument was like a part of him and he never set it down, and only paused in playing it when it was absolutely necessary. This made examining him both difficult but strangely enjoyable as well. The only person who seemed immune to Erik's monstrous charms was my colleague, Herbert West.

It was then that the nagging thought that was scratching at the back of my skull burst out. I looked at my watch and cursed as I dashed out of the room. West and Carnby were on my heels, but sadly we were all too late. Poor Dewart who had apparently awoken hours ago had done what any man would have done. Unfortunately in his attempts to free himself from the table restraints, the entire apparatus had upended and tumbled down on to the poor man. Apparently unable to obtain any leverage with only one leg, he had slowly been smothered.

As West and I attended to Dewart, Carnby ran off to inform the Chagnys. In his absence, we righted the table and repositioned Dewart, checking to make sure the straps were intact and tight. Then, without an afterthought, I lifted up the man's head and West plunged a syringe full of our green bioluminescent reagent into the base of his skull. Laying his head back down, I took up my pocket watch and my notebook and observed the progression of our patient as our reagent began to work. As always, the first reaction was an uncontrolled spasm of the entire musculature sending the body bucking wildly against the restraints. This was followed by a sudden period of calm in which the eyes and indeed all of the senses suddenly began to work again, sending the patient into frantic hysteria as previously silent inputs suddenly overwhelmed the brain with massive amounts of information.

As he lay there, eyes dashing about, Carnby, the Comtesse de Chagny and Eric walked into the room. The timing was unfortunate, for it was at this moment that Dewart entered into the next phase of the re-animation process, and it had absolutely nothing to do with the fact that Erik had forgotten to don his mask. Dewart's lungs began to work once more, and this, coupled with the sudden flood of sensory information to his brain, created an automatic response that we had seen time and time again. From Dewart's lips issued the most horrid of sounds, a cry of anguish so terrible, so soul wrenching that both Erik and his mother began to weep.

As Dewart collapsed into a heap of raving muscle, Erik turned to Carnby and spoke. "I thought you said he was dead?"

Carnby was either too stunned or too confused too answer either way. West looked at the trio with that curious half-cocked head that indicated he couldn't tell whether someone was joking or just being stupid. "He was dead!" he shouted as he straightened his coat and shirt. "I brought him back!"

Once we were settled, West and I began discussing options on how to deal with Erik's condition. Initially, we thought about transplanting Erik's head, but this direction was rejected primarily, because it did nothing to resolve the issue of Eric's face, but also because it relied heavily on the constitution of the donor body, and the suppression of various rejection processes. If we were unable to resolve the rejection problem, it would be unlikely that we could reverse the procedure. Therefore, we focused instead on transplanting significant amounts of skin and vascular tissue, primarily from re-animated donors. However, since the procedure we envisioned would require significant surgery, we quickly but crudely began to assess prospective blood donors. We assessed all of the patients, Carnby and even the Comtesse. Several of the patients were compatible, as was Eric's mother. Once she learned she was compatible, it was made clear to us that she was going to be his primary blood donor.

Our agreed upon plan was simple: after determining compatibility, we would systematically remove Erik's face and hands, and replace them with samples harvested from the re-animated. The rest of his body could be hidden by clothing. Unfortunately, the first part of the surgery would be the most experimental and the most painful. In order to confirm the compatibility of the reanimated donors, Erik would be subjected to three simultaneous transplants, one from each of the donors. These, we would do on his lower back, and in rather large sections. It was our hope that all would be compatible, but the reality we faced was that the odds of rejection, even with the reagent acting as a suppressant, were extremely high.

We began the first stage of surgery early one morning in one of the many bedrooms in the chateau, by intoxicating Eric with liberal amounts of brandy until he passed out. Carnby helped us strap him down to a makeshift table, while the Comtesse was set up in an adjacent bed. West commented on how poorly she appeared and she simply nodded and whispered that the strain of the last several weeks had made her extremely tired. West and I both knew that tiredness could not explain away the weight loss and unhealthy pallor she had adopted in the last few days, and I suspected that the disease that was ravaging her body was progressing rapidly.

Carefully, I removed four strips of skin from Erik's belly, while West went off to obtain replacement strips from our donors. Each donor was colored coded Blue, Red, Green, or White, so that there would be no mistake as to the origin of any successfully transplanted tissue. Carnby acted as a go between, bringing each strip up from West's laboratory to me as it became available. I worked as fast as I could, suturing in tissue first from Blue, then Green, then Red and finally White.

As I tied off my last piece of silk, I noticed that West had not yet returned from the catacombs to join me in evaluating the response of Erik's body to the transplanted tissue.

Leaving Carnby with explicit instructions, I dashed down into the catacombs and flew into West's lab. There, I found West violently pinned to the wall by the patient designated Green, but whom I immediately recognized as Dewart. The soldier's hand was wrapped around West's throat, dragging him up against the cavern rock. Grabbing a wooden chair, I smashed it against Dewart's remaining leg sending the man to the floor and West sliding back to the ground.

Brandishing the leg of the now shattered chair like a club, I helped West up while keeping an eye on his attacker who floundered, unable to right himself with only one leg. Having some experience with such uncontrollable patients, West and I proceeded to strap Dewart down to his bed, and then gag him as well. We checked on the remaining donors, who all appeared secure, and then returned to the surgery to monitor Erik's progress.

After a few moments, it was clear that Eric's body was rejecting three of the samples. The flesh around the transplants had swelled up, become red and warm to the touch. Agglutination of the blood between the recipient and the donated tissue was apparent, even with the reanimation agent acting to suppress rejection. Fearing a serious reaction West crudely ripped through my sutures and threw the offending tissue into a waste bin. He cursed as he studied the last transplant area which showed no signs of rejection. We had found a compatible donor; unfortunately our only compatible donor was August Dewart.

West ordered Carnby to follow him, and the young scholar soon returned pale and frightened. I had a sneaking suspicion of what he had seen, but medical procedure we were endeavoring to undertake allowed no time to coddle the meek. I took the two strips of tissue that West had carved out of Dewart and quickly sewed then into the vacancies created by the earlier rejection. As I finished, West appeared with a third strip and that was quickly installed as well.

We waited an hour. The tension was high, Carnby knew something unseemly had just happened, but either didn't or couldn't understand exactly what that was. I could see he wanted to tell the Comtesse de Chagny something, but he remained silent. For our part, West and I periodically checked the transplant sites. While the original donation seemed to be well received, we both feared that the re-animated tissue would complicate the procedure. Fortunately for both of us, the treated tissue showed no signs of initiating an adverse reaction. Without hesitating, I began to work on removing the skin from Erik's head while West left to obtain the replacement tissue.

I began my incision on Eric's chest just below the neck, and then made cuts that traveled over each shoulder heading toward his back. Then, carefully and with Carnby's help, we lifted Eric and I connected both cuts at a spot just between his shoulders. I then sliced from the back up his neck and over the rear of the skull. With care, I gripped both flaps and peeled the skin away from his body, much in the way that you would peel an orange, on occasion using my scalpel to slice through areas of difficult connecting tissue. Once I was over the shoulders and the crown of the skull, I had Carnby hold the body up as I pulled the now hood-like mass of skin up and off of our patient. The resulting skinless apparition was monstrous to behold. Thankfully, the Comtesse de Chagny had mercifully passed into unconsciousness before the bloody raw shape of her son's head was ripped out of his skin.

Moments later, West arrived with the replacement flesh, including the cartilaginous tissue we needed to construct a nose. I nodded, thankful that, for once, he had put medical care above experimentation. West had performed nearly the same cuts as I had, so once the nose tissue had been pinned in place it was only a matter of wrenching the new skin over the skull, centering the face into place and then trimming and suturing it at strategic places to take up slack. The whole procedure took less than an hour. After which we took a moment to admire our work. Erik's new face was not particularly handsome, but it was a vast improvement over his own. He was still bald, but at least now he had a nose, although this last feature was rather large and flat. Combined with the mustache and beard that had belonged to the Dewart, Erik looked like nothing so much as an operatic Mephistopheles.

Making sure that Erik was fully unconscious so that we could begin the next stage of the procedure, we were suddenly interrupted by a great and violent wailing, the source of which was obviously deep in the catacombs. West and I, accompanied by Carnby, dashed down the stairs to find Dewart free from his bonds and flailing about the room. Skinless from the chest up, the creature was like some ghoulish revenant who had come back to seek revenge on his tormentors. Furniture was thrown about the room, glass shattered, instruments flew, and, as we three moved in to subdue the monster, I saw it grab a slightly phosphorescent syringe, and the vial of glowing fluid that lay beside it. West and I could do nothing to stop what happened next. The syringe flew across the room like a dagger only to lodge in Carnby's right shoulder. The vial was thrown as well, shattering against the wall and spraying reagent across the other reanimates. Enraged and empowered either by the events or by overexposure to the reagent, the three patchwork soldiers ripped through their bonds and began to lurch violently toward us.

Knowing full well that a disaster had been set in motion, I grabbed Carnby and ordered us all back up the stairs. West furtively grabbed his medical bag and followed us. We could hear the creatures thrashing about the room as we stumbled frantically away. Hearing the screams, the few nurses that were on duty came rushing into the hall. I ordered them up the stairs as well, but they paused in confusion. It was then that the door to West's private lab burst open and the creatures began to stalk down the hall and into the ward. They were horrid visions of phosphorescent death, killing the other patients without pause or remorse. Worse were the traces of reagent that they carried with them, which seeped into the wounds of their victims, spreading the plague of arisen dead throughout the catacombs.

Overwhelmed, and with the nurses in tow, we reached the top of the stairs and slammed the door shut, bolted it, and then lodged a large masonry statue between it and the floor. The nurses fled out the front gate into the night. Carnby fled toward our surgery, while West and I immediately began to think about how to deal with an apparent rampant reanimation problem growing underneath our feet. Our ruminations were shattered when Carnby cried out that the Comtesse de Chagny was not breathing.

I sprung to her side and checked her vitals. She was cold, so very cold, with no heartbeat or pulse to be found. I cursed my eyes. The Comtesse de Chagny had not passed out at the sight of her son's surgery; she had succumbed to her cancer. I shook my head indicating that she had been dead too long, and that there was nothing conventional that could be done to save her.

West and I exchanged knowing glances, which Carnby caught. Never before had I seen such a look of resigned terror on a man's face. Helman Carnby knew what we planned on doing and knew that there was nothing he could do to stop us. Resigned, he slunk out of the room and left us to our own devices. What we did next needed to be done; it was what the Comtesse de Chagny had asked us to do; and it was what she would have wanted us to do.

Erik's surgery went well and, in the end, the skin transplants on his face and hands healed quickly and his recovery was rapid. He suffered a bout of melancholy over the loss of his mother, but he had been prepared for that event and overcame that tragedy as well.

As for the things beneath the house, we only ever opened the door once and then only briefly to add one last victim of our reanimation reagent to those who roamed below. Only Carnby, West and I knew the truth of what had happened that night, and we all agreed to keep it from Erik, believing that the less he knew the better.

We foolishly hoped that the catacombs would have contained their horrid secret, but it was not to be. As we tended to Erik in our snow-bound fortress, the moaning that had leaked out from the great door slowly ceased. We all suspected the worst, but all of us refused to open the door and venture below. Our suspicions were confirmed when word reached us from the nearby village. War crazed soldiers had pillaged the local towns, attacking and killing residents without mercy. Inevitably, one of these madmen was captured and hung for his crimes. When the body with its broken neck refused to cease moving, there was talk of necromancy and the superstitious peasantry quickly consigned the undying thing to a raging bonfire.

The winter held horrors for those in the trenches as well. Reports of diseased soldiers carrying out ghoulish acts on both sides of the lines were rampant and added fuel to the vile rumors of the German *Kadaververwertungsanstalt* or corpse-rendering works. Likewise, frequent were the reports that echoed those of the Angels of Mons, of a spectral lady in white with red gloves, who would roam the field of war, singing the most beautiful of operatic arias. Troops seduced by her siren song walked out into the no man's land between the trenches and were never seen again.

In March, the thaw was such that the four of us packed up what things we could and made our way to Paris by horse and cart. Carnby took what portions of the library he dared, and I know that West absconded with *The Pretorius Commentary on the Journals of Victor Frankenstein*. Erik took his violin, a tintype of his mother, as well as several volumes of music and librettos, but left the vast majority of his life behind.

Once in Paris, we met with the managers of the Paris Opera, and, with the aid of letters from his mother, he obtained a position in the orchestra under an assumed name. West and I returned to the front and served and experimented until the Powers called an end to hostilities. Carnby took passage to the United States and returned to California to study with his brother. I heard that, many years later, something untoward had occurred between the two and both were lost when their Oakland house caught fire.

Over the years, I corresponded with Erik. He was perhaps one of our greatest scientific achievements, and I longed to follow his progress. He quickly became something of a minor celebrity, renowned for his music, his baritone voice and wicked appearance, all of which allowed him to be cast in various productions concerning supernatural forces throughout 1918 and 1919. His last letter to me was dated from 1920, after his return from a tour of European capitals in which he performed as the Devil who travels to Tbilisi in Georgia and challenges a young farm hand to a musical duel. Sadly, the tour had seemed to take a toll on the young man. He had lost his voice, and the skin on his hands and face seemed to have aged dramatically in just a few weeks. He wondered if, after all these years, he could be undergoing a rejection of the transplanted tissue. I wrote back suggesting a course of treatment and the possibility of my coming to examine him personally. I never heard from him again and my inquiries at the opera house were ignored as well. Still, I treasure the review Erik had sent me from his London performance:

While some would suggest that the production currently on stage at the London Opera House caters to the less refined tastes of the populace, this critic finds that the performance of Erich Zann to be a significant contribution to modern operatic endeavors. Zann's performance as the Devil is complemented not only by his physical appearance but also by his nearly divine vocals. Moreover, his voice is complemented perhaps even surpassed by his technique in playing the violin. So magnificent is his bowing style that it is my humble opinion that those most magnificently delicate hands must have been a gift from God himself, or perhaps stolen from some fallen angel of music.

Frank Schildiner has fallen in love with the character of 1950s archeologist Jean Kariven, a dashing hero who investigates signs of hidden extra-terrestrial activities amongst Earth's long-lost civilizations, created by the popular French science fiction writer Jimmy Guieu. In this latest yarn, the dashing Kariven encounters...

Frank Schildiner: *The Tiny Destroyer*

Detroit, 1954

"I think you will discover that what I am to show you is of some interest, Dr. Kariven," Ikano Kato stated, lifting a small metal canister out of the Detroit Museum of Art's vault. The cylinder was slightly over a foot high, yet the powerfully built Kato was lifting it with some difficulty.

"When I received your request I was intrigued, especially since *le Frelon Vert* saved my resistance cell from that German Baron with the nasty dueling scars," Jean Kariven replied with a chuckle. "The nasty little man was never caught after the war, I am sorry to say."

"According to Mr. Reid's sources, he may be hiding in Japan. I do intend to search for him when I return home," Kato replied, fishing out a long, complicated looking key and opening the canister.

Kariven looked surprised and smoothed his pencil mustache unconsciously. "I had not heard of your plans to return to Japan, my friend. What of your partnership with Mr. Reid?"

Kato smiled briefly and began to open the cylinder, "We will still work together from time to time, but my country needs my help to rebuild. I could no longer ignore my responsibilities. Possibly, our sons will take up our mission and continue the battle someday. But you did not come here to reminisce; this is why I contacted you in London."

Kato placed a small figurine on the metal table and stepped back. The sculpture was about six inches tall and made from brown colored clay. Its legs and arms were short and thick, and its body was covered in what appeared to be a metal styled armor. But the most remarkable feature was its head—or better yet, the "helmet" of the sculpture, which resembled an old-fashioned diving helmet, though with goggle eyes instead of a porthole.

"A Dogu!" Kariven breathed, drinking in the remarkable sight. *"C'est magnifique!* Where did you get this item, my friend?"

Kato smiled again. "Oddly enough Mr. Reid discovered the cylinder in a hidden safe. His cousin, a former FBI agent named Martin, was killed in California. This canister, which appears to have been the property of a Dr. Melcher, was locked away safely. It puzzled us, so we resolved to contact an expert."

Kariven pulled a magnifying glass from his pocket and examined the statue. "A Dogu is, according to reports, a fertility figure of prehistoric Japan, specifically the eastern region. All, other than this one, were found broken, for some reason. However I do not believe they are fertility symbols..."

"Truly?" Kato asked, sensing Kariven was about to reveal something important.

"Yes," Kariven said, not looking up. "I believe they are a symbol of death. The intentional destruction of these sculptures was meant to ward off the destruction of the land. These tiny creatures were once weapons of great power..."

"Correct again, Dr. Kariven. For a human, you do have an eye for details," a voice stated from across the room. A tall, sparely built man, with short blonde hair, a black suit and dark sunglasses stepped into the light.

"*Mon Dieu!* Everywhere I turn, I encounter you! Will you, Polarians, ever leave us alone?" Kariven cried.

"You know of the Polarians and the Denebians?" Kato asked, shocked.

"Oh yes! I encounter them like the common cold," Kariven snapped. "Tell me, Polarian, what device have we stumbled upon now?"

The Polarian agent appeared unruffled by Kariven's outburst. "The Denebians have used your world in the past as testing grounds for some of their worst weapons. You should thank us for removing them."

"We do, of course, but your ancient war with the Denebians places all of humanity at risk," Kato said.

The Polarian nodded, acknowledging the statement matter of factedly. Then he continued, "A Dogu in ancient Denebian is a parasite that destroys the organism it inhabits. This device, loosed upon a world, could multiply endlessly and consume everything, eventually turning your planet into a lifeless rock."

"How horrible!" Kariven said, shaking his head. The Denebian weapons he had encountered were always frighteningly destructive! "What can we do to disarm it?"

"The lead-lined cylinder prevents the Denebians from locating the Dogu. Return it to its canister and I will take it to a special storage facility we maintain on your Moon. There, it will be harmless," the Polarian said, his tone as calm and emotionless as ever.

"I suspect you may have ulterior motives," Kariven said, looking at Kato, who nodded slowly. "Yet your people have always behaved benevolently toward humanity, so we will do as you say."

"Too late!" a woman said, stepping into the room and leveling a black rod at the Polarian. She was taller than him, with the icy beautiful sculpted face of an Egyptian Queen and long jet-black hair that fell to her shoulders. She would have resembled a fashion model, except for her pale green skin.

Kariven shrugged in a very French manner. "Where comes a Polarian, a Denebian must follow. No doubt you will start with threats, then attempt to kill us all."

The Denebian threw back her head and laughed. "For an upstart monkey, you're amusing, human. As Deputy Marshal of the Fourth Strike Force, I answer only to the High Scientist. He has allowed me to activate this Dogu should the opportunity arise. I have already done so."

"But you and your warriors will die as well!" Kato said, while slowly reaching beneath his jacket.

"No, we shall have left this misbegotten planet before the parasite consumes it. Farewell, humans!"

Upon that last statement, Kato fired his gas gun into the Denebian's face. She fell without a word.

"This is terrible," the Polarian said. "Once a Dogu is activated, even the Denebians can't stop it... Your planet and all life upon it are doomed..."

"How does the Dogu destroy worlds exactly? Tell me everything you know, it's our only chance!" Kariven said, his mind already forming a plan.

"The Dogu absorbs everything as a resource to reproduce itself. It grows exponentially and consumes every element. This one is drawing power from the very air we breathe right now. Soon, there will be two, then four, eight, sixteen, and so on until there is nothing left but Dogu!"

Kariven turned to his friend. "Mr. Kato, if you would be so kind—please use your rather impressive physical skills and break an arm or a leg off of this gruesome artefact."

"With pleasure," Kato replied and yelled, "Hiyyyaaaa!" as his foot lashed out and smashed into the Dogu. The figurine flew off the table and crashed to the ground, an arm and a leg from its left side shattering into pieces.

The stood and stared at the tiny, fallen figurine. It did not move, lying still and broken, completely inert. Several minutes passed and nothing changed.

"That was it?" said the Polarian, shaking his head, finally breaking the tension. "A simple blow and one of the Denebians' greatest weapons is destroyed? How did you know?"

"Simple enough. All Dogu found to date were broken. I surmised that the ancient Japanese determined that that was the simplest means of deactivating them. Our earliest ancestors appear to have been smarter than all of the Denebians and Polarians together," Kariven said. Kato began to chuckle.

"I wouldn't go that far, but we are grateful to you both," the Polarian said. Then he turned and noticed the Denebian was gone. "She has escaped, of course. I must pursue her. Farewell to you both."

"Let us hope she leads him away from our world," Kato said, picking up the broken figurine. "We could do well if both empires left Earth in peace."

"I fear that's unlikely," Kariven said. "Until that day, those of us who know the truth must ever remain vigilant. Now, I think we may safely dispose of the Dogu. I shall be happy if I never see another again!"

Stuart Shiffman, who penned the comical "The Milkman Cometh" in Volume 5, offers a new and amusing take—almost a spoof—on the murky world of spies, Istanbul, the Orient-Express, Nazis, Turkish coffee, madcap archeologists and English Lords in...

Stuart Shiffman: *Grim Days*

Istanbul, 1938

"This is a rather lovely view of the Golden Horn. The light is so wonderful near dusk..." said the tall, slim, blond man with the monocle to his hostess. His nose might be deemed a trifle larger than ideal, but he gave the impression of handsomeness and composure.

Indeed, this inlet of the Bosphorus sparkled in the twilight. There was an elegant view of the Topkapi Palace Museum in silhouette.

"As Chesterton's *Lepanto* says: 'From evening isles fantastical rings faint the Spanish gun, And the Lord upon the Golden Horn is laughing in the Sun.' You were very fortunate, Mrs. Rittenhouse, to have found such a villa, and one in a modern mode. Don't you think so, Spaulding?"

Lord Peter Wimsey addressed this last remark to a man with Levantine features sitting beside his majestic, middle-aged hostess. Captain Geoffrey Spaulding, a man with a fiercely humorous mustache and expression, and a scarlet tarbush perched on his dark curly-haired head, puffed on his cigar. His formal wear looked the worse for wear compared to the blond Englishman's own immaculate white tie and tails.

"We had discussed renting a Venetian villa, or some estate on the French Riviera," replied the lady. "Dear Geoffrey pushed for a hotel in Florida, but there is just nothing quite like the mystery of the East and the weight of centuries layered onto ancient Constantinople."

"Oh really, Mrs. Rittenhouse, it's more like the sewage of millennia when the wind is blowing towards the house," quipped Spaulding. "Some folks like that sort of thing, of course. Perfumiers charge a mighty pretty franc for Charnel no. 5."

"Oh, Geoffrey," giggled Mrs. Rittenhouse, "you mustn't tease us this way! Lord Peter will take you seriously."

"I would never take Captain Spaulding seriously," drawled the Englishman. Closer up, one could see that his butter-colored hair was being lightened by gray. "Being a notorious African explorer, he must find it hard to adapt again to our civilized modes of banter." He smiled a bit to show that it was all said in good humor. "Do you know my friend, Major Brabazon-Plank, Captain Spaul-

188

ding? He is currently leading an expedition up the Amazon, trying yet again to find a trace of Colonel Fawcett."

"Oh, I remember Plank—a rather wooden fellah, a chip off the old block, if I dare say so," replied Spaulding. "I suppose that it is better to go up the Amazon than be up the creek, but I usually find the major and minor faucets pretty easily by the bathtub."

"Oh, all these military men off on their missions of exploration!" exclaimed Mrs. Rittenhouse.

"They will be otherwise occupied soon," said Lord Peter quietly.

Spaulding's valet, Emanuel Ravelli, who looked like a music-hall idea of a curly-haired Italian rustic, whispered in the man's ear and drew him away in great haste. Mrs. Rittenhouse sniffed at this with the aristocratic hauteur of the neglected patroness.

Suddenly, Lord Peter no longer felt like trading banter any longer with the charlatan explorer. At the corner of his visual field, he caught sight of a serious-looking man in Turkish officer's uniform watching him. He was a man in his fifties, with iron gray hair in a severe brush-cut, whose hawkish nose seemed the prow of a warship.

"Colonel Haki, hello," said Lord Peter, going to shake his hand. "I did not expect to see you here!"

"He is an interesting fellow, that Spaulding," the man said to Wimsey, "and, I suspect, less of the charlatan and jester than the façade he presents to us. Have you thought, Milord, what a wonderful cover that might be for an intelligence agent, to be dismissed as being beneath anyone's notice, and yet to be able to travel widely and suddenly to all kinds of destinations?"

"No, I am afraid that it never occurred to me that the good Captain might be more than the clownish figure he presents."

"I am nonplussed that this is a new idea for you!" said the Turk. "It is axiomatic that you are seldom deceived by mere appearances, Lord Peter. Surely, this is not a pleasure trip for you. I had heard that you had married a couple of years ago, and now have children. Is the Lady Wimsey here with you?"

Lord Peter knew that the dour, but basically likable, Colonel Haki never heard gossip by accident. His old dossier must have been updated at the headquarters of the the *Milli Emniyet Hizmeti*, the Turkish National Security Service. It was as he had always suspected: Haki knew everything

"No, my wife did not come away with me this time, Colonel. I am here in response to an offering by a dealer in antique books and incunabula, in this case looking at acquiring a manuscript by Torquato Tasso."

"A shame," replied Haki. "One learns so much when one meets a man's spouse." He motioned Lord Peter to sit on a red art deco armchair, while he took the ottoman. "Please tell her how much I have enjoyed her novels—you will recall that I am an aficionado of the *romans policiers*. There has been little from her in the last year or so."

"Harriet has noted that she has had difficulty in continuing to write murder mysteries at a time when the greatest criminals have been nation-states which seem to commit their murders with impunity."

"She sounds like a woman of valor and wisdom. Although I had devised a perfect mystery plot of my own involving a murderous majordomo..." Haki thought for a moment. "We need to meet and speak more freely tomorrow, Lord Peter." He passed a slip of paper to the English aristocrat. "I know that you have a busy schedule, meeting with government officials and opposition leaders, and not book dealers, my lord."

Lord Peter was no longer surprised by the thoroughness of the Colonel's information. Over the last few years, the aristocratic investigator had spent a substantial amount of time in Continental Europe, acting as an unofficial attaché or on an occasional diplomatic mission for the Foreign Office. This little trip to the ancient seat of the Byzantine Empire was partially informational in nature, having been set by the Foreign Office, with the involvement of the Old Man of Military Intelligence, Sir Henry Merrivale.

"Yes, I know that you have the most *sub rosa* of assignments from a certain erstwhile former nautical gentleman," continued the Turkish officer.

Haki knows, thought Peter, *he knows that I am also one of former Lord of the Admiralty Winston Churchill's troublesome young men, even if I am more troublesome than young anymore. How interesting and deplorable.*

Tomorrow's meeting would be... fascinating.

Lord Peter gazed on the Hagia Sophia and slowly let out his breath at the beauty of the structure. He consulted the slip of paper again, to make sure that he had reached the correct address, and quickly crossed to the small café that Colonel Haki had designated. He snaked through some sidewalk tables and slipped into the comfortable shadows within.

Haki was there, in the rear of the café, with his back to the wall, smoking a *nargile*, a Turkish water pipe, already burbling away. His suit today was a cream-colored silk. He seemed less the vulpine secret policeman and more the sleek jungle cat.

Wimsey was intercepted by the café owner, a florid Greek apparently named Charlambides, also burbling. His café was the finest, he said, and he was infinitely honored by the Englishman's business; he had a cousin in America who was a famous and wealthy detective, and another in London's Soho who had a fish and chips shop. Before he recited the names of all his children with their school reports, they were greeted by the Colonel.

"Let the Milord sit, Nikko," said Haki, "and bring us coffee to start."

Wimsey took a chair at the small round iron-filigreed table, placing his hat—a silk-brimmed, black felt Homburg in the Anthony Eden style from Jno. Bodmin of Vigo Street, Royal Warrant as Bespoke Hatter to the Royal Family— and silver-headed walking stick there on the beaten brass of the tabletop.

"I see that you already have a pipe going, Colonel," he said, taking out his cigarette case bearing the Wimsey arms and flipping it open. "I have Morlands of Grosvenor Street on one side, and the more mundane Whifflets on the other. Morlands doesn't provide coupons, you see."

Lord Peter had devised an advertising campaign for them years before during his sojourn with Pym's Publicity, Ltd. He withdrew a Morlands and lit it from his lighter, adding to the fug in the café.

"I quite understand, Milord," replied the Colonel, drawing another puff from the *nargile*'s mouthpiece.

"So, Colonel Haki?"

"So, Lord Peter?"

The nobleman knew how well connected Haki was: he had been the intelligence chief for Syria and Palestine and, after the war, had become one of Kemal Ataturk's men. Zia Haki had been a deputy in the provisional government of 1919.

"Colonel, I don't have too much patience for your peculiar brand of misdirection," said Wimseym with a subtle twist of the mouth. "You intimated that you had information or knowledge of my activities.?"

"Indeed," said the Turkish secret policemen. "I know that you have been 'taking the temperature,' as it were, of our local notables towards the German and Italian regimes. You are among those Englishmen not satisfied with their own government's policies."

"Is that so, Colonel? I have not made any secret of my attitude towards those threnodies of failure, Neville Chamberlain and his cabinet of appeasers."

"On the other hand, if I may be so bold, you don't necessarily broadcast that fact *too* widely, Milord."

"After the Premier and Daladier stood by and let the Austrian *anschluss* happen, I don't have a lot of faith in their honor or intention to stand by and prevent the dismemberment of Czechoslovakia or any other small nation."

"You don't expect that the English Parliament will push back against the appeasers?"

"My dear Colonel, have you ever met any of the members of our parliament? Chamberlain and the Tory whip have them all intimidated. My friend Lord Ickenham had it right: 'As weird a gaggle of freaks and sub-humans as was ever collected in one spot. I wouldn't mix with them for any money you could offer me.'"

Wimsey paused. It wasn't quite true, he was friendly with a number of the troublesome young men that angered Mr. Chamberlain and Sir Edward Leithen so much.

"You are getting more information from me than I am from you, of course," he added.

Colonel Haki smiled and took another puff of his pipe.

"I have my own ideas about the National Socialists and Fascists, Milord. I even bought a copy of Herr Hitler's book, *Mein Kampf*. It occurred to me that it might shed a spot of light on all this... business. Have you read it?"

"Never had the time for that sort of reading," replied Wimsey.

It was not true. He had purchased a copy at Hatchards bookstore and had read it with growing horror, and thought it the worst sort of poisonous rot. Despite no longer being in his cricketing prime, he had taken it out to a field and batted it through the wicket. And that particular English-language edition was supposed to have been abridged and edited for content!

"I understand they give a copy to all the bridal couples over there," said Haki.

"Ah, I don't think it's that sort of book, Colonel. But I can't abide those bully types and their imitators: Oswald Mosley, Roderick Spode and the other British fascists—each of their movements symbolized by a different item of black clothing. Black shirts, shorts or coats—politics are more than a matter of choice of fashion."

"Do you expect war, no matter the efforts of Daladier and Chamberlain?"

Wimsey sniffed at the question.

"Oh yes, Colonel, I do, because the German Chancellor has an appetite that won't be satisfied by discrete nibbles at this or that county. The Premier seems to think that dissent with his policy of appeasement is unpatriotic, but I believe that dissent may be the highest form of patriotism. In fact, if patriotism means being true to the principles for which your country is supposed to stand, then certainly the right to dissent is one of those principles."

"I saw a revue once upon a time, where the comedian's antic premise was that war's damage could be forestalled by his special 'anti-war patent.'"

"What 'patent' was that, Colonel?" Wimsey took a deep pull at his cigarette and let the smoke slowly pour out of his lips.

"The comedian's proposal was that the soldiers of both sides should exchange uniforms. When the Germans see the Frenchmen in their German uniforms, they would think that their foes were Germans and not fire. And then the same with the French and all the others."

Wimsey laughed. "What about civilians caught between the armies?" he asked, raising an eyebrow.

"Oh," replied Colonel Haki. "I think that there, you have put your finger on the flaw in the comedian's patent for an end to war, Lord Peter!"

"On the night train to Munich," began Wimsey, on a new conversational spur line, "I discovered myself sharing a railway compartment with several archaeologists: Professor Horatio Smith of Cambridge University, a brilliant but absent-minded chap—I was at Eton and Balliol with his brother Sir George, the current British Ambassador to Germany—the American Dr. Henry Jones, Jr. and a French archaeologist, Professeur Aristide Clairembart..."

"Clairembart?" exclaimed Haki. "I remember him from before the War, when I was a senior intelligence officer in Syria and Palestine. Rather like a whippet with a white mustache and chin beard? He seemed rather dottering at first, back then, but turned out to be whippet-taut and quite durable. He was competing with Leidner for excavation permits in Syria and Mesopotamia. Is he still pursuing his phantom lost cities?"

"Very much so, Colonel. In fact, Clairembart was going on and on about the mysterious lost city of El Dorado in the Amazon, that old will-o'-the-wisp that claimed the life of Colonel Fawcett, as well as other jungle-lost sites of the Mayans in the Yucatan."

"That sounds like the Clairembart I knew. You should know that later, I discovered that he was providing intelligence to Colonel Dubois of the French Deuxième Bureau. Mind you, Leidner was doing the same for you British in Egypt."

"Really? Well, not a surprise, I suppose," said Wimsey with another drag at his cigarette. "It's all a matter of the Great Game, no matter who the adversary is. In any event, the esteemed gentlemen began to ramble conversationally hither and thither: a recent bit of urban legend about an English governess who was supposed to have disappeared from the Orient Express, and the usual odd political developments in the States. And then, there was talk about Mr. Bandicott, a rich American amateur archaeologist who discovered the tomb of the great Viking chieftain, Harald Blacktooth, in the Scottish Highlands..."

"If you don't mind my saying so, it sounds as if your company was well lubricated, Milord," said Colonel Haki, with a sly smile.

"I do believe that I remember, somewhat vaguely, that Clairembart had a credible bottle of Calvados that was passed about, and Smith had a flask of Scotch whisky in a tippling stick. But it was at this point that someone, whether Smith or Jones I cannot recall, brought up the notion that the current situation needed a new Scarlet Pimpernel to arise."

"A Scarlet Pimpernel?"

"Don't you remember? A heroic figure during the French Revolution. He rescued aristocrats from the guillotine under the very nose of Robespierre."

"A counter-revolutionary figure, then?" asked Haki.

"Don't play with me, Colonel. I know that you are acquainted with him as his biographer was also the authoress of some fine detective tales."

"Yes, perhaps I am," Haki acquiesced. "So this putative Pimpernel would be guiding out such assorted political dissidents, scientists, artists and racial enemies out from under the eyes of the Gestapo?"

"Exactly right, the idea being to put one in the eye of Reichminister Von Graum, the Chauvelin of our times," explained Wimsey. "We tried to think of a cover for this, which was rather a brain-beater at first. Then, Smith realized that a workable plan would be to get permission from the *Ahnenerbe* to excavate in search of an ancient Aryan civilization—which, naturally, is as much tosh and nonsense as could be."

"But consistent with Nazi Party doctrine!" Haki exclaimed. "I see! Do you think that Smith will do it—become a new Pimpernel?" He took a new puff from his *nargile*.

"That is the question, isn't it, Colonel? I wish that I knew the answer so that I could help him. Smith is intellectual and genteel, the seeming antithesis of the two-fisted adventurer like his colleague Jones. He even carries a photograph of Aphrodite Kallipygos in his wallet! I wouldn't be surprised if he did take it on, however, just to draw a line in the sand for the thugs and bullies."

"We need more people willing to place their lives and sacred honor on the line. Of course, those who do are not always on the same sides…" Haki looked thoughtful for a moment. "Have you ever heard the name 'Jimgrim?' No? Major James Schuyler Grim, at the time of the Great War, was an American working with British military intelligence, first out of Egypt, and then for General Allenby. He was my 'player on the other side,' my *bête noire*, during the war, particularly where Palestine was concerned."

"I was on the Western front at that time, Colonel."

"My adversary got to know me too well and could anticipate my countermeasures in Palestine and Syria following the Arab uprising. He slipped into our territory, interviewing people while posing as an American journalist before his people entered the war. Jimgrim even penetrated my intelligence offices in Jerusalem several times. We Turks thought that we understood the arts of suppression and extortion of the locals, being well-practiced over the centuries. That explained the hangings outside the Jaffa Gate during the war and how determined the Arabs and the Jewish settlers were to see the backs of us afterwards. Of course, after the armistice, and the British had control, and then the mandate, Jimgrim saw a different aspect of the situation there…"

"The moral of the story is therefore what, Colonel?" Wimsey put out his cigarette.

"War and secret intelligence does not provide morals because the story of war always continues, Milord. That is something for the priests and mullahs and the philosophers to determine. My point is that you must understand the psychology of the individual, the player on the other side."

"Ah," said Wimsey, "I am a mere parfait, gentil knight, Colonel Haki, and must do my duty and hold to my honor as well as I can."

"Do I presume that your squire Bunter waits outside?"

Wimsey rose to his feet, flicked away a few stray bits of tobacco from his suit, and took his hat and cane in hand.

"'Let me pack and take a train/And get me to England again,'" he quoted. "Rupert Brooke, you know. Thank you for your company today, Colonel."

He sketched a bow and handed some bills to the proprietor, pleasing Charlambides greatly, before walking out.

"Do you need anything, Haki Pasha?" asked the café owner.

There was a shot in the street before the secret policeman could answer. Nikko Charlambides sped out to the sunlight to see what there was to be seen.

There was a blond man in a dark suit laying in the street, a policeman standing over him. He could tell that the man in the street was not Wimsey.

Haki came up behind Charlambides's bulk.

"There is the Milord," he pointed out to the café owner, "with his manservant in the bowler hat. And there is the mysterious Captain Spaulding and his man Ravelli, pulling back from view—the men standing in the shadow of the other doorway."

"The dead man—he is a German spy?" asked Charlambides.

"It is impossible to say. I suspect that he is holding a Swedish or Argentine passport, or some such. Nevertheless it is impossible to arrest and detain people without absurd legal formalities." Colonel Haki turned to go back inside. "More of your excellent coffee please, my dear Nikko."

We don't often have the opportunity to publish a swashbuckler in Tales of the Shadowmen, *which is why Bradley Sinor's contribution, which brings together Alexandre Dumas' Milady and Rafael Sabatini's Captain Blood is particularly welcome, especially in a volume entitled* Femmes Fatales, *since there's hardly any villainess more beautiful and deadly than Clarice de Winter...*

Bradley H. Sinor: *The Screeching of Two Ravens*

The Caribbean, France, 1685/1625

Captain Peter Blood stared into the fog that had surrounded his ship for hours. The sea air was heavy and still, just as it had been since shortly after two British men-of-wars had been spotted closing in on the *Arabella*. Minutes later, a fog bank had rolled in out of nowhere, wiping the wind away and wrapping the ship like a heavy grey blanket.

Blood held a small knife in one hand and had been slowly whittling away at a piece of wood he had picked up from one of the ship's carpenter's barrels.

"I've never seen anything like it," muttered Jeremy Pitt, who was standing close to Blood. In the months since they had taken their freedom and the *Arabella*, the former ship master had become one of Blood's closest friends. "It's nearly noon and it looks more like dawn, and the ship feels like she hasn't moved an inch. The men are scared, and I don't blame them. But they trust you, Captain, and would sail into a dozen 20 pounders' fire if you asked them to."

The ship actually was moving, but barely, though it seemed that no one else but Blood had noticed it. He had been letting the shavings from his whittling fall into the water and watching them ever so slowly float, in a single line, back behind the ship. For a long time there was nothing else, then, in the distance, he could hear the faint crashing of waves on a beach.

"Listen!" he told Pitt.

"Shore?"

"Let's find out. Put one of the longboats into water and make sure the men are armed. I don't want to put my boots on solid ground and then find out that we are right in the middle of a picnic hosted by our old friend Colonel Bishop, and not be prepared," said Blood

The fog held the longboat only for 100 yards before it plunged freely into bright daylight. The shore was only a quarter of a mile ahead, the water slapping against the rocks in rhythmic pulsing. Blood looked back toward the ship but found only a wall of grey fog behind him.

"Make for those large boulders," Blood said. "We'll be sheltered from the wind and away from any prying eyes."

The area looked safe enough, but it was better not to take chances, especially since the only thing Blood knew about where they were was that it wasn't the Caribbean.

"Dodger, you and Harris stay with the long boat," said the Captain as he clambered onto the sand.

"Everyone else, split into two groups; one go north; the other south. Walk for ten minutes, and no more, then come back here," said Blood. "Don't get distracted by any local wenches you might see no matter how pretty they are."

"Aye, Captain," the men said, several of them laughing. Just being on solid ground seemed to buoy his crew's sprits; even Blood had to admit that he felt better away from the fog.

"Captain," yelled Pitt. "For a moment, I could have sworn there was someone watching us from the ridge. Older man, dark clothes, with a big hat, a staff, and an eye patch, a bird of some kind on his shoulder. But there's no one there now."

Blood motioned for Pitt to follow him. The two men went straight up the slight rise toward the trees, but there was no sign that anyone had been there for a long time.

The wind shifted, moving the trees, while the two men continued to walk. Blood was about to turn back when he stopped. A hundred yards ahead of the two men was a coach turned on its side; one of the two horses that had been pulling it was gone, the other struggling to get on its feet, but held down by the harness. A young man in tan and green livery lay across the front of the coach, sprawled forward like a marionette which had seen its strings cut.

There was a second man on the side of the overturned coach, jabbing his sword through the window at some unseen prey. His back was to Blood, and that was all the advantage that the pirate captain needed. He grabbed the man's leg and yanked, sending him flying off the coach to crash down hard on the ground. Having learned from bitter experience not to turn away from an advantage in a fight, Peter Blood kicked his opponent hard in the ribs, then again in the jaw.

Satisfied that his opponent would not prove any immediate danger, Blood turned his attention back to the coach, climbing onto its side.

"Is anyone there? I'm a doctor; I can help," he said, leaning his face in the window. A moment later he found the barrel of a pistol only an inch or so from his forehead.

"I would not advise you to move, Monsieur," said a stern female voice from the shadows. She held the pistol steadily and the look in her eyes said that, given the slightest provocation, she would fire. "I am not afraid to use this, especially not on an Englishman."

Captain Peter Blood took a deep breath and looked down at the woman who was holding the gun. She was in her mid-20s, her blonde hair was disheveled and her blouse had been ripped in a couple of places.

"Why don't you put that away and let me help you out of there?" said Blood, switching to French, though she did seem to have understood him in English.

"Why don't I just shoot you and then be done with it?" she replied.

"Because that pistol isn't loaded. If it were, I suspect you would have already blown that lout's head off," he said.

The woman looked at him for a moment, then smiled and lowered her head with a brief nod. The pistol vanished and she extended her hand for Blood to take. It was only a matter of a few moments to lift her out of the coach and onto the ground.

The quality of her dress and traveling cape, not to mention her manner, suggested that she was a woman of some position.

"Are you injured?" asked Blood. "I am a doctor."

"A medical man who isn't afraid to get into a bit of a tussle," she said looking at her unconscious attacker.

"One does what one has to," said Blood. "So, would you prefer we speak in English or in French, Madam?"

"English is such a gross language, but I'm a bit out of practice and it could not hurt to refresh my skills," she said. "So may I know the name of my rescuers?"

"Captain Peter Blood; my ship is the *Arabella* out of…the Caribbean," he said. "The other fellow is one of my crewmen, Jeremy Pitt."

"The Caribbean… A large place to call home," she said.

"What can I say," Blood shrugged. "And you are?"

"Clarice de Winter, Baroness Sheffield " she said.

"A pleasure, Milady. May I ask what happened?" said Blood. Though that much was fairly obvious to the captain, he wanted to hear her version of events; that would tell him a lot about his new acquaintance. He was curious to hear her side of it, especially if her tale did not match the one that he saw around him.

"I was traveling from the estate of my brother-in-law, when we were set upon by bandits. My coachman was able to lose them, thanks to some very fine driving on dangerously curved and uneven roads. Regrettably, at the moment that it seemed we had won free from them, the coach wheel hit something and turned over. Then that scum was on us."

"This looks like more than just a happenstance robbery. Were they after something special? I mean, besides the obvious things, gold, assorted loot… yourself?" asked Blood.

"I really don't know what you are talking about, Monsieur. I'm just a traveler who was set on by bandits. They were simply road scum," she said.

If there was one thing about Milady de Winter that Blood noticed at once, beyond her obvious beauty and poise, it was the intelligence behind her eyes. This woman was no vapid bit of smoke, as many noblewomen he had met before.

"Then why don't we start this conversation over and concentrate on the truth? You are not an idiot, Milady. I think you know why they attacked you." he said.

Her reaction was swift and came without hesitation; she slapped Blood hard on the left side of his face.

"How dare you have the gall to accuse me of lying, Monsieur! Is this the way a gentleman would act? I would have thought better of you. Obviously I was mistaken."

"Really, Milady? I would expect a somewhat more original reaction from you. Slapping me is so, so predictable," he said.

"And I do hate being predictable," she said.

.At that moment, Jeremy Pitt pulled himself up out of the coach, a small leather folio under his arm, which he passed to Blood.

"That is my property and I will thank you to surrender it right now," said the Baroness.

There were a dozen or so sheets inside; personal letters, along with two letters of credit that proved the woman in front of him had access to a great deal of money. However, it was the final letter that proved the most interesting; a thick wax seal weighted own the bottom of it as he unfolded the page.

"My written French is a little weak, but this appears to say, "The bearer of this document is acting on behalf of myself and this office. Give her all cooperation that she requires, without hesitation, under penalty of law. Armand Jean du Plessis, Cardinal Richelieu, state minister to Louis XIII, King of France. Impressive credentials, Madame, but a trifle out of date, if I do say so myself," said Blood.

"What do you mean?"

"I admit to not keeping up with the latest news, a bit difficult when you spend a lot of time at sea. But I seem to recall Louis XIII died some years ago, and his son Louis XIV now sits the throne of France," said Blood. "I'm frankly not sure who this Richelieu fellow might happen to be. The comings and going of politicians can get quite tiresome after a time."

"The King dead? Hardly! You are obviously misinformed," said Clarice de Winter. "As for Cardinal Richelieu, there are those who say that he is the most powerful man in France. If you will not help me under his authority, perhaps it might be simply a gentleman helping a lady in a time of great distress?"

"So you are trying to appeal to my gentlemanly instinct?" Turning to his companion, Blood said. "Jeremy, do I have any gentlemanly instincts? Now tell the truth."

"I suppose you do, when it suits you," said Pitt.

"So, will you help me? I may have spoken too harshly, Captain. There are times when one does not speak in such a way to newly-minted friends," she said softly. "I hope you will accept my apology. I am not a woman who trusts easily, but it appears that I do not have a lot of choices at the moment."

Blood reached down and took her left hand, lifting it to let his lips brush the back of her hand. There was something about this woman's manner, those emerald eyes of hers, that intrigued him, not to mention made him wary as Hell. Under other circumstances, Blood would have enjoyed matching wits with her, and even getting more than a bit physical, in an enjoyable way, but there was still the matter of what they were doing here

"Apology accepted. So why does this Cardinal of yours charge you with so much power? That document could be dangerous in the wrong hands," said the captain.

"I have, at times, acted as his agent on various matters. A month ago, he charged me to obtain an item for him—a certain wooden box," she said.

"And you chose not to ask why?" said Blood.

"With Richelieu, you ask only the things that you need to know in order to carry out the job that has come your way." Clarice de Winter took a few steps toward Blood, as if to show she was opening herself to him. "The box was in the hands of a baron named Mannering who is well known for collecting, shall we say, items that are supposed to not even exist."

"I presume that you were able to acquire this box," said Blood.

"Of course," she said, with the tone that said he should have never doubted that. "The acquiring was not at all difficult, and quite enjoyable," she punctuated her story with a slight smile. "Unfortunately, we were, as you see, intercepted and the box was taken."

"How audacious!" laughed Blood.

Baroness de Winter ignored the tone in Blood's words. "Yes, the Cardinal will not be pleased if I report failure. So, Monsieur, I throw myself on your mercy and ask for your assistance in regaining my property."

"Your property?" Blood arched an eyebrow at the woman and her ideas of ownership.

"Captain, hadn't we better be getting ourselves back to the ship? This whole thing doesn't feel right," said Pitt.

"No, Jeremy, we're going to assist Milady," said Blood. "The first thing that I want you to do is to help me tie our unconscious friend to yonder tree. Then draw your pistol and hold it at the ready while we have a little discussion with him."

"Aye, Captain!"

Clarice stood back, watching the two men work, a look of satisfaction on her face. "Captain, it may not be necessary for you to question this young man," she said finally.

Blood arched an eyebrow at her. "Really?"

"Now that I have a look at him, I think I know this face."

The prisoner could not have been more than 15 or 16 years old, hardly older than some enlistees in the navy that Blood had seen, both living and dead.

"You have a wide and diverse group of friends, in that case," said Blood as cheerfully as if he were discussing a beautiful rose bush.

Milady shot the pirate an angry glance. "I saw this man, along with what I presume were his companions in the attack. They came late one night to Mannering's estate, I could never find out why, but I know it was not a pleasant visit, for he was in a foul mood when they left. I did hear one of them say that if he changed his mind, they could be found at the Seven Shadows."

"The Seven Shadows?"

"An inn, a few miles from here," she said.

"Milady, you are a fountain of information," chuckled Blood.

Clarice walked five steps away from Blood, and then turned, a small pistol in her hand. She brought the weapon to eye level and aimed at the prisoner. Blood grabbed her hand and twisted the weapon away from her.

"I'm guessing this one is loaded, unlike your other weapon," he said.

"The man was intent on killing me; I simply wanted to make sure that he would have no other chances," she said. "If you were more observant, you might have noticed my second gun."

It was Blood's turn to smile this time. He dropped the pistol he had taken from her into his pocket, then reached in beneath her hair and pulled a dagger from a sheath that had been concealed down her back. Blood was fairly sure she had at least two other blades. Not that he had any problem with probing deeper beneath her garments, but Blood felt his point had been made. .

"I do not call you a gentleman, good sir," said Clarice.

"Call me what you will, just know that, like you, I am observant."

Blood waited a few seconds in the door to allow his eyes to adjust to the inside light. Just before he stepped over the threshold, he heard the screeching of two ravens. The birds were sitting on a fence post and Blood had the unnerving feeling that they were staring directly at him.

The Inn of the Seven Shadows was small, but well maintained, with outbuildings and several corrals. It was more a farm than a traveler's rest stop. There were two horses that matched Clarice's description of the mounts her attackers had ridden, tied up near the barn. Neither had been allowed to cool down or had been combed out; flecks of lather marked their coats.

"Innkeeper," called Blood as he stepped inside, studying the common area and finding no one in sight. There was an odd silence to the place for a few seconds, then he heard the sound of footsteps coming from a long hallway toward the back of the room.

"Good day, sir. Welcome to our humble abode. How can I be of assistance to a fine gentleman like yourself?" the man said, smiling and eyeing the new arrival warily.

"That all depends on what is in my pocket," Blood said, laying his arm around the shoulders of the innkeeper.

"Sir?" the innkeeper replied, not certain how to take the man's words.

"I have a pistol ball in one pocket and a coin bag in the other. Oh, the pistol ball is in a charged weapon," Blood told him, as casually as if he were speaking of new flowers he had planted, "One of them will be yours. Which would you prefer?"

"The coins," said the man slowly.

"Good choice. Answer me truthfully and they will be yours. Those two horses in your corral, I'm looking for the men who left them. Do you know who they are and where I might find them?"

"They left only an hour ago," the innkeeper stammered, "They were heading east toward the river on a pair of horses they paid me to keep here for them. Milord, I swear as God is my witness that I do not know their names or where they are going. I'm a simple man, trying to keep food on the table for my family."

Blood said nothing, then reached into his pocket, pulled out the coin bag and dropped a handful of coins into the innkeeper's hands.

"There, that wasn't hard. Now it might be best you forget that I was ever here," he said.

The innkeeper watched Blood disappear out the door before going behind the bar and pulling out a brown bottle. He pulled the cork out of it and swallowed nearly a third of the contents as he heard the sound of a coach rolling away and the screeching of two ravens outside his door.

"There, just to the right!" Blood looked in the direction that Clarice indicated. Just off the road, concealed by bushes, were two nut brown horses; hidden as much by the darkness that had fallen in the last hour as the shrubbery.

"If these do belong to the men we're looking for, I think it best that you remain here, Milady," he told her as he climbed down from the coach.

"Stay here? I think not," replied Clarice, who quickly joined him.

"I think I see a fire, maybe 50 yards inside the tree line," said Pitt.

"Jeremy, I want you to circle around and come in from the east. I think that it might be interesting to see what happens if her ladyship and myself just walk directly into our friends' camp."

The seaman nodded and vanished into the darkness.

"Normally, I would offer you my arm, milady, but in this case you will stay a few steps behind me, given the circumstances," said Blood.

For once Clarice didn't present an argument, either in word or expression.

Two men were sitting close to the campfire that Jeremy had spotted. Neither reacted or seven seemed to notice Blood's and Clarice's arrival. Before they could get close to the bandits, a grey wolf came out from between the trees and blocked their path.

The animal stared at the two but did not move. Had it not been for the sound of the animal's breathing, Blood could have easily been looking at a prime example of the taxidermist's art.

"Shoot it," said Clarice, her voice low and steady.

"Not yet," said Blood. Out of the corner of his eye he caught sight of a movement among the shadows, one that was gone before he could focus on it.

"No," repeated Blood, he pulled his gun and ran toward the animal, slamming the butt of the weapon t hard against the animal's nose.

The wolf howled and then jerked back before collapsing in a heap. In the darkness it was hard to say exactly what happened next, but moments later, it was not a wolf that lay on the ground, but a naked boy of perhaps 10 or 12 years, clutching his hands to his nose.

"That hurt," he screamed. "I think you broke my nose!"

"It's your own fault, boy!" said a deep-voiced figure, stepping out of the woods near Clarice.

It was the old man that Pitt had said he had seen on the shore: long coat, eye patch, a raven sitting on his shoulder while a second balanced on the head of a walking staff.

"I wasn't going to hurt them, Grandfather," the boy whimpered.

"Fenris, be quiet. You and I both know different," said the old man. "I swear that boy is going to be the death of me one day."

"And you are?" asked Blood.

"I have many names, Dr. Blood, as do you. I think you fully understand the reasons, as I'm sure Baroness de Winter does, herself, or should I call her..."

"Clarice de Winter will be sufficient for this evening," Blood's companion said quickly.

"As you wish, Milady," said the old man. "You may call me Odin, or if you are more comfortable with Merlin, I would answer to that name, as well as a number of others. The boy is my grandson, Fenris."

Blood arched an eyebrow at the old man.

This wasn't the first time that he'd run into someone who thought that he was a god or the anointed spokesman for one; most were gibbering idiots or part of the hierarchy of the Church. Sometimes it was hard to tell them apart.

Yet there was something different in this old man's manner. He had the same kind of intensity Blood had seen on a battlefield, usually by men who, if they didn't survive, would take a lot of their enemies with them.

"If you are who you are implying, then would I be wrong in assuming that you had some hand in what brought my ship here?" asked Blood.

"I have made no claims to being anyone, my dear captain, but it is obvious that you are as astute as I expected you to be," he said. "I think we had best be going."

The campfire had faded down to a small glow on the ground in front of the two men. Neither of the bandits looked up or gave any other sign that they were aware of the newcomers. Lying on the ground between them, its lid partially open, was a small wooden box, a curious design of ivory inlaid on its lid.

"That's it; that's the box that the Cardinal sent me after," said Clarice. "What has it done to these men?"

"Oh, that's simple," laughed Fenris. "They opened it."

"And just opening this box did that?" asked Blood.

"No, it was what was inside, what they saw," said Odin. "They saw the future, or what might be the future. Given their reaction, it probably wasn't very pretty. I would imagine it will be days before these two wake up—if they do at all. You never know what kind of animals might decide that these fellows would make a nice midnight snack."

"I suppose you are going to say that you made the box, and want it back," said Blood.

"I want it, but I definitely didn't make it. Let us say that it came from the Middle East and was old when I was a young man," said the old man. "And trust me, that was a very long time ago."

"You are probably lying through your teeth, but if you aren't, then I can see why the Cardinal wants that thing. There are those who would pay a hefty price for that knowledge," said Clarice.

Before either man could react, Clarice de Winter picked up the box and lifted the lid letting a sickly dull yellow glow appear. When she did that, her face went as pale as one who had left the land of the living. That Milady was not a woman who frightened easily had been obvious to Blood from the first moment he met her, but at that moment, he read pure terror and confusion on her face.

Blood grabbed the box away from her, snapping it closed.

"Are you all right?" said Blood. "Did you see something?"

"I saw darkness," she whispered, rubbing her neck, her fingers clinging there as if to protect herself from some unseen attack. "There was a sudden searing pain and then darkness."

Fenris' laughter was enough to drag Blood's attention away from his companion. "I think you had best give it to me; that's what I'm here for. Or I might have to eat you." The boy went to all fours and his transformation back into a wolf was too fast to follow. A deep, frightening growl emerged from the animal's throat just as Blood fired and Odin drove his walking staff hard against his grandson's side. The smoke from the pistol, the painful scream from the animal combined with the screeching of the ravens and was over in a matter of seconds.

"Is he dead?" asked Blood.

"Hardly," said Odin, his voice weak for only a moment. "Let's just say that he is going to have one mighty headache when he wakes up. He will definitely be in a very foul mood and hard to control. I suggest it is time for you to retire to more congenial climes."

"And get there how?" asked Blood.

Odin reached up to his shoulder and coaxed one of the ravens onto his hand. He whispered something to it and then the bird flew toward Blood and landed on the pirate's shoulder.

"My friend will show you the way."

"So, you got lost," said Blood.

Jeremy Pitt turned away from his captain and walked over to the edge of the deck, spending several minutes making sure that several lines were tied fast.

"Are you ever going to let me forget that?" he asked finally, a note of exasperation in his voice.

"Eventually, I suppose I will," smiled Blood.

He had found Jeremy wandering around the forest a few minutes after leaving Odin and Fenris. Together the two of them had bundled Clarice de Winter into the coach. She was still in something of a stupor, muttering half finished sentences. They had left her, along with the coach, at the Inn of the Seven Shadows. The innkeeper had not been pleased with his new guest, but seemed to accept that he had no choice in the matter.

"When she comes round, I have every confidence that she will spin a tale for this Cardinal which attaches no blame to her for not getting him his prize," Blood had told Pitt as they left.

On the beach, they found Odin's raven perched on the edge of the long boat. Almost as soon as the shore party had returned to the *Arabella*, the wind had shifted to let the ship move seaward. In what seemed less than an hour they breeched the fog and were again in familiar Caribbean waters.

"Good day, Captain" said a familiar voice.

Odin standing next to him did not surprise Peter Blood; if it had, he would not have given the old man the satisfaction of knowing it.

"You?" Jeremy Pitt made no attempt to hide the surprise on his face when he saw the old man.

"Me," nodded Odin.

"Somehow, I think the Caribbean is somewhat far from your usual haunts," Blood said casually.

"True, though my followers have been known to venture into this part of the world in the past," said the old man. "However, I've come because we have some unfinished business."

Blood cocked his head at Odin. "And what would that be?"

"I brought you to France for one reason. I could not seize the box myself, because of, shall we say, my nature. It has to be freely given to me. Neither Milady de Winter, the Cardinal, nor Baron Mannering were likely to do so. That's why I chose you," he said.

"And now you want it. Jeremy, go below to my cabin get the small leather bag, you know the one, it's on the floor under my work table."

"Aye, sir," Jeremy Pitt muttered.

"Given what it can do to people, it is best that the box be hidden away. The consequences of opening it might be catastrophic," said Odin.

"And you can be trusted with it? I have known a number of Norse and Swedes; the tales they tell of Odin don't inspire that much trust in you," he said.

"I could say the same thing about the tales they tell of you, Captain Blood. In only six months, you have become quite the notorious pirate," said the old man. "So you well know how a certain kind of reputation can work to one's advantage. I'm sure you've encouraged the spreading of somewhat exaggerated stories concerning your exploits."

That was true, Blood had to admit. Reputations were strange things, half truth, half dream with a generous drop of confusion mixed into the batter.

Pitt reappeared with the bag and passed it to Blood, who looked at it for a moment. Then, with all his might, he sent the thing flying out over the ocean. It struck the water, lingered on the surface for a moment and then vanished into the clear Caribbean depths.

"I think the best keeper for that thing, whatever it might really be, is in the hands of Davy Jones. It's not that I don't trust you, sir, but to be frank, I don't trust you or anyone with that thing," Blood said.

Odin chewed on his lip for a moment. Blood waited for his legendary fury to make itself known, but instead, the old man smiled and then laughed.

"Checkmate," said Odin. "I must admit that was not an action that I had anticipated. Well played, my friend."

Odin gestured toward the raven that had been quietly watching the whole affair from his perch on a wooden barrel. The bird hesitated, then leapt into the air and flew straight to Odin's wrist.

"Captain, may I wish you smooth sailing and strong winds at your back." Then he was gone as if he had never stood on the deck next to Blood.

The pirate captain stood there for a moment, and began to laugh.

Michel Stéphan, who lives in Brittany, loves the old black and white Universal movies featuring Frankenstein, Dracula, The Wolf Man, etc. This tale was written in homage to James Whale, for the words "Died 1899. Maddalena Ernestine, beloved daughter of..." are indeed carved on the tombstone of one of the most famous characters in horror fiction in his most celebrated film...

Michel Stéphan: *The Three Lives of Maddalena*

The 1790s

Diary of Maddalena Ernestine

Strangely, more things have happened to me during these last two months of my life than at any time previously. First, it was my encounter with Carmilla Karnstein who came to stay with us, one day in September, renting our little, first-floor bedroom. Then, there was my break-up—if the word is correct—with the man whom I had long considered as my brother, my sole confident and even my soulmate, Victor Frankenstein, who, the very day of his betrothal, did not even deign to look at me.

Victor and I grew up together; he is five years older than I, and comes from a wealthier family, but these differences never seemed to matter between us. He was like an older brother to me—the playmate who built a tree house for us in the woods belonging to Old Man Schluter, the student who taught me that life could sometimes be cruel, and that God could lack mercy towards some of His creatures.

I was the one on whose shoulder he cried during his first heartbreak, when he came to me, cursing all women, just because a girl from the village had tired of his favors.

When Victor went to university, his visits became more infrequent, but he never missed an opportunity to see me when his schedule allowed. We then spent a few, precious hours together, reminiscing about the good times we had had together, forever enshrined in our memories.

When Victor met Elizabeth, I was happy for them both. They were such a good match, and I liked to think that dear Elizabeth considered me as a true friend and not a rival. My relationship with Victor was too strong to be confined within the narrow limits of a love affair, and I think everyone understood then that we were truly inseparable.

When Carmilla came to live with us, Victor was already absorbed in his experiments, and it impacted his mood, but I never expected him to suddenly change so much. I always thought that Carmilla had something to do with it, but I could never bring myself to believe it completely. How could a being of mere flesh and blood, even one so strange, could exercise that much influence over another? Victor had changed so much that he failed to even recognize me. I had become invisible to his eyes, a total stranger. But Carmilla had also completely overturned my life. I did not believe one could experience so much fascination for another woman.

She had arrived early in the fall to live as a tenant in our house, for a period of time that would coincide with her mother's return to the family castle. Baroness Karnstein had left her daughter under the guardianship of my father, with a thousand recommendations and a sum of money which, as I found out later, was more than sufficient.

Carmilla was the same age as I, but she already seemed to know so many more things. I listened, fascinated, when she joined me in my room at night and we spent quiet time lying on my bed. The more I listened to her, the more it seemed that I knew nothing about her. Her very existence remained a mystery to me. What fascinated me the most was her intense gaze, and her booming laugh, which, coming from another girl's mouth might have seemed vulgar, but which, in hers, seemed fresh and beguiling. It was like an invitation to pleasure. Carmilla was very beautiful and, sometimes, I envied her. Despite her young age, I was sure that she had caused many suitors to lose their heads. I let myself be carried away by the sweet tone of her voice and slid slowly into a state of torpor that procured me the greatest happiness. This well-being only faded in the morning when Carmilla left me alone, but satisfied.

As he had done every year, Victor's father had organized a party in the gardens of their luxurious property in Visaria, and everyone in the village was invited. This year's event would also mark the engagement of Victor to Elizabeth. It was an opportunity for me to introduce Carmilla to them. She was beginning to be well known in the village. Her magnetism and beauty were a favorite topic of conversation. The distracted way she paid attention to the world around her and her ever-distant politeness might have passed for condescension or contempt, but she was so natural about it that the entire village seemed be in love with her. I was curious to see how her charm would operate on Victor. I had to introduce them to each other. I felt oddly compelled to do so. It had never occurred to me that this might endanger his engagement to Elizabeth. Or if it had it was entirely unconscious. My only intention was to bring together the two people whom I cherished the most.

But nothing happened as I had hoped. I began by finding Victor and offering him my warmest congratulations on his engagement; then I introduced Carmilla to him. There was an exchange of polite smiles, followed by a brief handshake. And, from that moment, it was also the end of a friendship that I thought would last forever.

After that day, Victor lost complete interest in me. I did not understand immediately what had happened. I still have not understood it.

The celebrations had barely begun and already Carmilla was impatient. She intimated with her beautiful smile that she was bored and wanted to leave. Victor, meanwhile, had long ago disappeared into the arms of his fiancée.

That day, I began to feel extremely ill.

It was as if all the calamities of the Earth had befallen me at once. The following day, I was forced to stay in bed when I learned of the upcoming departure of Carmilla. Her stay had come to an end and her mother had expressed \the desire to see her daughter soon. My world had collapsed.

Today, Carmilla is gone. I no longer exist for Victor and I think I will never have an explanation for it. If there is one, I hope I learn of it soon, for I feel that my end is nigh.

The two doctors who have examined me have failed to find the cause of my illness. My father wanted to find a third, more competent physician, but I told him that it was not worth it; he should not question the wisdom of the doctors. It is strange, but I am not afraid. I know that, for me, my life is at an end, but nothing truly ever ends. Everything has new beginnings. Maybe on the threshold of death, the human mind prepares you to face the ultimate void by making you delirious or feeding you fantasies to surround your last moments with a sense of well-being, but, honestly I do not believe that is the case.

I really think, especially in the last few days, that a great adventure is waiting for me beyond the darkness, and I am not afraid.

Diary of Carmilla Karnstein

The events that I have recently experienced had, for me, the attraction of novelty, but they still did not reconcile me with mankind, as they were unfortunately far too predictable.

The time I spent in Visaria enabled me to meet a girl, Maddalena Ernestine, who was quite pleasant, and to become her friend. Indeed, I was her confidante for several weeks. She told me her life story, her joys and sorrows. I was moved by it, so I decided to give her destiny a little helping hand.

The stories humans tell about us, creatures of the night, have always terrified them, which is only to be expected, since they have always seen us through the distorting prism of their own vices. I won't ever mention their religions, which condemn us as masquerading abominations from beyond the grave. Yet do we not offer the same eternal life that these worms are unable to grasp? They imagine they can oppose us with the impotent lamentations of degenerate mendicants or shake before our eyes their grotesque crucifixes.

Maddalena Ernestine lived in her dreams, contenting herself with a passionate love stifled by too many moral principles. I had to release her from that life, and I did. Her pathetic feelings will be transcended by death and turn to true love, which she could never have known before.

When she becomes one of us, she can finally live her passion with an intensity that only afterlife can offer. She will join her lover and they will be reunited for eternity. When I think of the moments of ecstasy that they will be able to share, I understand why churches curse us, we who have the power to accomplish such miracles.

My affection for her turned to pity the day I met her beloved Victor. What a waste, how many destinies severed by petty bourgeois morality!

It was easy enough for me to look into his eyes to erase all traces of Maddalena Ernestine from the mind of the young Doctor, so that he would not see it die. Besides, Maddalena Ernestine had been moping and wishing for death a thousand times before, without knowing what awaited her on the other side of that dark mirror. Her wish will be fulfilled. Those two deserve better than a meaningless romance in the land of the living.

She will be buried in her family crypt and, as usual, the doctors will find nothing sensible to say about the reasons for her death. Then, for several months, perhaps even a year, her heart will virtually stop, beating at a rhythm so slow that it is all but imperceptible to humans, who nevertheless know it as our only weak point and would not hesitate to stab her through it.

Her body will retain the brilliance of her youth until she wakes up and finally understand what wonderful opportunity I gave her. Maddalena Ernestine may then emerge from her grave to rejoin her Victor and the two shall forever be united.

Diary of Victor Frankenstein

Dr. Pretorius finally brought me the body. That madman wants me to create a female companion for the monster. I do not know if I can twice achieve the same success.

The body is in perfect condition. It is that of a girl of 19 who seems to be sleeping peacefully. However, there appears to be something defective about her heart. It does not respond quickly enough to electrical stimulation. So I took it out of her chest and asked Karl to get me a replacement.

Pretorius and I then began to prepare the body for the main operation.

The girl was an ordinary girl, with a physique that some might have even called ungrateful. However, when I bent over her to cover her face with gauze and bandages, I was suddenly transfixed by a strange vision. I saw a tree house and lots of Sun. Much sadness too.

But I digress. Karl is coming back. He looks pleased. I promised him 1000 crowns if he were successful. I think we will soon be able to start the operation.

(English adaptation by Jean-Marc & Randy Lofficier)

David Vineyard's contribution to this anthology is an exciting adventure romp, featuring a colorful cast of heroes and villains, reminiscent of an action movie of the 1960s. It finds its raison d'être *in one of Jules Verne's lesser known novels,* Mathias Sandorf, *which he wrote as a variation on the theme of* The Count of Monte-Cristo—*Verne greatly admired Dumas—while adding super-science to the mix. Like Edmond Dantes, Verne's hero, the eponymous Sandorf, is unjustly imprisoned and returns as a Captain Nemo-like science pirate, Dr. Antekirtt, whose lair is the prodigious island where our story takes place...*

David L. Vineyard: *The Mysterious Island of Dr. Antekirtt*

Antekirtta, 1954

The Captain swore steadily through teeth clamped on the blackened stem of his pipe as he fought the helm of the fishing boat. His breath, indeed everything about him, reeked of alcohol, and his eyes had the far-away, unfocused look of a man lost in drink. He was a burly black bearded man in a dark blue sweater and pea coat wearing a peaked cap pulled low over his red-rimmed eyes. Outside the wind howled at near gale force as the small craft fought through the rough waters of the Eastern Mediterranean.

Leo Saint-Clair stood in the shadows of the deck house, his keen, strangely colored eyes seeing through the darkness, picking out the details of the ship's bow as it plunged into the rough sea through the slanting wall of rain that whipped them. The tires roped to the bow as a guard were thrown like so many pillows by wind and sea. He studied the Captain dubiously, and thought about taking over the helm before they all drowned.

The Boy came through the hatch just then. He wore a slicker over an absurd outfit of plus fours and a blue sweater over a white shirt. His fair hair stood up in a cowlick in front, even in the downpour; the small white terrier that always accompanied him stood by his leg, shaking the excess moisture from his fur. Ordinarily neither the Boy nor the Dog should be on this voyage, much less the sodden sailor at the helm, but it was the Boy who had initiated this desperate adventure, and he was, after all, no ordinary youth, no more than Leo Saint-Clair, sometimes known as the Nyctalope, was an ordinary man.

"Good dog," the Boy chided as the dog shook off the last of the rain. He looked up apologetically at Saint-Clair, but the broad-chested man only glared on. He didn't mind the Dog or the Captain half as much as the Boy's obvious hero worship. Perhaps there had been a time when he would have welcomed that look—indeed had welcomed it from all comers, but now... Things had changed.

Mistakes were made; men made them and lived with the consequences, even heroes, and the more public the mistakes, the more painful the consequences.

"You shouldn't be up on deck in this blow," Saint-Clair said.

"Mr. Prince and Mr. Morane asked me to fetch you. Anyway, my dog and I are pretty fair sailors; you can ask the Captain..."

"What do they want below?"

"They have the charts out. They thought that, perhaps, a council of war..."

The Captain had begun to sing a vaguely obscene sea shanty of dubious origins in a low voice. He looked as if he would pass out any moment.

The Boy sensed the Nyctalope's concern. "I'll stay with the Captain," he boy volunteered. "We've weathered much worse storms than this. Anyway, this is practically sober—for him."

Saint-Clair nodded. He was less than reassured, but he had all of the drunken sailor he could stomach. He turned the collar of his coat up and pulled a cloth cap down over his hair. He stepped out in the storm, fought to close the hatch, and fell into the natural rolling walk of the sailor as he rode the storm. Even though his eyes could pierce the darkest night, the slanting rain meant he had to keep a keen watch.

Below, the cabin was lit by a yellow light, wan and sallow. Two men sat around a crude table. One was tall, lean, well muscled, with dark hair, steel-grey eyes and a pleasantly chiseled face. He wore a campaign shirt with epaulets and buttoned down pockets, the sleeves rolled up to reveal lean bronzed forearms. He looked up as Saint-Clair entered.

"Morane, Prince," Saint-Clair said, acknowledging his companions with a nod.

The second man was younger, not a great deal older than the Boy above. He was bronzed and weathered, with thick, near white hair and sharp blue eyes. He wore a blue pullover shirt and white denims. He was smaller than Morane, just below Saint-Clair's medium height. Despite his youth, he was a trusted agent of Interpol.

As Saint-Clair entered and shucked off his cap and coat in the close cabin, the younger man stood and took a blackened pot off the stove.

"Coffee?"

Saint-Clair nodded and straddled a chair resting his arms on the back. His chefs at home would be horrified by this foul steaming mixture, but the Nyctalope had drunk worse during his adventurous life. He thought of the foul tea served by his Nepalese guides at the roof of the world, or the potent Arab coffee served to him in Algeria, or even the black tea so popular in Chile, served in a covered metal cup...

Prince handed him a cup of foul-looking, thick black mud, and took his own seat. This was even worse than the tea he had drunk during the curiously formal ceremony of the caravan-sari along the Silk Road on the way to ancient, blue-domed Samarkand.

They had picked up Prince in Tripoli 15 hours earlier. The American Bonisseur de La Bath had suggested Prince to them when Morane's Scot friend, Ballantine, had been sidelined by a twisted ankle. So far, it seemed a good choice, though one could never be certain until the crucible of fire tested a man's flesh as well as his will. Saint-Clair would have preferred to have had the ex-OSS man with them, but the American had assignments for his CIA to worry about, and no time for what might prove a fruitless adventure.

"How's it look up top?" Bernard Prince asked.

Saint-Clair sipped the foul brew and shrugged. "Bad. We'll be lucky if the drunk doesn't run us aground."

Prince smiled. "I know he doesn't seem like much, but we're in good hands. He's a damn fine sailor."

"So everyone keeps telling me."

"Well," said Morane, "in any case, we have him. We might as well hope he's as good as they say—drunk or sober."

"A damn sight better drunk, I'd wager," Prince said, "than most sober. Anyway, this is a lucky little boat. I like her name, the *Cormorant*. Wouldn't mind having a ship of my own with that name someday."

"The Boy said something about a council of war," Saint-Clair said. He was feeling old in this company. Even the Captain was younger than he was, though he looked no older than Morane. Physiologically, he might be 30ish, but mentally... It was the heart, not the mind, that was artificial, and nearly immortal.

"Yes," Morane said. "I—we, were wondering if our 'friends' were very far ahead of us."

"They have half a day on us," Prince said, obviously a point he had made before Saint-Clair came down.

"And the same weather," Morane added. "And I can assure you that, whatever his other skills, the Yellow Shadow is no sailor."

"Nor that half-German-Chinese with him, I'll wager," Prince added.

"You're both forgetting Largo," Saint-Clair said. "He may sail a desk now, but he made his fortune running waters as rough as these as a smuggler, black marketeer, and running refugees—the ones he didn't drown whenever the authorities got too close. No, he's every bit as good as our drunken friend at the helm. Still, we can move faster in this fishing vessel than the freighter they're taking, and we can get in much closer. We should beat them to it, but not by much."

Prince seemed relieved. *More hero worship*, Saint-Clair thought. He would feel more secure if Prince and the Boy had more of Morane's reserve. He had had too many lives depend on his actions, and there had been too many dead in his wake. There was a time that didn't worry him, but now... His return to France from semi-self-imposed exile had been done quietly, as discreetly as a celebrity as he had once been could manage. Things changed, but governments still had needs. Malraux, a friend who had become an enemy, was now a friend

213

again--of sorts. Others had been forgiven, so why not a man as useful as the Nyctalope? Hadn't he saved countless lives during the war while seeming to collaborate? He was, after all, a legend, and the current government dealt in legends. The useful ones, at least. One advantage of being nearly immortal was the ability to outlive the tides of fortune. If he was no longer the living symbol of the old Imperial France that he once was, he still had his uses. A flag too old to be waved in public could still prove useful as a shroud for the Republic's enemies. And there were always enemies. Old and new.

"What do you think we'll find on Dr. Antekirtt's island?" Bernard Prince asked.

"Probably nothing," Morane said. "Nothing but legends."

"I don't know," Saint-Clair said. "There have always been rumors. Locals say the place is haunted. They won't even fish in its waters. Though you'd think all those pirate warships sunk back in 1884 would make for good fishing grounds. An artificial reef." He didn't add that he had been born only a few years before the great battle. He wondered what these men would say if they realized he had been at this game since 1897...

Prince leaned back. "I've heard the stories, but I never really believed them. Who was this Dr. Antekirtt?"

"A genius," Saint-Clair said. "He was originally a Hungarian patriot, Count Mathias Sandorf. He and his allies were betrayed when they tried to drive the Austro-Hungarian rule out of power back in 1867. They were sentenced to an inescapable prison, the Donjon at Pisino, a dreadful place above a deep cataract and a rushing river. They were left for dead, but they escaped. Of the three, only Sandorf made it to safety. Over the next 15 years, he became Dr. Antekirtt and created his fantastic island fortress of Antekirtta. Apparently, he was a genius of the first class, inventing many remarkable weapons, the likes of which are only now common. His fast little submarines, *Electric 1* and *2*, were said to be far ahead of their time, and his yacht, the *Ferrato*, a wonder. My father, a sailor himself, told me of both.

"Over the years, there have been attempts to visit the island and liberate its secrets, but they've always met with disaster. The last I know of was during the war. Himmler, that fantastic foul troll, followed one of his visions and sent an SS team to raid it... Skorzeny's men, though not led by Skorzeny himself, but by a man named Drax..."

"Hugo Drax?" Morane spoke up.

"Yes. That one. The one in the papers a couple of years ago over that rocket business in England. Those famous scars of his were from his visit to Antekirtta. He was the only one to escape alive, and barely at that. Anyway, since then, the place has had an even worse reputation, and it doesn't help that the currents are tricky and the natural harbors treacherous. Antekirtt no doubt knew a secret way in, but if he did, he didn't leave the secret with anyone."

"Tell me, Saint-Clair," Morane asked, "what do you think we'll find on Antekirtta?"

Saint-Clair shook his head. "I wish I knew, but I can almost promise that, at the very least, we'll find..."

"...Death," the Yellow Shadow said. "I think we can be certain that the island is a deadly trap."

Julius No, the strange half-German-Chinese, tapped his fingers on the top of the teak table in Largo's luxurious cabin. "I knew Drax. A fool, but a dangerous one. He spoke of terrors, and he was not a man given to such things. Those burns of his, he attributed to a fire-breathing dragon..."

"Ha!" Emilio Largo barked a sharp unpleasant laugh. "Booby traps perhaps, even wild animals. But dragons? Really, my dear Doctor!" Largo's dark eyes flashed with contempt.

"Dragons come in many forms," Dr. No said. Though he showed no anger, it was clear he disliked Largo and his manner.

The Yellow Shadow showed nothing, but inside he seethed. Why must he be plagued with such incompetent lieutenants? It was bad enough that devil Morane was involved in this, but to have to deal with these two... And that fool Tadeus who had tipped that damn Boy Reporter... He should have known better than to consult that brilliant mad Professor, who was one of the Boy's closest friends. Well, he had paid for his mistake with his life, though not at Monsieur Ming's hand, but too late to benefit him. By the time he had learned of the leak, the Boy had already approached French Intelligence, and they, in turn, Bob Morane; and the former air force Commandant had brought in the Nyctalope, and now Interpol in the form of the young but already formidable Bernard Prince. What a mess! What an unholy mess! Still, if the island held the secret he suspected... That was why he had brought Dr. No was along—and Largo, for his ships and his knowledge of the sea.

Bob Morane, that upstart Prince from Interpol, the Boy Reporter, and... Leo Saint-Clair... That was the wild card—Saint-Clair.

A light on the phone at Largo's left hand flashed red. The sailor picked it up. He spoke quickly in Greek, then hung up.

"We're there," he said. "No sign of anyone else, though in this storm... The Captain says we seem to be in a brief calm. I suggest we go ashore now before it blows up again."

The Yellow Shadow nodded, and rose. So far things were going well. Still, he felt a certain unease. He'd feel more at ease if he knew what as going on in the mind of...

...The Nyctalope leaped from the bow of the dory into the water and took the line to pull it toward shore. Prince dropped in the water on the other side and grabbed the line to help. In the boat Morane sat with a British-made Sten gun,

215

silenced like the ones used by the commandos during the war. The Boy held his dog under his coat in the stern, by the motor.

The storm had let up briefly, and they had taken advantage of that to come ashore. They had left the Captain back on the fishing boat, snoring raucously. Saint-Clair would have preferred to leave the Boy and the Dog with him, both to keep them out of the way and to watch the old souse. He was by no means sure the old reprobate would still be there when they returned. But he had been out-voted. It was the Boy wjo had brought them here, Morane pointed out, and Prince agreed.

Fools! This was deadly business, and no place for sentiment or adventure. Men might well die tonight—even boys.

They secured the dory and gathered their gear. Saint-Clair wore his si-lenced Browning in a shoulder rig under his pea coat and carried a silenced Sten gun like Morane. Prince was carrying a big Browning Automatic Rifle, the BAR, a gun that could shoot concrete to pieces. Even the Boy carried a 9mm automatic that he seemed quite familiar with. Only the Dog went unarmed, but even he was subdued, as if he, too, knew the danger that surrounded them. Both Saint-Clair and Morane carried heavy packs on their back, and Prince had one slung over his shoulder with extra ammo for the BAR.

They were ready for a fight.

They had landed on the northwest corner of Antekirtta. Monsieur Ming and Largo would have to utilize the natural inlet called Kencraf on the southwest side of the island, where the old lighthouse stood and the remnants of the pirate armada lay under the sea. Saint-Clair and Morane had opted for the route Drax and his men had taken after a U-boat had landed them ashore. The added bonus, in Saint-Clair's view, was a grizzly one. The Drax expedition had not been so long ago that there would be no signs of it. And, even if time had largely erased some of those signs, the Nyctalope's eyes would spot them. The trail of Drax's dead would warn them of any booby traps planted on the island, which might still be active and deadly, even after all these years.

They walked in the footsteps of ghosts, damned phantoms whose restless souls were lost to the winds of Antekirtta. Both parties were avoiding the small city Dr. Antekirtt had built and lived in. Their goal was the laboratory located near the center of the island, a Moslem fortress converted by Sandorf for his ex-periments.

Saint-Clair took the point. The island was almost certainly loaded with le-thal traps. His uncanny eyes were vital to their chances. If anyone could spot a trap... Morane had explained it succinctly: "The Nyctalope's eyes are our secret weapon. Whatever devices the Yellow Shadow may have with him, he and his associates will move slower—or risk a quick, violent death. We can beat them to it."

"To what?" Prince had asked. "I'm still not sure what it is that we're look-ing for."

"Power." It was the Boy who had spoken. "The Professor—well, as best as I could make out, he's not always clear, the original absent-minded genius—but he said that the man who came to him was asking about power sources. That's the real secret of Dr. Antekirtt, the power he harnessed. That's what we're looking for, I think, what Monsieur Ming and Dr. No are here for—the secret of Antekirtta."

"Power," Saint-Clair had said. "That's always what it's all about ultimately. Power to create—or destroy, pure unadulterated...

"...Power," the Yellow Shadow said.

Dr. No looked at Monsieur Ming, but said nothing. He knew what the Mongol was thinking. Antekirtta held secrets, perhaps one expecially dear.

They had come ashore in a fast boat lowered from Largo's ship, with a team of 12 armed and dangerous men recruited from the armies of minions at Ming's command. Hard men, cold-blooded, ruthless killers, every one. A match for most men—but for Morane—or the Nyctalope? Even in Hong Kong, Dr. No had read of the man Saint-Clair's exploits, and even if they had been exaggerated by the popular press—and they almost certainly were—he was still a dangerous foe. And while he knew nothing of the Boy, other than that he was a well known journalist despite his youth, and only had Ming's judgment of the man Morane, it was clear that this was unlikely to be an easy expedition.

The storm had laid while they came ashore—a good omen—but now the wind was freshening and the cold rain was beginning to whip up. A few minutes earlier, they could see the ruins of the old lighthouse on the point above the Kencraf inlet, but now it was growing darker. Dr. No, who despised the cold, regretted being here. Still, if Ming were right...

Largo was busy getting their gear ashore. He might be a greedy and dangerous ruffian, but he was a useful one. A tool, but a clever and useful one. When Blofeld had suggested him for the mission, the initial reaction had been doubt, but it was clear now he had been the best man for the job.

"We must move quickly," Dr. No said to the Yellow Shadow.

"But with care. I have no illusion that we are alone on the island. We cannot afford to imagine ourselves as ahead in this race. I will post men well ahead as scouts. They will gladly sacrifice themselves to any surprises the island has for us."

Dr. No nodded. It was a wise policy. Such men were only good for the fodder of these dangerous operations. In ordinary circumstances, neither he nor Ming would even be here—but this was no ordinary circumstance.

Largo was coming toward them. "We're ready." He carried a German Mauser on his hip in its wooden holster-stock, and, slung across his shoulder, an American Thompson machine gun with a drum, like the gangster he was. Ming carried a Walther P-38 in a holster under his coat, and Dr. No was unarmed. He considered his hands delicate tools and had no intention of harming them by carrying anything so crude as a gun.

The Yellow Shadow lifted his hand and waved three fingers. Three of his men split off from the others and moved ahead. The rain was now falling steadily and beginning to slant, as it had earlier. The wind off the sea was stiffer, picking up. Already, it was impossible to see their ship anchored in the inlet.

Largo took up a position behind the Yellow Shadow's three men. Another man, similarly armed, filed behind him, then Ming and then Dr. No and the rest of the men. There was a sort of overgrown trail leading up off the beach, and they took to that, rather than the rough country on either side. Even this was overgrown and rough going.

But, Dr. No could not help wondering, were they really...

"...alone?" Bob Morane was saying. "I don't think so."

The Boy had asked when they had stopped to rest. The white dog was in his lap, getting his ears scratched; Prince was squatting on a rock, checking the BAR. The rain was worse, but they had found an overhang of rock to the lea of the wind and were relatively sheltered. Morane reached out and tousled the Dog's wet head, and the grateful animal shivered playfully. "In any case, Saint-Clair is right. We must proceed as if Ming and the others are already on the island."

As if on cue, the Nyctalope appeared to the accompaniment of a flash of lightning and a clap of thunder. His hair was wild and wind-blown, and his features leaner and more drawn than on the photos and illustrations the Boy had seen from the hero's heyday. He was such a strange figure. According to rumors, he was virtually immortal, possessing an artificial heart, and had traveled to the four corners of the world—and beyond. If only half the stories than the man La Hire had written in the newspaper had some basis in reality, Leo Saint-Clair was nothing less than a Nietzschean *ubermensch*, a super-man, as much of the American comic-book variety as the intellectual one.

As he ducked to enter the shelter, he tossed something at their feet. Prince lay aside his rifle and picked the object up. It was an insignia, one with the distinctive lightning markings of the SS.

"We're on the right trail, at least," Saint-Clair said. "I found that about 20 yards ahead. There was more, but no sense disturbing the dead."

The Boy's head jerked up. The little white dog softly yelped as if he understood.

"A trap?" Morane asked, as Prince handed him the grim souvenir.

Saint-Clair nodded. "An old hunter's trick. Nothing extraordinary, save from what I can tell, it was activated by a crude electronic eye. Just a heavy log suspended from rope and the electronic tripwire. Spikes had been driven into the log and sharpened—perhaps even poisoned. This fellow..." he nodded to the insignia the Boy now held, "...was still hanging there after all this time—at least what was left of him. I saw signs that another man may have been injured. I can't imagine a man like Drax wasting much time on the wounded, so the body is likely close."

The Boy Reporter offered the insignia back to Saint-Clai, who shook his head. "Keep it. I've seen enough of them to last me a lifetime. From here on, we'll have to be doubly careful."

Prince nodded, again picking up the BAR. "Hadn't we better...?"

Morane nodded. "No sign it's letting up. I don't suppose Ming and his group are letting up either though. Once more into the breach, *mes amis*."

The Boy and Prince both laughed. To them, it was an adventure. A grand adventure. Saint-Clair shrugged. He had spent a lifetime in search of, and living adventure—more than one lifetime. It was never like the books. It was always earnest, and always good, and bad men and women died. The Boy's youth, Morane's courage, Prince's toughness, none of them were armor against the cold finger of death that waited for them at every turn on this island. He had killed, and he had survived. He had watched friends die, and he had taken vengeance. He knew the true face of adventure. A skull. A grinning, leering, humorless skull. He would be much happier if he knew where the Yellow Shadow and his party were. It was always safer to have the enemy in...

"...view," Emilio Largo was saying. "In my view, we're moving far too slowly. Perhaps you and the Doctor should stay back while I go ahead with a few of your men?"

The Yellow Shadow was not used to having his orders questioned. He didn't care for this Largo. He was a bully and a sadist, and there was more than a touch of cheap melodrama about him. Not that Dr. No was any better, but he, at least, had the restraint of his Asian blood. Largo was a vulgarian, a self-made man of the worst sort. Even if one admired his ruthlessness, there was a twisted quality about him, a perversion. Only Monsieur Ming's sternest command had kept the fool from bringing a woman along with them. Really, a woman on an expedition like this!

"We'll stay together," the Yellow Shadow said sharply. "Morane and Saint-Clair are both capable of lying in ambush for us, and picking us off silently. Morane may be a boy scout, but he's an efficient one, and the Nyctalope..."

"The Nyctalope," Largo virtually spat the word out. "A man who some say has an artificial heart and can see in the dark. What nonsense! Perhaps he was good—once. But he hasn't done anything since the war, that I know of. He's a has-been. And, anyway, if anyone believe those absurd stories, they would have to believe that the man is close to 80..."

Ming ignored the rant. He knew secrets that would leave the boastful Largo shivering in a corner, sucking his thumb like a cowering child. How could a man like Largo even imagine a man like the Nyctalope?

219

Though his mind was distracted, the Yellow Shadow was always aware of his surroundings. They had made their way about half a mile inland along the overgrown trails, and as yet encountered nothing that slowed them more than debris that had to be climbed over or gone around. There were few animals about, but the storm would have seen to that. Such creatures would take shelter and ride out the wild night. They had more sense than men.

There had once been a thriving village on the island, home to scientists and artists, but it had largely died out by the time of the Great War, and been largely destroyed by German bombers during the WWII, when they had carpet-bombed the island before the Drax expedition. No one seemed to know what had brought about the end of Dr. Antekirtt's little Eden, but Ming suspected that it was as simple as human nature. The good Doctor might have been a beneficent despot, but he was still a despot, and whatever pretense to democracy he had set up on the island, it was first and foremost his experiment, his dream. And when the dreamer dies—what becomes of the dream?

They had come to a fork in the trail. Seeking respite under an overhang of foliage, they studied the divergent paths.

"The question is," Dr. No said softly, "which is the road less taken?"

Largo snorted. "One way to find out." He signaled one of Ming's men toward the path on the left, and he took up his machine gun and boldly stepped toward the path on the right.

Ming started to stop him, then stopped. Let the reckless fool find out for himself. With a nod, the Mongol sent his own man to follow Largo's order. Largo was already halfway up the right path, sweeping the barrel of the Thompson ahead of him like a soldier on point.

"A brave man, our Signore Largo," Dr. No said with quiet sarcasm.

Largo disappeared first. It seemed quite a long time that he was gone. After a moment, they saw his figure reemerging, still swaggering, a nasty smile on his lips, a cigar clamped between his thick lips.

He stopped.

The Yellow Shadow tensed. Dr. No rested his delicate hands on the Mongol's arm.

Largo turned his head. He cocked it to one side, like a dog at an unexpected sound. In this storm, it was hard to hear anything. He turned back toward the main party. He took a step.

Paused.

Turned again...

"No!" It was Ming's sharp voice.

There was a flash of light. It was too weak for lightning.

Largo had half-turned as Ming had shouted at him. That saved his life. Almost.

He fell to the ground, screaming.

"Now we know the road forward," Dr. No said.

Largo was writhing on the ground, his hands to his face, still...

"...Screaming. I heard a human scream."

Saint-Clair froze, and behind him so did Morane, Prince, the Boy, and even the Dog.

Prince unslung his rifle and worked the action, Morane, like Saint-Clair, had recognized that the scream came from a distance. "Another of Antekirtta's traps," said the airforce hero as he relaxed.

"At least, we know we're not alone," Prince said, relaxing, a little teased by his reaction.

The little dog began a howl, but the Boy hushed him. "I'm sorry," the Boy began to say..."

"Don't be," Saint-Clair said. "I doubt they heard it, and even if they did, they already suspect we're here. And you can hardly blame the animal. That scream was almost inhuman. Either way, the pup is an advantage for us. His hearing and sense of smell are keener than my eyesight. He sensed something a few seconds before we actually heard the scream. I saw his hair bristle." It was the most human moment the Nyctalope had shown. Morane half expected to see him tousle the Dog's ears.

"Well," Prince said, "At least they're down a man. One more to our side."

The Boy was unexpectedly smiling. "I hope the Captain didn't hear that. He'll think he's having the terrors."

Even Saint-Clair chuckled. Then he turned serious. "I make them closer to shore than I would have thought," he said. "If the charts we have are accurate, we should be a few klicks from the villa and fortifications. I suspect we'll find more of Drax's party as we get closer, but we're ahead, and a wounded man will slow our adversaries a little more."

"Not for long. Ming is far from sentimental," Morane said, "but I agree, I think that scream will slow their pace if nothing else. God knows what the poor devil ran into."

Saint-Clair nodded. Ever since they had landed, he had felt a presence, as if they were being watched, and he was not given to hysterics or unease. This island had an uncanny effect on him, and he didn't like it. He didn't believe in demons, ghosts, or the whole pantheon of the supernatural, but he had seen more than his fair share of the odd and the unnatural, and this whole place stank of it. No wonder sailors avoided it. For the first time, he began to wonder if there might be something worthwhile to salvage from Antekirtta after all. Something still powered the electric eye that had killed Drax's man, at least as far back as the war, and, though he hadn't said anything to the others, the trap hadn't looked as if it dated from the last century when he had examined it. Antekirtta had supported some population longer than history suggested.

The storm had let up a little again, but if he was any judge, it was only another respite. Storms in this part of the world were notoriously fickle and likely to swirl around in complex currents, striking again and again until they blew themselves out. And this place was odd to begin with. Strange currents in the sea, and stranger ones in the sky. That was why they had abandoned Morane's original idea to use a helicopter, seeing as he was an ex-fighter pilot—why Ming and the others had come by sea too. Even a sea plane would have never navigated a landing in these waters, at the best of times. It was as if Antekirtta had been chosen to be as uninviting as possible to any intruder.

Taking the point, he swept the darkness, checking the little dog as they moved ahead. The animal's nerves were good. Fear kept you alive. For too many years, Saint-Clair hadn't known that feeling. It made him dangerous to himself and others. Since the war... Well, even an immortal had to grow up sometime...

They had been moving vaguely uphill for a while when, suddenly, he stopped. He raised a hand, but the others had already halted. They had seen the dead SS he had found and passed his remains quietly, keeping their thoughts to themselves, but since then, they had been a more sober crew.

The Nyctalope signaled the others to wait, and went forward. He slung the Sten gun under his arm and drew his Browning with the specially designed suppressor. He thumbed the safety off and went ahead on cat feet.

Then, he froze.

Slowly, he knelt down. He carefully moved some brush aside with his free hand.

There, in the brush, carefully hidden, was another electronic eye. He had come within a centimeter of tripping it. Noting its position, he stepped back several feet, then searched for a stone. Picking a good size one, he hefted it, waited a beat, then tossed it. It broke the beam from the electronic eye.

There was a flash of light.

The object up in the tree looked like a dragon's head in the darkness, even to his eyes. A beam of light like a flame leaped from it, and, directly across from its path, cut a swath though the side of a large tree. Smoke rose from the green trunk where the beam had struck. Had Saint-Clair broken that electronic eye beam, the "dragon's eye" would have cut him in two.

And it would have, if he hadn't noticed a bit of yellowed white in the dirt where the electronic eye had been.

It was another of Drax's unlucky crew—his half-buried skull to be exact.

The beam of light had decapitated the SS. Probably even cauterized the wound with its heat. Nasty.

Morane had come up quickly when he had heard the sizzling noise of the tree burning. "My God," he whispered.

"Yes," the Nyctalope said. "My sentiments exactly. Perhaps we should post a sign."

Morane whistled. "What in God's name?..."

The Nyctalope smiled. "Here be..."

222

"...dragons," Dr. No said. "As I warned Signore Largo, dragons." He was examining the device that had fired the beam of light and wounded Largo. It resembled nothing so much as a dragon's head until it was uncovered.

The Yellow Shadow had just sent Largo back on a stretcher made from some branches and his men's jackets. They were losing time, and Largo's scream had surely alerted the others. Normally, he would have killed the fool if for no other reason than his arrogance, and raising an alarm, but he wasn't sure if they could trust Largo's crew if word got back to them that he had murdered their leader. "He'll live, but he might lose that eye. Not so terrible a fate for a pirate I suppose."

Dr. No nodded. "This weapon is quite remarkable," he said, as if discussing a new specimen. "An electronic eye set it off. Largo must have tripped it. When you called out, he turned, and only caught a glancing blow along the edge of the optical nerve. If not, he might well have been decapitated. I've read of certain experiments, but nothing this advanced. The amplification of light through a jewel, usually a ruby I believe, to create such an intense beam that it can cut through the strongest metal—or flesh. You noticed the wound was cauterized..."

Ming was after bigger fish than weapons of light, but he made a note to have one of his men take the "dragon" back to the ship. Dr. No was still studying the weapon. The half-German-Chinese had recently run afoul of several tongs and only Ming's own Shin Tan had protected him from the vengeance of the Si Fan and others. With the money he had embezzled from the tongs, and what Ming was paying him, Dr. No had claimed to have purchased an island, a small key near Jamaica, where he planned to mine bat guano while indulging in his scientific curiosity—a brutal but clinical curiosity. Frankly the cold-blooded devil gave even the Yellow Shadow a chill. Still, the irony of Dr. No's planned self-imposed exile and this island fortress did not escape him.

"You think our competition is ahead of us?" Dr. No asked, as he reluctantly turned from the dragon weapon.

"Yes," replied Ming. "But I doubt they know what they are looking for. They have some vague idea I imagine... The man Saint-Clair is no fool, but since Tadeus knew little, he could give little away, and I doubt the eccentric Professor could tell them much, even if he wanted to. The man can't remember to match his stockings."

Dr. No shrugged. He, too, had been a victim of society's disdain for the pure intellect. One would think a man such as Ming, a scientist himself, would have more tolerance, but—Well, it hardly mattered. Soon enough, he would have his own little island fortress on Crab Key, well guarded by the mixed blood Chinese, crudely called 'chigroes,' whom he had carefully groomed as his servants with rewards weighed against harsh punishment. Once there, he was assured of his privacy. He couldn't imagine the British would be a problem—they seldom were in Hong Kong. So far, the only drawback involved birds. Birds! The Audubon society thought of Crab Key as some sort of private sanctuary. What nonsense, birds. In any case, he was confident that he could handle any British policeman they might persuade to look into his business. Perhaps, he would build his own "dragon" to keep the bird watchers and nosy policemen at bay. One more mobile and less clinical than this one. He was a traditionalist in many ways. Dragons should breathe fire, not beams of light, however deadly.

The rain had let up, though lightning still danced in the sky. More men had joined them from the shore, and the mood was nervous and tentative. Being willing to die for the Yellow Shadow and actually doing it were two different things. Largo's wound had cast a pall over the expedition.

"It has struck you of course that there is a conundrum here," Dr. No said

"A conundrum?" Ming replied.

"Yes. This—this weapon. It is not merely that it is advanced—Einstein didn't predict the electric eye until just before his work on relativity—indeed, it was that, and not his more famous work, that won his Nobel..."

"Your point?"

Dr. No paused, held his anger. "While Dr. Antekirtt was obviously a genius, and well ahead of his time, we must ask ourselves if he discovered some kind of self-replicating energy source... My dear Monsieur Ming, this Antekirtt—Count Sandorf—was last heard of before the beginning of the 20th century, but his weapons are still operational, and the electric eye is still connected to a source of power..."

Ming's bright dark eyes sparked. Yes! Fool that he was! Largo had distracted him. It was obvious. But that left one question: if the island's defenses were maintained—by who... or...

"What is it?" the Boy asked, watching as Morane carefully dug the earth out around the electronic eye Saint-Clair had found.

The Nyctalope shrugged. Morane had slapped his forehead, then, taking a hunting knife from his boot, had dropped to the ground near the electronic eye. Meanwhile, Prince was studying the "dragon" after taking it down from its hiding place.

"There are no wires" Prince observed. "So what powered it? I can understand the electronic eye tripping and firing it, but what powered it—or for that matter..."

Morane had finished digging out the electronic eye mechanism. He lifted it from the ground. It was no larger than a stake a surveyor might use, with the glass encased "eye" like a flashlight.

"No wires," Saint-Clair observed. Something stirred in his memory. He had encountered something similar once; power transmitted through the ether without wires, like radio or television signals

"Of course," said the Boy. "The Professor talked about this, but I thought he was babbling. Now it all makes sense." Even his pup was wagging his tail excitedly, as if he, too, sensed a mystery being solved. "Before I left, the Professor kept saying something about power through the air. I thought he was talking about airplanes or rockets or some such, but now..."

"Power through the air," Saint-Clair said.

Morane was examining the "dragon" now. "Here, see this small recess. It's a lens. A receptor. The eye activated it and also powered it. And there's another on the other side... Prince, put the weapon back, as close to exactly as it was as you can."

Prince did as Morane asked. Then the Commandant placed the eye back in the ground and waved them all back. He used his hand to break the unseen beam from the eye to the weapon. There was a flash and the tree was again scorched.

Prince removed the weapon again while Morane was careful to turn the eye away from the weapon. But it was Saint-Clair who had grasped the obvious. He moved quickly off the trail and thrashed in the bushes. The Dog barked excitedly until the Boy hushed him, but by then Morane, too, was thrashing in the brush.

"Here," said Saint-Clair. "About five feet away..."

"And another," Moraine said. "About six more feet in."

"I don't see..." began Prince.

"The Professor experimented with this once," said the Boy. "He nearly burned down the Diva's villa, but the idea was sound enough. Power, electrical power transmitted through the air without wires. The eyes act as transmission stations and focus the power. They don't look big enough to store it, so they carry the current from eye to eye and, when the beam is interrupted, it activates the weapon. They must be planted all over the island like this..."

It was Prince who saw the most obvious advantage first. "Then, if we follow them..."

"Back to the source," Morane said. "Of course, it will be rough going, but better than stumbling along looking for traps."

"Then, we had best move quickly," Saint-Clair said. "Ming and No aren't fools. They will think of the same thing before long."

"No doubt," said Prince, but he was laughing. He had seen the one thing the others had missed.

Morane and Saint-Clair looked at him as if he were mad, but the Boy suddenly began to laugh too. Even the little dog pranced as if he had gotten the jest.

"I don't get the joke," Morane said.

"Neither do I," added Saint-Clair.

But then Morane smiled broadly too. And to think, it had been his idea in the first place. Simpleton. And even as he smiled, he saw the same thought break on Saint-Clair's features.

They had an advantage the others could not duplicate. The Nyctalope's...

"...eyes," swore the Yellow Shadow. "Damn their eyes!"

His men crashed through the rough on either side of the path like so many elephants. Ordinarily, as stealthy as ninjitsu, the fear of the "dragons" had made them nervous, and nervous men were never stealthy. Still, even with that disadvantage, their pace had increased once they began to follow the path of the electric eyes.

Dr. No seemed to find it all amusing. The idea of power sent directly through the air had fired his mind.

"Of course, it was the great dream of the Slav genius, Tesla, to transmit power through the air, but while it is theoretically possible, the probability of overcoming the numerous problems and drawbacks stopped even his great intellect. Our Dr. Antekirtt must have indeed been a genius to not only conceive of the idea when Edison was still toying with filaments for his light globes, but to harness the power and overcome it. The potential as a weapon alone... Imagine..."

But the Yellow Shadow needed no lesser imagination to fire his vision. If the power could be used to trigger a simple light amplification weapon, then imagine if it was used directly. Not powering a toy, but directly used against an enemy. Already, he was considering the electronic eyes which were used to carry the invisible current. Was a few feet their limit, or could that be extended with a greater generation source? What if a nuclear reactor was available? He saw visions of entire cities in flames and the world on its knees—to him—alone. When Dr. No would no longerbe needed... Antekirtt's laboratory was such a dangerous place...

He closed the fist of his artificial right hand. He imagined Dr. No's skull crushed with that grip. Power, and his alone to wield. But in the shadows. Let others stand in the limelight. He preferred to manipulate his puppets from the darkness of anonymity. Vanity had been the downfall of others with the same dream. It would not be his.

An excited shout.

Another eye had been found.

He already knew the trail was leading to the fortress at the center of the island. That much was obvious. Where else would Antekirtt have built his generator but in the fortress of Antekirtta? And now, they had a safe path to that generator.

Only one thing concerned him. A small thing. A dangerous thing.

The man Morane was a fool, but one blessed with luck and remarkable cunning. Indeed he seemed to lead a charmed life, and now with this team of his... The Boy was nothing. The sailor? A mere drunk. The Interpol agent? A policeman, nothing more. But the other...

He knew the stories about the Nyctalope. An almost inhuman hero; the embodiment of Colonial France, a sort of living emblem. A ruthless soldier and

226

adventurer, a legend in the flesh. They had never met, but once before, a long time ago, in China, there had been a remarkable Triad of which the Yellow Shadow was one arm. Saint-Clair had almost single handedly smashed their plans. Ming had been forced to flee, to go underground. Saint-Clair had only been hours from not only destroying the Shin Tan and his plans, but from destroying him. That made him a deadly enemy. An enemy to be respected. Feared. Destroyed.

He would not rest until he stood over the body of the Frenchman, and cut out his artificial...

"...heart," Saint-Clair was saying. "This is the heart of the island."

They stood on a rise and looked down on the fortress of Antekirtta. It was a large structure, first built by Crusaders during the Second Crusade, and later conquered by the Seljuk Turks, who had made many improvements to the place, including a low outer wall that surrounded the main grounds. Inside, there was a courtyard with stalls and other small buildings around the inner walls, and to the southeast, a barracks—it couldn't be anything else—a building about three stories tall. There were other structures of equally obvious origin: a stable, downwind from the other buildings; an adjoining smith; what looked to be a munitions dump that apparently went underground; and the main structure or castle, a curious mix of Western and Eastern architecture, given a strange even Gothic appearance by the scuttling clouds above.

All of it deserted and quiet.

They made their way down the steep hill slowly. There was no sign of the Yellow Shadow, so they were ahead of the game. As they neared the ruins— there was no other name for them—the three men grew more cautious, and even the little dog seemed to sense the danger, keeping close to the Boy. No one spoke, but Saint-Clair could see the determination in Morane's face and the heightened awareness in Prince's eyes.

But there were no more traps. None they could see anyway.

The great gate was open, a heavy Moorish style door that now hung shattered by an explosion.

Again, no one spoke, but they all thought the same thing. Drax. He had made it this far, if no farther.

Saint-Clair entered first, the Sten gun unslung, moving through the center of the courtyard. It was overgrown and unkempt, full of shadows and pools of deeper darkness, gray even to his eyes. Behind him, Morane entered to the right, and Prince to the left, the Boy and the Dog behind them, the young reporter keeping an eye on their rear.

Nothing happened.

Saint-Clair spotted several electronic eyes, but they were inactive. Had Drax, and his SS, getting this far, deactivated them?

No.

Not Drax. And not Ming either.

And yet, one thing was clear. The electronic eyes within the fortress were as well cared for as those outside. They weren't alone. Eyes were watching them. Eyes that had chosen to allow them inside the fortress unassaulted.

So far.

Saint-Clair felt the hair on the nape of his neck stand up. The mystery of Antekirtta had long intrigued him. It had once been a sort of paradise, a haven for political refugees, artists, artisans, and scientists, then... Something had happened. Those who knew kept quiet. Antekirtt had died not too long after the great pirate battle that had ended his quest for revenge, and the island seemed to die with him. By the end of the Great War, it was known to be deserted, and by the Second World War, it was thought to be haunted. The fate of Drax and his men had only added to that myth. But was it a myth? What did hide on Antekirtta. Or who?

From the corner of his eye, he saw the Dog stop, sniff the air, stiffen. The animal's hair bristled as it had earlier.

Saint-Clair raised a hand. Morane stopped. Prince followed suit, using a hand to signal the Boy to stay back.

The party was at the great stone steps that led up to the main structure of the fortress, the original Crusader building. Like the rest of the place, it was overgrown and crumbling, and yet wasn't that a path well worn up and down the steps?

He scanned the shadows of the old building, seeking some movement, a hint of life, an ambush...

Slowly he began the ascent of the stone steps.

One.

So far no trap. Two.

He reminded himself to breathe. He could almost hear his heart beating. If someone had coughed, it would have sounded like a gunshot. Three.

Another two steps and he would reach a wide landing of sorts, then another half dozen steps to the main entrance.

And so far...

The figure came out of shadows so deep that even the Nyctalope's uncanny eyes hadn't seen him. One instant, there was nothing, then a flash of distant lightning and...

All three men swung their weapons toward the figure. The little dog barked once sharply.

The man seemed unaware of their weapons. He merely raised his hand, and spoke a single word...

"...Welcome," Dr. No said. "We should expect an unpleasant one."

That seemed obvious, but Ming nodded. Their progress had been exponentially faster once they left the main trail and followed the electric eyes, but it was still slow going, and the Mongol could not help but feel they were losing more than time. Experience had taught him the folly of arrogance, and he knew that men such as Bob Morane and Saint-Clair had not survived as long as they had by luck alone. The Yellow Shadow had known others who had crossed the Nyctalope's path and lived to regret it. That old business in China still stung, and if Dr. Natas held no grudges, and the one known as the Blue Scorpion had met final defeat at the hands of a brazen American engineer, Monsieur Ming had a long memory and desired pay back.

Perhaps this would afford him that opportunity. It was pleasant to think of Saint-Clair and Morane at this mercy...

One of his men came toward them swiftly. He spoke softly to the Mongol, his eyes cast down as was proper.

Ming turned to Dr. No.

"Just ahead. The fortress..." '

They moved quickly, but still with care. They were above the fortress in a copse of wood and well concealed, though they kept well back mindful of the Nyctalope's eyes.

The fortress lay in the shadows. It was still and seemed abandoned. They watched for several minutes, but saw no sign of movement. Flashes of distant lightning illuminated the courtyard. Low scuttling clouds created fantastic images. But nothing living moved.

Neither Dr. No nor Monsieur Ming dared to think they were ahead of the others. From here on the danger was only greater. One question remained in the forefront. What danger lay ahead? What lay unseen in the...

"...shadows," their host said. "For too many years, I have lived among the shadows of the dead."

He was a small man and, despite his age, obviously still fit. There was something of the athlete about his carriage, and a sense of tremendous energy and wit about him. His eyes were quick and saw more than they revealed. He had given them a queer name, but one Saint-Clair suspected was his own: Point Pescade.

His greeting had been perfectly designed to gain their attention:

"We must hurry, gentlemen. There is little time and we're all in grave danger..." Instinctively, Saint-Clair had turned to the direction the enemy was advancing from. "No, no, not them. There's far greater danger and little time. I have put this off too long, and now... Pray that there is still time. Come with me, gentlemen, and I will explain everything as quickly as possible."

He had told them about the mysterious "Dr. Antekirtt" and his war of revenge for the way he had been wronged, how Mathias Sandorf had used his genius, and the gifts of the island, to build a sort of scientific utopia after defeating his enemies, and then had been struck down by an enemy he could not have imagined.

As they talked, Point Pescade led them down a narrow stair into the catacombs located beneath the main building. Prince and the Boy agreed to keep watch while Saint-Clair and Morane followed the old man deeper into the darkness.

"How could he have known? How could he have guessed? Madame Curie was years away and Röntgen had yet to make his discoveries... How could the Doctor have begun to guess..."

Saint-Clair looked sharply at Morane. There was an unspoken agreement to let the old man tell his tale in whatever rambling way he chose. Obviously, the fellow was a bit dotty with age and loneliness.

As they moved deeper, they heard a curious hum, like some sort of giant generator, and they began to notice a radiant light emanating ahead of them. Before they could comment on it, they came upon a great room lined with giant machinery that resembled in many ways a generator, the source to the hum of power and light. Passing the giant generators, they came to a wall lined with panels and gauges, obviously monitoring the source of the power.

"And there, gentlemen, is the source of Antekirtta's power. You can't imagine how many hours the Doctor worked down here, how often I assisted him... Do you see, gentlemen, do you begin to comprehend? I myself installed that monitor after the last war... too late, too late..."

Saint-Clair followed the old man's pointing finger to the monitor in question and, suddenly, a chill ran up his spine.

"Marie Curie," Morane said, "Wilhelm Röntgen. The invisible enemy..."

"Radiation," Saint-Clair said.

"Aye," Point Pescade said sadly. "How could the good Doctor have known? Have guessed? He thought he had found the greatest boon to mankind since Prometheus gave us fire, and instead... At first, there were mysterious illnesses on the island, cancers, blood diseases, strange burns—we couldn't have known. Soon, people began to leave, and the Doctor's health began to fail as he wore himself out, down here, trying to discover the secret, all the time exposing himself to certain death—a slow, lingering death, that first claimed all he had loved, then his own life."

"My God!" Moraine said. "He built a nuclear reactor in the 19th century."

"No," Pescade said sharply. "No, gentlemen, not built one—found one. The entire island is a natural nuclear reactor, a volcanic wonder. That is what the Doctor found, but he could not have guessed..."

"...The price of the gift."

As they spoke, Morane had moved closer to a wall dominated by a large switch with bright red handles. It was quite big and would need two hands to pull it down. He reached out to touch it...

"No!"

Morane froze.

230

"Forgive me, but should you throw that switch without protective gloves and before I throw this switch..." Pescade indicated a large red button on the low panel before him... "You would receive a massive radiation burn to your hands, possibly fatal. You must remember this place may be a work of genius, but by modern standards... I fear I lacked the genius of my friend and mentor. It has been all I could do merely to maintain the island safely, and not even that..." He turned to Saint-Clair, locking his eyes with the man's uncanny orbs. "That was why I sent for you."

"Sent?"

"Indirectly, of course, but the bait was laid, and who else would be chosen for such a mission? No, there's no time for modesty. I needed a man of your caliber, even knowing that it would also draw other, more ruthless men. I needed to give you this."

The old man moved toward a closed cabinet which he opened. Inside was a large old book, stuffed with papers and wrapped in oil cloth.

"Doctor Antekirtt's journals, gentlemen. All his discoveries, all his wisdom. It's time to let the world be reminded of his genius, and time to carry these secrets away from this place before they're buried forever."

"Buried?" Saint-Clair asked.

"Buried," the Yellow Shadow repeated. He was smiling, his weapon aimed at the Nyctalope's chest. Behind him was Dr. No and several of his men, two of them closely covering Prince and the Boy. The little dog was nowhere to be seen.

"Don't tell me that you have failed to understand what this doddering fool was trying to tell you," Ming gloated. "My God, man, think. A natural nuclear reactor. These great generators... Perhaps you would care to tell them, Doctor?"

The Chinese glided forward like a great snake. He moved toward the switch where Morane had been standing. "No doubt you know the island is a natural nuclear reactor. To some extent, the entire planet is, but what you cannot comprehend is the simple fact that, in tampering with nature, Dr. Antekirtt upset the balance. Are you familiar with the term 'China Syndrome?'"

Morane had gone white. "Meltdown."

"Exactly," Ming said. "Meltdown. The entire island collapsing on its core, a tremendous explosion and a release of radioactive gasses. No doubt, the island will cease to exist. The geologists who monitor such things will put it down to a volcanic eruption, but... Tell me, how long do you estimate?" he had spoken to Point Pescade.

"Should I fail to throw that switch? A few hours. It controls the rods which help to cool the reactor which the volcano powers. They're failing, but should hold out a little longer..."

231

"So that you have time to give our friend Saint-Clair here Antekirtt's note-book?. Such a waste. For the greater glory of France? What a joke. No, no the good Doctor and I have better things to do with this gift." Ming was gloating.

The Nyctalope was seemingly at ease, but beneath the exterior, every muscle was tense. He could feel the tension build, and knew that his moment, the moment of action, was near. From the corner of his eye, he had seen the Boy's little dog in the shadows. He might be small, but could provide a diversion, and all Saint-Clair needed was one moment. If only the animal waited for the right moment.

Dr. No was standing by the switch now. "So this decides all our fates? Throw the switch and the island lives for another few hours, leave it and..." He smiled thinly and reached out for the switch.

Let the old man keep silent, Saint-Clair thought.

Dr. No put both hands on the switch.

Point Pescade moved a single step, hiding the red button with his body.

Dr. No threw the switch.

Then, everything happened at once.

The Chinese-German scientist was jolted; his body became an arc of light and fire, his hands almost ablaze. An inhuman scream escaped his lips. For a moment, he hung there before his body broke contact. Then, still screaming, he ran from the room, holding his burning hands in front of him.

The little dog leaped forward and sank his teeth into the ankle of the guard behind the Boy.

Bernard Prince ducked and drove his elbow back into the breast bone of the man guarding him. The fellow folded like cardboard as the Interpol agent's hand chopped down on his exposed neck.

The Nyctalope drew one of his Brownings and calmly shot the guard who was screaming at the little dog between the eyes.

Bob Morane leaped and knocked aside Monsieur Ming's gun as it fired. There was a momentous struggle, then the bigger man forced Morane off. Moving faster than he would seem capable of, the Yellow Shadow was off through the catacombs, following Dr. No. The Nyctalope lunged to follow him.

"Saint-Clair!"

It was Prince. He was pointing at the control panel.

Point Pescade was slumped against it. A red stain ran down the front of his shirt. Saint-Clair recognized the dark color of heart's blood.

He and Morane kneeled by the fallen figure. While the aviator checked the wound, Saint-Clair cradled the old man's head.

"Take it easy. We'll get you to help... Prince, press this red button and throw that switch..."

"No," Point Pescade said, his voice curiously strong. "No. It's better this way. Don't bother, son, I know a fatal wound when I... Promise me that you will

232

get the Doctor's papers away. You must decide what to do with them. I'm too close. That's why I chose you. Please, promise me you will..."

But that was the last thing he said—in this world.

Ming and his men gave them no more trouble. With the island's protection cut off, they made quick work of returning to their boat, and much to Saint-Clair's surprise, when they reached the *Cormorant*, the Captain was halfway sober and the engines warm. They were underway in a matter of minutes.

The first pink tint of dawn was teasing the horizon in the east when, to their south, the Sun rose with a vengeance. There was a flash of light so bright that, for an instant, they could see through the flesh of their hands to the very bone, and then the sky was filled with fire and rubble as the island disintegrated as if it had never existed.

At Saint-Clair's command, they grabbed the gunwale. In the next moments, a roar like the Heavens themselves had opened hit them, and then a wind, hot as the Devil's breath, sent the boat rocking and the waves rolling under them.

It would be a near thing, the Captain had told them, but they could outrun the worst of the tsunami that would follow the island's destruction.

The Boy and the Dog went below first. It had been a long day. Prince went next, a single finger raised in salute as he did. Morane lingered for a moment. The diary of Doctor Antekirtt lay on the engine housing. He looked at it for a long time, then at Saint-Clair.

"Coming below?"

"In a minute." Saint-Clair watched as Morane went below.

The island, at least the place where it had been, was dark once more. In the east, the Sun was now a promise rather than a hope.

He lifted Antekirtt's notebook. In this journal were answers that men had sought for centuries. And it would soon be in the hands of his own beloved France, perhaps heralding the dawn of a new century of French power and greatness...

But at what price?

Slowly and with deliberation, he tore the pages from the notebook. He tossed them to the seven winds and watched as they fell to the surface of the still roiling sea.

And when he was done, he went below. For the first time in a long time, he felt human, he felt part of something. There was such a thing as redemption, even for men who could not die in the ordinary way of mortals.

For the Nyctalope, the dawn had come again after too long a darkness.

Brian Stableford brings his momentous alternate history epic, The Empire of the Necromancers, *to a conclusion of sorts in this sixth and final segment, which brings the action back to where it started, that is to say in London. Readers wishing to get better acquainted with some of the characters should check Brian's remarkable translations of Paul Féval's ground-breaking novels* John Devil, The Vampire Countess, Revenants, *and* The Black Coats *saga.*

Brian Stableford: *The Necromancers of London*
(Being the sixth part of
The Empire of the Necromancers)

The Story So Far

In Paul Féval's John Devil *(Black Coat Press, 2005), that legendary pseudonym is adopted by Comte Henri de Belcamp in support of his mother's career as a notorious member of London's underworld, where she is known by her maiden name, Helen Brown. After attempting to rescue her from an Australian prison camp Henri takes news of his mother's death to his long-estranged father, the Marquis de Belcamp, in the small town of Miremont, and is reconciled with him. Meanwhile, Henri is secretly engaged in financing the construction of an unprecedentedly powerful steamship with which he intends to rescue Napoleon from St. Helena and conquer India; in pursuit of this plan, he takes over a secret Bonapartist organization, the Knights of the Deliverance. Henri is assisted in this project by his long-term companion Sarah O'Brien, the daughter of a murdered Irish general.*

When a potential traitor to the Deliverance, the opera singer Constance Bartolozzi, is murdered in London, the case is investigated by Gregory Temple, the senior detective at Scotland Yard, assisted by his junior, James Davy. John Devil is identified as the murderer. Temple strongly suspects that the person behind that name is Helen Brown's son, known to him as Tom Brown, but the evidence seems to point to Temple's former assistant, Richard Thompson (who is secretly married to Temple's daughter, Suzanne). Actually, James Davy—who is another of Henri de Belcamp's many aliases—has framed his predecessor, exploiting the account of his methods Temple has published in a book on the art of detection. Henri/Davy persuades Thompson to flee to France, where Suzanne is a guest at the Château Belcamp, but he is captured and convicted of the Bartolozzi murder.

When Henri is reconciled with his father, Sarah rents the so-called "new château" on the Belcamp estate under the name of Lady Frances Elphinstone. Henri commissions the murders of his dead mother's wealthy brothers, but there is one further obstacle to the fortune Henri intends to collect by this means, in the name of Tom Brown: Constance Bertolozzi's daughter, Jeanne Herbet, who also lives in Miremont. Jeanne is the designated heir of both brothers, neither of whom knows which of them is her father. Henri falls in love with Jeanne after impulsively saving her life, and decides to marry her fortune rather than murdering her.

Henri eventually marries Jeanne under the alias of an English entrepreneur, Percy Balcomb, in which guise he slips out of the jail where Henri is supposedly confined. Henri is in prison because the obsessive Temple, having failed to prove that he murdered General O'Brien or Constance Bartolozzi, found out where the bodies of his hired killers were buried. Temple has obtained this information from the drunken mistress of the vertically-challenged petty criminal Ned Knob, who was a witness to the murders and disposed of the bodies. Ned had also schooled the false witnesses at Richard Thompson's trial, using members of a troupe of vagabond actors.

On the eve of Thompson's execution, Henri inveigles his way into Newgate Prison, helping him to escape by taking his place. When Temple tries the same trick, Henri confronts his nemesis in the condemned cell, almost driving him insane by telling him that Tom Brown is not, after all, one of his pseudonyms but an actual half-brother, sired by Temple. After escaping in Temple's place, however, Henri finds that everything is going awry. The Deliverance is betrayed, his new steamship is destroyed, and his mother has returned from Australia, accusing him of having abandoned her. He finds it politic to commit suicide—or, at least, to appear to do so.

Part One of The Empire of the Necromancers, "The Grey Men" (in Tales of the Shadowmen 2, Black Coat Press 2006) picks up the story four years later, in November 1821. Ned Knob, now directing the acting troupe, is unexpectedly confronted with his predecessor in that role, "Sawney" Ross, who has been hanged but now appears to be alive again, though somewhat slow-witted. When the reanimated Ross is collected by a diminutive French physician, Germain Patou, Ned follows them to a boat where they are met by a man in a Quaker hat like the one Henri wore in his guise as John Devil.

After being knocked unconscious, Ned wakes up in Newgate and is interrogated by Gregory Temple, now working for the secret police. Temple is supposed to be investigating a series of body-snatching incidents, but his attention has been caught by a report of the Quaker hat. Following his release, Ned tracks Patou to a house in Purfleet. There he renews his acquaintance with Henri and witnesses the resurrection of a man from the dead using an elaborate electrical technique recently discovered by a Swiss scientist.

The demonstration is interrupted when Henri's ship is attacked by a rival group under the command of the only one of the reanimated Grey Men to have recovered all his faculties: a person who styles himself General Mortdieu. Mortdieu's hirelings seize the electrical apparatus from the house, taking it to *their own ship, the* Outremort. *Ned is arrested again, but makes a deal with Temple. As the* Outremort *is about to depart from her berth in Greenhithe, a three-cornered battle develops between Mortdieu's hirelings, Henri's followers and Temple's men. The fight eventually arrives at an impasse, but a hastily-contrived treaty permits Mortdieu to sail away, taking Patou with him.*

In Part Two, "The Child-Stealers" (in Tales of the Shadowmen 3, *2006) Gregory Temple is woken one night by Henri, who tells him that they must join forces, at least temporarily. Temple's grandson has been kidnapped from the Château Belcamp, where Thompson and Suzanne are now resident, along with two younger children of much richer parents; one is the son of Henri and Jeanne, the other the son of the former Sarah O'Brien, now the widow of a German Count.*

Temple and Henri set out to make their separate ways to Miremont, where Temple has to break the news to Jeanne that she is not a widow. Henri is de-layed and Temple has to respond to the first ransom note with no one to help him but Ned Knob. He is taken prisoner in his turn. Temple's captors are mem-bers of a long-dormant society of heretic monks known as Civitas Solis, *who are even more interested in securing the secret of resurrection than in the ransom money that will help finance their exploitation of it.*

Henri's delay has been caused by his traveling under the name George Palmer, in which guise he was involved with a vehm (a secret society of vigi-lantes) at the time of General O'Brien's murder, and in whose eyes he is still a wanted man. Having made his peace with the vehmgerichte, however, Henri is able to attack Civitas Solis *and liberate Temple and the captive children before disappearing again, intent on joining forces with* Civitas Solis *in the expectation of using them as he had formerly used the Deliverance.*

*In Part Three, "The Return of Frankenstein" (*Tales of the Shadowmen 4, *2007), set in the vicinity of Spezia in Northern Italy in the summer of 1822, Ned Knob has been commissioned by Gregory Temple to keep watch on a villa rented by Victor Frankenstein, the original inventor of the technology of resur-rection carried forward by Germain Patou, and his friend Robert Walton. Fran-kenstein is about to resume his own experiments, aided by a group of Englishmen headed by Lord Byron and Percy Shelley. Ned is also reporting his findings to Henri de Belcamp.*

Ned is not the only spy interested in Frankenstein's work. He is ap-proached with an offer of cooperation by a man who calls himself Guido, who eventually turns out to be a Magyar working for a reputed vampire—one of "na-ture's Grey Men" rather than a legendary bloodsucker. He also meets a burly but uncommonly articulate Grey Man who is somewhat resentful of being por-trayed as a murderous "daemon" in the sensationalized version of Frankens-tein's story that Robert Walton issued by way of Mary Shelley; Frankenstein's first creation prefers to think of himself as the Adam of a new race and is at-tempting to negotiate a reconciliation with his creator. Ned has a less amicable

236

encounter with a fanatical warrior monk named Malo de Treguern, who appears to be working for a more orthodox and more inquisitorially-inclined arm of the Roman Church than Civitas Solis.

Owing to the interaction of these various interested parties and Percy Shelley's collapse as a result of a wound inflicted by a member of the local militia, Frankenstein's villa is besieged and his attempts to renew his experiments are thwarted. Frankenstein and most of his associates escape, but will have to find a more hospitable spot to resume work. Ned hears of Shelley's death by drowning a few days later, but does not believe the rumor.

In Part Four, "The Vampire of Paris" (Tales of the Shadowmen 5, *2007), set in the Autumn of 1822, Gregory Temple visits the aged Jean-Paul Sévérin, who was once one of the best swordsmen in France, in quest of information regarding Germain Patou, offering to trade information regarding an alleged vampire that Sévérin, his son-in-law, René de Kervoz, and Patou once encountered—an encounter that was responsible for Patou's initial interest in the biology of resurrection.*

The female vampire in question, known as Comtesse Marcian Gregoryi, has returned to France, seemingly no older although two decades have passed; she has hired Robert Surrisy as her lawyer with a view to buying the new château at Miremont. Coco-Lacour of the Sûreté, Malo de Treguern and Lord Byron also take an interest in the matter. Temple and Sévérin are attacked by hirelings of the Comtesse's associate, Guido, who is similarly intent on finding Patou and who attempts to kidnap Sévérin's grand-daughter in order to force information out of the old man. The attempt is thwarted by Frankenstein's first creation, who is now going by the name of Lazarus.

With Lazarus' aid, Temple tracks the master vampire who employs the Comtesse as his cat's-paw to Miremont, but is outmaneuvered by him and tricked into introducing him into a party held in the new château; he and the other guests—who include Byron and the enigmatic Colonel Bozzo-Corona—are saved in the nick of time by Sévérin and Malo de Treguern, whose timely intervention puts the vampire to flight. Temple and Byron make a brief but friendly contact, and admit to one another that they both have agents on a ship named the Belleville, *bound for the Caribbean....*

In Part Five, "Where Zombie Armies Clash by Night" (Tales of the Shadowmen 6, *2009), set in the early months of 1823, Ned Knob is cast adrift in a small boat after the* Belleville—*the French ship in which he has traveled to the Caribbean in search of Germain Patou and General Mortdieur—is captured by the pirate Amédée Desart, master of the* Cayman. *He finds himself in the company of Marie Laveau, a* vaudou *priestess originally from New Orleans, who has plans to represent her self as a reincarnation of the ancient Tairo Queen Anacaona and plant the seeds of a* zambo *empire in northern Haiti. She expects rescue by the zambo, but it is actually Mortdieu who picks them up in the Out-*

remort, *delivering them into the heart of a multi-sided conflict in which the advantage shifts with hectic rapidity.*

Marie mounts an exhibition of zombie production with which she hopes to secure her prestige, but is shot by a mestizo *sniper at its climax, forcing Mortdieu to go inland in quest of Patou, from whom he is temporarily estranged. Before Patou can return, however, Mortdieu's refuge is attacked and taken by a fort led by Desart and Lord Byron's associate, Edward Trelawny, who was also on the* Belleville, *commissioned to make a deal with President Boyer of the Haitian Republic,. Having captured the* Outremort, *Desart sets out to sea again, having divided his crew into three—but having over-reached himself, has to flee Boyer's navy.*

Ned renews his acquaintance with Sawney Ross before Mortdieu takes advantage of an opportunity to capture the Cayman, *and then sails with him to execute the terms of a pact that the Grey General has made with Boyer's captains—which turn out to be the destruction of the pirate stronghold of Tortuga by cunning means. With that done, the basis appears to be in place for an alliance between Mortdieu and Patou, Marie Laveau and Boyer, with Byron and Trelawny's plans pushed to the sidelines.*

Now read on...

London, 1823

Chapter One
Waiting for the Night Mail

November 1823 had turned out to be unseasonably cold, and the members of the thin crowd awaiting the arrival of the evening mail coach from Dover were all huddled in the coffee-shop next door to the Post Office, sitting as close as possible to one or other of its two black-leaded stoves. One man, however, had stationed himself slightly apart from the two clusters, alone at a table. He was muffled by a greatcoat, a scarf and a capacious felt hat, with a coffee-pot and a white china cup before him. The dregs had long since gone cold.

The coach was late—unsurprisingly, given that the chill of the night must have frosted all the ruts and potholes in the road into jarring solidity, and that a freezing fog had settled that must be even worse in open country than the streets of London, though not quite as smoke-laden.

When a slender but not unmuscular individual came over to the table where the lone man was sitting, carrying a fresh coffee-pot and a clean cup, the latter looked up gratefully, although he did not allow the concealing scarf to fall from the lower part of his face. The gratitude vanished from his eyes, though, and he scowled behind the scarf. The benevolent newcomer was not a waiter.

"Good evening, Mr. Temple," the newcomer said, politely. "Or should I say 'good morning,' given that it's past midnight? Do you remember me?"

Gregory Temple cursed the mention of his name, although it had been spoken in tone so soft and silky that he doubted that any other members of the patient crowd had heard it. "I remember all the hirelings who bore false witness against Richard Thompson, with the intention of sending him to the gallows for a crime committed by John Devil," he said. "Given the chance, I'd bring them all to their due reckoning—and be sure to keep them from the kind of evasion accomplished by Sawney Ross. You have a damnable nerve approaching me, Mr. Hopkey."

"You can call me Sam," the actor said, as he sat down and poured out two cups of coffee for himself and the secret policeman. "And I'll freely admit that I was never comfortable with that affair. I've been to the Old Bailey half a dozen times in all, but always to secure an acquittal, save for that once. John Devil took care to snatch Thompson away from the noose, though—for which you might be a little grateful. You've forgiven Ned Knob, after all, and taken him into your service."

"I've forgiven no one," Temple growled, although he picked up the full cup readily enough, and put the hot brim to his lips gratefully, "and I know full well that Knob didn't send you, for he's still in the Caribbean with your old master, trying to play the diplomat in the founding of a zombie empire."

"Might I ask how that work is going?" Sam Hopkey said, with the ghost of a smile on his lips.

"None too well, as you doubtless have your own means of knowing," Temple retorted. "Limehouse is swarming with sailors returned from the Americas, and they all turn up at Sharper's eventually, although many must be disappointed to find it metamorphosed into Jenny Paddock's Cabaret Theater. I hear that your slut has pretensions now to be a tragedienne, although I doubt that she was playing Phaedra tonight."

"You have no right to call Jeanie a slut, sir," Sam Hopkey replied, with a certain dignity. "We might not have solemnized our union in church, but we're as faithful a couple as you'd find at one of the Duchess of Devonshire's affairs, and far more so than any you'd find in jolly George's rotten court."

There was no scope for denying that, so Temple merely said: "What do you want, Mr. Hopkey? Best hurry—the coach will be here at any minute."

"Not a chance, Mr. Temple," the wiry man replied. "It'll be another half-hour at least, on a night like this. As you must have guessed, I'm here on Tom's behalf."

Temple had guessed, but he was still intrigued. He had lately had some slight contact with a representative of *Civitas Solis*—the man who styled himself Giuseppe Balsamo—and the fact that Tom Brown, alias Henri de Belcamp,

239

thought it necessary to make separate contact suggested that the latter's plan to become an influential figure in that shadowy organization was faring no better than Germain Patou's plan to secure a haven in Haiti where he could resume his necromantic vocation with all possible fervor and efficiency.

"John Devil and I might have forged a brief alliance in the recent past," Temple said, "but we are not friends. Any information you give me, I am likely to use against him. I'm even more eager to send him to the gallows than you and your doxy."

"Tom told me that you would be gruff and surly," Sam replied, calmly, "but he told me not to take any notice, because you know as well as he does, in your heart of hearts, that you're both on the same side now, facing the same adversaries with the same heroic spirit. He says that no matter what you might say aloud, you're no more committed to the King and Parliament than Ned Knob is."

"He has a damned cheek, then," Temple opined, wrathfully. "I'm loyal to my country—and Parliament has not yet made up its mind. Canning used to be the most ardent of the enemies of Jacobin science, but now he's in charge of the nation's destiny, he knows better than to play the bigot."

Although Lord Liverpool was the Prime Minister, everyone knew that George Canning was the man in charge of the Tory party and the government. Sam merely smiled at the mention of the name, though. "I've played the bigot myself, on stage," he said, "and the opposite too. Mr. Canning's a fine actor, but I know the art too well to trust anything he says. If you think that his Commission of Inquiry intends to make a fair report of the affair at Fyne Court, you're a greater optimist than I took you for."

Temple scowled, although he knew that if Tom Brown were now in London—as he surely must be, if Sam Hopkey had come here on his behalf—then he had ample means of finding out what was going on, even in the wilds of the Quantocks. He would know, just as Balsamo had, that Victor Frankenstein, whom Lord Byron had hoped to escort to the Americas, had instead accepted an invitation from Andrew Crosse and Michael Faraday, the most prominent English pioneers of electric research now that Humphry Davy was dead, to stage a demonstration at Crosse's home in Somerset—and that Canning had set up a commission to investigate the claims that Frankenstein had made regarding the resurrection of the dead, in which selected parliamentarians would associate themselves with members of the Royal Society. Temple was due to take charge of the escort that would accompany the commission's members to Fyne Court in less than 36 hours time.

"That's none of your business, Mr. Hopkey," Temple growled, "nor of John Devil's."

"It's everyone's business, Mr. Temple," Hopkey replied, flatly. "If the world is to be turned upside-down, there's not a man, woman or child within it who doesn't have an interest at stake. This is the 19th century, Mr. Temple—

what you call common people are no longer prepared to let their fate be decided by aristocrats and mill-owners, especially in matters of life and death. I didn't come to quarrel with you, though, or to issue challenges. I came to give you information that you direly need to know. For one thing, Szandor and Addhema are in England, probably in London."

Temple knew that Addhema was another name by which Countess Marcian Gregoryi was known in what was assumed to be her native land—or the native land of the person she had once been. He had not known, however, that the vampire and his minion were in England, and Sam was right to judge that it was information of which he and his superiors were in need.

"It was only to be expected," he said, ungraciously. "They're as eager to take possession of Frankenstein and his secrets as Byron and *Civitas Solis* are."

"Not to mention half the governments in Europe, now that credulity is beginning to dawn," Sam said. "It's not just Limehouse that's swarming with sailors returned from the Caribbean. Patou may still be in trouble, but Marie Laveau's publicity has spread. If Canning were to prove willing, in spite of pressure from the Church, England might steal a useful march on her rivals. It's not just Frankenstein that Szandor might be after, though, according to Tom. He sent me to warn you that you may well be in danger yourself."

"I doubt that," Temple said. "The vampire had the opportunity to kill me in Miremont, and refrained."

"It's not the vulgar peril of assassination that threatens you," Sam Hopkey told him. "The vampire might have intended to capture you as well as the Colonel at the Grafina von Boehm's château—and Szandor's probably not the only new enemy whose attention you've attracted."

"It was Byron that Szandor intended to capture," Temple corrected him. "The rest of us were merely bystanders."

"That's possible," Sam insisted. "Tom believes, however, that it was Byron he intended to *seduce*, along with the Grafina. The man he probably intended to *capture* was Colonel Bozzo-Corona—he presumably believed that he already had you, having hobbled you and set you aside for later collection."

"Why would the vampire want to capture the Colonel?" Temple could not help asking, genuinely curious. "Surely not because of his wealth, if he had Sarah von Boehm in his sights."

"According to Tom," Sam said, "the Colonel is considerably richer than the Grafina, although his fortune is much better defended. It wasn't the Colonel's money that interested Szandor, but his antiquity—and Tom believes that Szandor's interest might well have aroused the Colonel's in its turn. It's not your influence as a secret policeman, which seems to be almost annihilated, that interests other parties now, in Tom's opinion—merely your stubbornness in having lived so long, while giving no sign of any conspicuous loss of your mental and physical prowess."

Temple was genuinely puzzled. He had had cause to wonder himself at the remarkable fashion in which the aged Jean-Pierre Sévérin had conserved his skill and acumen, but he had not thought to include himself in the same category. It was Sévérin that he had come to meet from the Dover coach, although he did not know yet why the Frenchman had asked him to be there. "I thought that Szandor was interested in means to secure and prolong life-after-death, and regarded the living as mere prey," he said.

"That was not what he told you when you met him," Sam said, so confidently that Temple knew that he or his master must have had an eye-witness report of the encounter. That could only have come from one person.

"Is Lazarus in England too, then?" Temple asked. He had lost track of Frankenstein's first Grey Man after the affair at Miremont, and had had no news of him since. "Is he the one you're warning me against?"

"No—he still seems intent on forging a reconciliation with his maker. The people of whom Tom commissioned me to warn you to beware are Balsamo and Sarah von Boehm."

"In other words, *Civitas Solis* and the remnant of the *vehm* that took up arms against them when they kidnapped Jeanne and Sarah's children. I can understand why it might be in John Devil's interest to make me wary of both, if he's engaged in some sort of power-struggle with Balsamo—but I've had no indication of hostility from either party." He did not think it politic to add that he had received overtures of friendship from one—and he knew, in any case, that overtures of friendship from a man like Balsamo might easily conceal intentions of a very different sort.

"The proposed demonstration at Fyne Court has become a significant focus of interest, Mr. Temple," the actor told him, with an expansive flourish of his right arm. "The attention of all those working in the cause of Enlightenment, as well as all those working against it, is focused upon it for the moment. If Faraday returns to the Royal Institution suitably enthused and duly licensed to begin his own experiments, London will become the Necromantic capital of the world, with material and intellectual resources that far outstrip anything that Germain Patou and Marie Laveau might contrive in Haiti, let alone those that *Civitas Solis* can presently call upon, given its current state of disarray. Frankenstein's technique is not, however, the only topic of interest whose urgency has been revived by recent events, especially in the ranks of the older Secret Orders. There is more than one kind of potential immortality, Mr. Temple, and more than one way to approach their investigation. You already know that the Commission you will be escorting will include several individuals with secret agendas. Tom advises you to be wary, and to be exceedingly careful in deciding who your friends are."

"I always am," Temple said. "As I've already told you, I certainly don't count John Devil among them. Lazarus, on the other hand…"

"…Has his own ambitions, and makes his alliances in accordance with his own ends."

Temple recalled that the Grey Men's New Adam had admitted something of the sort, but it was hardly necessary. As with Szandor, Lazarus' first priority had to be the interests of the dead-alive, not the living. To the extent that the two sets of interests coincided, he seemed as reliable an ally as any, but if ever there was a conflict, he might be as redoubtable an adversary as any…except, perhaps, Szandor, who was certainly gifted with uncanny powers of delusion and apparently possessed what Temple had decided to call "dividuality:" the ability to divide his person into two. Balsamo, Sarah von Boehm and Colonel Bozzo-Corona, on the other hand, were bound to be interested, first and foremost, in means of prolonging life rather than surviving death; if the methods of modern science were to replace those of the ancient alchemists in that search, that would be the principal focus of their attention—but modern science required empirical observation and experimentation, which would require subjects: living ones, in this instance, rather than dead ones.

Temple still could not believe that he might be as interesting, in that context, as Séverin, or the Colonel—or Balsamo himself, if he were more than a mere impostor—but what Sam was saying was certainly worthy of some thought…unless, of course, John Devil were extending this lure to him precisely in order to deflect him from other concerns and paths of Inquiry. That, he knew, was perfectly possible.

"We all make alliances according to our own ends," Temple told his unwelcome companion, brusquely. "Which is why I will make none with you or your master. Since you've brought me a message from him, I'll give you one to take back: while I still have duties to perform, I shall carry them out to the best of my ability, but if and when I am free once again of immediate obligations to crown and country—which might be very soon, if my superiors' patience runs out—then I shall resume the hunt for John Devil, and pursue it doggedly."

"Alone?" Sam queried.

"If necessary," Temple stated—but he knew that he was being disingenuous. He would not be alone; he had been promised all possible support by the Comtesse de Belcamp, with the sole provision that he did not pursue his chase to the death. Jeanne was interested in capture, not annihilation.

"Tom asked whether you would consent to meet with him," Sam Hopkey continued, after a slight pause. He was obviously not hopeful that his offer would be accepted.

Temple was, in fact, hesitating over the wisdom of uttering the refusal that leapt to his lips, and wondering whether it might be more profitable to accept, when there was a rumble of wheels outside, and the night-coach from Dover was heard racing into the Post Office forecourt.

The waiting crowd rose as one man, and not merely because they had been waiting for so long. The postillion was sounding his horn, and the blast was an alarm signal, intended to summon help. Something was amiss.

Having longer legs than Sam Hopkey, Gregory Temple reached the door first, three or four strides ahead of any of the people who had been huddling closer to the stoves. He bounded out into the street and set off across the courtyard as the coach pulled up, the four hoses steaming and the wheels squealing like souls in torment as the brakes were applied.

Uniformed employees were already emerging from the Post Office itself, and one of them shouted: "What's wrong?"

"Wounded man inside!" cried the coachman. "We were attacked!"

"Highwaymen?" queried a second official. "In 1823! On the Dover Road! Impossible!"

Temple's heat was already sinking, however. He knew that the word "impossible" had virtually lost all meaning, precisely because it was 1823. For the moment, he was far less concerned with the plausibility of highwaymen attacking a mail coach on the Dover road than with the identity of the wounded man. Jean-Pierre Séverin, he knew, was not a man to submit meekly to any kind of attack—but even a man reputed to have been the best swordsman in pre-Revolutionary France could not be expected to be able to defend a mail coach against bandits armed with pistols. It was easy enough to image the ex-morgue-keeper responding chivalrously to a challenge and being shot down in consequence.

The first official reached the flank of the coach ahead of Temple, and pulled open the door. There were only three passengers inside, one of whom was sprawled on the floor between the benches while the other two pored over him with evident concern. There was blood on the floor and on the stricken man's clothing.

None of the three, however, was Jean-Pierre Séverin. The man lying on the floor, having been bloodily slashed on his upper right arm, not far from the shoulder, was Malo de Treguern, Knight of the Order of St. John Hospitaller—another ancient who would inevitably have responded with violent chivalry to any demand to "stand and deliver!"

Temple shoved the Post Office official out of the way, and forced the two concerned passengers to sit down. "Monsieur de Treguern!" he said, urgently. "What happened? Was Séverin with you? What has become of him?"

Malo de Treguern opened his eyes, as if slightly surprised to discover that the coach had reached its destination. "Mr. Temple!" he said. "Thank God you're here! You must summon reinforcements immediately. We were stopped on the road. Séverin and I tried to fight. We expected to take them by surprise, but they were ready for us. They took him, Mr. Temple—the cowards led him on, then dropped a net on him. They dared not face him, even though he only had a stick, and not a blade. I too had a staff, but…"

Temple had been examining the wound. "You've lost a lot of blood, Monsieur de Treguern," he said, "but you'll live, with luck and God's favor. We'll have you in St. Thomas's in no time." As he spoke, he looked at the official, who nodded. A stretcher was already being brought out, and its bearers were well used to sprinting to the hospital. Highwaymen were exceedingly rare nowadays, but traffic accidents were becoming increasing common, as if by way of compensation. The number of people run down by coaches and carriages in the London streets was dizzying to contemplate.

"Why are you here, Monsieur?" Temple asked, as practiced hands transferred the injured man from the floor of the church to the stretcher.

"Séverin is not to blame," Treguern stated, in a hushed but determined voice. "I insisted on accompanying him. We have not become firm friends since our adventure at Miremont, I admit—but once two men have fought as comrades against monsters, there is a bond between them. He was coming to warn you that Comtesse Marcian Gregoryi has crossed the channel, doubtless to pursue her evil schemes in London. He has information about her master, gleaned in Paris...as have I. He saw the virtue of our traveling together—not virtue enough, alas!"

By the time this speech was finished, Temple was trotting alongside the stretcher as it was being carried through the bitterly cold streets in the direction of St. Thomas's Hospital. He could see Tower Bridge in the distance, its candle-lit towers looming out of the mist as if suspended in mid-air.

"I will come to see you tomorrow," Temple promised, relenting in his pace, and then turning back. The coachman, he knew, would be able to tell him exactly where the attack had taken place, and the Post Office would be glad to lend him a horse once he made his identity known. The Postmaster would summon constables and guardsmen to take up the chase I his wake, but he wanted to make a start as soon as humanly possible, before any tracks that the coach's attackers had left behind could be obscured.

Sam Hopkey was waiting by the carriage.

"Don't go, Mr. Temple," said the actor, obviously having guessed his intention. "It might be a trap—they may want you too, remember, whoever they are."

"Séverin is my friend," said Temple. "He's also a foreign national on English soil; I'm honor bound to protect him from harm, and to pursue anyone who seeks to injure him." To the Postmaster he said: "I'm Gregory Temple, late of Scotland Yard. I need your best horse."

"He's being saddled as we speak, Mr. Temple," the official said, along with half a dozen others. "Should my men go with you, or should I save the horses for yours?" Temple's name was obviously not unfamiliar to him, although it might have been if he had been a younger man, and he was obviously not to be deterred from offering full assistance by rumors of madness.

"Save the horses for the constables," Temple said. "The guardsmen will bring their own, when they come." He turned to the coachman, who was still catching his breath. "Where?" he growled, tersely.

"Between Blackfen and Crayford," the driver replied, "not far from Hall Place. There were at least six, perhaps ten—not common blackguards, but skilled swordsmen. They might have killed the warrior monk, if they'd wanted to, but were content to put him out of the fight. He said as much himself."

"They'll be differently inclined toward you, Mr. Temple," Sam Hopkey said. "If you go charging in without a dozen men at your back, you'll likely meet the same fate as the Frenchman."

"Only if they're expecting me," Temple said, as the saddled horse was brought forward. "I'll travel faster alone, and might have to wait ten minutes and more for any reinforcements at all, let alone a dozen men. If your master turns out to be behind this caper…"

"He's not, sir," the actor protested, vehemently. "This is far more likely to be Balsamo's doing."

So there's definitely a rift in the Civitas Solis *lute,* Temple thought, as he climbed on to the horse's back. *Henri has not mastered that organization as easily as he mastered the Deliverance—which is doubtless why he has taken on the mantle of Tom Brown again, to muster the raggle-taggle army of the London Underworld.*

He urged the horse forward. He was not wearing spurs, but the animal was a veteran post horse, loyal and willing. It set off at a fast trot, and accelerated to a gallop within a dozen strides. Temple headed for Bermondsey at top speed. The coach had covered nine-tenths of its journey before being attacked, practically on the outskirts of the capital. That meant that its assailants had had time already to have fled into one or other of the city's rookeries—but would they have done that? Would they have dared, if they were indeed adversaries, rather than hirelings, of John Devil? More likely they had gone to Dartford, in order to make use of the river to reach a more distant destination.

Temple knew that he was being something of a fool in leading the pursuit on is own, but he had been inactive for some time, and had not forgotten that Jean-Pierre Sévérin had saved his bacon in Miremont, when he had done more harm than good himself by unwittingly taking the vampire into the new château. He had a debt to repay, to himself as well as to the Frenchman.

The horse was a magnificent specimen, perhaps not one of the fastest in the world but certainly one of the sturdiest. Its stamina did not flag as it covered the miles of the Dover road, passing through Greenwich and Eltham like a cannonball, swathed in the fog as if by a cloud. Beyond Eltham there were no more street-lights, and the three-quarter Moon was only visible at present as a pale glow lighting the mist, but the horse had been this way many times before; it knew the road, and was confident of its footing, even on the frost-ridged carriageway.

The mist began to crystallize out and sink to earth as frost while Temple made progress. The Moon became more distinct by the minute, and the stars began to peep through; the sky above the fog was almost free of high cloud. Temple knew that dawn would be a long time coming, given the season, but there was light enough to let him see, and the layer of sparkling white frost covering the highway and the objects to either side of it assisted him in that task.

By the time he reached the place where the mail coach had been attacked, there was no danger of him missing the residual evidence of the assault, which showed almost as clearly as it would have done on freshly-fallen snow. Temple was convinced that he could pick out Jean-Pierre Séverin's footprints, and those of Malo de Treguern, left when they leapt down from the vehicle, armed with a cane and a staff, to battle the marauders. He dismounted and tethered the post horse to a bush, then swiftly located the spot where the Hospitaller had been interrupted and wounded, but did not pause to examine the blood-stains flecking the thin layer of rime. He pressed on, following Séverin's footprints to the point where they too reached a confused terminus, beneath the overlapping boughs of two venerable trees.

He looked up then, to see where the net that Treguern had mentioned might have fallen from—and realized his mistake.

The trap had been re-set, and his detective skill had led him straight into it.

The net fell again, and caught him in its toils. He struggled hard to throw it off, and might have succeeded had he had a minute longer—but the bandits had not left their trap to do its work unaided. Shadowy forms emerged from the pools of darkness beneath the trees, and reached out to grapple with him. One, at least, was armed with a wad of German tinder steeped in some sweet-smelling substance.

Realizing what the substance must be intended to do, Temple held his breath and tried to continue the fight—but he was outnumbered by at least four to one, and would have succumbed within a matter of seconds had the contest not turned into a brawl, in which his immediate assailants seemed to be fending off an attack by another party.

The battle took place in silence; no one barked any orders or expressed surprise in curses. The whole affair had a supernatural feel to it, as if none of the combatants, save for Temple himself, was fully human—but that was probably an illusion, caused by the fact that his exertions had forced him to take a tainted breath.

He struggled to retain consciousness, but his mind became dizzy and it seemed that the world began to spin around him.

His one regret, as he fell into unconsciousness, was that he had not been able to obtain a single useful clue as to who had tried to capture him, or who had tried to stop them, or who was likely to triumph in the ensuing conflict.

Chapter Two
Beyond the Dover Road

Gregory Temple had fallen unconscious in the course of his investigations on several previous occasions, and had even been the victim of chemical narcotics more than once. When he began to come round, therefore, his first lucid thought was that he ought to conceal his condition, to feign unconsciousness in the hope of overhearing something that might be to his advantage.

He could hear someone moving about—more than one person, if the discrimination of his hearing could be trusted—but no words were spoken. After a little while, the evidence of one of the movers faded away; the individual had either left the scene or become very still.

As to what "the scene" might be, Temple was only able to make a few deductions. He was lying on a dusty wooden floor, too stable to be the deck of a boat—although the sound of water lapping could be heard not far away. If he was in a dwelling or storehouse of some kind, it had to be on a shore, probably that of the Thames. He was lying under a thick blanket, but his hands and feet were not bound, so there was a possibility of mounting a swift and effective action against his captors if he could work out where they were positioned. He began to tense and flex his muscles, but without stretching his limbs in a fashion that might disturb the blanket in a revealing fashion.

He decided, in the end, that the second individual that he had heard moving had indeed gone away, even though he had not heard any door opening or closing, and that the other was situated to his right, some three or four feet away, in a wooden-legged chair of some sort. There was no evidence, so far as his closed eyes could tell, that the place in which he was being held was brightly lit, but he assumed that there must be at least one candle burning close at hand, in order that he might be watched.

When the time seemed ripe, he tried to cast off the blanket and rise to his feet with a single fluid movement, and began reaching out toward his mysterious watcher even before he opened his eyes. The sound he emitted thereafter, however, was not a snarl as he launched himself forward aggressively, but a groan, as a reflex educated by long habit made him pause, forbidding his arms to act aggressively against the woman who was seated in an armchair beside an unpolished table—which did indeed bear a candle, positioned so that its light would fall upon a supine body in the location he had just escaped.

He groaned because he thought that the reflex had betrayed him: that what he saw was not really a woman at all. He recognized her, having seen her twice during his most recent excursion to Paris and its environs. It was the individual who called herself Countess Marcian Gregoryi, alias Addhema—the vampire's minion.

248

Had she been carrying a weapon, she could easily have shot or stabbed him while he hesitated, but she was not, and obviously had no such intention. Her hands were holding an open book, which descended slowly to her lap as she looked up at him, mildly.

He tried not to meet her eyes, knowing what magic there was in them, and how completely he had been deceived by her master's mesmeric art at Miremont, but it was not easy. In that matter too there was a reflex at work—a reflex guided by an innate capacity for lust that he had not entirely put away, in spite of his advanced age.

The pretended Countess—or Comtesse, or Grafina, according to her arena of operations—was very beautiful. "Do you intend to strike me, Mr. Temple?" she asked, in perfect English. "That seems a trifle ungrateful, given that my men saved you from…well, doubtless not a fate wore than death, but a fate that would surely have proved inconvenient to you."

Temple's reflexive pause became a frozen hesitation—and he realized that he was, indeed, very cold, although there was a stove next to the table, whose coals were still bright. The space was not easy to heat, for it was some kind of warehouse, capacious enough to defy the stove's efforts even if its rear door not been standing open, letting in the pale light of dawn.

Countess Marcian Gregoryi did not appear to be feeling the cold, however; she was clad in a think woolen coat and a fur wrap, but even that might have been a disguise. Did vampires feel cold at all?

"Pick up your blanket, Mr. Temple," said the Countess. "Keep warm—the daylight does not promise much relief to the frozen world."

Recognizing the wisdom of the advice, Temple did as he as told. "You claim that you saved me from the trap that was set for me?" he said. "Who, then, disposed the net for a second time?"

"I don't know," she said. "The men who drugged you were mere hirelings, of course, and did not know themselves who issued the order, else I'd have got the information with very little effort. I do know that they took your friend Séverin to Purfleet, with instructions to deliver him to a barge. I've sent Guido after them, with instructions to follow the barge to its destination, if he can. They're playing a dangerous game, whoever they are, because they'll be heading into the heart of Tom Brown's territory if they go upriver, and I can't imagine that they'll head for the marshes."

Having swathed himself carefully in the blanket, Temple said: "And why did you save me—if indeed you did?"

"I can hardly blame you for your mistrust," Addhema said, "after that fiasco in Miremont—but we have nothing against you on that score. If you were not a hunter in the pay of the state, we would have nothing against you at all, but you understand now, I think, what kinds of prejudice we have faced in the past, and still face, in our fight for survival."

"You might not be a literal blood-drinker," Temple retorted, "but if there is any truth at all in what Séverin has told me, you are certainly a killer."

"I don't deny it," she told him, equably, "but I plead self-defense. Do you imagine that men have not tried to murder me, in spite of my camouflage? But you have made alliances with murderers before, under the pressure of circumstances. Tom Brown has certainly contrived as many deaths as I have."

"My grandson and his son were threatened by the same malefactors," Temple said, dully. "It was a rare circumstance, in which the enemy of my enemy became my principal hope of attaining my goal—but we are not and never will be friends, and I consider you in the same light, even if some of your present enemies are also ill-disposed toward me. I do not make alliances with vampires."

"You were willing to make an alliance with Frankenstein's first Grey Man," Addhema pointed out, "and your employee Ned Knob seemed actually to like him, if Guido is to be believed. Now that you know that Szandor and I are merely Grey Men created by the hazards of nature, why should you be unduly troubled by the reputation that legend and superstition have foisted upon us? Szandor took advantage of you in Miremont, it's true—but can you really blame him? He took care not to hurt you. Indeed, when your friends attacked us, we were content to slip away without hurting anyone, rather than make a fight of it. The *vehmgerichte* have been after us ever since, and Colonel Bozzo-Corona has begun inquiries of his own that might prove equally inconvenient. Our hopes of making common cause with Lord Byron have been dashed, for the moment. We were tempted to take ship for Haiti to seek out Marie Laveau, but Faraday and his self-styled Necromancers of London are closer at hand. Faraday is the real prize in the game as it presently stands—there's a man who can easily put the likes of Germain Patou and Balsamo's antique alchemists in the shade! What a triple alliance might be forged between him, Frankenstein and Szandor!"

"If a triple alliance is formed," Temple opined, "Andrew Crosse will be the third member. He, after all, is brokering the potential friendship between Faraday and Frankenstein. Darwin is dead, alas, and the Lunar Society little more than a memory, but England has enough great men of science not to need your master—or you, his second self."

"Second self? We're not quite as closely allied as that, Mr. Temple—although you'd doubtless find the terms of our relationship interesting, if you were to open your mind to the Inquiry."

"Is that why you've taken me captive?" Temple demanded.

"Captive?" she echoed, mockingly. "Why, Mr. Temple, we haven't taken you captive, but merely freed you from potential captivity in someone else's hands. You're as free as a bird. You're not bound, and the door stands open not 15 meters away. No one will attempt to inhibit your movements—unless you surrender to the violent impulse that overtook you while you were still lying down, feigning unconsciousness. For the time being, you and I are on the same side, whether we make any formal alliance or not. We both want the parliamentary commission to reach Fyne Court safely, and to be dazzled by a successful demonstration of Frankenstein's technique. You might not be as fully committed, as yet, to the cause of the dead-alive as your associate Mr. Knob and your mercurial adversary John Devil, but you're a man of reason, a champion of deductive logic who does not stoop to using rhetoric as a means of sustaining belief when the evidence becomes challenging."

"What are you looking for in London, Addhema?" Temple demanded.

"What we have long been looking for everywhere else," the beautiful countess replied. "The secret of immortality...or, if you prefer, of eternal undeath. We are presently working on the assumption that the secret we need is not the same secret for which *Civitas Solis* and the Bavarian Illuminati have long been searching. Although there would be a certain esthetic symmetry in the discovery that an effective method of maintaining God-given life were also effective in maintaining the second life that some individuals achieve, naturally or artificially, *after* death, we have no reason to expect that to be the case."

"God-given life?" Temple echoed. "Do you believe in God, then?"

"Not in the kind of God that would declare us an abomination, a blasphemy against His dictates—but who knows what plans the divine mind might have for the future progress of humankind, if there is indeed a God?"

"Malo de Treguern believes that information to be contained in the revelation of the scriptures," Temple said.

"But you doubt it, Mr. Temple," Addhema countered. "Scriptures tend to rush to judgment, which is why they are always being augmented, reinterpreted and replaced. Even so, Treguern's scriptures are not averse to the idea that the dead might rise from their graves, in the flesh, in order to build a Millennial Kingdom on the Earth."

Temple's gaze went to the book resting on her lap, but it was not a Bible. Nor was it a copy of the anonymous *Frankenstein*. It was printed in Gothic script, apparently in German, but it seemed to be a recent text, more likely a philosophical treatise by some follower of Leibniz or Kant than some romance by Ludwig Tieck or the Baron de la Motte Fouqué.

"Show me your true form," Temple whispered, forcing his voice so that she would be able to hear him. "Show me what lies behind your *camouflage*."

Countess Marcian Gregoryi laughed lightly. "Do you still believe that I am a skeletal monster, like the one that Séverin thought he saw, on the night that his daughter killed herself, or the one that René de Kervoz thought he saw when he believed that he had shot me in the head? Do you think that I am a mere husk, more dust than flesh, and that what you see before your eyes is but glamour? You have no idea, Mr. Temple, what Grey Men and Grey Women might be capable of making of themselves, given time and education...just as you have no idea what living men and women might make of themselves, given the same resources. You are on the brink of discovering something of your own inner re-

251

sources, just as Colonel Bozzo-Corona appears to be…but you are still blinded, as he is, by your preconceptions, by ideas that you have long taken for granted, although the only basis they have is the strength of your conviction. We are more alike than you imagine, Mr. Temple—but I am older than you are, although appearances are deceptive. Szandor is older still….and there may be Grey Men even older, who have greater skill in concealing themselves, just as there are may be living men even older than Saint-Germain and the Jew, unhampered by the superstitions that have shackled those two. Szandor does not like that idea overmuch, but he has always had a tendency to vainglory. I find it intriguing, don't you?"

Temple had heard of the Comte de Saint-Germain and the Wandering Jew, just as he had heard of Giuseppe Balsamo before the man currently using that name had introduced himself, but he had never believed in either and suspected that Addhema was teasing him. All he said aloud, however, was: "I am not a supernatural being. I am merely a living man who happens to have grown old."

"I am not a supernatural being either," the vampire countess retorted, "but merely a woman returned to life after death, who appears not to have grown old. I wish you well, Mr. Temple—for the moment, at least, we have the same enemies. Be careful, I beg you. Keep Frankenstein and Faraday safe, if you can." She stood up as she was speaking, and gathered her fur wrap more tightly around her shoulders and neck, as if she were indeed fearful of catching a chill. "The Sun is up, as you can see," she continued, "and vampires prefer the dark. I must bid you farewell."

For a moment or two, Temple wondered whether he ought to arrest her, or at least make the attempt—but he had no charge to bring against her that could possibly be proven in a court of law and he was, in any case, more than half-inclined to believe her when she said that it had been her men who had saved him from the predators who had sought to trap him in the same net that had trapped his friend. For that reason, he simply let her walk out of the door and move off into the gathering but still-gloomy light of day.

After a short pause, he followed her, eager to know where she might be headed—but when he arrived in the doorway and peered out, she was nowhere to be seen. He had to wonder whether he had been the victim of mesmerism, at least to the extent that he had allowed her to make her escape, but there was no use crying over spilled milk.

He set off to walk along the shore of the river, heading westwards. At the first possible opportunity, he hailed a boatman who was steering his skiff toward the port. He still had money in his pouch—at least Addhema was no cutpurse—and he paid for passage to Tower Bridge.

"Has there been any unusual traffic on the river of late?" he asked the boatman.

"Not that I've noticed, sir," the boatman replied, "but this is the Thames, after all, where the usual is a broad church. Were you thinking in terms of conspirators or ghosts?"

"Conspirators," Temple said, firmly. "Germans, in particular, or other Eastern Europeans."

"No, sir," said the boatman. "I've seen nothing of that sort."

"And what of John Devil the Quaker?" Temple asked. "Is he up to his old tricks again?"

"The rallying cry is said to have been broadcast in Jenny Paddock's," the boatman admitted, "but I never go to such places myself—I'm an honest man, sir."

Every thief and scoundrel in London declared himself to be an honest man, Temple knew—and many of them, he suspected, actually believed it, being far readier to see the motes in their neighbors' eyes than the beams in their own— but he judged by the boatman's weary tone that he, at least, was an ignorant individual who preferred to nurture his ignorance rather than take the risk of knowing too much.

From Tower Bridge, Temple set off in the direction of St. Thomas's Hospital, where he found Malo de Treguern abed, evidently weak but fully conscious.

"What did you find out, Mr. Temple?" the Knight of St. John enquired. "Do you know what has become of Jean-Pierre?"

"No, alas," Temple confessed. "I nearly fell into the same trap myself— and I must confess to some slight surprise that you were spared."

"Spared?" Treguern queried, looking down at his bandaged arm. "They could have killed me had they wanted to, I suppose, but they certainly did not spare me. I've sustained worse wounds, in the days before the revolution, and lived to tell the tale, as I certainly hope to do again, but I'm no longer a young man."

"That," said Temple, "is exactly why they might have taken you—but they were bravos acting under orders, and probably knew no more than I did that you would be accompanying Séverin. Why were you with him?"

"I heard that he was coming to England, with information relating to the vampire. I had information of my own, from the Church's informants. Like him, I thought you should be apprised of it. Szandor and Addhema are in England. Byron having departed from Europe, their attention is now directed toward Victor Frankenstein again. Whether they intend to harm him, I cannot tell, but I am certain that they want to know his secret, and that they would use it if they could."

"I believe they would," Temple agreed. "And you would go to any lengths to prevent that, I assume?"

"I am sworn to uphold God's law," the warrior monk stated, proudly, "as you are sworn to uphold the law of England. Neither, I think, extends any tolerance to vampires or necromancers."

Temple frowned. "For the moment," he said, "Victor Frankenstein is under the protection of His Majesty's Government. Whether he will remain so depends on the outcome of an official Commission of Inquiry. I ought to remind you, Brother Malo, that the Roman Church has no authority on English soil."

"In this instance," Treguern relied, "the Roman Church and the Church of England are in perfect agreement. Even your dissenters have no truck with necromancy. There is a Bishop on the Commission of Inquiry, is there not?"

Temple nodded, unsurprised that the information in question had been communicated to the Knight of St. John. "The Bishop of Salisbury," he confirmed. "Along with three members of the House of Commons, Robert Hastings, Stephen Southborne and John Medstead—two Tories and a Whig—and three men of science: Thomas Young, Peter Barlow and William Snow Harris. Michael Faraday would undoubtedly have been included had he not already involved himself with Crosse's trial as an enthusiastic supporter. I do not know how many of them, apart from the Bishop, have strong religious convictions of one sort or another, but I suspect that God's acknowledged servants might be in a majority"

Malo de Treguern expressed his satisfaction with this judgment with a mere nod.

"That might not be of any great consequence," Temple added. "The genie is out of the bottle. Grey Men are being manufactured by the score, if not by the hundred, in Haiti, and it is only a matter of time before the practice spreads to Cuba and New Orleans. If the information transmitted by our diplomats is reliable, experiments are being conducted in Paris, Leipzig, St. Petersburg and Constantinople. This is the 19th century—religious objections tend to be set aside once the prospect of profit puts in an appearance, and governments have scented potential advantages in labor and in war. The only prospect worse than failing to seize an advantage in such matters is that of seeing others seize and exploit it instead. The competition has already been joined; the only question now is who will win; I believe that the parliamentarians will have been apprised of that, and that their scientific colleagues would not require any such formal instruction. The commission's report will not be as reflexively negative as you might hope."

"Do not be so sure, Mr. Temple," the knight said. "In any case, the commission's report might be a minor matter of provocation. God has intervened before, with flood and fire, when blasphemy and corruption threatened His plan."

"There are many who would agree with you that London is the new Sodom, and Paris the new Gomorrah," Temple conceded, "but the world is larger now than it was once imagined to be, and it would require a vast volcanic eruption to consume them both, and other dens of iniquity besides. Men of your kind are ever avid to preach that the world's doom is imminent, but they have never been correct before. To make matters worse, from your point of view, *Civitas Solis* might gain the upper hand even within the Church, if its reignited research into the principles of longevity bears fruit."

Treguern looked at him long and hard, despite his evident weariness. "Have you been in recent contact with the man who calls himself Giuseppe Balsamo?" he asked, shrewdly.

"Yes, less than a week ago," Temple replied. "We are not friends, though. His associates arranged the kidnap of my grandson, in the course of a plot to capture Henri de Belcamp, alias Tom Brown—Germain Patou's one-time collaborator."

"Balsamo and his associates are dangerous heretics," said the warrior monk, "but the Vatican has their measure. They did capture the man you call John Devil, if the information transmitted by *our* diplomats is reliable, but he gave them the slip not long afterwards. They're searching for him high and low—low being the more likely eventuality."

"He has friends in many strata of society," Temple observed. "He undoubtedly has the ear of the Duchess of Devonshire as well as that of Jenny Paddock, and has probably doffed his Quaker hat to King George more than once. His mother taught him well, but she betrayed him in the end, although he swears that she was mistaken, and that he never intended to leave her for dead. On the last point, at least, I believe him—he did love his mother, and valued what she and Thomas Paddock taught him far more than the formal education for which his father paid."

That was not the information for which Malo de Treguern was fishing. "Was it his agents who attacked the mail coach, do you think?" he asked.

"Unlikely," said Temple, although he did not want to tell the Churchman about Sam Hopkey's warning. "If I had to bet, my money would be on the Grafina von Boehm's *vehmgerichte*. They're the most aggressive of all the interested parties—although it would smack of ingratitude, after you and Séverin came to their rescue at the new château in Miremont. Their resurgence is rumored to be due to the active involvement of the Bavarian Illuminati—who originated, I believe, as a splinter-group of *Civitas Solis*."

Treguern's brow was furrowed and he was biting his lip. "I could imagine them pinking me, but scrupulously leaving me alive," he said. "They have a peculiar notion of chivalry, more Romantic than Roman—but Séverin is cut from different cloth. They'll get nothing out of him."

"I doubt that information is what they want," said Temple, thoughtfully. "They might well be interested in his experiences as a morgue-keeper, but it's his own apparent possession of an innate elixir of long life that intrigues them far more. While they can't lay their hands on Saint-Germain or the Jew..." He trailed off, provocatively.

Treguern's eyes narrowed, testifying to the fact that the names were not unknown to him, and their mention in connection with the present affair not entirely unexpected, but he rose no further to the bait than that. Like so many other players in the game, he did not regard Gregory Temple as an enemy, but nor did he regard him as a wholly trustworthy ally. "On that score," the monk said, "they might have done better to take me as well, if they could; Séverin and I are much the same age. How old are you, Mr. Temple?"

"Old enough for my name to have become legendary, in certain circles," Temple admitted, "but I do not drink the blood of virgins, or feed gluttonously on the life-force of young men, else I'd have sucked the likes of Ned Knob and Sam Hopkey dry some years ago—and Tom Brown too, had I ever laid hands on him long enough to do it."

"You must not speak like that, Mr. Temple," the Churchman told him. "Even jests can be blasphemous. I beg you to keep the Bishop safe when you escort your charges to Somerset, and not to be blinded yourself by whatever you see at Fyne Court. I would go with you if I could, and will follow when I can."

"I would rather you did not, Monsieur de Treguern," Temple said. "My duty is complicated enough as it is."

"No, Mr. Temple," Treguern retorted. "Your duty is perfectly clear and perfectly simple—it is your doubts that are clouding your judgment."

Chapter Three
Fyne Court

The next day, Temple and four agents of Lord Liverpool's secret police met the members of the Parliamentary Commission at Paddington Green, from which westward-bound coaches set off at regular intervals, mostly bound for Bath or Bristol. The convoy that was to carry the expedition would take the Bath Road, and then depart from that city in a south-westward direction, heading for Taunton, and ultimately for Broomfield, the site of the ancestral home in which Andrew Crosse had installed the finest electrical laboratory in England.

The commissioners, along with their servants and other companions—Hastings and Medstead were traveling with young women who were not their wives, as MPs far from their constituencies sometimes did when on official business—were divided into four carriages. One of Temple's agents was instructed to ride with each carriage, seated next to the coachman. Temple rode a horse, sometimes at the head of the column and sometimes at the rear. The party changed horses twice before making its first substantial stop in Reading, and four times more before eventually reaching Bath, where it made an overnight stop.

Temple was perfectly sure that *Civitas Solis* and at least one other organization must have spies among the women and the servants accompanying the commissioners, and perhaps among the commissioners themselves, but there was no way to identify them. His own men took care to eavesdrop on as many conversations as possible, and to report their substance back to him, but he did not expect anything to come of that, save for an estimate of the likely temper of the discussion that would follow Frankenstein's demonstration, if it were to prove successful.

At least three of the seven commissioners appeared to be convinced that it would not be successful, and that the whole affair would prove to be nothing but a hoax, but those who took the possibility seriously seemed direly suspicious of the whole business. The Bishop, in particular, freely expressed the opinion that if an appearance of life were to be returned to a corpse after death, the only possible cause would be its possession by a demon. He declared himself ready, materially and spiritually, to perform an exorcism if necessary, both to prove the point and rid the world of the demon in question.

So far as Temple could judge from snatches of overheard conversation, it was the parliamentarians rather than the scientists who were most prepared to approach the question with open minds, ready to weight up the evidence presented to them. Whether or not the scientists were sincere Christians, their commitment of faith to the science they knew seemed unwavering, and two of them—the aging Young and the much younger Barlow—seemed to take it for granted that death was irreversible, and that whatever they saw when the demonstration was mounted would most probably be a hoax of some sort, achieved by means of trickery. Temple heard Young opine that the trickery would likely be mesmeric in kind, but Barlow would not even admit the honesty of mesmerism as a technique or an art.

At dinner that evening, in Bath's finest coaching inn, the Bishop addressed the whole company on the subject of the Devil's wiles, and the possibility of an all-out assault by the legions of Hell on the human world, which had fallen too far into apostasy, thanks to the blasphemous ravages of Jacobin science. Temple noted, however, that although most of those present nodded politely, the men of science were definitely opposed to the Bishop's views and the members of parliament seemed distinctly dubious. There was no talk of mesmerism while the company of travelers was at table, but there was a good deal of skeptical talk about progress, with Medstead the Whig seeming only a little less doleful in that regard than the two Tories.

Material progress, according to Medstead, might well be linked to the progress of mores, but that did not mean that it was an unalloyed virtue in itself. Like most Whigs, he maintained mental balance-sheets whose accounts were scrupulously made up in terms of utilitarian calculations of arithmetically-expressed pros and cons. Not surprisingly, however, his remarks made no inroads in the Tories' assumption, as voiced by Hastings, that technological progress was a mere fad, which served to deflect attention away from the moral progress that was humankind's collective vocation, and that the moral progress in question had to be based in a sound understanding of humankind's past and a ready appreciation of the causes of human folly.

The scientists, not unnaturally, saw things differently. Young, in particular, agreed with the Bishop that progress in morals had reached its terminus in the teachings of Christ, which would have improved human society long ago had the mass of men ever been inclined to follow them, but contended that great strides had yet to be taken in the matter of progress in knowledge and the understanding of the natural world. All three of the men of science professed belief in natural theology: the doctrine that the proper study of mankind was God's creation, and that every discovery of new phenomena and the laws controlling them brought the minds of men closer to the mind of the God who had designed and ordained those phenomena.

But if I read the Book of Genesis right, Temple thought, *death was no part of God's original plan, at least so far as sentient and willful beings were concerned. It was a punishment that he inflicted on Adam and Eve for disobeying His instruction not to eat of the Tree of Knowledge. Perhaps it was always His plan—or His hope, at least—that knowledge would eventually lead humans back to a remedy for the plight, by one means or another. And perhaps God took care to ensure that there would be a choice of such means, in order that humans would have to take responsibility for the architecture of their own fate.*

He said none of that aloud, though; it was not his place. He contented himself with listening carefully to as many of the discussions taking place around the table as he could. There was little profit to be gained by such eavesdropping, however, from an intellectual as well as a political point of view. Eventually, as his overloaded head began to swim, he cursed himself for his insatiable curiosity. A wiser man, he thought, might have abandoned all philosophizing about progress long ago, having discovered that it did not lead anywhere but around in circles

On the following day, the expedition's own progress—construed in a purely practical sense—became much slower, the roads leading westwards from Bath having not been maintained as well as the highway connecting that city to the capital. It was by no means unknown for such roads to become quite impassable between late December and early March, but the cold snap that had descended upon the country in the last few days had arrived in the wake of a relatively dry and balmy spell, and the frost did not linger long in the ground once the Sun came up. The gradual ascent into the Mendip Hills posed difficulties, but the four carriages were the sturdiest that government money could hire, and there were no major mishaps apart from the customary instances of lameness among the 16 horses, which did not slow them down overmuch in site of the relative infrequency of relay stations.

Temple maintained his vigilance, in spite of a near-total recent lack of natural sleep, but there seemed to be no sign of danger, and the commission's members seemed quite safe in their apparent relaxation. Their relaxation was manifest—a tendency Temple had often observed in London-dwellers when they left the capital for the country. It was as if they were making a crossing from one world to another, where time slowed in its pace and the inert mass of the past reasserted its dominance over the seductive magnetism of the future.

If the conversations of the scientists and parliamentarians ever took on a sinister edge, it happened while Temple was out of earshot; he saw and heard nothing but everyday pleasantries and friendly banter. He continued nevertheless to watch the road like a hawk, and to listen in on the conversations going on inside the carriages, even though both exercises had come to seem like wasted effort. Nothing was said that might have betrayed an individual who was not what he claimed to be, and there were no armed confrontations, even on the minor roads taken by the carriages in order to avoid the city of Bath entirely, its temporary and permanent inhabitants having been reduced to penury and crime, wittingly or not, by dire and stubborn circumstance.

Even though no attempt was made to interfere with the convoy, Temple was heartily glad to see the rooftops of Fyne Court appear. The house was said to have been built during the reign of Charles I, but had obviously been extensively modernized, Andrew Crosse's taste for the contemporary obviously extending far beyond his scientific adventures. Crosse had the local reputation of being a wizard rather than a man of science, intent on mocking God by aping His creation of a human being out of common clay, but Temple knew how easily gaudily-clad rumor may outstrip dull reality in the eyes and memories of men; for that reason, Temple supposed that Crosse was merely a rich man who had taken up electrical science as a hobby, much as his ancestors might have taken up the study of astrology or alchemy, and that he was much misunderstood by his neighbors.

The arrival was inevitably hectic, with trunks being transported from the carriages into various quarters of the house according to the instructions of Crosse's butler, a typical domestic tyrant named Caddick. Temple and his men were, of course, given rooms in the servants' quarters, although Temple was immediately summoned to meet Andrew Crosse and his guests in the library.

Temple found four men gathered there. He recognized Michael Faraday, and had no doubt which of the four was Victor Frankenstein. Crosse, in his capacity as host, was the first to address him. "Your reputation precedes you, Mr. Temple," he said, "and we're very glad to have you here. With such a famous detective on hand, no one will be able to suspect us of any trickery. Welcome to the inaugural gathering of the Necromancers of London—for we hope to move our endeavors to a town house soon enough, where we shall find it much easier to obtain the equipment we need."

Not to mention a much readier supply of corpses, Temple thought, as he bowed.

Crosse introduced his companions then; the man Temple did not know was identified as an old friend whom Crosse had not seen for some years, but whose presence was exceedingly welcome: George Singer.

"Singer's passion for electrical science was even greater than mine at the outset," Crosse explained. "It was he who first introduced me to Mr. Faraday, ten years ago, and Faraday, in his turn, who arranged for me to give a lecture in London in 1814, where I met Percy Shelley and his wife-to-be. It was through Shelley, of course, that I initially made the acquaintance of Dr. Frankenstein. We have been correspondents for some years, although I am not the avid traveler my father was—he frequented the court of Louis XVI for a while, where he made the acquaintance of Ben Franklin."

Temple shook hands with all four men, gravely. Faraday, a young and slender man, seemed to be bubbling over with excitement and enthusiasm—so much so, in fact, that he barely devoted a second of his time to Temple before returning to his interrupted conversation with Crosse. Crosse was older—almost forty, to judge by appearances—but more aristocratic in his bearing, seemingly able to look down tolerantly upon his less well-born companion, even though he was a full inch shorter. Singer, who seemed a little older than Crosse, was more reserved and somehow less conspicuous; for the moment, he seemed to have been slightly edged out of the conversation, and his attempts to strike up a dialogue with Frankenstein appeared to have been inhibited by the latter's morose anxiety.

"I believe that you have met an employee of mine," Temple said to Frankenstein, for want of any more profitable subject. "Edward Knob."

Frankenstein did not seem to recognize the name immediately, but it eventually struck a chord in his memory. "The young man who came to Shelley's aid in San Terenzo," he said, nodding glumly. "Shelley took quite a shine to him, as I remember—he recognized him as having attended at least one of Davy's lectures, although Mr. Crosse's performance must have been before his time. Was he a policeman, then?"

"Not exactly," Temple replied, "but he has his uses. He is in Haiti now, with Germain Patou and Marie Laveau, but I am expecting him to return in the new year."

"With exciting news, I hope," Singer put in. "Rumor always exaggerates, I know, but if the tales regarding Mademoiselle Laveau have any truth in them at all, she must have access to a useful traditional wisdom of which we know nothing. Given that Patou has already obtained a measure of success comparable to Victor's, there is reason to hope that he might be making further progress."

"Indeed," Temple agreed. "If you'll forgive the impertinence, Dr. Frankenstein, might I ask whether you have had any contact since you were in Spezia with the product of your own success, who now goes by the name of Lazarus."

"There has been some communication between us," Frankenstein reported, warily. "Why do you ask?"

"Is he expected to arrive here in order to witness the demonstration?"

Frankenstein frowned. "He expressed a desire to be here in a letter," he admitted. "I replied that I did not think it wise—but he has become so headstrong that I cannot imagine that he will pay much heed to my opinion."

"To be perfectly frank," Temple said, "I would not have been displeased to find him here. I have talked with him briefly, in Paris, and I believe that he would help to protect you if he could. There are, alas, other parties from whom you might need protection."

"The mysterious Count Szandor?" Frankenstein asked, probably having obtained the name from Lazarus.

"Possibly," Temple conceded, "but I am more anxious, for the present, about members of two secret societies: *Civitas Solis* and a Bavarian *vehm*. Both have agents in London as we speak, and almost certainly have spies here. My men and I will do our utmost to prevent them taking any hostile action, and they may well be here only to observe and report, but I must ask the four of you to be careful of your own security. Much might hang on the outcome of your demonstration. Are all the preparations well in hand?"

Crosse smiled at the delicacy of that question. "We have three dead bodies, obtained by legal means with the consent of the next of kin, which have been immersed in the baths," he said. "The first should be ripe for revival tomorrow. As to what mental condition they might be in, if the resurrections are successful, I cannot tell—but if we are fortunate, one at least will be capable of speech."

"Yes indeed," Singer agreed, "but I fear that we cannot answer for what they might say, if one or more of them turns out to be loquacious." Temple glanced at him briefly, trying to fathom the wry smile that played upon his lips, but immediately returned his attention to the Swiss scientist, who seemed to be eager to address another question to him.

"I believe, Mr. Temple," Frankenstein said, "that you met some of Patou's Grey Men before he fled Purfleet. Did they include the self-styled General Mortdieu?"

"Yes," said Temple. "Ned Knob had more contact with him than I, as he had with his old friend Sawney Ross, sufficient to form a strong impression of the General's ambitions, but not form any elaborate notion of his intended plan of action."

"What else did he learn?" Faraday asked, curiously.

"He claims that he watched a demonstration very similar to the one you intend to mount, which was half-successful. The body returned to life, and was able to remember a name—but nothing more than that, alas."

261

"I'd settle for that, if need be," said Faraday. "Once the principle is firmly established, before a host of unimpeachable witnesses…"

Temple was not at all sure that the seven men he had escorted from London were "unimpeachable," but he would not have dreamed of saying so. "Has there been any untoward or unusual occurrence in the vicinity of the house in the last few days, sir?" he asked, addressing Crosse.

"There have been poachers on the estate," Crosse reported, "but that's not unusual, considering that the cold weather has arrived. The village is abuzz with gossip, of course, much of it hostile—but I have not been confronted directly, and I don't expect any trouble. There have been a number of burglaries in local country houses, but we have been spared. Ghosts have been seen, but that's not unusual either, in view of the prevailing tension—servants are very amenable to hysteria."

"Ghosts?" Temple queried—although he knew that the remark about burglaries was more likely to be symptomatic of the presence of hostile forces.

"Oh yes—all country houses of any antiquity have their contingent of ghosts, whether or not they've been modernized. The house was built in 1634, but all the descendants of Odo de Sante Croce, who came to England with William the Conqueror, are supposed by the superstitious to have taken up residence along with my nearer ancestors, including the Sante Croce who was killed at Agincourt. Ghosts of knightly ancestors are inherently more exciting, are they not, than those of 18th century scholars and travelers? I've never seen any ghost myself, of course, and nor has Cornelia, my wife—we have servants to do that for us. Even Caddick has never seen one, although Cook has, and you'd be hard-pressed to find a serving-maid who hasn't."

Temple frowned. "Sometimes," he said, "living men can be mistaken for ghosts, especially if they pose as such. Please tell me if any further sightings are reported by your servants."

"I will," Crosse promised. "Shall we go down to dinner now?" he was addressing his guests, not Temple, who was not dining with the commissioners in the main hall but with the servants in the kitchens.

The ex-detective recognized the question as a tacit dismissal and withdrew. He expected, at any rate, to pick up more in the way of interesting gossip in the servants' quarters and he was not mistaken. Caddick was on duty upstairs, so there was no one to suppress the servants' natural garrulousness; Temple sat quietly to one side, listening to as many overlapping voices as he could. The situation was further confused by the fact that servants were coming in and out all the while, having carried out missions upstairs, and were eager to report on events in the principal dining-room. Apparently, the Bishop as not on his best behavior, and had already undertaken to lock horns with the Devil, in the form of sententious speeches that Crosse and Faraday had greeted with more mockery than alarm. The rules of hospitality, however, forbade host and guests alike to go too far in the matter of giving offense, so the banter had apparently retained a surface of good humor.

As usual, the servants' dinner lasted even longer than the one upstairs, because the servants on duty had to eat in shifts. Temple had to answer the call of duty three times himself, to check in with his men, who had been set to work shifts at various sentry posts. Every time he had to leave he made a brief tour of the surrounds himself but once dark had fallen the visibility outside became very poor.

As in London, there was a freezing mist, but this time there was a cloud layer above it, which maintained the humidity and opacity of the atmosphere. Beyond the area dimly illuminated by the light filtering out of the windows of the house, the gloom was impenetrable. That made Temple feel very uneasy, although he certainly did not envy the lot of any spy posted to watch the house in such inhospitable conditions.

On three occasions Temple bumped into servants in unlit corridors and vestibules inside the house. On the first two occasions, the individuals with whom he collided were maids, who were full of apologies as soon as they realized that he was not one of their customary colleagues, but on the third and last occasion, it was a man who bumped into him, who made no apology at all but made haste to be gone. He must have known the layout of the house, for he had vanished as if into thin air by the time that Temple reacted to the fact that a folded piece of paper had been thrust into his hand.

After two minutes of futile pursuit, the detective paused by a lantern in one of the principal corridors in order to unfold the note and read it. It was, inevitably, unsigned, but its contents were as disturbing as they were enigmatic.

The note read: *SINGER DIED IN 1817.*

Any other recipient of such a note might immediately have thought in terms of ghosts, but Temple had had experience of circumstances that he immediately likened to the present ones.

"Szandor!" he whispered, biting his lip anxiously. "Is he here already, and already as close to Frankenstein as can be? If so, no wonder his minion was at such pains to persuade me that he is not my enemy."

Chapter Four
Interview with the Vampire

It did not take Temple long to find a pattern in the responses he received to his questions about George Singer. The older retainers remembered him well enough from the time when he and Crosse had been fast friends and collaborators in experimentation, but their memories became strangely vague when they were asked about the circumstances that had parted the two men, or what Singer had been doing since 1817.

When Temple explicitly suggested to Caddick that rumor had reached London of Singer's death, Caddick immediately agreed that some such rumor had gone around the neighborhood, and had caused "the young master" some grief, but hastened to add that the sorrow had been more than counterbalanced by the universal joy at discovering the rumor to have been untrue.

"I will not liken his return to that of the prodigal son, sir," said Caddick, sententiously, "for that would verge on blasphemy, but I can guarantee that if Cook had had a fatted calf to hand, its throat would have been cut without delay."

"I see," Temple said—but the hour was very late by then, and he thought it best to retire to the tiny attic room he had been given, in order to sleep before deciding what action to take. As was his habit, he placed a loaded pistol beneath his pillow before lying down.

He fell asleep as soon as his had hit the pillow, or so it seemed, and his sleep was deep enough for him to have not the slightest idea how long he had been unconscious when he was suddenly awakened by a cold touch.

His first instinct was to reach for the pistol, but he found it gone. There was an abrupt crack as a flint was struck, and a wisp of German tinder ignited, which was immediately touched by an expert hand to the wick of a wax candle.

The light was held in such a position as to illuminate George Singer's face from below.

"Count Szandor," Temple said, immediately, in an attempt to surprise the other. "Have you come to drink my blood, or merely to spill it?"

"You know perfectly well that I wish you no harm, my friend," the so-called vampire said. "I removed the gun for my own protection, not because I have any intention of using it. Did you recognize me, or were you warned?"

"I was handed a note," Temple admitted, reluctant to lie because the alternative claim would have been a facile boast. "I was not quick enough to identify the person who gave it to me."

"Tom Brown's man, I assume," the other replied. "The others would take pride in leaving you completely in the dark—which is, I admit, one of the reasons why I would rather enlighten you. I give you my word that my only purpose here is to aid Frdankenstein's demonstration as fully as I can. If it succeeds, then I intend to maintain the identity of George Singer, and to become a member of the company that Faraday is already calling the Necromancers of London. Crosse has been so delighted to have his old friend returned that it would be impossible to convince him, now, that I am not the man he believes me to be, while Faraday and Frankenstein are avid for all the support they can obtain. Your gaze, I knew, would be much harder to deceive in the long term."

"You might count yourself fortunate, then," Temple said, pensively, "that Jean-Pierre Séverin is not here...nor Malo de Treguern."

"I bear Séverin no ill-will for what happened at Miremont," Szandor-as-Singer said, "and might have cause to be grateful to him for the reminder of my limitations. Treguern will, I suppose, always be my enemy, but even he might be more amenable to reason than he thinks, when his faith finally begins to crumble under the unbearable stress of reality. The immediate point is, however, to convince you that you should let my plan proceed—and, indeed, that you do your best to support it if the clowns of *Civitas Solis* or the Prussian dolts take it into their heads to interfere."

Temple did not challenge the vampire's reference to the hirelings of the *vehm* as Prussians rather than Bavarians; he was aware of the intricacies of middle-European exploitation. All he said was: "I might take a deal of convincing."

"A good deal more than Lord Byron, no doubt," the other conceded, as he settled himself comfortably into the wooden chair set beside Temple's meager dressing-table, having placed the pistol on the table-top. "Alas, His Lordship is out of reach at present, as is his loyal ally Shelley—who is still alive, by the way, not yet a Grey Man like his dear friend Keats. Even so, Mr. Temple, you are not without a hint of the Romantic about you—as befits the adversary of John Devil. The latter would be an easier recruit to my cause, I suppose, but my ambition now is to emerge from the Underworld to which I have been too long confined. I do not simply want to masquerade as George Singer for the duration of a festival—I want to become George Singer, in order to take up the cause of electrical science where he was forced to leave off by a stupid aneurism. I want to work with Faraday and Crosse, as well as with Frankenstein, for I believe that there is no quadrumvirate in all the world that could make faster and further progress in this revolution."

"And you want my help to do that?" Temple said, skeptically.

"If possible, yes—or at least your agreement not to interfere. You represent His Majesty's secret police, and I would far rather work within their protective cordon than without it. I have been a fugitive for far too long, regarded by the living as a deadly enemy and obtaining neither succor nor support from my own sad kind. In time, I fully intend to take Faraday, Frankenstein and Crosse into my confidence, in order that they might profit from my accumulated knowledge as I might profit from theirs, but I judged it better not to complicate this week's demonstrations unnecessarily. The last thing I want, however, is to be unmasked in inconvenient circumstances—and that is why I am coming to you beforehand. I readily confess that I fear your skill and enterprise, and hence your opposition. Clearly, I was right to do so, even though you appear to have needed a nudge from your arch-enemy to put you on the track. I do not come empty-handed; not only have I information to offer in return for your co-operation, but the services of an agent with far greater expertise in espionage than anyone else in your employ."

"The Countess," Temple guessed.

"Exactly so. She has played the spy before, of course—she was as useful to Bonaparte, in her own way, as the legendary Fouché."

"But she is merely you puppet, is she not?—an extension of yourself rather than an independent individual. Can she really work for me as a spy while you play Singer's part at the heart of Faraday's necromantic adventure?"

"She is certainly my apprentice," Szandor replied, "more the creation of my mesmeric powers than her own will. Initially, I set out to shape her as a companion in my loneliness, and would have been more-or-less content had she remained a puppet or a slave, but she is more than that now. She is no mere extension of my own personality, and is capable of fully autonomous action. I am all the more proud of her, and myself, for that."

"Who is she, really?" Temple demanded. "And who are you?"

"Your questions are based on false grounds," the vampire told him, "But I shall give you honest answers. You think you want to know who we were when we were alive, assuming that we are, in some sense, still the same individuals now—but even though I retain some of the memories of the man who inhabited this body when it was alive, I am not him. The Countess retains none of the memories of her living predecessor, so she might, I suppose, be reckoned a purer individual than I. In one way of reckoning, she really is Madame Marcian Gregoryi, for Marcian Gregoryi was the name of my living predecessor—a name that I discarded when I decided to become Count Szandor Tzingaryi. In another sense, my companion is Addhema, a female equivalent of Adam, into whom new sentience was breathed by my mesmeric authority when her predecessor's body reverted to common clay."

"So the Bishop is right: you are not humans reborn or resurrected, but demons who have put on borrowed human flesh?"

"*Demon* is such a harsh term, Mr. Temple—and if it is supposed to imply that we are minions of Satan, accursed followers of a self-appointed anti-God, we are certainly nothing of the kind. If the consciousness that emerges to inhabit a new-born babe as it grows to childhood is to be reckoned a creation of God rather than a vile possessor, I cannot see why Addhema and I should not be accorded the same privilege—but I confess that I do not know quite what I am, any more than you can be sure that you know what manner of being you are. I am, however, as enthusiastic to find out as any former victim of superstition and dread who has glimpsed a glimmer of enlightenment and is avid to follow that star."

"Mortdieu claims that he is no longer NapoLeon Bonaparte," Temple said, reflectively, "for all that he has the same vaulting ambition—but if Ned's judgment is reliable, Sawney Ross is definitely still Sawney Ross, however sour his complexion may be."

"I would be surprised if Ross makes that claim himself," Szandor retorted, "but he would be entitled to the delusion, if he so desired."

"You have met other representatives of nature's Grey Men," Temple said, his tone making it a statement rather than a question. "Have they told you that they are not the same men now as they were when they were alive?"

"Some have," the other reported, "but the oldest of them have forgotten everything save for their own self-deceptive legends. The Jew insists that he was cursed by Christ on the road to Golgotha, Saint-Germain that he was the greatest of all the alchemical followers of Hermes Trismegistus—but the Jew is no older than 600 years, and Saint-Germain no older than 200. You have no idea how I have yearned to meet Cain, Pythagoras or Apollonius of Tyana—or any of the old Greek demigods—but the sad truth is that Grey Men are mortal too, whether they develop from the living or from the dead, by what might or might not be variations of the same basic metamorphic process."

"You think that Saint-Germain and others like him are merely Grey Men whose predecessors did not die?" Temple asked, curiously

"I cannot be certain about the two examples in question, but I know that there are—or have been—Grey Men who claim that they never died. How they can be certain of that, I don't know, although I suppose they can be certain that their bodies were never buried. But what, exactly, is death, Mr. Temple? Is it the cessation of the heartbeat, the exhaustion of the breath, or merely the extinction of consciousness within the body? If it is the last, then a man might die without his heart ever ceasing to beat, or without ever ceasing to draw breath—but if it is a matter of the suspension of consciousness, do we not die every time we go to sleep, only to rise again, perhaps less identical to our former selves than we admit? Perhaps our dream-selves reformulate us every night—and perhaps, when duplication becomes impossible, they succeed in creating a substitute, different in character and in potential from its predecessor."

"Possessed, for instance, of greater *mesmeric authority*?" said Temple, echoing the phrase the other had chosen.

"I am not at all sure how exceptional I might be in that regard," Szandor told him. "Lazarus seems to have no such power, and trustworthy reportage credits none to Mortdieu—but their second incarnations are very young, as yet. Then again, Mesmer's discoveries barely scratched the surface of the phenomenon that he mislabeled animal magnetism, and present-day practitioners of hypnotism are similarly groping in near-darkness. The secret report that Franklin and his associates prepared as a result of their investigation of Mesmer is only a little more honest than the one that was published, but at least it admits that the power of suggestion is greater than anyone had imagined, whether or not there is any tangible fluid on which it might be exercised. I am uncomfortably aware of the possibility that, if there were greater mesmerists abroad, they as could easily hide from me, or persuade me of their non-existence, as I can hide from common men, or persuade them of my non-existence—but I will not allow that awareness to inhibit my ambition to try my powers in a spirit of disciplined experimentation, with collaborators of the highest intelligence."

"Your apparent shapeshifting is due to the power of suggestion, then?" Temple deduced. "You have not actually remolded your flesh in Singer's image?"

"You are attempting to draw a distinction that is far too explicit," the vampire told him. "Sight is a less trustworthy sense than humans, in the grip of their dependency, are ready to assume. Seeing is believing, you say, without knowing how truly you speak. Once a belief is securely planted, sight proceeds in association with that belief. Children must learn to see in order to bring a coherent image of the world out of the confusion that surrounds them, and what they learn to see, or not to see, depends on what they are taught to believe, and what they are taught not to believe. Your eyes are not passive instruments, Mr. Temple, but active seekers of form and meaning; nor is your mind a blank canvas awaiting sensory paint, but a net set to trawl an understanding that is largely pre-existent. When I appear to dissolve into a cloud of dust or a wisp of mist, or fade into a near-fleshless skeleton, I do not really evaporate or shrink—that is merely your mind's way of coping with the seeming paradox of the rude destruction of its own confabulations. I am no mere illusion, Mr. Temple—I really am George Singer, insofar as Singer any longer exists, and am becoming more comfortable in that guise every time Andrew Crosse looks at me with the gladness that comes from having a friend that he once believed dead returned to him alive. In the same way, the lovely Addhema, whom I made in the image of my ideal of beauty, really is Countess Marcian Gregoryi, in all the glory of her precious flesh, and she becomes even more herself every time a man looks at her and finds her beauty wondrous."

Temple was not at all sure that he understood the implications of these claims, but he was glad of the information, which he took to be honest. There were more pragmatic issues at stake, which he needed to address. "What do you intend to do tomorrow, Mr. Singer?" he said. "You are not here simply to observe, I think."

"I am here to assist," the vampire replied, equably. "I am here to do what I can in order to ensure that Frankenstein's demonstration is the spectacular success that he, Faraday and Crosse desire so dearly."

"Mesmerically?"

"Of course—but not by means of trickery. It is no part of my plan to persuade the audience that they have seen something that has not actually happened. That would defeat my object."

"So you intend to exert your mesmeric authority upon the resurrected man?"

"I do—except that the first subject Frankenstein has chosen is a female, little more than a girl. He selected her on the basis of her youth and the condition of the corpse, rather than her sex, but I am pleased with his choice. I believe that I shall find it easier to render a young female articulate than an old man."

"And what will you have her say?" Temple wanted to know.

"Ideally, whatever she pleases—but if it should transpire that her mind is virtually blank, devoid of accessible memory or tangible ambition, then I shall do my best to put words in her mouth. You need not fear that any words that I implant will lack politeness and piety; I need the demonstration to succeed in every possible sense."

Again, Temple was ready to believe him—but there were other matters still to be addressed, while the opportunity was there. "Why did your rivals kidnap Jean-Pierre Sévérin?" he asked.

"I don't know," the vampire replied, "But if my guess is worth more than yours, I'd wager that they want to engineer his metamorphosis into a Grey Man, and chose him because they believe that nature has already primed him for such a transformation. If they fail…well, you already know that they tried to trap you too, and I'd also wager that you warned Treguern to beware when you visited him in the hospital, having concluded that the bully-boys missed an opportunity in wounding him and leaving him behind."

Temple did no bother to confirm that Szandor would have won his bet. "My superiors would never agree to any alliance with vampires," he said.

"Of course not," Szandor replied. "That is way I have come to you. Your superiors will, I suppose, be less ready to dispense with your services if you can tell them that the most beautiful woman in London is in your personal employ, and if you can make deft use of the information she supplies. No one need know that she has returned from the dead, and she is more than capable of making any such accusation seem absurd if it is leveled in her presence. I am offering you a lifeline with which to shore up your precarious position, Mr. Temple—you might do well to take it, else you might be forced to retire from the game…or enter into Tom Brown's employ."

Never, Temple thought—knowing, of course, that that was exactly what he had been intended to think, in spite of the old proverb counseling a man to prefer the Devil he knows to the Devil he does not. He knew, too, that what his visitor had said about the fake Countess was also true about the fake Singer; any public accusation that he or any other person might make regarding Singer's true identity could easily be made to seem absurd in the presence of the man in question, who would have Crosse's testimony to back his imposture. And yet, had not Jean-Pierre Sévérin demonstrated that a sufficiently rapid hand could defeat even a mesmerically-authoritative eye?

As if he were party to Temple, private thoughts, the vampire resumed his discourse: "You are doubtless thinking that you thwarted my plans once, and might do so again—and so you might, if you were sufficiently dexterous. I invite you to wonder, however, whether Sévérin and Treguern might have done more harm than good by bursting in when they did at Miremont. Treguern would have been unhappy to see an alliance forged between myself and Lord Byron, and the *vehmgerichte* would certainly not have been glad to see one forged between myself and the Grafina von Boehm, but you have little sympa-

269

thy for either. On the other hand, you and your masters might yet have reason to be direly displeased that Colonel Bozzo-Corona has been alerted to shades of light and darkness whose existence he had not previously suspected. Like Saint-German, he had become convinced by his own legend, and had committed himself to it in a fashion that was not entirely sane. How Séverin's captors would have loved to trap the Colonel in a secure net! Now that he is alert, though, he is more likely to trap them. He has made alliance with Tom Brown before, in the guise of the Gentlemen of the Night; were he to do so again…"

"Colonel Bozzo-Corona is a much respected man," Temple said, furrowing his brow as much in anxiety as puzzlement.

"So he is," the ersatz Singer agreed, "but he is three-quarters grey already, and a more avid vampire than I ever was, at least in monetary terms. There's no miser like a grey miser, Mr. Temple, and none more dangerous—especially if he has the army of the *Habits Noirs* at his beck and call."

Temple knew better than to protest that the *Habits Noirs* were an item of urban folklore, although he had never heard any suggestion that Colonel Bozzo-Corona was involved with them. "Still," he said, slowly, "I would be a fool to believe that you could possibly have the interests of the living, rather than the interests of the dead-alive, at heart."

"You'd be a fool if you were to believe that the two do not coincide, at least in this instance," the vampire retorted. "There are men of ill-will among the ranks of the dead-alive as well as the living, and I mount no defense of the likes of Mortdieu, who dreams of conquest—but there are men of good will too, perhaps in as high a proportion as among the living. I am not asking you to trust me, Mr. Temple, but only to bear with me for a little while, in order to determine whether we might both profit from a better understanding."

Get thee behind me, Satan! Temple thought—but he could not muster the conviction to say it aloud, or to mean it. Perhaps that was the effect of the vampire's steady stare, but whatever the source of the belief might have been, the detective was certain in his own mind that Count Szandor was not Satan, nor any minion of the Lord of Hell. Szandor was a creature who had come into the world like any other, unaware of his own origins, nature and potential. The flesh he inhabited had died once, but it was alive again now, and fully entitled to the consideration due to living, thinking individuals. He was not a demon, nor a monster—perhaps less so, in fact, than John Devil the Quaker, with whom Temple had once reluctantly called a truce. Gregory Temple was a secret policeman now, and everyone knew that secret policemen had to make occasional pacts with their adversaries, for the sake of the greater good.

"I make no promises for the longer term," Temple said, finally, "but for the time being, I won't attempt to denounce you before tomorrow's demonstration, or make any other move against you."

"And if the *vehmgerichte* or *Civitas Solis* should make a move?" the vampire prompted.

270

"They're foreign agents operating on English soil," Temple said, firmly. "It would be my sworn duty to prevent them, just as it would be my duty to arrest any agent of Tom Brown's."

"There's no need to worry about Tom Brown," the false Singer assured him. "He's set against *Civitas Solis* and the *vehm* alike. He might stir up a little mischief, that being his nature, but he's not about to lend any material support to our adversaries. And that, I think, concludes our business for now, Mr. Temple. If all goes well, we shall certainly talk again—and you'll also have the opportunity to question Addhema at your leisure. For now, I'll bid you goodnight—we shall both need sleep if we're to be fully awake tomorrow."

About that, at least, the vampire was right, for Temple could feel the extent of his exhaustion. He was not displeased when the candle-light went out, snuffed by a subtle breath. Nor was he surprised that he did not hear the door of his little room open or close, that absence leaving behind the suggestion, if not the suspicion, that he had been visited by a ghost.

Chapter Five
The Demonstration

The next time Temple was woken up it was by one of his own men, anxious that he was late in making a scheduled round. Having ascertained that his pistol was safe beneath his pillow, Temple made haste to get dressed, and ate a swift breakfast in the servants' parlor. Then he checked his men, making certain that each of them knew exactly what his duties were to be between nine in the morning and midnight before sending those who had not yet slept to bed.

Once again, he made his own tour of the house's surrounds, shivering in the cold morning air, but there was nothing to be seen outside the house, and he still had no idea which of the people within it might be agents of foreign powers. All he could do was wait, and hope that he could react quickly enough if anything untoward did occur.

The demonstration being scheduled to take place at noon, Frankenstein and his associates were busy in their laboratory, making preparations. The members of the Commission of Inquiry were at a loose end, and occupied themselves as they pleased. The Bishop insisted on taking a walk in the fresh air, but it was a little too fresh for most of his companions, so the scientists busied themselves in learned discussion while the parliamentarians—including those who had brought companions from London—investigated the possibility of obtaining sexual favors from Fyne Court's serving girls. So far as Temple could tell, they had little success; Somerset folk did not, in the main, accord much status to Members of Parliament, and Messrs. Hastings, Southborne and Medstead were not conspicuously equipped with any personal charisma.

One way or another, however, the time dragged by until the moment came for the interested parties to assemble in what was known as "the small drawing-room," where chairs had been neatly set out in four rows. The first row was reserved for the members of the commission, the second for a number of other invited guests from the surrounding area, including representatives of the Taunton Literary and Philosophical Society. The third row was occupied by selected members of the guests' households, including two young wives and a female "housekeeper," who added a little feminine glamour to the proceedings. Temple and his men had been allotted chairs in the fourth row, along with Crosse's wife and children, but Temple preferred to stand at one side of the improvised stage, while posting one of his men opposite and another at the room's main door, situated opposite the stage.

Crosse brought Frankenstein and his other co-conspirators into the room through a door behind the stage. He was carrying the corpse to be reanimated cradled in his arms, and did not seem to find the burden excessive. It was not until the girl had been laid on the table that her shroud was removed, revealing her to have been some 13 or 14 years of age. She was not naked, but had been clad in a loose-fitting chemise in order to offer token protection to her modesty.

She had been plain rather than pretty, with the muscles of a farm-girl rather than the slender arms and delicate hands of a lady of leisure, but death had not marred her unduly. Temple had been told, privately, that she had drowned, but had not been long immersed in the water following her demise, and might even have been revived had those who pulled her out known how to proceed in that regard. Temple felt sorry for her parents and siblings, none of whom were present, but also felt a slight tug of hope at the thought that life might yet be returned to the corpse.

The girl's body was still damp, and rather glutinously so, by virtue of having been immersed in a special solution for some time, but it was rapidly wired up to a complex electrical apparatus including a series of Voltaic piles. Before switching on the electric current, however, Frankenstein carefully introduced two fluids into the corpse, one red and one clear, using a clyster.

The hush of expectation that had descended seemed to stretch as the anticipation as prolonged, but Frankenstein was finally ready for the administration of the crucial shock. The day was bright now that the morning mist had cleared, and the room's windows faced south, so the sunlight streamed into the room in full measure, adding a suggestion of everyday normality to events that might have looked far more sinister if carried out in a gloomy cellar or an eerie attic.

The first shock only caused the corpse to shudder convulsively; when it was over, the body gave no more sign of life than before. The second was more effective, but not in any particularly striking sense. The shudder died away, but only to give way to movements of a less abrupt kind, like the stirring of a sleeping body in the grip of a bad dream. A third administration was necessary, however, and even then the reanimated corpse could not sit up unaided; Crosse had to lift her up, and he continued to support her.

When she had first been laid down, the girl had seemed more off-white than grey, in spite of a certain discoloration of her skin, but she was noticeably darker in complexion now. Her eyes were open, and the whites stood out quite clearly to the sides of the near-black iris and jet black pupil, within the shadowed orbits.

She stared at the assembled crowd, and seemed to be able to see them, although her waxen features registered no flicker of surprise, delight or anxiety. A tremor ran through the assembly regardless; some, at least, had already seen more than they expected.

Frankenstein had stepped back, his work done, and Faraday was also content to stand by, watching and waiting. It was George Singer who stepped forward to examine the girl closely, picking up her limp hands one by one and staring into her face. His eyes met hers, and interrogated them. His voice it was, too, that began to ask her questions.

"Do you know where you are?" he asked her—although that did not seem to Temple to be the logical place to start.

The dead girl hesitated, as if unsure how to move her mouth or activate her vocal cords—but in the end, her lips parted, and she whispered: "No."

"Can you tell us your name?"

There was a further hesitation. Temple realized that Crosse and his associates had made no attempt to introduce the girl to the crowd, and that even he had not been told her name—the name, that is, with which she had been baptized when alive. It hardly mattered; the word that was eventually formed, seemingly with some difficulty, by the grey lips was: "No."

George Singer seemed oddly pleased with that reply, although Temple heard several members of the audience emit sighs of disappointment.

"Do you remember anything at all?" the vampire continued.

This time, the hesitation was extended, but Temple thought that the grey girl was undergoing a manifest change as the crowd watched with bated breath, almost as if she were recovering herself...or entering into herself. Her gaze became keener and more intelligent, her stance surer and more self-composed. She drew back from the arms that had been holding her up, standing of her own accord—and she looked into George Singer's eyes, as if she recognized something within them.

"You too have died," she said, "but you have mastered the art of appearance."

Singer seemed severely discomfited by this remark, and Temple knew that he would never have made her say any such thing by means of dictation. Temple also knew, however, that the statement would sound like perfect nonsense to almost all the members of the audience.

"What do you remember?" Singer persisted.

"I remember darkness," the girl replied. "I remember the water—the cold, cloying water. I remember death's embrace—but I am glad to be back in the world of space and time. Is that what you want me to say? Are those the words you are trying to put into my mouth? Am I your slave, to do your bidding?"

Temple had tensed all his muscles, ready to act. He knew that the vampire's plan was going awry—that the mesmeric authority that he was trying to impose upon the dead girl was meeting a determined rebellion, and not merely rebellion, but a measure of resentment and contempt. Whatever spirit had come to take possession of the corpse was stronger than anyone, including the vampire, could have expected. The detective could see, however, that George Singer was intrigued as well as anxious, eager to know what this unexpected newcomer might have to tell him, even though the script that he had written had been torn up and thrown away.

"No, my dear," Singer said, with the utmost tenderness, "you are not my slave, and are not required to do my bidding. You are a free agent, like any other sentient being, with the power of choice—but you're a stranger here, for all that you have lived before. I beg you to be patient, and docile, until you understand what is happening around you."

Again, there was hesitation—and then the grey girl laughed. It was a sardonic laugh, with as much mockery as amusement in it.

That was too much for the Bishop of Salisbury. He leapt to his feet, brandishing a crucifix in his right hand and a Bible in his left, and began to intone a rapid formula of exorcism, in the Latin of the Roman church rather than the English of his own. Temple reckoned that he might be lacking a bell and a candle, if the rite were to be performed to perfection, but he assumed that it would not be utterly lacking in efficacy, if exorcisms had any efficacy at all.

The latter question was difficult to determine. The grey girl certainly reacted to the Bishop's intervention, but not as any demon, resentful but cravenly intimidated by the power of God, might have been expected to react. "Why should I begone?" she asked him, quietly but firmly. "Can you believe that the world is yours, and that you alone have the privilege of determining what it can and shall contain? Do you not understand that you are nothing more than a mere larva, bearing within you the seed of something strange? Begone yourself, you poor pathetic fool!"

Perhaps, Temple thought, if the grey girl had had a weapon to hand, she might have used it in conjunction with her final dismissal, but she was barehanded, and possessed of no more strength than the frail body she inhabited. All she could muster was a gesture, half-contemptuous and half-bellicose: a mere symbol of aggression.

To at least one of the members of her terrified audience, however, that symbolic gesture was sufficient to warrant a violent reply.

Temple's own men, disciplined by long training, merely reached for their cudgels without taking them out—but Stephen Southborne had brought a dagger to the séance, in case of need, and he drew it. With a single fluid motion, which spoke of practice, he hurled it, aiming for the grey girl's breast.

The vampire would not tolerate that; with a lightning movement, he snatched her out of the path of the flying blade. It missed the resurrected girl by a foot—but Singer was not the only one who had obeyed a protective impulse. Victor Frankenstein had leapt forward, intending to snatch her out of harm's way himself, but had found her already gone, and he stumbled, leaning forward with his arms outstretched.

The dagger struck him in the neck, and buried itself deeply, while red arterial blood spurted forth to either side of the embedded blade.

Southborne went as pale as a ghost, and Hastings had to prop him up to prevent him falling in a swoon. The ladies present were not the only ones who gasped or screamed. Even the vampire seemed stunned; the hands that had reached out so forcefully to pluck the intended victim out of the way relaxed their grip and fell nervelessly to his sides.

The grey girl's mocking contempt changed to raging wrath upon the instant. She leapt away from Singer, shoved Michael Faraday aside, and hurled herself from the stage as if to attack the audience. Few of the crowd's members were still seated, but chairs tumbled in every direction as some moved to their left and others to their right, desperate to get out of her way.

Temple was by no means calm, but he had sufficient self-control to take note of the absurdity of the situation. The girl was no more than five feet tall, slender and weak, while there were many in the crowd who stood nearly a foot higher, with well-toned muscles and the vigor of sportsmen—and yet, not one of the men in the assembly had the courage to take a stand. What they saw coming at them, with their educated eyes, was no mere creature of flesh and blood but a monster, perhaps released from Hell.

Again, Temple wondered whether the girl might have struck out with lethal force had she had a club or a sword, but, as things were, she merely attempted to strike those within reach with the flat of her hand, as if to slap their faces as a punishment for impertinence. None of the attempted blows landed; her intended victims were too quick in their evasions.

The Bishop of Salisbury fell over bruisingly, and so did Peter Barlow, among others, but all of them were tumbled by the jostling elbows or flailing arms of their fellow living men, victims of mere confusion. The grey girl did not lay a hand on anyone as she moved through the four rows of scattered chairs— and once she was through the crowd, she headed straight for the door.

One of Temple's men was guarding the door, and now he did draw his cudgel, spreading his arms and bracing his knees in a street-fighter's crouch.

"Don't hurt her!" Temple howled.

He only meant to instruct the man to handle her gently when he seized her, but the man construed the order differently, and stood aside. The door was standing ajar; there must have been servants gathered beyond it, eavesdropping on the momentous affair—but they were already fleeing. When the girl snatched at the door-knob and drew the batten wide, there was no one visible in the corridor beyond.

Within a second, the girl had disappeared.

In the meantime, Faraday had picked himself up and had joined Andrew Crosse and George Singer, crouching over Frankenstein's fallen body.

"Follow the girl, but *don't hurt her!*" Temple cried to the guardian of the door, as he ran to Frankenstein's side. He knew as soon as he arrived beside the fallen man that there was no hope for him—or, at least, no hope for his life.

"Pick him up!" Faraday instructed Crosse and Singer. "Take him to the laboratory! We must immerse him as soon as possible, even before we draw the dagger from his neck."

Temple did not hesitate; while Crosse and the vampire did as they were told, he turned to the crowd, and posed himself in such a fashion as to forbid any interference. The Bishop of Salisbury was still down, nursing his bruises, but Robert Hastings made as if to protest. "Hold hard!" Temple told him. "You came for a demonstration, and you shall have more than you bargained for, if you consent to wait. Those of you who still suspect trickery will have your final doubts dispelled."

"You must catch and destroy that demon, Mr. Temple!" was Hastings' only reply.

"She has done no harm," Temple said. "I'd rather arrest Mr. Southborne, and commit him to the assizes on a charge of manslaughter, but I dare say that he will claim privileged immunity, since he is on parliamentary business here—and besides, the crime of manslaughter might need to be redefined by parliament, if the Necromancers of London can bring Frankenstein back from the dead."

The Bishop was on his feet by this time, and seemed to be on the point of preaching an angry sermon to Temple and anyone else who would listen, but the room was already emptying as the crowd dispersed.

Having satisfied himself that there was nothing more to be done in the drawing-room, Temple hurried after Faraday and his companions, and reached the laboratory in time to see Frankenstein's body being immersed in the same bath of fluid from which the girl's body had been removed. There were two other tanks nearby, each containing a male corpse, but neither body had been as fresh as Frankenstein's by the time the treatment had begun, and they seemed very somber by comparison.

"Have you learned his technique well enough to bring him back?" Temple demanded of Faraday.

"I believe so," Faraday replied. "We can but try."

The false George Singer took Temple's arm and drew him aside. "That did not go as well as I had hoped," he said, when they were out of earshot of Faraday and Crosse. "I had not expected to meet with such resistance, and had a very different performance planned. Who would have thought that a corpse could be revived so swiftly, with a seemingly-mature intelligence? We must interrogate her together, when your men bring her back; there's much to be learned here."

"*If* they bring her back," Temple said, grimly. "They'll not be the only ones searching for her, and if she falls into the hands of the Germans or the Churchmen, they'll want to keep her for themselves—unless, of course, you can exert your mesmeric authority over *them*."

"I'll do what I can," the vampire said, "but we'll need to keep an eye on Frankenstein too—if he can be revived, with his mind relatively unimpaired, he might be the most valuable witness of all to the mysteries of his own condition."

"The Commission of Inquiry is spoiled, though," Temple observed. "For one of its members to kill the man under investigation, even by accident, is fatal to its pretentions. The Bishop's antics can be set aside, but not Southborne's. He could not have done more had he been secretly commissioned to wreck the investigation."

"Perhaps that's so, in a purely technical sense—but if the members can be persuaded to extend their stay here long enough to watch three more revivals instead of two, imagine what an impact the testimony of Frankenstein might have, delivered from beyond the grave! Imagine what a tale they'd carry back to Canning and the King!"

"If theatricality is what you want," Temple told him, a trifle bitterly, "you might do worse than reveal yourself, and regale the audience with anecdotes of your checkered past."

Singer shook his head. "More than human I might be," he said, "but I'm greatly outnumbered here, without my lovely counterpart to charm my adversaries. I do hope the girl will come to no harm—there are people here, more lethally armed than the idiot Bishop and the headstrong parliamentarian, who might prefer to kill her rather than question her."

"Whatever you might think of the Bishop," Temple said, "there will be many members of that audience who believe that he proved his case—that the girl really was possessed by a malevolent demon. Southborne was probably not the only one who felt a reflexive urge to destroy her. Are you quite sure yourself that the intelligence which took such rapid control of her, in spite of your own efforts, was *not* a demon?"

"As sure as I am that I'm not a demon myself," Singer replied, wryly. "I dare say, though, that this is not the first time such a mistake has been made. Find the girl, Mr. Temple, if you can—I must play my part here."

Temple did not care for the implication that he was under the vampire's orders now, but he was eager to discover what progress the search was making, so he went out in search of his men.

There was no shortage of witnesses to tell him which way the chase had gone, at least while he was still in the house and its shadow, but once he reached the wooded part of the estate he had to use his talents as a tracker.

Recently dead though she was, the grey girl was evidently agile, for she had crossed the boundary wall of Fyne Court's grounds and disappeared into thicker woods, with at least half a dozen men in her wake.

Five minutes after clambering over the wall himself, Temple met someone coming the other way, apparently having abandoned the chase. It was not one of his own men, but one who had traveled with the expedition as Southborne's valet.

"I apologize for my master's hot-headedness, sir," the man said, as he approached the detective. "It was recklessness, not malice. He is exactly what he seems to be."

"Unlike you, I presume," Temple said, looking the man up and down.

"I wondered whether you had identified me when I gave you the piece of paper," the other replied. "We've met before, alas—but Tom was pressed for time, and had to take what opportunity he could to intrude a spy into the party. The others did no better, I think—you've doubtless spotted the German by now, and you must have known already that Snow Harris is in the pocket of *Civitas Solis*."

All of this was news to Temple, but he did his utmost not to show a flicker of surprise, while he tried to figure out where he might have seen the valet before. Sharper's seemed by far the likeliest venue, and the memory eventually clicked into place.

"I've seen you playing the villain to Sam Hopkey's hero," Temple said, trying to sound as if he had never been in doubt about it, "and you're doubtless another veteran of the Old Bailey. How did you know that Singer is an impostor?" He was careful not to say *vampire* in case he, too, might give away far too much.

"Tom knew witnesses to his death who had not been suborned. When he heard of his alleged return, he knew that Szandor must be involved, and that Crosse must have been hypnotized into forgetfulness. You will not seek to have me arrested, I hope, Mr. Temple—I've done nothing against the law, and have done you a good turn. Tom's orders were to protect you, and to trust you if alliances had to be made. The foreigners are the real enemy."

"I don't doubt that the *vehmgerichte* and Balsamo's followers are Tom Brown's enemies just now," Temple retorted, "but I'm not so sure that they're mine, even though one or other of them may well have taken Séverin by stealth. Why have you given up chasing the grey girl?"

"Given up, sir?" the other queried. "I haven't given up—I'm just looking elsewhere. Whatever that creature is, it doesn't lack cunning. If I were in her place, I'd have doubled back already. Your men aren't exactly subtle in their procedures, if you'll forgive the observation."

"And what will you do with her if you find her?"

The other raised an eyebrow, mugging as if he were onstage in Jenny Paddock's cabaret theatre. "Do you take me for one of the pantomime villains I play, sir? Do you imagine that my mind is bent on rape? I can assure you that I'll be the perfect gentleman, as solicitous as a benevolent uncle."

"You mean that you'll help her escape—all the way to London, if you can."

The valet shrugged. "Won't be easy, sir," he said, "given that I'm more-or-less alone. You wouldn't care to come to some arrangement, I suppose—just between ourselves?"

"No, I wouldn't," Temple said, through gritted teeth—although he was not entirely certain of the wisdom of his reflexive hostility.

"There's gratitude for you," the valet replied, seemingly unoffended. "Watch out for the vampire, sir—he's a tricky one, by all accounts." And with that, he continued on his way back toward Fyne Court, leaving Temple alone with the chatter of birdsong and rustlings in the undergrowth that might have been anything at all.

Chapter Six
A Voice from Beyond

Temple stood where he was for three minutes more, listening. There was no sign of anyone else returning from the hunt, and the girl's pursuers had passed out of earshot, probably on a wild goose chase.

Satisfied that there was no point in continuing, Temple turned to follow Southborne's valet, and nearly jumped out of his skin. The grey girl had obviously been standing behind him for a minute or more, waiting for him to turn round.

"I believe I need your help, sir," she said.

"Yes," he said, a trifle numbly, "I believe you do,"

"I heard you shouting to the men who were chasing me, instructing them not to hurt me," she said, explaining her decision to approach him, "but I don't know who you are."

"Gregory Temple," the ex-detective told her. "I'm in the employ of His Majesty's government. I escorted a seven-man commission here from London, to bear witness to your resurrection."

"My resurrection?"

Temple hesitated, then said: "Yes—that's what has happened to you. Were you not aware of that?"

"Are you saying that I really did die? That it was not a dream?"

"Yes—you were drowned."

"Murdered?"

"An accident, I believe. Do you have any reason to think that you might have been murdered?"

"No." The denial did not seem certain.

"But you remember who you are—were—now? You've recovered your memory?"

The grey girl stared at him, quizzically. "I'm not the person I remember," she said, echoing what Szandor had told him, and what General Mortdieu had apparently told Ned Knob. "Yes, I do remember her—but she was a feeble thing. I feel quite different now. I feel...but I don't have the words to describe it. I do have words that aren't my own, though...words that were somehow *put into my head.*"

"By a mesmerist," Temple told her. "He was intent on controlling you, and expected to find you far more vulnerable than you were. He had a script all prepared for you, but you wouldn't respond to his prompts. Perhaps his attempted insistence brought forth an instinctive resistance of some sort. He did save your life, though, when that fool Southborne threw the dagger."

"Yes," the grey girl said, vaguely. "He talked about supplying me with words before..."

"Before?" Temple queried. "Before you died, you mean? You had met him before?" Suddenly, he wondered very forcefully whether the girl's drowning had been something other than an accident. If so, it would not take much imagination to guess who might have been responsible, whether directly or indirectly.

"It was prophesied that I would die," the girl said, still seemingly lost in something akin to a dream, albeit with elements of cruel reality contained within it. "It was also prophesied that I would emerge from the chrysalis of death as a different kind of being, as unlike my old self as a butterfly is to a caterpillar."

So she had already been primed, Temple thought, *with the sentiments she expressed to Hastings and the Bishop—they merely failed to emerge on cue. Szandor was taking no chances; he intended to rig the entire exhibition—but if he was prepared to commit murder to do it, I ought to bring him to justice, if I can.*

There were, however, more urgent matters at hand. What was he to do with the girl, now that she was in his custody? How could he keep her safe, and away from all the other parties avid to interrogate her?

"Are you cold?" he asked her.

She nodded to indicate that she was, although she did not seem entirely certain. She knew, at least, that she ought to be feeling the cold.

Temple took off his jacket and wrapped her in it. He could not immediately think of any place of safety to which they might go, let alone any in which he could leave her while he attended to his duties back at Fyne Court. "What's your name?" he asked

"I *was* Helen," she replied.

"Well, she-who-was-Helen, we need to find a hiding-place for you. If your memories are intact, you must know the neighborhood far better than any of the people chasing you just now—perhaps better than the servants at Fyne Court. Is there anywhere close at hand where you might be safe, until I can help you get away?"

"I know these woods," she said. "They won't catch me here. Her father was the finest poacher in the county." She spoke with pride; presumably, that was not an idea that Szandor had planted in her head.

"In that case," Temple said, "We need to arrange a meeting place— somewhere to which I can bring a carriage, or at least a pair of horses. Can you ride?"

"Of course I can," she replied. "They don't own a horse, but her father and her brother have worked in stables. She's ridden a post horse—they're the fastest."

"That's good," Temple said. "Horses it shall be. Pick a good spot, where we won't be seen."

"Take the Taunton road," she said, after a moment's pause for thought. "There's a broken signpost by a sunken path, about a mile from the Court. Take the sunken road, as far as the ford in the hollow. Wait there—I'll try to make sure that you haven't been followed before I show myself. Best not wait for dusk, though—it's a treacherous place in the dark."

Once they were mounted, Temple thought, it would be very difficult for anyone to chase them, provided that their horses were fit enough and fast enough. "I'll get away when I can," he promised, "but it probably won't be before noon."

She took off his jacket and handed it back. "Best return as you came," she said. "I'll be fine, I think. I do feel the cold, but…I'm not sure that it can harm me now."

Temple hesitated, wondering whether it might not be better simply to take the girl back to Fyne Court, and protect her there as best he could—but he was even more convinced now that he could not trust the vampire, and was certainly not about to put his trust in Southborne's valet. While Szandor was disguised as Singer, he could not count on Crosse or Faraday either. He cursed his misfortune in being so far from the capital. If only the Necromancers of London had been invited to do their work close to home, instead of being exiled to a supposedly safe distance!

Frankenstein, he knew, would not be ripe for revival for at least 72 hours, and perhaps considerably longer. He might have time to get the girl to London and return, although that would certainly violate his instructions and put his official position in even greater jeopardy. He needed a secure hiding-place much nearer to Fyne Court, from which he could come and go at will.

"Go, then," he said to the girl. "I'll come when I can. I'll do everything possible to keep you safe."

The grey girl disappeared into the undergrowth, sand Temple went back to the house. It was a further hour before his men returned, quite empty-handed. Crosse had volunteered to mobilize his servants to beat the woods, but Temple had declined the offer, saying that it would be better not to frighten the girl, and that the wisest course was simply to send someone to wait for her at her parent's house, to which she would undoubtedly return.

It took the detective until 2 p.m. to make his preparations with what he considered to be necessary discretion—by which time he had reason enough to borrow a pair of horses, ostensibly in order to relieve the man he had sent to the village.

He waited for a full hour at the appointed place, but the girl never showed up. Eventually, he returned to the house cursing his bad judgment, but privately convinced that someone else had captured her. If so, she had not been brought back to the house.

The agents of *Civitas Solis* were unlikely, in Temple's judgment, to have any kind of priory nearby, but that did not mean that they did not have friends in the vicinity, especially if William Snow Harris had already been affiliated to their cause. If that really were the case, Harris would undoubtedly take it upon himself to sound out Faraday and Crosse with a view to their recruitment—but with luck, he would try to sound out Singer too, and get more than he bargained for.

Temple did relieve the man he had left at Helen's old home, but instructed him to send another man out as soon as he got back to Fyne Court, so that Temple need not be too long away. He used the interval to question Helen's parents about her life, and about any strangers she might have met in the days leading up to her death. Of the latter matter they clamed to know nothing at all, but they answered all of his questions as one might expect of a poacher and his wife confronted with the former cream of Scotland Yard: evasively and with a great deal of suspicion.

Once he was back at Fyne Court, Temple set about interviewing the members of the Commission, to determine what their thoughts might be on the matter of continuing and completing the Inquiry. Six were immediately willing, being curious themselves as to what might become of Victor Frankenstein—Southborne, in particular, expressed a strong interest in seeing him revived—and the seventh, the Bishop of Salisbury, was easily convinced that there was God's work to be done in any event, albeit best done in a quieter fashion than he had so far contrived.

Eventually, Temple found an opportunity to talk to George Singer again. "What did you do to that girl?" he demanded.

Singer seemed to consider a flat denial, but then shrugged his shoulders. "Nothing too terrible, as you have seen," he answered. "If I contrived her death, it was in the knowledge—or, at least, the conviction—that it would not be irreversible. It appears that I was more successful than I hoped in planting seeds of suggestion in her mind prior to death, in the hope that they would enhance her capacity to return. Sometimes, I even surprise myself. Have you caught her, then?"

"I think Balsamo's followers might have spirited her away."

"Really? I thought you capable of outwitting them—but no matter. Tomorrow might go better; I had no opportunity to plant any seeds in the minds of the other two poor fellows. On the other hand, they might not revive at all, and if they do, their mental faculties might be beyond the reach of my talents as a mesmerist, redoubtable though they are."

As things turned out, however, the second day's demonstration did not go well at all. The attempted resurrection failed completely. That would have disconcerted Faraday and Crosse in any case, but it was doubly disconcerting in the circumstances, for they could not be sure that they had not erred in some respect, where Frankenstein would have succeeded.

"We have his instructions," Faraday opined, in Temple's presence, "but not his genius. He would have displayed a surer touch—of that we may be certain."

"But the method works," Singer put in. "Given that, you will surely succeed—if not tomorrow, then some time thereafter."

"But dare we take the risk of trying to restore Frankenstein to life, until we have made certain that we are capable of success?" Crosse asked

"Dare we take the risk of *not* making the attempt?" Singer countered. "We did not expect to reach this situation, but now that we have, the members of the spoiled Commission of Inquiry must still be satisfied—and I cannot see that we can satisfy them now, except by bringing Victor back to life. The gauntlet has been thrown at our feet, and we are honor-bound pick it up. We must meet the challenge."

"What do you think, Mr. Temple?" Crosse asked, although Faraday frowned at the notion of consulting a layman on what he considered to be largely a matter of science.

"My first duty is to protect the Commission," Temple said. "I suspect that my superiors might judge that I have already failed in that—but I have a corollary duty to protect the demonstrators who are presenting their evidence to the Commission. In that respect, I wonder whether there might be any danger to Frankenstein in trying to revive him too soon?"

"Too soon?" Faraday muttered. "Like Singer, I'm more afraid of leaving it too late."

"If the fluid and moderate electrical excitation do not restore his pulse, however, we dare not take him out of the womb," Crosse said. "Not tomorrow, at any rate. Even the poor soul we lost today showed slight signs of life before fading into oblivion."

"Some sort of bodily circulation is definitely necessary to restored life," Singer stated, without specifying the reasons for his certainty, "but I'm confident that Frankenstein will recover that more rapidly than the common run of the dead. We shall be glad to have him in reserve, if the third trial fails—no one will pay much heed to that, in the circumstances; the denouement will depend entirely on the fourth act."

He was correct in his estimation; the third trial also failed, although it came within a whisker of success. The dead man revived sufficiently to sit up, but not to stand upright or to talk, and soon lapsed into inertia again. No one seemed to care; many of the observers invited from outside the Court had not even bothered to turn up. The exhibition that everyone wanted to see was the unscheduled fourth one, when Victor Frankenstein would be brought back from the dead—or not.

Faraday and Crosse seemed to be divided in their opinions as to the wisdom of trying to revive Frankensein a mere three days after his death, but that gave Singer a casting vote of sorts, and his mind was made up.

"Three days is a propitious interval," the vampire said. "It carries symbolic meaning for the Bishop, and for his supposedly-devout companions. Besides, the freshness of the body might well be more important than the length of exposure to the preliminary treatment. If we fail, we shall still have the possibility of trying again, but if we succeed…well, think of that, gentlemen. What if we succeed?"

The Necromancers of London could not prevail against the Vampire of Szeged; his arguments would probably have been sufficient even without his additional means of persuasion—and so it was that the audience assembled for a fourth time on the afternoon following the second failure, abuzz with anticipation.

There had been no sign of the grey girl anywhere in the neighborhood, but Southborne's valet had taken the trouble to tell Temple that Tom Brown had been alerted to the circumstances, and would have the roads west of the capital under careful surveillance. "He'd better pray, then," Temple had observed, sourly, "that they have not taken her to the Bristol Channel to put her aboard a boat or a ship." The spy had not had any reason to dispute that possibility.

The audience for the demonstration was larger than any of its predecessors, several of the household servants having found excuses to be in the room, and many of the Commission's hangers-on, including the two whores, having also worked their way into the company. Victor Frankenstein had become a famous man, albeit as a Gothic villain whose shady reputation was akin to Lord Byron's notoriety. No one doubted that his return from the world beyond would be a momentous occasion, or that any news he might bring back from the afterlife could be anything other than significant. The Bishop was not the only person carrying a crucifix, though, and there was actually a queue of people wanting his blessing before the ceremony began.

The general procedure was identical to the three previous occasions, but it was conducted with a manifest dignity that increased its ritual air. As on the first day, it required three administrations of electrical current to restore any semblance of life to the corpse, but, as on the first day, three sufficed.

The room was filled with a pregnant silence as Crosse and Singer lent the individual who had been Victor Frankenstein the support he needed to sit upright. Singer was not so quick to ask questions this time, however; he remained at Frankenstein's side, but watched as if mesmerized himself while the new Grey Man surveyed the audience with his bleak but trenchant gaze.

In the end, it was Faraday who stepped forward to ask: "Do you know me, Victor?"

The Grey Man turned his head in order to study Faraday carefully. There was a long pause before he finally said: "Yes."

Temple repressed a perverse urge to giggle.

"Who am I?" Faraday asked, innocently.

"Michael Faraday," said the Grey Man, forming the syllables slowly, almost as if he were uncertain of the use of his vocal apparatus.

"And who are you?" Faraday asked.

After another pause, Frankenstein said: "Victor."

Temple could not help noting that Faraday had already called him by that name, but the scientist seemed to be satisfied that the response was no mere echo.

"Do you remember what happened here three days ago?" Faraday asked—unwisely, in Temple's opinion. The detective looked at Southborne; the latter's face was quite white, as if he fully expected the living corpse to point an accusing finger at him, in the fashion of a ghost in a stage melodrama.

"We brought the girl back to life," was Frankenstein's answer. Perhaps, Temple thought, he had not had time to form a memory of what had happened thereafter.

"We did," Faraday confirmed. "And now, we have performed the same service for you—with even greater success."

The Bishop of Salisbury stood up, much more self-controlled now than before. "Might I ask a question, Mr. Faraday?" he asked, his voice only slightly tremulous.

Faraday had no option but to agree.

"Where have you been for the last three days, Doctor Frankenstein?" the Churchman asked.

Frankenstein fixed the Bishop with a basilisk stare. "Do you want to know what Hell is like, Your Eminence?" he asked, evidently gaining swiftly in facility as he made further use of his tongue. "Can you not be patient for a little while longer?"

That is not Frankenstein speaking! Temple thought. *If it is not a demon, then it is someone or something which seems to be masquerading as a demon—but why?* His gaze went reflexively to the vampire, who had only just moved away from Frankenstein slightly, perceiving that the Grey Man was no longer in need of support. Singer seemed as puzzled as Temple was himself, presumably for the same reason.

The Bishop was trying hard to remain unintimidated. "Yes," he said, bravely. "I would like to have testimony of what Hell is like, from the mouth of one of its denizens, recently emerged."

"Why," said the Grey Men, "this is Hell, nor am I out of it."

Temple knew perfectly well, as more than half the audience members must have done, that the Grey Man was quoting Marlowe's Mephistopheles—a mocking ploy surely calculated to increase the suspicion that this entire scene had been staged, and was all trickery. He wondered, momentarily, whether Frankenstein might possibly have been slain by a stage dagger, and whether the blood he had shed might have been fake.

Something is wrong here, he thought, *but what on Earth is the motivation behind it? This is not Szandor's doing, for he wants the Commission to make a favorable report, in order that he might insinuate himself into the company of the duly-licensed Necromancers of London.*

He could not help remembering the possibility that Szandor had mentioned to him, that there might be vampires even older than he, who could deceive him as easily as he could deceive the living.

The scientists seemed uneasy at this turn of events, and Thomas Young took it upon himself to intervene. "How does you present state of being differ, in terms of your sensory perceptions, from the one you knew before?" he asked, having first solicited permission by raising his hand.

"I am still learning to use my faculties," the Grey Man said, in a pensive tone, as if to imply that this was a question he permitted himself to take seriously. "It will take time, I think, to learn this new way of being and overcome my own bewilderment. I suspect that there is much to be learned, but I cannot tell, as yet, what it might be."

William Snow Harris stood up then, either to continue speaking on behalf of science, or to play a role on behalf of *Civitas Solis*. He did not bother to ask Faraday's permission before asking: "How does it feel, Doctor Frankenstein, to have been resurrected from the dead? Are you glad to have been returned to life?"

"Feel?" the Grey Man repeated. "Am I glad? How do I know? Do you think my feelings are comparable with yours? Can you imagine that I might be able to use the words my predecessor knew to describe an experience that your language has never had occasion to represent? We shall need a new language now, Mr. Harris."

"You know my name," Snow Harris observed, dully.

"You were formally introduced to my predecessor," the Grey Man pointed out, "as were Mr. Hastings, Mr. Southborne, Mr. Medstead, Mr. Young, Mr. Barlow and, of course, His Eminence the Bishop. The memories are a trifle dim, at present, but they are intact, I think." He seemed to be collecting himself, testing his muscles and his mind alike. His eyes had lingered on the Bishop after pronouncing his title, and he suddenly said: "May I ask *you* a question, Your Eminence?"

The Bishop still had a grip on his courage. "Yes," he said.

"Was Lazarus possessed by a demon when he came forth from the tomb?" the Grey Man demanded.

"Lazarus came forth in answer to Christ's call," the Bishop replied.

"And how do you know," Frankenstein countered, "that I did not?"

The Bishop looked around, as if fearful of finding Christ lurking somewhere in the room.

Would it be any greater surprise if he were? Temple wondered.

Whether it was his courage or his ingenuity that failed him, the Bishop made no reply.

"The Age of Miracles is over," Hasting stated, flatly.

"Nonsense," the Grey Man retorted. "It has hardly begun. Unless you mean that the resurrection of the dead has henceforth been a matter of rare and random chance, without perceptible causation. If that is what you signify by *miracle* then yes, the Age of Miracles is over, and a new Age has begun, in which resurrection will be a matter of technique and artistry, and life after death will cease to be a mere flickering phantom, putting on flesh and purpose."

This is more than Szandor could have hoped for, Temple thought, realizing that the tide was turning, having only feigned an intention to ebb. *What weight can the Commission's verdict have, now that the dead-alive have an advocate of their own as compelling, in his own way, as General Mortdieu.*

No daggers were being thrown this time; even if Victor Frankenstein's reputation had not gone before the Grey Man, he would have cut a far more imposing figure than the poor bewildered child.

Put him in a suit and top hat instead of a shroud, Temple thought, *and he might address the House of Commons, or the House of Lords, on his own account, challenging them both to assess him as a demon or a miracle of virtue...or a man of science still.*

"And what do you intend to do with your new life, Doctor Frankenstein?" Temple was momentarily surprised to find that he had asked the question aloud.

The Grey Man turned to face him. "Gregory Temple," he said, as if struggling to recall the name. "The guardian of the Commission...and public safety. You have met my...the person who calls himself Lazarus. You have heard his account of his intentions. Mine are, I fear, just as vague. How can I know what intentions I might ultimately have until I know what possibilities might lie before me? For the moment, what can I do but ally myself firmly with Mr. Faraday, Mr. Crosse and Mr. Singer, in order to investigate myself, and the possibility of saving others from oblivion, as I have been saved?"

Temple had no alternative in mind, but others apparently did, for the door through which the grey girl had fled three days before was suddenly thrust open, and three men costumed as monks came in. They were carrying swords. Only

287

one of the three pushed back his cowl, permitting Gregory Temple to recognize him as the man who called himself Giuseppe Balsamo.

"Have no fear, my friends," Balsamo said, addressing the audience. "The house is more secure by far now than it was when it only had Temple's four men and your own servants to guard it against the Prussians. I can give the Necromancers of London safer conduct by far than His Majesty's secret police, and with better motives. I must politely request the rest of you to pack your bags and leave within the hour. You are, I fear, in danger from more than one source, and I cannot guarantee the safety of such a large and ill-assorted company."

Temple's men were looking at him for a lead. He signaled to them to stand and wait, taking no overt action for the time being. He was obliged to step forward himself, however, and confront the upstart monk. "You are on English soil, Signor Balsamo," he said, "and I am the recognized authority here. I must ask you to withdraw, and take your men with you."

"This is no mere national concern, as you know very well, Mr. Temple," Balsamo replied. "I belong to no nation, but to the Brotherhood of Humankind."

"You belong to a company of brigands and child-stealers," Temple retorted. "Whatever delusions you have carried forward from the past, you are no better now than Tom Brown's company of criminals or the Illuminati's *vehm*. There is no legitimate authority here but the Crown's." So saying, he drew his cudgel—and his four men drew theirs. He was not foolish enough to think he had the numerical advantage, though, and was not surprised to see at last a dozen members of the audience, masters and servants alike, lay bare an assortment of blades, Not all, he knew, would be affiliates of *Civitas Solis*—but Balsamo would not have made a move had he not thought the situation controllable in the short term.

The wild cards were, however, the four men standing on the stage. Balsamo must have thought that he had a good chance of commanding their obedience—but he might not have been aware of George Singer's imposture, and he certainly had no idea whatsoever of what the Grey Man might do. That was the heart of his gamble.

What the Grey Man actually did was to turn around, pick up a heavy Leyden Jar, and hurl it, with amazing force, directly at Giuseppe Balsamo's head.

Balsamo ducked, but the damage had been done, in symbolic terms. Southborne's valet was not the only man who immediately leapt forward to tackle the invading monks, and Temple's men did not wait for a signal this time. Within half a second, the riot was in full swing.

Chapter Seven
Order out of Chaos

Temple's duty was explicit in the orders he had received from his political masters: to protect the members of the Parliamentary Commission from any harm. That was the purpose of the first orders he howled to his men, instructing them to gather the seven members of the Commission together and to deploy a phalanx around them, to the extent that it was possible for five men to do that.

In practice, of course, it was by no means so simple. For one thing, the members of the Commission were concerned for their companions and servants, and wanted to keep them close, swelling the ranks of those potentially in need of protection considerably. For another, some of the members, and their servants too, were avid to defend themselves, and had weapons with which to do it. Temple had no hesitation in allowing the three members of parliament to join his protective cordon, although he immediately set out to assert his authority over them, in order to keep them in formation. He had only a second's hesitation about allowing Southborne's valet to do likewise; for the moment, it did not matter in the least that the man was in the play of John Devil. Snow Harris's servant, on the other hand, Temple immediately disarmed, and found the time to whisper in the scientist's ear that if he manifested the slightest gesture of support for the warrior monks, he would be knocked out and carried to safety as luggage, to be charged with treason at a later date.

In fact, Snow Harris seemed to be as astonished by the turn of events as anyone else, and glad enough to cleave to his immediate fellows rather than his rumored associates. Without any sign of internal dissent, therefore, the company was formed up, and Temple then directed his attention to getting it safely to the main door of the room and through it. His intention was to make for the stables, if that were practicable, or to find a redoubt that could be suitably barricaded if escape from the grounds proved impossible.

The first part of the operation proved easy enough, there being no organized resistance to it. There were a number of minor brawls taking place between the tumbled chairs and the door, but it proved easy enough for Temple and his fellow point-man to clear all obstructions from the way, without engaging in any earnest combat. Temple was not in the least surprised by that, for he did not suppose for a moment that *Civitas Solis* cared a fig for the members of the Commission; their target was, and had always been, the Necromancers of London—and, most particularly of all, the resurrected Victor Frankenstein.

In different circumstances, Temple might well have taken a stand with Crosse and Faraday, to make certain of their escape, but he could not do that. Indeed, he was barely able to spare a couple of backward glances, as he shepherded his flock toward the door, to see what had become of Frankenstein and his companions. He was unsurprised to see, even at a glance, that it was George

Singer who had taken charge of that party, nor that, once Singer had a blade in his hand, it would be direly difficult for anyone to get past him. Neither Crosse nor Faraday was armed, but the Grey Man had shown that he was capable of fighting, and several of Crosse's household servants had immediately rallied to their master's support, making the whole company a fighting-force to be reckoned with, especially on what was effectively home ground. As Temple ushered his own people out into the corridor, therefore, he was able to observe that Crosse's party was making a similarly disciplined retreat through the door behind the stage.

Balsamo had obviously not been bluffing when he claimed that the house was surrounded; there were more monks' habits to be seen in the corridors and even more outside the house—but none of their wearers attempted to attack Temple's company, being content to retreat from them and melt away, intent on discovering and seizing other prey.

Temple brought his charges to the stable complex without anyone sustaining or dealing out any harm more dangerous than a bruise. He supervised the harnessing of the two largest carriages in the garage, and the saddling of a dozen extra horses, rudely pushing back other guests intent on making their own escape, demanding that they wait their turn. One of two protested that he was stealing their horses, to which he replied that he was requisitioning them in the name of the crown, and that they would be able to recover them from the constabulary in Taunton, that being his immediate objective as a place of refuge. When the carriages were loaded, however, and the majority of the horses mounted, he delegated authority for the convoy's safe conduct to his second-in-command, intent on returning to the house.

"That might be unwise, sir," Tom Brown's man said, leaning down from the horse on to which he had climbed. "I should be able to find help closer at hand than Taunton, and you might do better to return with half a dozen experienced brawlers at your back."

"Too late, in all probability," Temple told him. "Go—and if you return with half a dozen would-be brawlers at your back, don't expect to find me in sympathy with you."

He watched the convoy until it was safely through the gate, and then turned back, heading for Crosse's laboratory. At first, the only people he met in the corridors of the house were other escapees intent on following the Commissioners with all possible haste, but he eventually found his way barred by two sword-bearing monks, who had been delegated to form a kind of rearguard while their fellows attempted to storm the laboratory. He knew that he was close to Crosse's lair, but could not see the laboratory door as yet. The sound of raised voices informed him that the battle was not yet finished, however, and an overheard reference to a battering-ram suggested that Frankenstein's followers had barricaded the door, ready to withstand a siege.

Time was pressing, Temple knew. Help would arrive eventually, from Tom Brown's men if not the constables from Taunton—and the agents of the *vehm* would also oppose their rivals fiercely, if they had not been taken out of the equation in advance. Some kinds of assistance, Temple knew, might create more problems than they solved, in the longer term, but the immediate objective was clear enough: to prevent *Civitas Solis* from kidnapping Victor Frankenstein and the Necromancers of London.

It was with that thought in mind that Temple squared himself for a flight, holding out his truncheon in a threatening manner. "I am an officer of the Crown," he informed the two men blocking his way, dutifully. "To cross swords with me is to advertise your eligibility for the gallows."

"You'd have to catch us first," replied one of the monks, unmistakably an Englishman.

"He's just an old man," the second monk observed, as if to bolster his companion's confidence, before addressing Temple directly, saying: "Back away, old man—there's no disgrace in a retreat from superior forces." He too was speaking English like a native.

"Don't kill him," said a voice that came from behind Temple, which certainly did not belong to an Englishman. "This one we should take alive."

Temple suspected that the sentiment behind the instruction was not respect for English law, and was not entirely glad to hear this order—but he was quick to seize whatever slight advantage it might offer him. Satisfied that the two men ahead of him would at least hesitate before trying to run him through, he attacked them without warning, swinging his cudgel in a manner that was by no means as reckless or random as it must have seemed.

The detective was conscious as he moved of the fact that he *was* an old man, but he remembered the fight that Jean-Pierre Séverin had undertaken on his behalf in the grounds of a Paris hotel, and knew that old reflexes can sometimes make up in skill what they lack in promptness. He cracked one of his adversaries on the side of the knee, sending him sprawling on the floor, and smashed the other on the right elbow, disabling his sword-arm. With his free hand he shoved the second man back against the wall, and was past him in a trice, long before the man behind him could take any constructive action. *There!* he thought. *I'm not ready for my dotage as yet!*

He did not even bother to look back to see what the third man was doing; he simply ran on, determined to attack the besiegers of the laboratory from behind even if he were being pursued. He would have undoubtedly have carried out this rough-hewn plan, had he not had occasion to pass an open door, through which a weighted rope was suddenly thrown to tangle his legs.

On another occasion, he might have evaded the inexpert cast, but he was traveling at full tilt for fear of his presumed pursuer, and the slightest loss of balance was always likely to be fatal. He stumbled to his knees, and although he braced himself with his arms, ready to spring up again, he was not given the chance.

Suddenly, there seemed to be monkish habits all around him, and hard blows descending on his back and shoulders. He sustained at least four impacts to the body before his skull was struck, causing him a great deal of pain. When the head was struck, however, he did not lose consciousness, being merely dazed and agonized. Once again, he was acutely aware of his age, and the diminution of is forces attendant upon it, but he also felt a near-supernatural stubbornness, an iron determination not to give way to the multitudinous pains clawing at his body and mind.

He was aware of being picked up and carried awkwardly into the room from which the rope had be thrown, then dumped on a settee. He was abandoned there, not knowing whether to be grateful or to feel insulted that his adversaries did not even think it necessary to knock him unconscious.

"We'll come back for him later," said one of the Englishmen.

Temple was aching too badly in too many places to be able to pull himself together immediately, and contented himself with gripping his injured head in his bloodstained fingers for at least five minutes. He kept his eyes open, not without difficulty—there was blood trickling down his forehead too, and the pain was literally blinding—but all he could see was a confusion of blurred shapes. To begin with, there was a great deal of noise, but it abated by degrees, and the shapes gradually coalesced into items of furniture.

Finally, certain that he was alone and unguarded, Temple blinked away a few bloody tears and made a Herculean effort to raise himself into a sitting position. He succeeded, but at some cost, and had to maintain immobility for a few minutes more, gathering himself all over again. When he could finally see clearly, his first glance told him that the room was still empty—but his second picked out a human form recently arrived in the doorway.

The newcomer's eyes met his, and the other—who might otherwise have passed on—immediately hurried into the room.

"Mr. Temple!" said a Grey Man that Temple first mistook for Victor Frankenstein. "Are you badly hurt?"

Temple blinked again, and his gaze traveled over his interlocutor's dust-stained riding-costume and grey features with mute incomprehension. "Lazarus?" he said, finally. "Is that you?"

"Yes it is," replied Frankenstein's Adam. "We've arrived too late, it seems—but I've brought help, if there's any assistance that can usefully be given. Do you know where my maker is?"

"He was in the laboratory, I think, only a few minutes ago—ten or fifteen, perhaps. I had the impression that he was barricaded in, with Faraday, Crosse and the vampire."

"Vampire?"

"Count Szandor, now masquerading as George Singer, Crosse's old friend and former colleague. Are they not there? Has the door been forced? Have the mad monks taken them?"

"No," Lazarus replied, "they're no longer in the laboratory—but the door has not been broken down, and what has become of them I cannot tell. I gather that the demonstration was not a success."

"Oh yes," Temple said, forcing a sardonic laugh. "It was a tremendous success. Had it been more modest, events would presumably have transpired in far better order. *Civitas Solis* would never have risked an open assault had the prize not seemed too tempting to resist. You know, I suppose, than your maker is now a Grey Man himself, more immediately articulate than any of his kind, with the possible exception of General Mortdieu?"

"I knew that he had died and was due to be resurrected," Lazarus confirmed, bending over to examine Temple's head-wound more carefully with his eyes and fingers. "I came as rapidly as I could, with what assistance I could gather." As he spoke the final words he turned to look at someone else who had come along the corridor, and was now framed in the doorway. It was Jean-Pierre Séverin. Like Lazarus before him, the great swordsman hurried forward as soon as he recognized Temple.

"I'm sorry, my friend," the Frenchman said. "Had we got here a mere ten minutes earlier…but the Comtesse's men are scouring the house and grounds. If they cannot catch up with Balsamo's brigands there, they will soon be on their trail."

"The Comtesse's men?" Temple echoed, in frank bewilderment.

Séverin blushed slightly behind his white beard and moustache. "It's the strangest alliance imaginable," he said, "but it was the Comtesse's men who freed me from the Germans who sent hirelings to capture me on the Dover Road, and Lazarus persuaded me to accept a truce while there are greater matters at stake."

"Don't worry, old friend," said Temple, with a hollow laugh. "The Comtesse is in my direct employ now, it seems, and I have somehow become fast friends with her master, the vampire. Had I succeeded in reaching the laboratory where I believed he and Frankenstein to be under siege, I would have fought with him shoulder to shoulder, in spite of what happened at Miremont. Do you know whether the Commissioners reached safety? They were on the Taunton road."

"We came from another direction," Lazarus told him, "but have no fear—the Commission is irrelevant now. Open warfare has been declared, and it only remains for the various armies to mobilize and take up their positions. Wellington will take a stand himself, no doubt, with 10,000 redcoats behind him."

"It might come to that, now," Temple admitted. "If we could capture a few of Balsamo's men and bring them to trial…"

293

"I doubt that Mr. Canning is ready for that, as yet," Lazarus told him, moving back after satisfying himself that Temple's head-wound, though bloody, was superficial. "We'll do far better if we can recover Frankenstein, Crosse and Faraday, and establish the Necromancers of London at the heart of the Royal Institution, with or without the mysterious Mr. Singer."

Temple made as if to get to his feet, but his limbs were not yet ready to support him without excessive complaint. "That fool Southborne," he muttered. "If he hadn't panicked at the sight of the grey girl...have you any news of her, by the way?"

"None," Lazarus admitted. "The events of the first demonstration were reported to us, but we have no idea what happened to the subject after her escape from the house."

"I saw her briefly," Temple told him. "We arranged to meet, so that I could get her to a place of safety, but she didn't make it to the rendezvous. I seem to have failed in every possible respect but one—although my superiors will doubtless be pleased to hear that I did my duty according to my orders."

A third man came in then, but this one barely glanced at Temple before addressing himself to Lazarus. "The Grafina is negotiating a treaty with Tom Brown's men," he announced.

Temple recognized the man as Guido, the vampires' principal mortal hireling, and was slightly surprised to see him rather cheerful. "What are you so pleased about?" hee growled.

"Why should I not be glad?" Guido retorted. "The opposition has been tempted to a reckless move, and thus helped enormously to establish a common cause between the rest of us. We had presumed that Balsamo and Belcamp would make their peace, and might even make a treaty with the Illuminati, at least while their Prussian dupes were forced to operate on alien soil. Now, *Civitas Solis* stands alone, with everyone against them—at least for the time being. It's only a few short months since my master stood alone, without a friend in the world, but he will be the lynch-pin of a mighty alliance now, if..."

"If only you can find him," Temple growled. "Is Malo de Treguern with you, perchance?"

"Alas, no," said Lazarus. "The Church has its own politics, and it does not matter how much the Knights of St. John hate the heretics of *Civitas Solis*—they will never join forces with an army as seemingly diabolical as ours."

"I'm not at all sure that I shall join it myself," Temple said, "if John Devil is a member of its High Command."

"With all due respect, Mr. Temple," said Lazarus, politely, "we do not really need you. You would not be half as useful to us as Séverin."

Temple immediately looked up at the Frenchman, who did not let him down. "I stand with Mr. Temple," he declared, stoutly. "I will follow his counsel."

Guido shook his head, as if to signify that it was quite irrelevant, but Lazarus looked at him disapprovingly and said: "If we cannot find Frankenstein, there is no center around which we might form. I am not the only articulate Grey Man in Europe, by any means, but none of us has Frankenstein's status and importance. While he and Faraday are missing, along with Crosse and Szandor, the greater part of the genius of this affair is lost. We do need Séverin—and Mr. Temple might be useful too, if he is willing to help us even for a little while."

If *Civitas Solis* have the men of science," Guido said, confidently, returning to the door as he spoke, "we'll get them back in no time at all, with or without the two old men. The alchemists might outnumber our own small company, but once Tom Brown's resources are added to ours, we can locate and storm any hidey-hole where they might have taken refuge."

"I wish I could believe him," Lazarus said to Temple, as he moved toward the door in his turn, "but we have no idea what resources *Civitas Solis* might have in the vicinity, and their expertise in hiding dates back centuries."

Once the Grey Man had gone, Jean-Pierre Séverin sat down on the settee beside Temple. "This is direly confusing," he said. "I came to London to warn you that the vampires were in England, fully expecting that you and I might join forces to hunt them down together and dispose of them forever. Now, it seems, they are doing all they can to help us, in a war against enemies I never knew I had."

"They didn't know they were your enemies either," Temple told him, "until their curiosity was aroused. We've lived too long for our own good, it seems; people have begun to look askance at us, sensing something unnatural. It will do us no good to protest that old age has merely been kind to us, because that is the precise object of their research. As an Englishman and a policeman, I have His Majesty's secret agents behind and beside me, but as a Parisian, you, alas, have no one to turn to but the likes of Vidocq."

"I have René de Kervoz behind and beside me," the Frenchman muttered, "and I have received an offer of assistance from Colonel Bozzo-Corona. While I am on English soil I have you, too, Mr. Temple, do I not? If we cannot hunt vampires together, we can still act as one in some other worthy cause."

"You do have me," Temple conceded, "but, as you can see, I'm likely to be as useless to you as I am to Lazarus and his allies. I don't have your uncanny skill in a fight, so I have little to bring to any partnership."

"But I don't have your renowned intelligence," Séverin countered. "It's my opinion that if anyone can figure out a path through this maze of confusion, and bring order out of its chaos, it's you—not Michael Faraday, or the boastful Count Szandor, or even my old friend Germain Patou, but you. We might make a powerful team, my friend, even in a contest full to overflowing with younger men, secret societies and the ranks of the dead-alive"

Temple finally contrived to stagger to his feet. "You're very kind," he said, "but my bruises are telling me, in no uncertain terms, how far past my best I am, in spite of my seeming resilience. Since younger men than us—and deader ones—seem to have this matter in hand, for now, I suggest that we go down to the servants' pantry to discover whether Cook and Caddick have survived the battle. Either way, we'll be fed and watered, ready to fight another day, if the chance or necessity arises."

"Agreed," said the one-time fencing-master, helping Temple to hobble to the door. "Just show me the way."

Chapter Eight
The Necromancers in London

When Gregory Tremple finally completed the discomfiting business of making his official report, he hastened to St. Thomas's hospital, where Jean-Pierre Séverin was waiting for him at Malo de Treguern's bedside. The great swordsman had already told his compatriot the full story, and Treguern, his curiosity sated, was now protesting loudly against the injustice of his doctors.

"They say that I am an old man," the knight protested. "They think me half-mad, because I wear the Hospitallers' cross so proudly, and owe such fidelity to the Order's ideals. They will not let me go, although the wound no longer troubles me, for fear that it will open again. I have shown them all my other scars, but they will not believe that I have the same healing power now that I had then."

"They might be right, my friend," Temple told him, touching the fingers of his right hand to his own wounded head. "At any rate, you cannot blame them for their anxiety. They are not convinced, as yet, that wounds they have formerly taken to be mortal no longer mark a necessary end to human life."

Treguern took exception to that. "If you are implying that I might be turned into an abomination if I should happen to die," he said, "I must object in no uncertain terms. I would like you to give me your word, Mr. Temple, that you will oppose as sternly as you can any attempt to resurrect me after my death. I will not suffer this body to become the abode of a demon."

"I'll give you my word, for what it's worth," Temple replied, "but now that I've seen and heard two further example of the dead-alive, I'm more convinced than ever that there is no principle of evil at work here. I do not claim that the dead-alive are intrinsically virtuous, nor do I deny that some might be more dangerous in their new state of being than they were when alive, but they are thinking beings, capable of moral judgment and entitled to moral consideration. If I were to die…"

"You should not say such things, even in jest," Treguern insisted, cutting off the sentence. He would doubtless have said more, but was interrupted himself by the arrival of another visitor: an old man wearing a quilted coat and a woolen scarf, who seemed a trifle unsteady on his feet as he walked, but whose eyes were bright, penetrating in their gaze.

Temple and Séverin both recognized the man, but it was Malo de Treguern who actually addressed him by name, saying: "Colonel Bozzo-Corona! What on Earth are you doing here?"

"I am in London on business, traveling with my beloved grand-daughter. little Fanchette. When I heard that one of my oldest friends, a warrior knight, was lying in a hospital bed far from his native Britanny, in danger of dying alone, how could I not come to see him? But I see that you do have friends, and the finest imaginable: a great swordsman and a brilliant detective. I'm delighted to see you again, Monsieur Séverin, Monsieur Temple."

Temple bowed, following Séverin's example.

"You have had quite an adventure, I hear," the Colonel said to Temple. "I had adventures myself once, but I am too old now—every affair I undertake seems likely to be my last. We cannot simply lie down and let fate take its course, though; it is the nature of a man to strive, and, if necessary, to fight."

Temple did not know what to say, but Treguern was more forthright. "Have you, too, come here searching for the elixir of life—or, at least, the secret of progressing to an unholy artificial afterlife?" he asked.

"Me?" said the Colonel. "No, I'm fully reconciled to my own fate—but I still have business matters requiring my attention. Business is the curse of the modern era, don't you think? An evil, but a very necessary evil. A man must have ambition, and ambition, nowadays, requires business. No matter how much we might regret the fact that mere money has become the measure of everything, and that the sheer beauty of a treasure no longer counts for anything by comparison with its market price, we can but accept it…and without money, one cannot do good works, can one, Frère Treguern?"

"One does not need money to do good works," Treguern replied—as the Colonel must have known that he would. "It simply makes them easier to perform."

The Colonel smiled. "You must let me help you, my friend," he said. "Come and stay with me when the doctors release you—I have rented a very comfortable house in Hampstead village. You would be welcome there too, Monsieur Séverin—and you must come to dinner soon, Mr. Temple. We old men must stick together, must we not? The mere passage of time has given us common cause and united our interests."

Temple thanked the Colonel kindly, although he did not see how he would be able to find time for mere socializing until Balsamo's brigands and their presumed prisoners had been located—a task that had so far proved beyond the scope of Tom Brown, let alone the secret police and the vampire's agents. He was distracted, however, when a young orderly came up to him and handed him a folded sheet of paper, before returning in haste without waiting to be questioned as to its origin.

With the collective gaze of three pairs of curious eyes upon him, Temple unfolded the note. *SHARPER'S AT SIX*, it read, in its entirety. Temple did not doubt that it was an invitation, if not a summons, nor did he doubt that it came from Tom Brown—or, at least, that it had been sent with John Devil's knowledge and approval.

"What is it?" Sévérin asked.

"Official business," Temple muttered.

"A state secret!" said the Colonel, marveling. "Why, how exciting. Are you on the trail of Faraday's abductors? That news caused great consternation in the scientific circles of Paris, I can assure you. If the agents of the Terror had not cut off Lavoisier's head during the Revolution, he would be under 24 hour guard today."

Ignoring this strangely ambiguous item of whimsy, Temple said: "I must go." He raised a hand to interrupt Jean-Pierre Sévérin before the other could make a formal declaration of his intention to accompany the man whose bosom companion the now considered himself to be. "I need to go alone," he added. "There is no danger—but there might be, if I were to take anyone with me."

He did not give Sévérin time to argue, nor either of the others time to comment further, but hurried off.

He walked across Tower Bridge at a brisk pace, and then hired a cab to take him home. He knew that it would take time to make himself up, and then to get to what was nowadays Jenny Paddock's Cabaret Theatre.

He did not make himself up as Solomon Green, the character he had invented specifically for use in the den of iniquity in question. Too many people now knew that Green had been Gregory Temple in disguise. Instead, he made himself up as a sunburned sailor, with every appearance of 20 years' experience in the slave trade. That was the guise he presented to Jenny Paddock when he approached her counter and demanded a tot of rum.

He was served by a young girl, who could not possibly have seen through his imposture, but he saw from the corner of his eye that the mistress of the establishment was looking at him quizzically, and hurried away into the shadows, selecting the same sheltered vantage-point from which Solomon Green had formerly observed the comings-and-goings in the heart of the criminal Underworld.

He had been in the booth for ten minutes before two other individuals sat down to either side of him. They were wrapped up very warmly, having just come in from the icy cold, with felt hats pulled down low over their features and scarves over their mouths. They did not unwrap themselves to display their faces, and left it to Temple to summon the waitress and order two glasses of gin. Neither of them, to judge by their contrasted height and build, could possibly be Henri de Belcamp. One was too bulky by far, and even the smaller of the two was a little too tall and not sufficiently slender.

"Thank you for coming, Mr. Temple," said the smaller of the two, in a voice not much above a whisper, but nevertheless quite distinct. "Tom has given us all a guarantee of safe conduct, so you need have no fear."

For a moment or two, Temple could not identify the voice, and when he did, he was not quite ready to believe it. "Szandor?" he said, interrogatively.

"In person," the vampire replied. "You must have been worried about me, in spite of the Countess's confident assurances that I would be safe. Please tell her, when you next see her, that her confidence was not misplaced."

Temple had only seen Countess Marcian Gregoryi once since his return to London, but he was, indeed, due to see her again very soon. She had already demonstrated her talent for gathering information interesting to the agents of the Crown, and Temple was no longer so sure that his masters would dispense with his services at the slightest excuse.

"Have you escaped from *Civitas Solis*, then?" Temple asked.

"They never caught us," Szandor replied, blithely. "Fyne Court was built in the 17th century, when Jacobean tragedies were still being performed in London's theaters. It was a time when priests' holes and secret passages were *de rigueur*, along with the ghosts of knightly ancestors. When Balsamo's men were able to get into the laboratory—without the necessity of breaking down the door—they found us gone, as if vanished into thin air. We thought it politic to lie low thereafter, though. Our hopes of conducting our research openly, in the confines of the Royal Institution, had been badly dented, if not actually dashed by the fiasco."

"So you threw in your lot with John Devil," Temple growled.

"We have not thrown in our lot with anyone, Mr. Temple," said the other man, speaking for the first time. "We are conducting our own investigations in our own way."

Again, Temple had difficulty identifying the voice. Again, his conclusion seemed more guesswork than reasoned confusion. "Lazarus?" he ventured.

The other actually laughed. "I suppose we are similar now," he said. "There is a certain justice in that, I must reluctantly admit."

"Frankenstein," said Temple, dully. Once, the thought that he was in a booth in Will Sharper's Grog Shop, sandwiched between a vampire and a man returned from the dead would have terrified him. Now, it seemed almost a relief to know that his drinking companions were no petty criminals.

"Tom Brown differs from his erstwhile friends in *Civitas Solis* and his erstwhile enemies in the *vehm*," the vampire said, "in that he is no monopolist. I do not say that he is not a profiteer, but he really does not want to have the afterlife securely within his own gift. He is a Romantic heart."

"And you believe that he is a better protector than His Majesty's Secret Service or the Duke of Wellington's legions?" Temple asked, bitterly, knowing full well that the answer was yes.

"We would like to have your amity as well, Mr. Temple," Frankenstein said.

"Indeed we would," the vampire said, supportively. "Of, at least, your undertaking not to join forces with Malo de Treguern or Colonel Bozzo-Corona."

"The Colonel told me himself, only a few hours ago, that he was here in London on business, and had no interest in the afterlife," Temple said, although he had not really believed it at the time, and was even less convinced now that Szandor had brought up the Colonel's name.

"Business with the Gentlemen of the Night," the vampire confirmed. "But there's probably not a man in their ranks who does not owe a double allegiance to the All-Father and John Devil. We live in a world of confused loyalties, Mr. Temple—which can sometimes break a man in two, if he's not careful. Please tell the Countess to mobilize all her resources to the task of keeping track of Colonel Bozzo-Corona and his shifty soldiers—and you might do worse to put some of your other men on to him as well. He's deluded as to his origins and nature, of course, as we have all been in the past, but his mind is exceedingly sharp, and he's an extraordinarily clever and patient planner. Unlike Tom, he is most certainly a monopolist, and one who stops at nothing."

"Is that what you brought me here to tell me?" Temple asked, unable to sound grateful, although he felt a trifle curmudgeonly on that account.

"We brought you here to reassure you as to our health," the Grey Man put in, "and to let you know that, whatever other crimes Balsamo might have committed, he is not presently holding any significant hostages."

"How are you, Dr. Frankenstein?" Temple asked, with genuine curiosity. "Have you mastered your new faculties and feelings? Do you know yet what you are, and what you might make of your second lease of life?"

"I'm making progress," the Grey Man told him.

"What about the girl?" Temple asked. "Have you managed to recover her from *her* captors?"

"No, alas," said Szandor. "We cannot even be sure that she was captured, although I know how much it would wound you to think that she missed her rendezvous with you of her own accord. Tom will find her in the end—and he has agreed that when he does, he'll hand her over to us in order that she and Victor might compare notes and assist in one another's re-education."

"You cannot trust him," Temple said, flatly. "Treachery is in his bones; it's all he can do to prevent his *alter egos* from betraying one another."

"That's as may be," the vampire replied, equably, "but who can we trust? We can only go forward as best we can, careful not to betray our own destiny."

"You, a vampire, speak of destiny now?" said Temple. "You speak approvingly of men who are not monopolists, and disapprovingly of men who are. It's difficult to believe that you're the same skeletal figure I talked to in Miremont."

"Change is possible for all of us, Mr. Temple," the other murmured. "Even for you. You know as well as we do that the world has already been turned upside-down; the question that remains is whether we can adapt ourselves to the new order. I am determined to do so, and so are my friends."

"You do know, don't you," Temple said to the Grey Man who had once been Victor Frankenstein, "that this man is not George Singer, but a Grey Man of sorts, camouflaged by mesmeric glamour?"

"Yes, I do," Frankenstein replied. "He is my brother now, or my half-brother, at least; we are alike in the most important matter of all. Who else is there in London who can give me a sound education in the art of life after death?"

Temple looked up as someone materialized at the table bearing a tray, and set out another round of drinks, almost as if in answer to the Grey Man's question.

"Compliments of the house, gentlemen," said the newcomer, who was not the little waitress but Jenny Paddock herself. "Mr. Hopkey apologizes for the fact that he has not time to say hello, but he is making himself up for tonight's performance." The hostess was looking directly at Temple, evidently able now to see through his disguise.

"Mr. Hopkey is neither here nor there," Temple told her, coldly. "What of John Devil's apologies?"

"My husband is dead, sir," Jenny Paddock replied, striking an offended pose, "and I'll thank you not to insult the name of my poor, dear Tom under his own roof."

Temple was not entirely sure whether the "Tom" she had in mind just then was Thomas Paddock or Tom Brown.

"Thank you, Mistress Paddock," the vampire put in. "My friend meant no offense. Once we've drunk these down, we'll be on our way—we all have our ships to catch, literally or figuratively speaking."

"You'll miss the performance," Jenny Paddock said, seeming genuinely wounded by such neglect. "That would be a shame, for *The Vampyre* is a fine melodrama, rumored to be based on a story by Lord Byron himself."

"I saw the first performance of the original production at the Porte-Saint-Martin," Szandor said, smoothly. "I was seated directly behind Monsieur Nodier and Monsieur Dumas. Without meaning any disrespect to Mr. Hopkey's troupe, I doubt that they could better that occasion. I no longer like the play as much as I did then—the Byronic image of the vampire has grown a little stale, has it not?"

"As you please, sir," said Jenny Paddock, stiffly.

"It's a pity that Sawney Ross and Ned Knob aren't here to see their protégés perform the play," Temple observed, obedient to a mischievous whim. "You and he were intimate at one time, I believe, Mistress Paddock—at least until Pretty Molly came between you."

The hostess did not deign to reply to that, but returned to her counter with her dignity seemingly intact.

301

The three men reached out for their glasses, in no particular hurry. Temple would have downed his without ceremony, but Szandor raised his, with the unmistakable gesture of a man about to propose a toast.

Temple paused and waited. The Grey Man followed his example. Temple wondered, vaguely, whether Grey Men were capable of getting drunk. He supposed not, on the assumption that alcohol probably did not have the same effect on dead-alive as on living flesh.

"To the Necromancers of London!" Szandor declared, still speaking in his curiously distinct whisper. "Long may they thrive!"

"To the Future!" added the Grey Man who had once been Victor Frankenstein. "Long may it last!"

Feeling compelled to complete the ritual, Gregory Temple only hesitated a moment before saying: "To Life! Long may it retain the empery of the flesh!"

No one objected; everyone drank. As the fiery beverage assaulted his throat, Gregory Temple could not help but wonder whether his words were mere wisps of straw, about to be blown away by the irresistible tide of destiny and the marvelous discoveries soon to be made by the Necromancers of London.

Credits

Secrets

Starring:	Created by:
Raposa (Diego de la Vega)	Johnston McCulley
Madeleine (Jean Valjean)	Victor Hugo
The Wolves	Paul Féval
Co-Starring:	
Monseigneur Myriel	Victor Hugo

Written by:
Roberto Lionel BARREIRO was born and lived in Buenos Aires, Argentina, for 30 years. Then, following the call of love, he moved to Chile where he resides right now. He has worked as a journalist for various magazines from Argentina, Chile, Spain, Cuba and even the USA. His first love is his wife and two kids. His second love is comics, movies, pulps and all kind of pop culture from around the world. This is his first contribution to *Tales of the Shadowmen*.

What Rough Beast

Starring:	Created by:
Hugo Danner	Philip Wylie
Judex/Vallières	Louis Feuillade & Arthur Bernède
Sâr Dubnotal	*Anonymous*
Gianetti Annunciata	*Anonymous*
Von Meyer	Seabury Quinn
The Colossus	Clark Ashton Smith
The Ghouls	H.P. Lovecraft
The Ape Demon	E. Hoffman Price
The Tentacled Demon	Seabury Quinn
Co-Starring:	
Abednego Danner	Philip Wylie
General Broulard	Humphrey Cobb
Nathare of Vyones	Clark Ashton Smith
Tom Shayne	Philip Wylie
And:	
Joiry	Catherine L. Moore

Written by:
Matthew BAUGH is an ordained minister who lives and works in the Chicago area. He is a longtime fan of pulp fiction, cliffhanger serials and old time radio. He has written a number of articles on characters like Zorro, Dr. Syn, Jules de Grandin and Sailor Steve Costigan. He has had stories published in *The Green Hornet Chronicles, More Tales of Zorro, Six Guns Straight From Hell, The Avenger Chronicles* and *The Phantom Chronicles*. He is a regular contributor to *Tales of the Shadowmen*.

What Doesn't Die

Starring:	Created by:
The Bride	William Hurlbut & John Balderston
	& James Whale
	based on Mary Shelley
Doctor Omega	Arnould Galopin
Also Starring:	
Nikola Tesla	
George Westinghouse	

Written by:
Thom BRANNAN has had stories published in Permuted Press' *Robots Beyond* anthology, in Library of Horror's *Wolves of War* (with Victorya C.) and will have a story featured in the soon-to-be-released *The Green Hornet Chronicles, Vol 1*. His work can be seen at DarkTomorrow.net. This is his first contribution to *Tales of the Shadowmen*.

Faces of Fear

Starring:	Created by:
Christiane	Jean Redon
Freddy Krueger	Wes Craven
Judex	Arthur Bernède & Louis Feuillade
Dr. Crane	Bill Finger & Bob Kane
Dr. Genessier	Jean Redon
Dr. Orloff	Jesus Franco

Matthew DENNION lives in South Jersey with his beautiful wife and new baby daughter. He currently works as a teacher of autistic students at a Special Services School. Matt has been a huge fan of the works of Edgar Rice Burroughs ever since he first picked up *A Princess of Mars*; he is also a big follower of Sherlock Holmes, Doc Savage, Spider-Man, Batman, and James Bond. This is his first published story and his first contribution to *Tales of the Shadowmen*.

Nadine's Invitation

Starring:	Created by:
Lady Marguerite Blakeney	Emmuska Orczy
Countess Nadine Carody	Jaime Chávarri, Anne Settimó & Jess Franco
Colonel Bozzo-Corona	Paul Féval
Lecoq	based on Paul Féval & Emile Gaboriau
Dr. Siger Holmes	based on Arthur Conan Doyle
Count Dracula	Bram Stoker
Co-Starring:	
Percy Blakeney	Emmuska Orczy
Alice	Philip José Farmer
The Darcys	Jane Austen
Duke of Holdernesse	Arthur Conan Doyle
Baron Tennington	Edgar Rice Burroughs
The Delagardies	Philip José Farmer
Baron de Musard	Philip José Farmer
And:	
Rue Morgue	Edgar Allan Poe
Calyx Bar	Louis Feuillade & Arthur Bernède
Cordon Jaune	Ian Fleming

Written by:
Win Scott ECKERT Win Scott Eckert holds a B.A. in Anthropology and a Juris Doctorate. He is the editor of and contributor to *Myths for the Modern Age: Philip José Farmer's Wold Newton Universe*, a 2007 Locus Award Finalist for Best Non-Fiction book. He has contributed to *The Avenger Chronicles*, *The Captain Midnight Chronicles*, *The Phantom Chronicles 2*, *The Green Hornet Chronicles* (which he also co-edited), and the forthcoming *More Tales of Zorro*. He was a regular contributor of Wold Newton essays and stories to *Farmerphile: The Magazine of Philip José Farmer*, and he was honored to provide the Foreword to the new 2006 edition of Farmer's seminal "fictional biography," *Tarzan Alive: A Definitive Biography of Lord Greystoke*. Win's latest books are the encyclopedic two-volume *Crossovers: A Secret Chronology of the World*, and the Wold Newton novel *The Evil in Pemberley House*, about Patricia Wildman, the daughter of a certain bronze-skinned pulp hero (co-authored with Philip José Farmer). He is immensely pleased to appear in all seven volumes of *Tales of the Shadowmen*.

Fiat Lux!

Starring:	Created by:
Quentin Travers	David Fury
Henri-Jean de Sainte-Claire	based on Jean de La Hire
Rochefort	Alexandre Dumas
The Invaders	Larry Cohen
Co-Starring:	
Leo Saint-Clair	Jean de La Hire
And:	
The Watchers' Council	Joss Whedon
The Papyrus of Manetho	Edgar P. Jacobs
Also Starring:	
Cyrano de Bergerac	
Cardinal de Richelieu	
Marquis de Cinq-Mars	
François de Thou	
Manetho	
Akhenaton	
Merira	

Written by:

Emmanuel GORLIER lives in Puteaux, near Paris, with his wife and three children. He has been a fan of science fiction since the first grade and a devoted player of *Dungeons & Dragons* for 30 years. That is probably why he became a tax accountant. He has contributed to *Enter the Nyctalope* and *Tales of the Shadowmen*.

Lurching Towards Camulodunum

Starring:	Created by:
Sâr Dubnotal	*Anonymous*
Naïni	*Anonymous*
Helen Vaughan	Arthur Machen
Rudolph	*Anonymous*
Becky Sharp	William Makepeace Thackeray
Clarke	Arthur Machen
Villiers	Arthur Machen
Jacques Courbé	Clarence A. "Tod" Robbins
Francis-Aytown	Bram Stoker
Randolph	Lloyd C. Douglas
Richard Upton Pickman	H.P. Lovecraft

Charles Delaware Tate	Dan Curtis, Sam Hall
	& Violet Welles
Pierre Rodin	Micah Harris
	based on Robert Bloch
Co-Starring:	
Dr. Robert Matheson	Arthur Machen
Ranijesti	*Anonymous*
Basil Hallward	Oscar Wilde
Dorian Gray	Oscar Wilde
Lord Henry Wotton	Oscar Wilde
And:	
The Judge's House	Bram Stoker
Kadath	H.P. Lovecraft
Also Starring:	
Paul-Jean Toulet	
William Butler Yeats	
Aubrey Beardsley	

Written by:

Micah HARRIS is the author (with artist Michael Gaydos) of the graphic novel *Heaven's War*, a historical fantasy pitting authors Charles Williams, C.S. Lewis and J.R.R. Tolkien against occultist Aleister Crowley. His most recent publication is the novella "On the Periphery of Legend" in Volume 2 of *Jim Anthony, Super Detective* for Ron Fortier's Airship 27 Productions. 2010 will see the release of his first comic *book* book (as opposed to *graphic novel* comic book), *Lorna, Relic Wrangler* with Loston Wallace, illustrator of Harris's *The Eldritch New Adventures of Becky Sharp.* He is a regular contributor to *Tales of the Shadowmen.*

The Robots of Metropolis

Starring:	Created by:
Tiziraou	Arnould Galopin
Denis Borel	Arnould Galopin
Doctor Omega	Arnould Galopin
Rotwang	Fritz Lang & Thea Von Harbou
The Volkites	Tracy Knight, John Rathmell,
	Maurice Geraghty & Oliver Drake
Fred	Arnould Galopin
Co-Starring:	
Unga Khan	Tracy Knight, John Rathmell,
	Maurice Geraghty & Oliver Drake
The Fredersons	Fritz Lang & Thea Von Harbou

Metropolis	Fritz Lang & Thea Von Harbou
The earthquake ray	Tracy Knight, John Rathmell,
	Maurice Geraghty & Oliver Drake

Written by:
Travis HILTZ started making up stories at a young age. Years later, he began writing them down. In high school, he discovered that some writers actually got paid and decided to give it a try. He has since gathered a modest collection of rejection letters and had a one-act play produced. Travis lives in the wilds of New Hampshire with his very loving and tolerant wife, two above average children and a staggering amount of comic books and *Doctor Who* novels. He is a regular contributor to *Tales of the Shadowmen*.

Death to the Heretic!

Starring:	**Created by:**
Bruce Wayne	Bob Kane & Bill Finger
Alfred Pennyworth	Bob Kane
	& Jerry Robinson
Indiana Jones	George Lucas,
	Philip Kaufman
	& Lawrence Kasdan
Prof. William Omaha McElroy	Earl Barret,
	Robert C. Dennis
	& Charles R. Rondeau
Leo Saint-Clair (The Nyctalope)	Jean de La Hire
Amelia Peabody Emerson	Elizabeth Peters
Radcliffe Emerson	Elizabeth Peters
The Anubis Gang	Paul Hugli
Co-Starring:	
Dr. Hugo Strange	Bob Kane & Bill Finger
Ted Grant	Bill Finger & Irwin Hasen
Dr. Francis Ardan	Guy d'Armen

Written by:
Paul HUGLI has a degree in Zoology, and has written for everything from *Cracked* magazine to general interest pamphlets, and for most of the first, second *and* third tier adult magazines. He is the author of three published "adult fantasy" novels, and the acclaimed *Traci Lords Companion*. He has also been employed as a science/math instructor, and as a "Floor Manager" at a local "Gentleman's Club." In addition, he once owned/managed Destiny Bookstore, which dealt in SciFi, comics and adult "fantasy" magazines, for 30 years. He

now has three novels in the works. This is his first contribution to *Tales of the Shadowmen.*

Will There Be Sunlight?

Starring:	Created by:
Colonel Bozzo-Corona	Paul Féval
Robert Thomas	Lester Dent
El Pecoso (Pecos Allbellin)	Harold A. Davis
Baron Vardon	Harold A. Davis and Lester Dent
Gaspard Zemba	Walter Gibson
Irma Caber (Irma Peterson)	H.C. McNeile
Dolores Valencia (Dolores Borenza)	Walter Gibson
Natasha Malakoff	H.C. McNeile and Gerard Fairlie
Jean Lumière (John Sunlight)	Lester Dent
Julius Freyder	H.C. MacNeile
Rosa Klebb	Ian Fleming
Prosecutor (Serge Mafnoff)	Lester Dent
Stalin's Aide (Makaroff)	Lester Dent
Co-Starring:	
Reverend H. Briefenstein	Ladislas Fodor & Marc Behm
Dr. James Caber	Lord Dunsany
Professor Moriarty	Arthur Conan Doyle
Darvin Rochelle	Walter Gibson
Claud Caber (Carl Peterson)	H.C. McNeile
Urania Caber	Philip José Farmer
John Clay	Arthur Conan Doyle
Dr. Stewart (Fu Manchu)	Arthur Conan Doyle and Sax Rohmer
Karah Stewart	August Derleth
Césarine	Grant Allen
Antonia Lashley (Toni Lash)	Lester Dent
The Red Knife (Frunzoff Nosh)	Lester Dent
Sherlock Holmes	Arthur Conan Doyle
Fantômas	Pierre Souvestre & Marcel Allain
And:	
The Black Coats	Paul Féval
Nemirovitch Beauty Salons	Robert Hill

The Golden City of the Very Highest	H.R. Haggard and Lester Dent
The Borgia Pearl	Arthur Conan Doyle
Peterson's Pup-Food	P.G. Wodehouse
The Sons of the Feathered Serpent	Lester Dent
The Brigand's Painting	Paul Féval
Also Starring:	
Joseph Stalin	

Written by:
Rick LAI, a regular contributor to *Tales of the Shadowmen*, is a computer programmer. During the 1980s and 1990s, he wrote articles expanding on the Wold Newton Universe concepts which have since been collected by Altus Press as *Rick Lai's Secret Histories: Daring Adventurers, Rick Lai's Secret Histories: Criminal Master Minds, Chronology of Shadows: A Timeline of The Shadow's Exploits* and *The Revised Complete Chronology of Bronze*. Rick resides in Bethpage, New York, with his wife and children.

The Sincerest Form of Flattery

Starring:	**Created by:**
Diabolik	Angela & Luciana Giussani & Zarcone
Dr. Garrick (Fantômas)	André Hunebelle & Jean Halain & Pierre Foucaud based on Pierre Souvestre & Marcel Allain
Co-Starring:	
Eva Kent	Angela & Luciana Giussani & Zarcone
Ginko	Angela & Luciana Giussani & Zarcone
Fantômas (Mexico)	Guillermo Mendizábal & Gonzalo Martre
Fantômas (Argentina)	Julio Cortazar
Kriminal	Max Bunker & Magnus
Killing	Pietro Granelli & Rosario Borelli
Satanik	Max Bunker & Magnus
And:	
The Depository Bank of Zurich	Dan Brown

Written by:
Jean-Marc & Randy LOFFICIER, the editors of the *Tales of the Shadowmen* series, have also collaborated on five screenplays, a dozen books and numerous translations, including *Arsène Lupin*, *Doc Ardan*, *Doctor Omega*, *The Phantom of the Opera* and *Rouletabille*. Their latest novels include *Edgar Allan Poe on Mars* and *The Katrina Protocol*. They have written a number of animation teleplays, including episodes of *Duck Tales* and *The Real Ghostbusters* and such popular heroes as *Superman*, *Doctor Strange* and created the Mayan detective series *Tongue*Lash*. Randy is a member of the Writers Guild of America, West and Mystery Writers of America.

Big Little Man

Starring:	Created by:
Miguelito Loveless	John Kneubuhl
Nurse Ratched	Ken Kesey
Co-Starring:	
James West	Michael Garrison
The Toyman	Don Cameron & Ed Dobrotka
Professor Moriarty	Arthur Conan Doyle
John Sunlight	Lester Dent
Sumuru	Sax Rohmer
Lecoq	Emile Gaboriau
Paladin	Sam Rolfe & Herb Meadow
Bulldog Drummond	Herman Cyril McNeile
Fantômas	Pierre Souvestre & Marcel Allain
Count Manzeppi	Charles Bennett
Walter Jameson	Charles Beaumont
Karl Glocken	Katherine Anne Porter
Robert Morane	Henri Vernes
Dennis Nayland Smith	Sax Rohmer
Dr. Cyclops	Tom Kilpatrick
Voltaire	John Kneubuhl
Antoinette	John Kneubuhl

Written by:
David McDONNELL, the "*maitre'd* of the science fiction universe," has dished up coverage of pop culture heroes for more than three decades. Beginning his professional career in 1975 with the weekly "Media Report" column in *The Comic Buyer's Guide*, he joined Jim Steranko's *Mediascene Prevue* in 1980. After 31 months as *Starlog*'s Managing Editor, he became that pioneering SF magazine's longtime Editor (1985-2009). Simultaneously, he served as Editor of *Comics Scene*, *Fangoria* and *Action Heroes* as well as numerous *Star Trek* li-

censed publications and movie one-shots (James Bond films, *Aliens*, *The Shadow*, *Willow*, etc.). Born in Altoona, PA's Mercy Hospital, he lived with his family in Fort Bayard, NM (1960-63) and dressed in a home-made Jolly Green Giant costume one Halloween. This is his first contribution to *Tales of the Shadowmen*.

The Apprentice

Starring:
Simon Templar (The Saint)
Malko Linge (S.A.S.)

Created by:
Leslie Charteris
Gérard de Villiers

Written by:
Brad MENGEL lives in Australia, with his wife, daughters and dog. Over the years, he has worked as a barman, teacher and librarian. Currently, he is engaged in a study of the "Aggressors," the often violent action adventure series of the 1970s, 1980s and 1990s, such as *The Executioner*, *The Destroyer* and *The Punisher*, which he plans to turn into an encyclopaedia and one day publish. He was a contributor to *Myths for the Modern Age: Philip Jose Farmer's Wold Newton Universe*.

The Beast Without

Starring:
Catherine Levendeur
Bisclavret

Created by:
Sharan Newman
Marie de France

Written by:
Sharan NEWMAN is a medieval historian and author. Rather than teach, she chose to write novels set in the Middle Ages, including three Arthurian fantasies and ten mysteries set in 12th-century France, featuring Catherine LeVendeur, a one-time student of Heloise at the Paraclete; her husband, Edgar, an Anglo-Scot; and Solomon, a Jewish merchant of Paris. The Catherine Levendeur mysteries have been nominated for many awards. Sharan won the Macavity Award for best first mystery for *Death Comes As Epiphany* and the Herodotus Award for best historical mystery of 1998 for *Cursed in the Blood*. The most recent book in the series *The Witch in the Well* won the Bruce Alexander award for best Historical mystery of 2004. This is her first contribution to *Tales of the Shadowmen*.

Legacy of Evil

Starring:
Sir Dennis Nayland Smith

Created by:
Sax Rohmer

Dr. Petrie	Sax Rohmer
Captain Georges Sauvin (*Le Poisson Chinois*)	Jean Bommart
Fah Lo Suee	Sax Rohmer
Fu Manchu	Sax Rohmer
Also Starring:	
T.E. Lawrence	

Written by:
Neil **PENSWICK** was a successful theatre writer in the North of England. He submitted material for various television shows and was on the short-list to write for *Doctor Who* when it was cancelled in 1989. He adapted his script entitled *Hostage* as one of Virgin's New Adventures (1993). In recent years, Neil has written for a range of television series including thrillers, Sunday-night family viewing, a drama-documentary, and, for the first time, and contradicting his Leonard Cohen type reputation, a situation comedy. He is currently short-listed to write for a popular BBC TV children's series and has also been mentored by the brilliant and hugely talented Phil Ford and written an original three-part scary children's series. He is a regular contributor to *Tales of the Shadowmen*.

The Masquerade in Exile

Starring:	**Created by:**
Dr. Daniel Cain	H.P. Lovecraft
	& Stuart Gordon
Dr. Herbert West	H.P. Lovecraft
Helman Carnby	Clark Ashton Smith
Christine Daae, Comtesse de Chagny	Gaston Leroux
Erich Zann	H.P. Lovecraft
August Dewart	August Derleth
Co-Starring:	
Raoul de Chagny	Gaston Leroux
Emile René Belloq	George Lucas,
	Philip Kaufman
	& Lawrence Kasdan
Eric Moreland Clapham-Lee	H.P. Lovecraft
Randolph Carter	H.P. Lovecraft
Etienne-Laurent de Marigny	H.P. Lovecraft
The d'Erlettes	Robert Bloch
Dr. Septimus Pretorius	William Hurlbut
	& John Balderston
Dr. Victor Frankenstein	Mary Shelley

Erik	Gaston Leroux
And:	
Le Culte des Goules	Robert Bloch
Miskatonic University	H.P. Lovecraft
Don Juan Triumphant	Gaston Leroux
Also Starring:	
Alan Seeger	
Marquis de Sade	
Dr. Harold Gillies	
Dr. Alexis Carrel	
Dr. Charles Guthrie	

Written by:

Pete RAWLIK holds a B.S. in Marine Biology and manages monitoring projects in the Florida Everglades. He has been a fan of the Lovecraftian fiction since his father sat him on his knee and read him Lovecraft's *The Rats in the Walls*. His fiction has appeared in *Talebones*, *IBID* and *Crypt of Cthulhu*. His literary criticism has appeared in *The New York Review of Science Fiction* and in *The Neil Gaiman Reader*. This is his first contribution to *Tales of the Shadowmen*.

The Tiny Destroyer

Starring:	**Created by:**
Jean Kariven	Jimmy Guieu
Ikano Kato	George W. Trendle
The Polarians	Jimmy Guieu
The Denebians	Jimmy Guieu
Co-Starring:	
The Green Hornet	George W. Trendle
Dick Martin	Robert Kehoe & Harvey Gates
Dr. Melcher	Robert Kehoe & Harvey Gates

Written by:

Frank SCHILDINER has been a pulp fan since a friend gave him a gift of Phillip Jose Farmer's *Tarzan Alive*. Since that time he has published articles on *Hellboy*, the Frankenstein films, *Dark Shadows* and the television show's links to the H.P. Lovecraft universe. He is a Senior Probation Officer in New Jersey and a martial arts instructor at Amorosi's Mixed Martial Arts. Frank resides in New Jersey with his wife Gail and two cats. He is a regular contributor to *Tales of the Shadowmen*.

Grim Days

Starring:	Created by:
Lord Peter Wimsey	Dorothy L. Sayers
Mrs. Rittenhouse	George S. Kaufman
	& Morrie Ryskind
Captain Geoffrey T. Spaulding	George S. Kaufman
	& Morrie Ryskind
Emmanuel Ravelli	George S. Kaufman
	& Morrie Ryskind
Colonel Haki	Eric Ambler
Nikko Charlambides	based on Dashiell Hammett
Bunter	Dorothy L. Sayers
Co-Starring:	
Harriet Vane (Lady Wimsey)	Dorothy L. Sayers
Major Brabazon-Plank	P.G. Wodehouse
Sir Henry Merrivale	John Dickson Carr
Sir Edward Leithen	John Buchan
Prof. Horatio Smith	Anatole de Grunwald,
	Roland Pertwee,
	A.G. Macdonald,
	& Wolfgang Wilhelm,
	based on Baroness Orczy
Dr. Henry Jones, Jr.	George Lucas
	& Menno Meyjes
	& Philip Kaufman
	& Jeffrey Boam
Prof. Aristide Clairembart	Henri Vernes
Colonel Dubois	Pierre Nord
Eric Leidner	Agatha Christie
General Von Graum	Anatole de Grunwald,
	Roland Pertwee,
	A.G. Macdonald,
	& Wolfgang Wilhelm,
	based on Baroness Orczy
Mr. Bandicott	John Buchan
Harald Blacktooth	John Buchan
James Schuyler Grim (JimGrim)	Talbot Mundy
And:	
Jno Bodmin	P.G. Wodehouse
Morlands cigarettes	Ian Fleming
Whiffletts cigarettes	Dorothy L. Sayers

Written by:
Stuart SHIFFMAN is a native New Yorker long resident in Seattle, where he attempts to say dry and uncovered in moss. He regrets having to give up the Manhattan apartment on the 101st Floor of the Empire State Building and his autogyro. He is a long-time science fiction fan, winner of the Trans-Atlantic Fan Fund in 1981 and the 1990 Hugo Award for Best Fan Artist, Sherlockian and Wodehousian and has contributed cartoons, illustrations and articles to *The Baker Street Journal* and *Plum Lines and Wooster Sauce*. Stu has written on alternate history and is a member of the judging panel for the Sidewise Award for Alternate History. He lives with Andi Shechter, book reviewer and past chair of Left Coast Crime, in a hobbit hole with too many books. He is a regular contributor to *Tales of the Shadowmen*.

The Screeching of Two Ravens

Written by:
Bradley H. SINOR is a native New Yorker long resident in Seattle. His stories have appeared in numerous science fiction, fantasy and horror anthologies such as *The Improbable Adventures of Sherlock Holmes*, *Ring of Fire 2* and *The Grantville Gazette*. Four collections of his short fiction have been released: *Dark and Stormy Nights*, *In the Shadows*, *Playing with Secrets* (along with stories by his wife, Sue Sinor) and *Echoes from the Darkness*. His non-fiction work has appeared in a variety of magazines and anthologies. He is a regular contributor to *Tales of the Shadowmen*.

The Three Lives of Maddalena

Starring:	Created by:
Maddalena Ernestine	William Hurlbut & John Balderston
(The Bride)	& James Whale
Carmilla Karnstein	Sheridan Le Fanu
Dr. Victor Frankenstein	Mary Shelley
Elizabeth	Mary Shelley
Dr. Septimus Pretorius	William Hurlbut & John Balderston
	& James Whale

Written by:

Michel STEPHAN was born and lives in Brittany with his wife and two children. He has been a fan of science fiction, fantasy and horror since age 10. He loves Universal monster movies (especially the *Frankenstein* series), sci-fi serials and collects Aurora model kits. He has submitted stories to Black Coat Press's French sister imprint, Rivière Blanche and has previously contributed to *Tales of the Shadowmen.*

The Mysterious Island of Dr. Antekirtt

Starring:	Created by:
The Captain	Hergé
The Boy	Hergé
His Dog	Hergé
Leo Saint-Clair (The Nyctalope)	Jean de La Hire
Bob Morane	Henri Vernes
Bernard Prince	Michel Greg
	& Hermann Huppen
Monsieur Ming (The Yellow Shadow)	Henri Vernes
Dr. Julius No	Ian Fleming
Emilio Largo	Ian Fleming
Point Pescade	Jules Verne
Co-Starring:	
Hubert Bonisseur de La Bath (OSS 117)	Jean Bruce
Bill Ballantine	Henri Vernes
Mathias Sandorf (Dr. Antekirtt)	Jules Verne
Hugo Drax	Ian Fleming
The Professor	Hergé
Ernst Stavro Blofeld	Ian Fleming
Dr. Natas	Guy d'Armen

The Blue Scorpion	George F. Worts
Pointe Pescade	Jules Verne
And:	
Antekirtta	Jules Verne
The Si Fan	Sax Rohmer
The Shin Tan	Henri Vernes
Also Starring:	
André Malraux	
Heinrich Himmler	

Written by:
David L. VINEYARD is a fifth generation Texan (named for his gunfighter/Texas Ranger great grand-father) currently living in Oklahoma City, OK, where the tornadoes come sweeping down the plains. He has useless degrees in history, politics, and economics, and is the author of several tales about Buenos Aires private eye Johnny Sleep, two (nearly published) novels, several short stories, some journalism, and various non-fiction. He is currently working on several ideas while battling with a three month old kitten for household dominance and the keyboard of his PC. He is a regular contributor to *Tales of the Shadowmen*.

The Necromancers of London

Starring:	**Created by:**
Gregory Temple	Paul Féval
Sam Hopkey	Paul Féval
Malo de Treguern	Paul Féval
Jean-Pierre Sévérin	Paul Féval
Countess Marcian Gregoryi	Paul Féval
Count Szandor	Paul Féval
Victor Frankenstein	Mary Shelley
Helen	Brian Stableford
"Lazarus"	Mary Shelley
Giuseppe Balsamo	Alexandre Dumas
Colonel Bozzo-Corona	Paul Féval
Guido	Brian Stableford
Jenny Paddock	Paul Féval
Co-Starring:	
Henri de Belcamp (Tom Brown, John Devil)	Paul Féval
Germain Patou	Paul Féval
Also Starring:	
Michael Faraday	

Andrew Crosse
Bishop of Salisbury
Robert Hastings
Stephen Southborne
John Medstead
Thomas Young
Peter Barlow
William Snow Harris
Marie Laveau
General Mortdieu (Napoléon)

Written by:
Brian M. STABLEFORD has been a professional writer since 1965. He has published more than 50 novels and 200 short stories, as well as several non-fiction books, thousands of articles for periodicals and reference books and a number of anthologies. He is also a part-time Lecturer in Creative Writing at King Alfred's College Winchester. Brian's novels include *The Empire of Fear* (1988), *Young Blood* (1992), *The Wayward Muse* (2005), *The Stones of Camelot* (2006), *The New Faust at the Tragicomique* (2007) and his future history series comprising *Inherit the Earth* (1998), *Architects of Emortality* (1999), *The Fountains of Youth* (2000), *The Cassandra Complex* (2001), *Dark Ararat* (2002) and *The Omega Expedition* (2002). His non-fiction includes *Scientific Romance in Britain* (1985), *Teach Yourself Writing Fantasy and Science Fiction* (1997), *Yesterday's Bestsellers* (1998) and *Glorious Perversity: The Decline and Fall of Literary Decadence* (1998). Brian's translations for Black Coat Press include numerous Paul Féval titles, Paul Féval fils' *Felifax the Tiger-Man*; three Jean de La Hire's *Nyctalope* novels; Marie Nizet's *Captain Vampire*; Ponson du Terrail's *The Vampire and the Devil's Son*; several volumes of the works of Maurice Renard and J. H. Rosny Aîné, and other books by Charles Derennes, Henri de Parville and Villiers de l'Isle-Adam. He is a regular contributor to *Tales of the Shadowmen*.

TALES OF THE
SHADOWMEN

Volume 1: The Modern Babylon (2005)
Matthew Baugh: *Mask of the Monster* - Bill Cunningham: *Cadavres Exquis* - Terrance Dicks: *When Lemmy Met Jules* - Win Scott Eckert: *The Vanishing Devil* - Viviane Etrivert: *The Three Jewish Horsemen* - G.L. Gick: *The Werewolf of Rutherford Grange* (1) - Rick Lai: *The Last Vendetta* - Alain le Bussy: *The Sainte-Geneviève Caper* - Jean-Marc & Randy Lofficier: *Journey to the Center of Chaos* - Samuel T. Payne: *Lacunal Visions* - John Peel: *The Kind-Hearted Torturer* - Chris Roberson: *Penumbra* - Robert Sheckley: *The Paris-Ganymede Clock* - Brian Stableford: *The Titan Unwrecked; or, Futility Revisited.*

Volume 2: Gentlemen of the Night (2006)
Matthew Baugh: *Ex Calce Liberatus* - Bill Cunningham: *Trauma* - Win Scott Eckert: *The Eye of Oran* - G.L. Gick: *The Werewolf of Rutherford Grange* (2) - Rick Lai: *Dr. Cerral's Patient* - Serge Lehman: *The Mystery of the Yellow Renault; The Melons of Trafalmadore* - Jean-Marc Lofficier: *Arsène Lupin's Christmas; Figaro's Children; The Tarot of Fantômas; The Star Prince; Marguerite; Lost and Found* - Xavier Mauméjean: *Be Seeing You!* - Sylvie Miller & Philippe Ward: *The Vanishing Diamonds* - Jess Nevins: *A Jest, To Pass The Time* - Kim Newman: *Angels of Music* - John Peel: *The Incomplete Assassin* - Chris Roberson: *Annus Mirabilis* - Jean-Louis Trudel: *Legacies* - Brian Stableford: *The Empire of the Necromancers* (1)

Volume 3: Danse Macabre (2007)
Matthew Baugh: *The Heart of the Moon* - Alfredo Castelli: *Long Live Fantômas* - Bill Cunningham: *Next!* - François Darnaudet & J.-M. Lofficier: *Au Vent Mauvais...* - Paul DiFilippo: *Return to the 20th Century* - Win Scott Eckert: *Les Lèvres Rouges* - G.L. Gick: *Beware the Beasts* - Micah Harris: *The Ape Gigans* - Travis Hiltz: *A Dance of Night and Death* - Rick Lai: *The Lady in the Black Gloves* - Jean-Marc Lofficier: *The Murder of Randolph Carter* - Xavier Mauméjean: *A Day in the Life of Madame Atomos* - David A. McIntee: *Bullets Over Bombay* - Brad Mengel: *All's Fair...* - Michael Moorcock: *The Affair of the Bassin Les Hivers* - John Peel: *The Successful Failure* - Joseph Altairac & Jean-Luc Rivera: *The Butterfly Files* - Chris Roberson: *The Famous Ape* - Robert L. Robinson, Jr.: *Two Hunters* - Brian Stableford: *The Empire of the Necromancers* (2).

Volume 4: Lords of Terror (2008)

Matthew Baugh: *Captain Future and the Lunar Peril* - Bill Cunningham: *Fool me once...* - Win Scott Eckert: *The Atomos Affair* - Micah Harris: *The Anti-Pope of Avignon* - Travis Hiltz: *Three Men, a Martian and a Baby* - Rick Lai: *Corridors of Deceit* - Roman Leary: *The Evils Against Which We Strive* - Jean-Marc Lofficier: *Madame Atomos' XMas* - Randy Lofficier: *The Reluctant Princess* - Xavier Maumejean: *A Wooster XMas* - Jess Nevins: *Red in Tooth and Claw* - Kim Newman: *Angels of Musics 2: The Mark of Kane* - John Peel: *Twenty Thousand Years Under the Sea* - John Shirley: *Cyrano and the Two Plumes* - Steven A. Roman: *Night's Children* - Brian Stableford: *The Empire of the Necromancers* (3).

Volume 5: The Vampires of Paris (2009)

Michelle Bigot: *The Tarot of the Shadowmen* - Matthew Baugh: *The Way of the Crane* - Christopher Paul Carey & Win Scott Eckert: *Iron and Bronze* - G. L. Gick: *Tros Must Be Crazy!* - Micah Harris: *May The Ground Not Consume Thee...* - Tom Kane: *The Knave of Diamonds* - Lovern Kindzierski: *Perils Over Paris* - Rick Lai: *All Predators Great and Small* - Roman Leary: *The Heart of a Man* - Alain le Bussy: *A Matter Without Gravity* - Jean-Marc Lofficier: *Madame Atomos' Holidays* - Randy Lofficier: *The English Gentleman's Ball* - Xavier Maumejean: *The Most Exciting Game* - Jess Nevins: *A Root That Beareth Gall and Worms* - John Peel: *The Dynamics of an Asteroid* - Frank Schildiner: *The Smoking Mirror* - Stuart Shiffman: *The Milkman Cometh* - David L. Vineyard: *The Jade Buddha* - Brian Stableford: *The Empire of the Necromancers* (4).

Volume 6: Grand Guignol (2010)

Christopher Paul Carey: *Caesear's Children* - Win Scott Eckert: *Is He in Hell?* - Emmaneuel Gorlier: *Out of Time* - Matthew Baugh & Micah Harris: *The Scorpion and the Fox* - Travis Hiltz: *The Treasure of theUbasti* - Rick Lai: *Incident in the Boer War* - Roman Leary: *The Children of Heracles* - Jean-Marc Lofficier: *J.C. in Alphaville* - Randy Lofficier: *The Spear of Destiny* - Xavier Maumejean: *The Man for the Job* - William P. Maynard: *Yes, Virginia, There Is a Fantomas* - John Peel: *The Biggest Guns* - Neil Penswick: *The Vampire Murders* - Dennis E. Power: *No Good Deed...* - Frank Schildiner: *Laurels for the Toff* - Bradley H. Sinor: *Where the Shadows Began* - Michel Stephan: *The Red Silk Scarf* - David L. Vineyard: *The Children's Crusade* - Brian Stableford: *The Empire of the Necromancers* (5).

WATCH OUT FOR
VOLUME 8: AGENTS PROVOCATEURS
TO BE RELEASED EARLY 2012

Lightning Source UK Ltd.
Milton Keynes UK
UKOW02f2043210915

259000UK00002B/196/P